**Two brand-new stories in every volume...
twice a month!**

Duets Vol. #43

"If you seek escapist fare, sensuality,
romance and a good story, look no further..."
than talented Temptation author Jamie Denton, says
Under the Covers. Joining her this month is new
writer Holly Jacobs with the delightfully funny
I Waxed My Legs For This? Enjoy!

Duets Vol. #44

Popular Jacqueline Diamond returns to Duets
this month. *Romantic Times* notes she always
"delivers a wonderful romance...and combines
it with a quirky cast of characters." Paired with
Jacqui is Isabel Sharpe, "a name to watch in the
romance genre for her excellent characterizations
and smooth plotting," says *Affaire de Coeur.*

Be sure to pick up both Duets volumes today!

Excuse Me? Whose Baby?

"So, what's going on?"

Jim asked, leaning back in his chair.

Dex wished she were anywhere but here. The law office was decorated in such intense black and white that humanity seemed like an intrusion. Then, from a back office, she heard a baby cry. If it went with the decor, it must be a baby penguin.

"Well," Burt Page said, folding his hands atop his desk, "this is an odd situation. I have Dr. Saldivar's will here. You're both named."

"But why?" Dex couldn't imagine that Dr. Saldivar would leave her so much as a test tube.

Jim shook his head. "I don't understand, either."

"It has to do with Ayoka," said the attorney.

"Who?" Dex asked.

Burt cleared his throat. "She's the, er, baby."

"What baby?" Jim glanced at Dex. "If Dr. Saldivar adopted a child, what could that possibly have to do with either of us?"

"Ayoka isn't adopted. She's yours. Uh...both of yours."

For more, turn to page 9

Follow That Baby!

Busted!

"Melanie," Joe said quietly. "Could you tell me why Barbara's room looks like a guest room with a crib thrown in instead of a nursery?"

Melanie looked into his eyes, so tired of lying she wanted to throw up. "Well, Joe...after her father died, I...couldn't bring myself to—"

"The husband's out." Joe gestured over his shoulder like a baseball umpire.

"Out?" Melanie raised her eyebrows. *Uh-oh.*

"I've eliminated him. He never existed." He pressed a finger to her mouth when she would have protested. "I won't lie to you again, Melanie. Please do the same for me."

She scrunched up her face in an agony of indecision. How much more would he swallow? Not much, from the look of him. But she couldn't break her promise to—

"Di-buh! Di-buh!" The baby's triumphant shriek pulled Melanie's head around. She gasped. Stared in horror. *Oh no. Oh no.*

Duncan, alias Barbara, walked toward them, diaper held aloft in a victory salute, evidence of her deception bared for all the world to see.

For more, turn to page 197

If you purchased this book without a cover you should be aware that this book is stolen property. It was reported as "unsold and destroyed" to the publisher, and neither the author nor the publisher has received any payment for this "stripped book."

HARLEQUIN DUETS

ISBN 0-373-44110-X

EXCUSE ME? WHOSE BABY?
Copyright © 2001 by Jackie Hyman

FOLLOW THAT BABY!
Copyright © 2001 by Muna Shehadi

All rights reserved. Except for use in any review, the reproduction or utilization of this work in whole or in part in any form by any electronic, mechanical or other means, now known or hereafter invented, including xerography, photocopying and recording, or in any information storage or retrieval system, is forbidden without the written permission of the publisher, Harlequin Enterprises Limited, 225 Duncan Mill Road, Don Mills, Ontario, Canada M3B 3K9.

All characters in this book have no existence outside the imagination of the author and have no relation whatsoever to anyone bearing the same name or names. They are not even distantly inspired by any individual known or unknown to the author, and all incidents are pure invention.

This edition published by arrangement with Harlequin Books S.A.

® and TM are trademarks of the publisher. Trademarks indicated with ® are registered in the United States Patent and Trademark Office, the Canadian Trade Marks Office and in other countries.

Visit us at www.eHarlequin.com

Printed in U.S.A.

Excuse Me? Whose Baby?

JACQUELINE DIAMOND

4-18-08 Donation

Harold D. Cooley Library
Nashville, NC

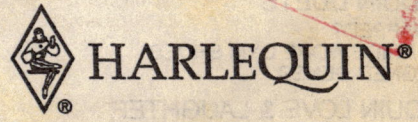

TORONTO • NEW YORK • LONDON
AMSTERDAM • PARIS • SYDNEY • HAMBURG
STOCKHOLM • ATHENS • TOKYO • MILAN • MADRID
PRAGUE • WARSAW • BUDAPEST • AUCKLAND

Dear Reader,

Small colleges are delightfully offbeat places where eccentric personalities can bloom. Perpetual students like my heroine, Dex, live in a world apart from the rest of us, so for her I dreamed up Clair De Lune, California, and De Lune University for *Excuse Me? Whose Baby?*

I practically grew up on a college campus. My school in Nashville, Tennessee, was affiliated with Peabody College for Teachers, where my mother was an art professor. I later attended Brandeis University in Waltham, Massachusetts.

My hero, Jim Bonderoff, needed a different brand of individuality from Dex, so I created a household of ex-marines with literally no holds barred! I enjoyed seeing how these two different realms meshed in my new book and I hope you will, too.

Please write me at P.O. Box 1315, Brea, CA 92822!

Sincerely,

Jacqueline Diamond

Books by Jacqueline Diamond

HARLEQUIN DUETS
2—KIDNAPPED?
8—THE BRIDE WORE GYM SHOES
37—DESIGNER GENES

HARLEQUIN LOVE & LAUGHTER
11—PUNCHLINE
32—SANDRA AND THE SCOUNDREL

In loving memory of Ambrose "Joe" Mercier
and his wonderful sense of humor.

1

"Your lawyer called."

Dex Fenton was trotting down the creaky wooden steps of the English building, carrying a pile of essays she'd just collected from a Shakespeare class, when she heard Professor Hugh Bemling's remark.

Lawyer? Whose lawyer was he talking about?

The thin, bearded professor stood in his office doorway, cleaning his glasses with his shirttail. Shaking back a mass of flyaway brown hair that threatened to block her vision, Dex looked around the hall, but she didn't see anyone else he could have been addressing.

"I don't have a lawyer," she ventured.

"Well, a lawyer called and asked for you," he said.

Dex tried to ignore the sinking sensation in her stomach. She didn't know any lawyers and she preferred to keep it that way. Nevertheless, she refused to let herself be intimidated by anyone, ever. "Did you catch his name?"

"I wrote it down." Hugh, who regularly got lost in the library stacks and had addressed Dex as Dixie for her first three months as his teaching assistant, fished through his pockets. He dragged out a laundry receipt and his campus health card before handing her a crumpled note.

Dex squinted at the ink-smeared letters. "'O wavy

hair, O beauteous maiden,'" she read, and stopped. Obviously, this was not a telephone message but a poem of an embarrassingly personal nature.

Hugh's cheeks, or what was visible of them beneath his gray-flecked facial hair, flushed bright red as he snatched back the paper. "That's...some random thoughts I jotted down. I can't think where I put your message."

Dex adjusted her stack of essays. "I'm sure it was for someone else." And so was the poem, she hoped. "I'd better get going. I'll have these graded by Monday."

"Have what graded? Oh, the papers, yes." Hugh patted his shirt pockets. "I know that note's here somewhere. Let me check in my office."

"Thanks, Hugh, but you don't need to..." She didn't bother to finish. He was already gone.

There was no point in waiting. Once inside, he would get so busy pawing through piles of journals that he'd forget what he was looking for.

Anyway, Dex had another job to do. In addition to assisting the professor, she made ends meet by working as a campus courier.

She'd earned a B.A. and a master's degree in English, but her parents, both college professors, weren't impressed. Dex had completed the coursework for her Ph.D., but found herself stuck on writing her dissertation.

She just couldn't seem to work up much enthusiasm for it. Or, maybe, for becoming Dr. Dex Fenton and having to leave the friendly environs of Clair De Lune, California, to take whatever college teaching post she could scrape up.

So she worked two part-time jobs and rode a bicycle and lived in an efficiency apartment over a garage. Most of the time, she rather enjoyed things the way they were.

Out in the sunshine, she hurried around the brick building to the bike rack, where she stuck the essays into her bike's side compartments and put on her helmet. She hoped she had enough room left to carry today's campus deliveries. Fortunately, today was Friday, usually a light mail day.

As she mounted her bike and set off, a few jacaranda blossoms drifted onto Dex's arm. Some of the lavender petals, which appeared every spring as sure as the swallows came back to Capistrano, clung to her pink sweater and blue jeans.

"O wavy hair, O beauteous maiden." Spring was certainly getting to Professor Bemling, Dex thought. He was a cute guy, if you liked absentminded forty-year-olds. At twenty-six, though, she considered him too old for her.

The kind of guy she wanted was in his early thirties, with sun-streaked dark hair and alert brown eyes. He gave the impression of being tall, although he wasn't quite six feet, and he had slim hips that moved with a sensuous rhythm.

She shook her head. Why on earth was she thinking of a man she wanted nothing to do with?

The main section of De Lune University was laid out in an old-fashioned rectangle, its symmetry marred only by the jutting addition of the glass-and-steel faculty center. Dex was passing that facility, which was probably why her mind had gone skittering across memories from a crisp evening four months ago.

The holiday faculty party had featured mistletoe

and dance music, tipsy flirtations and a general letting-down of inhibitions. In an eggnog-induced blur, she'd felt a man's dark eyes catch hers with unexpected intensity.

He'd asked her to dance and laughed at everything she said. She didn't resist when he whirled her onto the patio.

He'd smoothed her unruly curls with both hands, then kissed her senseless. It was all so blurry, so sensational and so...insane. Dex pedaled faster, trying to put the scene, and the memory of what had followed, behind her.

Half a quadrangle farther, at a rear entrance to the administration building, she banged on the door. This was the squirrely abode of Fitz Langley, the maintenance and communications supervisor.

"Hey, Fitz!" she yelled. "Got any stuff for me to deliver?"

The door rattled and shook as the rusty lock stuck. Finally, it wrenched open and out poked a head worthy of mounting on a hunter's wall. A shaggy chestnut mane framed a broad leonine forehead, a flattened nose and a mouth that could roar but rarely did.

The door opened wider under pressure from Fitz's short, stubby frame, and he handed her two padded envelopes and a box. "Most of the stuff's already been delivered, but these just came in. By the way, some lawyer called you."

Dex got that sinking feeling again. Apparently an attorney really was looking for her. And looking hard.

Could someone be suing her? If so, he'd be sorely disappointed. Her two jobs barely paid enough to scrape by, and she owed a pile of student loans that would become due the moment she finished her doctoral dissertation. Whenever that might be.

"What lawyer?" she asked. "Has he got a name?"

"I e-mailed you."

"I only check my mail when I enter grades in the computer." Dex was annoyed by e-mail, phones, answering machines and anything else that interrupted her thinking. Not that her thinking was terribly profound, but how was it ever going to get that way if things kept jangling and blipping at her? "Can't you just tell me?"

"Once I input data, I erase it from my personal memory banks." With a shrug, Fitz vanished into his lair.

Dex strapped the deliveries onto the back of her bike. As she pedaled off, she wondered if someone could have died. She hoped not. And left her money. She still hoped not.

Her parents in Florida were both in excellent health, as far as she knew. She called them infrequently, since they listened only when she had some accomplishment to dazzle them with. Still, she would have heard if they were ill.

Her only other close relative was her younger sister, Brianna, a precocious twenty-four-year-old magazine editor. If anything happened to her, it would be her husband calling, not a lawyer. Dex was certain they had no Midas-touched great-aunt who might have popped off. In fact, no rich person had ever crossed her path except once, and she would just as soon never see or hear from him again.

As if to remind her of that one lapse, she found herself again passing the faculty center, going in the other direction. Dex gritted her teeth and sped up.

She didn't know what had gotten into her that night. He was the wrong sort of man for her entirely. Too bold. Too confident.

She needed someone gentle and understanding, someone who could offer the warmth she'd missed while growing up. Even at the holiday party, she'd known she was making a big mistake. Yet in the arms of Mr. Hot Stuff, she'd been transformed into a hormone-charged Jezebel.

The only fortunate aspect to the whole night was that no one had noticed the man entering and leaving Dex's apartment. In Clair De Lune, the walls might not have ears but everyone else did, and took notes, too.

She rounded a corner and jerked the handlebars to avoid colliding with two lovesick students standing on the sidewalk, their jean-clad legs entwined, their lips locked and their hands earnestly groping each other. Spring was, of course, the mating season among primates enrolled at De Lune University.

At the art department, Dex raced up the steps and, with a brisk greeting, set the box on the secretary's desk. Some days she stuck around to chat, but today she was sure she could hear those essays grumbling in her saddlebags. And then there was the annoying question of why that lawyer might be calling her.

She left one of the envelopes at the music department and headed to the science complex, which was located in a separate quadrangle. Her last delivery was for the fertility research center.

As soon as she entered, she noticed something odd. Usually the place had a sterile look, with the receptionist sitting alone at her desk. Today, however, professors, graduate students and technicians formed solemn clumps in the pale peach entryway.

Dex spotted a doctoral student she knew. "Hey, LaShawna, what's going on?"

The tall African-American woman swung toward her. Instead of giving an upbeat greeting, LaShawna Gregory hugged her clipboard as if it were a life preserver. "It's Dr. Saldivar. She's had an accident."

"An accident?" Dex had never heard of an explosion occurring in an infertility lab. Except maybe a population explosion. "Here?"

"No, in India." Unshed tears glimmered in the young woman's eyes. "She was due back yesterday from a medical conference but..." She bit her lip. "We keep hearing rumors. Something about an elephant."

Helene Saldivar was a brilliant researcher who helped couples have kids. Tall and rawboned, the woman strode through life, her manner brisk but kindly. "Her patients must be upset."

"Her patients?" said LaShawna. "She doesn't actually treat any..."

The receptionist marched over and plucked the envelope from Dex's hands. "Sorry to interrupt, but there's still work to be done around here."

Dex nodded guiltily. "I hope the accident isn't serious," she told the graduate student, and hurried out. Eager to start grading papers, she sped along the three blocks from campus to the apartment she rented from the retired dean of comparative literature.

Amid a block of pastel-painted bungalows and pineapple-shaped palm trees on Forest Lane, Dean Marie Pipp's dark-shingled home lurked like an escapee from a Grimm's fairy tale. An overarching eucalyptus blocked most of the sunlight from the yard, where spindly herbs dominated the flower beds.

Across the street, little old Mrs. Zimpelman stopped trimming her roses and waved to Dex. Then she dialed her cell phone and made a call to one of her gossipy friends. Mrs. Zimpelman reported all the comings and goings on Forest Lane as if it were Avenue of the Stars.

Dean Pipp, by contrast, minded her own business. Today, however, she must have been watching through the window. When she saw Dex, she came onto the porch, her fringed shawl quivering in the light breeze.

"Yoo-hoo, my dear!" she called. "You have a telephone message!"

Dex already had a good idea whom it was from.

THE LAW FIRM of Page, Bittner and Steele occupied the seventh floor of Clair De Lune's tallest professional building. It was served by four elevators, two of them out of service and the third dedicated to floors eight through twelve.

Dex waited in the lobby for a ridiculous length of time. She wished she'd stopped to eat lunch, but Dean Pipp, whose farsighted eyes could scarcely decipher her own spidery handwriting, said the attorney needed to see her either at one or at once, which in this case amounted to the same thing.

"It's some important fellow downtown," she'd said. "You know, the firm of Something, Something and Something. Mr. Something ran for mayor last year, didn't he? It's his partner Mr. Something who wants to see you."

"Page, Bittner and Steele," Dex had deciphered

when she took the note. It was a prestigious partnership. What on earth could they want, and why the urgency?

Curious and tired of the constant messages, Dex had hopped on her bike and headed for the firm.

Across the marble-floored lobby, the revolving door swung into action. Although she was blinded by a burst of sunlight reflecting off the glass doors, she heard awed murmurs from the other elevator hopefuls, as if a celebrity had entered the building.

Dex's vision cleared. Toward the elevator bank strolled the confident figure of the town's self-made multimillionaire, who also happened to be one of De Lune University's biggest benefactors and a visiting member of its computer faculty.

His body was toned and lean. His brown hair retained a hint of sun bleaching, even though it was years since he'd given up surfing for long days running his computer software firm and long nights making women very, very happy.

James Bonderoff was known for his sophisticated lifestyle and, judging by the pictures in the local newspaper, his exquisite taste in women. He preferred gorgeous executives and professional women, all of whom looked terrific getting in and out of his expensive cars.

He didn't usually go for women with crinkly hair who tended toward plumpness. He probably didn't even remember Dex.

James gave the group a puzzled smile. "Something wrong with the lifts?"

At that moment, the only working elevator opened. The crowd parted like the Red Sea to let him enter.

Dex tried to duck back, but she was standing too

close to the doors. The crowd swept her in, right next to the last man on earth she ever wanted to see again.

He smelled of sunshine and expensive aftershave, and he wore his silk suit as casually as if it were jeans and a T-shirt. Beneath the elegant fabric, there was no mistaking the muscular build of the man. Especially since the crowd was mashing her right into his pecs.

In the enclosed space, his dominant presence aroused a prickly combination of uneasiness and longing. There was too much of him, Dex decided. The legs were too long, the shoulders too broad, the face too sculpted.

She couldn't imagine herself rolling around in a delirium of sweaty ecstasy with such a man. Or rather, she didn't want to imagine it, because she *had* done it and regretted it ever since.

A tall woman on the far side of the elevator gave Jim a come-hither look and flirtatiously finger combed her hair. Dex was impressed. She couldn't drag her fingers more than two inches through her tangled mane without the aid of a blowtorch.

As they stopped at floor after floor, the occupants dispersed. For the last leg, there were only two people in the elevator.

Dex edged away from Jim, keeping her gaze averted. With luck, he'd go striding off at the seventh floor, never to be seen again.

"Don't I know you?" The remark rumbled through her nervous system. She felt his breath whisper across the crown of her head, which was all he could see.

What the heck? Lifting her chin, she met his eyes squarely. "You might say that."

She could see at once that she'd misjudged the distance. She was closer than she'd thought, so close that when the elevator stopped, the tiniest stumble brought her against his arm.

She drew back in time to glimpse surprise on his face. And recognition. Oh, heavens, not recognition!

"Didn't we—?" Jim stopped in mid faux pas.

"That was my twin sister," Dex said. "The one who does stupid things at faculty parties."

His face registered confusion. Curiosity. Doubt. When the doors opened, Dex hurried to exit, forestalling further conversation.

The name of the law firm blazed from glass doors dead ahead. Apparently the partnership took up the entire seventh floor.

"Paying a visit to your lawyer?" Jim asked. He was very close to Dex's ear, or else his baritone reverberated at a particularly sympathetic frequency.

"My lawyer?" Good heavens, what kind of budget did the man think she had? "Well, you know how it is. Between the personal trainer, the live-in hair stylist and the full-time guru, I had to let somebody go. So I decided to come fire my lawyer."

Her humor fell flat. His silence, possibly offended or merely bored, followed her through the glass doors. She'd made another great impression, Dex thought uneasily.

The law office, she discovered as she entered, was decorated in such intense black and white that humanity seemed like an intrusion. Then, from a back office, she heard a baby cry. If it went with the decor, it must be a baby penguin.

On sighting Jim, the receptionist snapped to attention. The only other person present was a young man tending the plants. He stared at Dex's chest so hard that he accidentally watered the file cabinet.

"Mr. Bonderoff!" the receptionist said. "This is an honor. And you must be Miss, uh, Fenton. Mr. Page is waiting for you."

"For which one of us?" Dex asked.

"Both," the woman said.

"The two of us?" Jim seemed as taken aback as she was. "There must be some mistake."

"Why, no," the woman said. "Please, go right in."

Dex and Jim exchanged glances. This, she realized instantly, was a mistake. Those dark eyes of his plugged into her as if he were installing his software directly on to her hard drive.

They had only one thing in common, she reminded herself as she dragged her gaze away, one stolen night, slightly tipsy but not full-out drunken. She didn't want a repeat. She also couldn't imagine what possible involvement a lawyer might have.

"Does this guy represent you?" she asked.

Jim shook his head. "My company has its own legal department in-house. I'm as mystified as you are."

Now they had two things in common, Dex mused.

Following the secretary's directions, they crossed the salt-and-pepper tile and entered an office the size of a roller rink. The black-and-white theme was no more appealing here, Dex found, even when expressed in a diamond-pattern carpet and a gleaming black desk.

A wall of windows overlooked the shake-shingle and red tile roofs of downtown Clair De Lune. One tidy block after another of low buildings spread in all directions, some constructed of Spanish-style white stucco, others of funky wood. Even from this height, she could make out window boxes overflowing with petunias and geraniums.

She wished she were outside, anywhere but here. James Bonderoff's nearness was proving even more disturbing than his absence had been.

From behind the massive desk emerged a man with stooped shoulders and pale eyes. "Burt Page," he said. "We've met." He held out his hand to Jim.

"Oh, yes. Chamber of Commerce breakfast last month, right?" Jim returned the handshake.

"What's this all about?" Dex asked.

"Ah, Miss Fenton. Please have a seat, both of you."

Jim draped himself over a chair. Dex perched on an identical one and had to prop her gym shoes on a crossbar because her feet didn't reach the floor.

"Well." Burt Page folded his hands atop his desk. "This is an odd situation."

"What is?" Jim asked.

"It's about Helene Saldivar," said the attorney. "You do know her?"

"I've funded some of her research," the millionaire said.

"That's your only connection with her?"

Jim cleared his throat. "She ran some, well, private medical tests for me. As a favor." Quickly, he added, "She's a fine person. Nothing wrong, I hope?"

Instead of answering, the lawyer said, "And you, Miss Fenton? You knew her as well, I believe?"

"Sort of." Dex squirmed. The kind of contact she'd had with Helene Saldivar wasn't something she cared to discuss in front of James Bonderoff. "I heard she had some kind of problem with an elephant."

"I'm afraid so." The lawyer shuffled a sheaf of papers on his desk. "It seems that, while she was in India, she suffered a coronary."

Jim frowned. "She had a heart attack?"

"It was an unfortunate coincidence," said the attorney. "Although it's not uncommon for a motorist to suffer an attack and crash the car, it's the first time I've heard of anyone being stricken and falling off an elephant."

"Is she going to be all right?" Jim leaned forward, his hands clenched. What kind of tests had she run for him, anyway? Dex wondered.

The lawyer stopped rattling the papers. "I'm afraid the accident was terminal."

Dust motes swirled against the white wall behind him as silence reigned. After a moment, Dex said, "You mean she's dead?"

Page nodded. "I have her will here. You're both named."

"But why?" She couldn't imagine that Dr. Saldivar would leave her so much as a test tube. Dex had simply become, at the doctor's request, an egg donor to help out some of her desperate patients.

Then she remembered with a jolt that, according to LaShawna, Dr. Saldivar didn't treat patients.

"I don't understand, either." Jim's voice had a hoarse quality. "What's going on?"

"It has to do with the disposition of Ayoka," said the lawyer.

"The elephant?" Dex peeled off a loose bit of fingernail polish. The rose-colored flake dropped onto the black-and-white carpet, where it stood out like a neon sign.

"No, no." Burt Page cleared his throat. He stared at his desktop, then at the ceiling, then out the window. "Ayoka isn't an elephant. She's the, er, baby."

2

NORMALLY, Jim's brain worked on multiple tracks like the quantum computer—which so far was only theoretical. He could solve so many problems simultaneously that his brain must be operating in various universes. In none of those universes, however, did Burt Page's comments make any sense.

"What baby?" he asked. "If she went to India to adopt a child, what could that possibly have to do with either of us?"

"Ayoka isn't adopted." The lawyer's Adam's apple made a noteworthy trip up his throat. "She's yours. Uh...both of yours."

Dex's face went white. She swayed in her chair.

Jim caught her arm to steady her. As he did, a strand of her scouring-pad mane brushed his cheek. It smelled like herbal shampoo, he noted in a daze.

The woman bore only a faint evolutionary resemblance to the type of ladies he usually dated, yet she aroused a powerful male response. Four months ago, she'd sent him spiraling out of control. Jim Bonderoff was a man who never lost control.

He'd luxuriated in her spontaneity and her ample curves. She didn't fit the image of a wife and mother that he'd formed in his mind, yet he'd begun to think, for the first time in years, that perhaps he should stop trying to control every aspect of his life and simply trust his instincts.

Then she'd announced that she was leaving town and had declined to give any forwarding address. He'd been bitterly disappointed and had contemplated pursuing her to the ends of the earth.

A few days later, his common sense had reasserted itself. She was obviously the wrong woman for him, and both of them knew it. So he'd taken steps to make sure he would never lose control that way again.

Now, however, her warm presence penetrated all the layers of his consciousness. He ached to cup that pointed little chin and to touch her wiry hair, which straggled in all directions as if spread across a pillow. Not to mention what he'd like to do to those rosebud lips.

"Are you all right, Miss Fenton?" Burt leaned across his desk. "Perhaps I should summon a doctor."

"I'm all right." Dex wiggled out of Jim's grasp. "And there's no need to prop me up, either."

"You were sagging," he said.

"Wrong."

"Swaying, then."

"Catching my breath," she snapped.

Jim wondered what had gotten into him. Hair spread across a pillow? Rosebud lips? Barbed wire and fangs were more like it.

"You were saying?" he prompted the lawyer.

"Dr. Saldivar gave birth to a daughter nine months ago," Burt said. "She's called Ayoka, which I understand is a Yoruban name meaning 'one who causes joy all around.' Annie for short."

This was interesting, but pointless. "I still don't see

how she could be my child," Jim said. "Dr. Saldivar and I never—" how was he going to phrase this diplomatically? "—strayed from the vertical."

"But she did conduct some tests of a personal nature, isn't that right?" Burt leveled him a man-to-man gaze. Having served in the Marines, Jim knew what it meant. *This has to do with your manhood. It's a guy thing. Don't make me spell it out in front of the lady.*

Jim made the connection. He hadn't wanted to accept that this baby might actually be his but, when confronted, he could hardly deny it.

All of his adult life, he had considered fatherhood an impossible dream. After suffering a double attack of the mumps in adolescence, he'd feared he might be sterile.

Out of sympathy for others with similar problems, he'd begun donating money to fertility research.

About a year and a half ago, he'd mentioned the subject to Dr. Saldivar at the dedication of a new wing of the university's fertility research center, which he'd funded. She'd offered to test his sperm discreetly.

A short time later, Jim had learned that he was potent enough to father a whole brood. His sperm, Helene had told him, practically leaped out of the test tube like little dolphins.

Apparently she'd kept a few of those dolphins for her own use. The realization hit him hard. He made an uncharacteristic choking sound. "I'm the father?"

Burt folded his hands on the desk. Instead of answering directly, he said, "As a young woman, Dr. Saldivar didn't want children, so she had her tubes tied. As the years went by, however, she changed her mind, but the operation couldn't be reversed. I suppose you might say that her biological alarm clock went off."

"Okay, she needed a father for her baby and she chose me, without my consent," Jim acknowledged. "But you said she had her tubes tied. If she couldn't produce an egg, then who..."

He stopped. Inside the room, the silence coagulated. Outside, a car horn *ayoogaed* the Lone Ranger theme.

Even a man with a brain like a very old computer, or possibly a set of Tinkertoys, could get the picture. Jim looked at Dex. She picked at her fingernails, her gaze averted.

"That's right," Burt said. "Miss Fenton is the mother. Biologically speaking."

Dex stopped shredding her manicure and addressed the lawyer. "I never authorized such a thing. We'll put her up for adoption, of course. That was why I donated my eggs, to give some loving parents a much-wanted baby."

Give her up? Until this moment, Jim had been oblivious to the fact that he had a daughter, but he knew immediately that he wasn't going to let strangers raise her.

He'd wanted a child for years. Not, admittedly, out of wedlock, and certainly not with Dex Fenton. But fate, in the form of Helene Saldivar, had taken matters out of his hands.

"Don't you even want to meet her?" Burt was saying.

"No," said Dex.

Jim felt a sneaking sense of regret that this fireball didn't care about her own baby, but perhaps it was for the best. "I'll take her. Sight unseen. If I have a daughter, I'll accept full responsibility."

"What do you know about raising a child?" Dex demanded. "Can you change a diaper? Do you know anything about burping a baby?"

"I can learn," he said.

Burt raised both hands in a paternalistic gesture. "Perhaps it would help if you met Annie. She's with her nanny in the other room."

Jim remembered hearing a baby cry earlier. Now he couldn't wait to meet her. "Absolutely! And she's going home with me. I'll change a diaper right here on your desk if I have to."

The attorney's nostrils flared. "That won't be necessary. Miss Smithers! You can come in now!"

DEX FOUGHT against showing the slightest weakness. The last thing she needed was to get dizzy and have Jim grab her again. It wasn't fair that a mere mortal could light fires with his fingertips.

She didn't want him to touch her, and she didn't want to see this baby. If she did, Dex might make a decision that would be catastrophic for the little girl.

Every child deserved a loving home with parents who were capable of nurturing her with laughter and tenderness. No decent mother would condemn Annie to life with an arrogant playboy posing as a father. Nor would she take the baby herself, when she knew that inside her hot-tempered exterior lay a heart of ice.

Dex had been raised by parents who didn't know how to love, only how to approve or disapprove. Often she heard their voices in her mind critiquing her every action, and in her own tone when she corrected a student. She would never inflict such a parent on an innocent baby.

An honest person didn't shrink from admitting her shortcomings. What Dex wanted most, the loving family she'd never known, was beyond her ability to create. But she was capable of a selfless act. She would save Annie from a similar fate.

She steeled herself as a rake-thin woman entered the office, pushing a stroller. Strapped inside, with hair frizzing into a halo and a plump body wiggling to get free, was...Dex.

A tiny Dex. A nine-month-old Dex, all set to make the same mistakes as she blundered through life, to quail before the same unkind children who teased her about her adolescent chubbiness, to be scorned by the same self-centered teenage boys and to cry herself to sleep at night.

Annie needed a home with parents who could shield and support her. She deserved to grow up happier and with a greater capacity for love than the mother she resembled down to the smallest spiral of her DNA.

"It's amazing." Leaping from his chair, Jim went to crouch beside his daughter. "She looks exactly like me."

"Like you?" Dex couldn't believe it. "Since when do you have curly hair?"

"Oh, that." He shrugged off the comment. "Haven't you noticed her eyes? They're mine. You can't miss it!" Unstrapping Annie, he lifted her to his shoulder.

Silently, Dex conceded the point. The baby did have piercing brown eyes like his, not her blue ones. Still, it was a small resemblance.

Entranced at rising to such heights, the baby giggled and waved her arms. Nonsense syllables bubbled up. "Ga ga da da ba ba."

"Did you hear that?" Jim demanded. "She said Dada!"

"You're fantasizing," Dex countered.

"I suggest the two of you come to some agreement between yourselves," Burt said from behind his desk. "In her will, Dr. Saldivar explained the baby's genesis and recommended that you receive joint custody since she has no close relatives. I suppose you could battle this out in court, but I doubt that would be in the best interests of the baby."

Nor of Dex's pocketbook, either. In fact, the battle would be lost before it began, since the best legal representation she could afford would be a student from De Lune University's law school.

Last year, the campus legal aid center had handled a disputed family case in which, if she recalled correctly, the father ended up with custody of his mother-in-law and the judge took home the baby. Or, at least, that's the way it had sounded in the campus newspaper.

"There's no question about it. I'll take charge from here." Jim turned to the nanny. "Miss Smithers, I'd like you to work for me."

"That can be arranged." The nanny frowned at the baby in Jim's arms and whipped out a comb. "Just a minute, sir." Standing on tiptoe, she dragged the comb through the baby's crinkled hair. It stuck after two inches.

"Naturally, I'll match your salary," he said. "You'll get the same benefits and retirement plan as my other employees."

"Dr. Saldivar's salary would not be adequate. I'm well aware of who you are, sir." Without waiting for his reply, the nanny produced a bottle marked Curl Relaxer and spritzed it over Annie's head. The baby let out a wail and clapped her hands to her scalp. "No, no, no!" Miss Smither's scolded. Pushing the tiny hands away, the nanny yanked the comb through the locks. "She's lost her headband again. I think she must eat them."

"Was Dr. Saldivar underpaying you?" Adjusting his grip on Annie, Jim wiped a blob of curl relaxer from his cheek.

"Dr. Saldivar had to make do on a researcher's income. You don't," the woman responded tightly, and from her purse produced a plastic headband with gripper teeth. "Now hold still, Ayoka." She clamped the thing across the baby's temples and scraped back the hair. Tears welled in the little girl's eyes.

"I'm willing to raise your salary if you're being underpaid," Jim said. "But only if you're being underpaid."

Dex couldn't stand it any longer, not when tears were rolling down the baby's cheeks. "Don't you touch her!" she yelled at Miss Smithers. "You horrible woman, can't you see that headband is hurting her?" Racing across the room, she removed the plastic band from Annie's head and shoved it into the nanny's grasp.

"I won't have a child in my charge going around with messy hair." The nanny looked down her nose at Dex's own frothy mane.

Jim stared in surprise at the tears on his daughter's cheeks and at the viselike headband. "I didn't even notice," he said.

"Of course you didn't!" Dex retorted. "You're not a father any more than I'm a mother. And neither is this poor excuse for a nanny. The child needs a real family."

"I can learn," the millionaire said quietly. "As for Miss Smithers, she and I have been unable to arrive at a mutually agreed-upon salary, so her services won't be needed."

"Cheapskate," muttered the woman. After collecting her spray bottle from a polished table, where it left a moisture ring, she marched out of the room.

Squirming to watch her departure, Annie slid lower in Jim's grasp. Her left shoe dropped to the floor, and a strap on her yellow sundress fell across one pudgy upper arm. In another minute, her outfit—which was much too flouncy and fussy, in Dex's opinion—was likely to fall off entirely.

"Here, I'll take her." Without waiting for permission, she slid her hands under the little girl's arms and transferred the baby to her own shoulder. Annie nestled there contentedly. "For the record, I *like* your hair, babycakes."

Jim smiled. "I have to admit, she does resemble you a little." He didn't seem to notice the wet spot the baby's mouth had left on his zillion-dollar suit.

"Resemble me?" Dex wanted to chew him out, but it was hard to stay angry when she held this cooing bundle in her arms. "She *is* me." To the lawyer, she said, "A person is entitled to custody of herself, isn't she? Well, look at us."

"She's half you," Jim conceded. "And half me, Dex. You've already said you don't want her."

"I want what's best for her. A good home, not a cold mansion the size of a hotel." The campus had buzzed with descriptions of Jim's hilltop residence since he hosted a scholarship fund-raiser last fall.

"Maybe you think she belongs in your apartment?" he replied. "A single room over a garage with clothes strewn everywhere and nothing but tofu in the refrigerator?"

"I wasn't aware you two were previously acquainted," Burt said.

Jim halted with his mouth open, then closed it quickly. Dex could feel herself blushing.

The irony wasn't lost on her. She and this man had once made wild, earthshaking love—five months *after* the birth of their daughter. That had to be a first.

Not one that she cared to discuss with this lawyer, however. "We've met," she said.

"I have a compromise to propose." Jim held out a finger to Annie, who grasped it and took a tentative, tooth-free bite. "You don't believe I can be a good single parent. Okay, I'll prove it to you."

"How?" Dex didn't want to compromise, but she was in no position to dictate terms.

"Move in with me for a few days," the man said. "I'll take Annie on a trial basis, and you can watch to make sure I provide a proper home."

"If you'd like to hire another nanny, there's a registry in the area," Burt said.

"I'll have my secretary contact them," Jim said. "In the meantime, my butler and my maid can fill in when I'm not available. And Miss Fenton can help, too, if she wishes."

"I don't see how you're going to prove you can make a home for her." Dex's arms tightened around Annie. "Your butler and your maid will help out?

And then you'll leave her to a hired nanny? It's just not acceptable."

Not to mention that she had no desire to put herself in the middle of this man's life. She had her own life, modest as it might be. And her privacy. And her sanity.

"The situation is only temporary," Jim responded. "I expect to be married soon."

Dex went hot and cold, then hot again. He was going to be married? Surely he didn't mean to her! But if not, then to whom?

"Congratulations," Burt said. "The way people gossip around Clair De Lune, I'm surprised I hadn't heard the news."

"I like to play my cards close to my chest," Jim said.

"When did this happen?" Dex demanded, and only the presence of the lawyer restrained her from pointing out that, as recently as the Christmas party, Jim had been fancy-free.

"Nothing has happened, exactly." He folded his arms with an air of confidence. "I've had an informal understanding for years with my high-school sweetheart. She's a psychology researcher in Washington, D.C. Three months ago, I popped the question. She hasn't given me an acceptance, but it's only a matter of time."

Dex did some mental arithmetic. That was only a month after they'd spent the night together. Why had he suddenly decided to propose to this long-distance amour?

It was true that Dex had given him the brush-off when he asked to see her again. That didn't excuse his rushing to propose to someone else.

"Just because you might or might not be engaged has no bearing on custody," she said. "Annie needs parenting now, not whenever your fiancée gets around to giving you an answer."

Jim's dark eyes probed hers. She felt, as she had at the Christmas party, the intensity of his will. "I think we should hold this discussion over lunch," he said. "In private."

Burt glanced at his watch. "Good idea. I don't mean to hurry you, but I have another client arriving in a few minutes. By the way, I can have Ayoka's furnishings and clothes delivered to your house this afternoon if you like, Jim."

"That would be fine. Dex?"

She hated the sense of being herded like a wandering sheep. Also, she wasn't crazy about the prospect of spending time alone with Jim Bonderoff, even if it involved free food.

But she had a responsibility to make sure Annie found a proper family. Dex lifted her chin defiantly. "Sure," she said. "I'd be happy to talk."

3

JIM ALMOST WISHED he'd brought his European sedan instead of his sports car. It was hard fitting Annie's car seat into the back, and a real challenge wedging and strapping the stroller and Dex's bike half in and half out of the trunk.

Nevertheless, once he got into the driver's seat, he enjoyed squeezing his long legs against Dex's soft warmth. There were advantages to being cramped.

He chose not to question his physical response to her too closely. That night of the faculty party, he'd blamed it on a few too many drinks. Today, he ascribed his reaction to that delirious spring fever known locally as Clair De Lunacy.

All this had nothing to do with Nancy Verano, his soon-to-be fiancée. She was a special case, apart from day-to-day reality.

"So," he said as he whipped out of the parking garage into a break in traffic, "what was that business about you going away? When you told me that, I got the idea you were moving. Otherwise I'd have called."

"I meant I was going away for Christmas vacation." She squirmed as far to the right as possible. His knee still grazed her thigh, and he didn't bother to move it.

"You're sure you weren't trying to get rid of me?" he persisted.

"Would you be angry if the answer's yes?"

"Not angry," he answered. "Puzzled."

They flared through a yellow light and picked up speed, heading toward the town's outskirts. The wind coming through the window made Dex's mane dance around her head like a living thing. "Puzzled as to why I didn't utterly succumb to your charms?"

"Actually, you did," Jim reminded her.

"It was the eggnog," she said. "President Martin made it himself. He loads it with booze."

Jim had made the same excuse to himself, but hearing it from Dex bothered him. Not that his ego was bruised by the possibility that a woman might embrace him while drunk and reject him when sober.

Still, he'd experienced blissful sexual abandon with this woman, and all indications had been that she'd felt the same way. So why didn't she want a rematch?

"It wasn't necessary to make excuses," he said. "I can take no for an answer."

She frowned. "I don't know why I misled you. It's just that you're not my type."

She wasn't his type, either. At least, he hadn't thought so until he got to know her.

For someone so small, Dex had a luscious body, full-breasted and slim-waisted. Jim recalled one particular position, when he'd lain on the floor while she lowered herself onto him. They'd both cried out in pure agonized pleasure.

"We certainly fit together well enough," he said.

"I'm not like the women you usually date," she said.

They roared through the arching wrought-iron gates of Villa Bonderoff. "How would you know?"

"I've seen your picture in the paper at society goings-on," said the unwitting mother of his child. "Your dates are always tall and skinny."

"Really? I hadn't noticed." Jim tried to picture Nancy. His former high-school sweetheart was taller than Dex, definitely, and he didn't think her breasts were as big, although they'd never gone far enough for him to find out for sure.

He couldn't see her very clearly in his mind. It was odd, since they'd known each other for twenty years.

The driveway swooped uphill, winding between low trees. Although he'd built the house four years ago, Jim never lost his awe at veering around a corner and catching sight of the white Mediterranean-style swirl of rooms and balconies.

"Wow." The syllable burst from Dex, followed by the dry comment, "Not exactly cozy."

"Annie will have plenty of space and lots of toys." He swung to the right, bypassing the front guest-parking bay. "The best schools and camps, and a horse if she wants one."

"Is that what you think makes a kid happy? Possessions?" Dex demanded.

"I realize we have different lifestyles." Jim chose not to harp on the shabby state of her apartment. "But wealth doesn't preclude love, you know."

She sat in silence as the car turned into a side driveway that led to the six garages. The butler had left the station wagon outside in one of the striped parking spaces, and Jim slotted the sports car next to it.

He wondered if Dex's reticence meant he'd scored a point. He hoped so, because he wanted this child more than he'd ever wanted anything, and that was saying a lot.

Annie bubbled with glee as he got out and lifted her from the car seat. Those big brown peepers of hers darted from his face to Dex's, and then across the sweep of pink bougainvillea tumbling over a retaining wall.

"I called ahead to have my butler fix lunch," he told Dex as she joined him and Annie on the pavement. "He promised he'd send someone out for formula and baby food."

"Someone?" Dex trooped alongside as Jim strolled toward the house, taking three steps for every two he made. "How many people work here?"

"Not many," he said. "There's Rocky, the butler. And the gardener and the maid."

"Do they live here?"

"They have apartments over the garages."

"They sound like kindred spirits," she said.

Unaccountably, Jim felt a prick of jealousy.

They mounted a curving stone staircase from the driveway to the garden above. The many levels of the site had been one of its primary appeals, although Jim had experienced some regrets later when he saw the problems it created for Rocky. His butler had lost a leg while serving in the Marines.

Still physically fit at forty-one, Rocky hated having anyone give him special treatment, though. He'd always been tough, and he still was.

Come to think of it, Rocky probably figured kids ought to be treated like Marine recruits. For the first time, Jim felt a twinge of worry at the possibility that Annie might not fit into his household quite as easily as he'd assumed.

If Nancy didn't agree to marry him, he supposed he would have to hire a nanny on a long-term basis, but he didn't like the idea. Dex was right about a child needing to be with people who loved her.

At the top of the steps, his guest paused to drink in the profusion of flowers peering shyly from a rock garden. There were primroses and petunias, pansies and dianthus and something yellow and daisylike whose name he didn't know.

"This looks so natural," she said. "It's beautiful."

"My landscape architect designed the whole thing, right down to—" Jim frowned at a major weed sprouting near the edge of the bed. "Well, not that."

He made a mental note to mention it to Kip LaRue, the gardener. It wasn't the fellow's fault he was sometimes inattentive. He'd been lucky to survive a helicopter crash that left him with head injuries three years ago.

Jim's household was a testament to his early years in the Marines. He'd made rough-and-ready friends then, and now he employed some of them.

He was glad he'd called ahead to alert them to Annie's arrival. Surely at least Grace, the maid, would warm to the little creature.

The smell of disinfectant hit Jim as he opened the side door that led into a sunroom. Dex wrinkled her nose, and Annie stuck out her tongue.

"What's that smell?" Dex asked. "Never mind, I recognize it. Is somebody sick?"

"Not that I know of." Jim regarded the glass-topped ice cream table set with expensive china. "It looks like we're going to eat in here."

If not for the smell, it would have been a lovely place for lunch. The high-ceilinged room had tall glass windows, a couple of designer trees and a profusion of hanging ferns and fuchsias. Filtered green light gave the air a magical quality, as if it hovered in another dimension.

Someone, however, had scrubbed the flagstone floor with disinfectant and applied liberal doses to the walls. Jim hoped this wasn't Grace's idea of how to prepare a house for a baby, but he suspected that might be the case.

"Can we open a window?" Dex blinked, and he saw that her eyes were red-rimmed from the fumes.

"Sure." When Jim transferred the baby into her arms, Annie grabbed onto her mother like a baby monkey. He had to admit, the kid had strong ideas about whom she belonged to. "Do you have allergies?"

"Not usually. I may be allergic to your house, though," Dex said.

As he cranked open the tall windows, Jim hoped she was joking. "My maid gets a little carried away sometimes with the cleanser. She used to be a Marine drill sergeant."

"Are you serious?" Dex buried her nose in Annie's cheek.

"She mustered out four years ago."

Before he could explain further, the interior glass door crashed open. It hung on such well-oiled hinges that the slightest push made it crunch into the wall. As always, he jumped, and so did his guest.

A wheeled tray clattered through, covered with domed dishes and a small silver dish mounded with puréed fruit. It was pushed by a big man in camouflage fatigues.

"Attention!" shouted Rocky Reardon, drawing himself up to his full six-foot-five. "Mess is served!"

Dex's entire body quivered as if the sound had set her vibrating. Annie clapped her hands over her ears. "Ow," they both said.

Jim glanced anxiously at his butler. In the five years that Rocky had worked for him, the man had maintained strict discipline. Since he treated Jim as his superior officer, this posed no problems. But where would he put a baby in the chain of command?

"Rocky, this is Annie," he said. "I hope you two will get along."

Rocky's gaze fixed on the little girl. It was a quelling look that had once set recruits' knees to trembling—Jim's included.

"Ba ba?" said the baby, unafraid, and held out one hand to him.

"She likes me." Wonder trembled in Rocky's voice. "Look how little she is! Sir, she's the spittin' image of you. Only a whole lot cuter."

"You like babies?" Dex peered at him. Jim had to admire the way she refused to back off even when faced with this mountain of a man.

"Yes, ma'am," said Rocky. "I sometimes take care of my nieces and nephews. Can I hold her?"

"Sure." She waited as the butler walked stiffly across the room. People never suspected that Rocky had an artificial leg unless he chose to take it off and wave it at them, which he'd only done twice—once during a bar fight and another time when the maid demanded he cook hash the way they used to serve it in the Marines.

Rocky cradled the infant. From this great elevation, Annie studied her parents. "Whee!" she said.

"I could feed her in the other room," the butler suggested. "I'll hold her on my lap, since we don't have a high chair yet. She'll be perfectly safe, ma'am."

"I suppose that would be all right." Dex clasped her hands, as if worried but unwilling to insult the man.

"Grace went out for supplies, ma'am, but I processed this fruit here." With his free hand, Rocky scooped up the silver bowl. "It's all-natural canned peaches, no additives."

"Thank you, Rocky," Jim said.

"Yes, sir." The man shifted as if trying to figure out how to salute with a baby in one hand and a bowl of puréed fruit in the other, then settled for a nod and left the room. Jim was relieved. He'd been trying for years to get his butler to stop saluting.

Dex peeked under one of the domes. "This meal looks great."

"Help yourself." Jim removed another of the covers.

Rocky hadn't had time to prepare anything hot, but he'd done a fine job on the triangular tuna-salad sandwiches with the crusts trimmed. They were topped by sprigs of mint and accompanied by scoops of homemade potato salad.

They sat down with their plates and glasses of iced tea. A couple of times, Dex looked toward the door as if trying to see where Rocky had taken the baby, but by now they'd vanished into the depths of the house.

It occurred to Jim that a woman who'd just met a child, particularly a child she intended to give up for adoption, shouldn't be so concerned about its well-being. He wondered if Helene Saldivar had shown this much devotion, especially in light of her selection of Miss Smithers as nanny.

"What are you thinking?" Dex asked after downing a couple of rapid bites.

"I was wondering what kind of mother Dr. Saldivar made," he admitted.

"Cold and calculating," she replied promptly.

"I didn't realize you knew her," he said.

"So you agree? About her personality, I mean?"

He recalled Dr. Saldivar as he'd last seen her, at a fund-raiser last fall for the fertility center. "She did seem aloof, but I assumed it was her professional demeanor." Yet, knowing that she'd borne his daughter not long before the fund-raiser, he found it amazing that she'd been able to hide that fact. What a bizarre woman. "You're right."

"She must have been warped," Dex said. "She lied without compunction."

"On the other hand, you've been known to shade the truth yourself." Jim downed a sandwich and helped himself to seconds.

"You mean about moving away?" Dex said. "I panicked. So did you."

"Excuse me?"

"You mean it's a coincidence that you ran off and proposed to another woman one month after we...made each other's acquaintance?" she said. "You can't expect me to believe that!"

Jim frowned. He hadn't seen anything odd about proposing to Nancy a month after loving, and losing, Dex. It had seemed perfectly natural.

He'd planned to marry Nancy for a long time, but their careers had gotten in the way. Especially hers.

She'd left Clair De Lune to teach at a small college in Alaska, then jumped at an offer of a university position and research grant in Washington.

Along the way, she'd refused to accept any help from Jim. A word in the right ear, and she could have been working much closer to home. She'd wanted to succeed on her own merits, though, and he respected her decision.

Somehow the years had slipped away without his realizing it. He hadn't wanted to press her and hadn't felt any particular urgency about getting married. Not until recently.

"I figured nature was telling me something," he mused. "That I was ready to settle down."

She stared at him. "You can't mean that you had any settling-down thoughts about me!"

No, he didn't mean that. Did he? Jim tried to recall exactly what he'd been thinking and feeling four months ago, but he couldn't.

He wasn't accustomed to self-examination. For heaven's sake, he was on top of his life, his business and, above all, himself, so why flail around in search of renegade emotions? "Certainly not. The timing was purely coincidental."

"I see." Having cleaned her plate, Dex eyed the plates of carrot cake, cheesecake and chocolate mousse arrayed on the cart's lower shelf. "Do you always have three desserts?"

"Rocky didn't know what you liked," he said. "So he gave you a choice."

"I have to choose?"

"Have all three. There's more in the kitchen." Jim watched in amazement as she took him at his word, plopping three plates onto the table.

He couldn't remember the last time he'd seen a woman eat one dessert, let alone three. None of the skinny executive ladies he sometimes dated did, and as for Nancy...well, he couldn't remember.

They hadn't spent much time together since she'd moved away five years ago. Mostly they saw each other on holidays, when she came to visit her parents, or when he went to Washington on business.

It was time to get back to the subject that had brought him and Dex together. "How did you meet Dr. Saldivar, anyway?"

Busy making short work of the carrot cake, she didn't immediately answer. She approached eating, like everything else, with total absorption.

Jim flashed back to their night of lovemaking. She'd brought him alive in ways he hadn't known were possible. Her mouth, her hands, her breasts had excited him almost past bearing.

"One of my jobs is campus courier," Dex said, serenely unaware of the direction of his thoughts. "I met her while delivering mail to her department. I don't remember how the subject came up, but she said she needed a donor to help some of her desperate patients have children. So I agreed."

"Maybe she was sincere," he said. "Initially, anyway."

"Dr. Saldivar didn't see patients," Dex said.

"She didn't?"

"I found that out today. That's why I'm so angry. It was a con job, pure and simple." She patted the corners of her mouth with her cloth napkin. "How about you? How exactly did she get her hands on your sperm?"

The way she phrased the question was so startling

that Jim choked on a bite of sandwich and went into a coughing fit. Before he could recover, Dex hopped up, ran around the table and grasped him from behind.

As he struggled to break free, he felt a fist prod into his stomach. Three short thrusts against his solar plexus threatened to launch his entire set of internal organs into outer space.

"Should I call the paramedics?" she shouted.

Somehow, perhaps because his life depended on it, he managed to wheeze, "No." After a couple of swallows of iced tea, he added, "Not unless you plan to attack me again. Then I might need a stretcher."

Dex resumed her seat. "It's called the Heimlich maneuver."

"I've heard of it. I just didn't realize it was a new form of assault." He waved away her response. "I'm kidding. It's a good skill to know, but you were too quick off the launching pad. I could have coughed that food up by myself."

"Better safe than sorry," said Dex.

He didn't have a response. Not a coherent one, anyway. Instead, as soon as he caught up on his breathing, he returned to her earlier question. "You asked about Helene."

"Maybe I shouldn't have." Dex quirked an eyebrow. "What went on between the two of you really isn't my business."

"Me and Dr. Saldivar?" He felt like coughing again, but restrained himself. "Not even remotely. Besides, don't you think I'd have questioned her motives if she suddenly whipped out a vial and preserved a specimen?"

"She could be very persuasive."

He laughed. "I suppose so, but in my case, she was doing me a favor. Making sure I was fertile."

"Why?" Dex asked.

It was disconcerting, the way she asked such personal questions without blinking. It threw him off balance, and Jim wasn't accustomed to anyone else getting the upper hand. Or forming one into a fist and plunging it into his midsection, either.

"There's no need to go into details," he said. "If you're going to be living here, we need to respect each other's privacy."

"Whoa!" She stopped halfway through the slice of cheese cake. "I haven't agreed to that."

So she wanted to play hardball. Well, Jim was a master at that game.

"Fine. I'll have my lawyer draw up the custody papers, you can sign Annie over to me, and that'll be the end of it." He folded his arms and leaned back to await the fireworks.

4

INSTEAD OF ARGUING, Dex regarded him calmly. "What amazes me is that a man who has everything could be so selfish."

In his outrage, Jim forgot about maintaining the upper hand. "What makes you say that?"

"You just want Annie because she's got your genes," Dex said. "You can't love her, because you don't know her. And since you're planning to get married, you can have plenty more children. Your wife probably won't be crazy about taking care of a stepdaughter, anyway. So why deny her to some family whose empty arms are aching?"

Jim allowed himself a rare moment of self-searching. *Was* he simply latching onto this baby because her eyes matched his?

No, he decided. If he brought to fatherhood the same determination that had enabled him to build his business into a billion-dollar enterprise, he could make this child the happiest person on earth.

"My daughter will be privileged and loved and special," he said. "Ask any of my employees what I'm like. Did you know I was voted Clair De Lune's boss of the year?"

"A child isn't an employee." Dex regarded him coolly. Why wasn't she as impressed by his accomplishments as all the other women he met? Jim wondered.

"As her mother, I can't let Annie stay here without a fight. I realize that if I get the campus legal aid center involved, I'm likely to end up with custody of Rocky and you'll have to marry my landlady. But I owe it to my conscience to try."

Jim remembered the scrambled custody case in question. He hated to admit it, but although his firm had high-priced attorneys on staff, he was terrified of the legal aid center. Its bumbling amateurs had a gift for turning cases so inside out and backward that judges temporarily lost their bearings.

"All I'm asking is for you to move in for a week," he said. "Observe me in action. See for yourself how happy our daughter will be." The word *our* made him lose his train of thought. How had that slipped out?

"No," Dex replied. "I have a home, as little as you may think of it. And friends. And a life. For all you know, I might even have a boyfriend."

"Do you?" he demanded, then wondered why the prospect disturbed him. After that one night of bliss, he'd accepted that he and Dex weren't destined to roll around in the bedroom together again, even though it felt like sheer heaven.

"No," she admitted.

Jim's relief lasted only until he remembered the real subject of their discussion. After setting his plate on the cart, he leaned forward earnestly.

"If you don't want to move in here, fine," he said. "Leave Annie with me for a while and then see for yourself how she's doing. If you truly find that I'm unsuited to care for her, I'll give her up."

She shook her head. "You won't. It's a ploy."

"I'm not a liar." He meant what he said. Still, Jim was forced to concede he wasn't sure he could give up his daughter if push came to shove. "In any case, if we fight it out in court, a judge is unlikely to force me to put Annie up for adoption. At best, we'd get joint custody. Is that what you want?"

A wistful expression touched her face, and for a second, yearning shone in Dex's eyes. Then she swallowed hard. "I'm not the nurturing type."

"Then give me a chance." Jim knew when to press his point. "I promise, if the arrangement really isn't working, I'll agree to an adoption. In either case, Annie gets a home and you're off the hook."

"I'll have to think about it."

Far back in the house, male and female voices rose in a dispute. Grace must have returned from the grocery store, and judging by the noise, she and Rocky were disagreeing about the baby.

Jim wished Dex had left the house before the argument erupted, since it didn't speak well for his household. However, she hadn't, and he needed to resolve it. "Excuse me for a minute."

"I'm coming, too." She scrambled alongside him into the hallway.

He could make out the words clearly now. Rocky was saying, "What idiot sterilizes disposable diapers? For Pete's sake, you can't put bleach next to a baby's skin!"

"I'm not putting it next to her skin, you pie-faced moron!" the maid boomed. "I'm applying it to the outside of the diaper. This gizmo's probably loaded with germs!"

"The chief assigned me to baby detail, not you. Get away from her," Rocky growled.

"Are they always like this?" Dex asked as they hurried through the large, gleaming kitchen.

"Occasionally," Jim admitted. "I think they miss being in action."

At the entrance to the utility room, he halted. Dex wiggled into the doorway beside him, her hip brushing his thigh. He squelched the impulse to swivel and pin her against the door frame and instead focused on the scene in front of him.

On a changing pad atop the washing machine lay Annie. Before her fascinated gaze, the hulking butler and the nearly six-foot-tall maid, who at thirty-seven was as buffed up as she'd ever been, squared off in a tug-of-war over a disposable diaper. Mercifully, Grace had already set down her bleach bottle, right next to a spray can of antiseptic.

"Give it here!" shouted the maid, and yanked the diaper away from the butler. So caught up were the antagonists that they failed to notice the new arrivals.

Rocky grabbed the diaper and gave another jerk. The fibers parted and the diaper ripped raggedly in half, sending them both stumbling.

"See what you've done?" snapped the butler. "Now go wash the latrines. No wonder a knucklehead like you never made sergeant major!" He reached for another diaper from an open plastic carton.

"Don't you dare let one of those contaminated things touch that sweet little baby's bottom!" roared Grace.

"I'll do as I please." Rocky patted the diaper against Annie's knee, which was the closest part of her anatomy. "So what are you going to do about it?"

Jim cleared his throat to announce his presence, but it was too late. An infuriated Grace butted headfirst into Rocky's stomach, bowling him over with a huge *oof*. On the washer, Annie clapped her hands in delight.

Still doubled up, Rocky grabbed the maid by the waist. He flipped her over his shoulder and sent her sliding onto the floor with a *splat*.

"That's enough!" Jim said.

The pair stopped, breathing heavily. From her position flat on her back, Grace glared at him. Rocky didn't look pleased at the interruption, either.

"Permission to speak freely, sir?" he said. "This is between Sergeant Mars and myself."

He had a point. Jim generally allowed his staff to work out their own differences. They were, after all, competent adults.

As he weighed the situation, Dex hurried across the utility room to the changing station. "Neither of you knows the first thing about babies."

"Do you?" Jim couldn't resist asking.

"I baby-sat all through high school." She pulled another diaper from the package. "First of all, you don't need to sterilize disposable diapers."

Rocky beamed. Grace's mouth twisted in dismay as she got to her feet.

With a speed and ease that left her audience in awe, Dex grasped Annie's ankles, lifted her little bottom and whipped off the old diaper from beneath her sundress. In milliseconds, the baby was cleaned and rediapered.

"Awesome." Grace dusted herself off.

"As for you—" Dex swung toward the butler "—leaving a baby unattended in a high place is very dangerous. You should never even take your hand off her while she's being changed."

Now both staff members appeared crestfallen. Jim had never seen anyone take on his ex-Marines and win, hands down. He couldn't resist a sneaking admiration for this diminutive whirlwind.

"We'll do better in the future, ma'am," Rocky said.

"You bet you will!" Dex released an exaggerated sigh. "Like it or not, I'm going to have to move in here until you two complete basic training." She shot a stern look at Jim. "Did you plan this?"

He shook his head. "Honestly, no."

She handed him the baby. "Try to keep out of trouble while I go pack a few things, will you?"

"I'll drive you, ma'am," said Grace.

"Thanks, but I've got my bike," she said, and departed, leaving them all stunned.

After a moment, Rocky said, "She's quite a woman, sir."

"I'm afraid we don't know the half of it yet," said Jim.

DEX'S LEGS pumped as she cycled along University Avenue. She kept her head down and aimed for speed, trying to work off those three desserts.

Jim lived on the northeastern edge of town, where the Claire De Lune flatlands began to rise into the foothills of the San Gabriel Mountains. The university was located due west of his house, also on rising ground.

Much of the land in this part of Clair De Lune remained undeveloped due to the uneven terrain, so there wasn't much traffic for Dex to contend with. Which was a good thing, with her mind in turmoil.

Had she really agreed to move in with Jim Bonderoff? The man was maddeningly arrogant—boss of the year, indeed!—and knew less than nothing about children. He also had an endearing smile, brown eyes touched with mischief and a masculine way of moving that made her want to chuck off her clothes all over again.

The plan was insane.

Even more inexplicable was Dex's reaction to Annie. From the moment she'd met her daughter, she'd felt as if the child were a missing part of herself.

It was ridiculous, of course. For the child's first nine months, Dex hadn't even known of her existence. Had Helene Saldivar not suffered an untimely death, Annie might have grown up and even wandered across Dex's path, unrecognized and unremarked.

No. I'd have realized the moment I saw her, no matter where, that she was me. Or, at least, half me.

Rounding a bend in the curving road, Dex spotted the redbrick university dorms ahead on her right. She'd lived there for four years and still missed the camaraderie with her dorm mates.

She would miss her little apartment and her friendship with Marie Pipp, too, when she finished her dissertation and found a teaching job. There was practically no chance of landing one at De Lune U., which hired only experienced full-time teaching staff.

Her parents, on the occasions when they communicated with Dex, harped on the point that it was time to finish her dissertation and launch a stellar career in academe. They would agree, one-hundred percent, about putting Annie up for adoption.

What if I don't want a stellar career in academe? What if what I really want is right here?

But she couldn't have it. She was in no position to raise Annie herself, even if Jim would agree. As for the man who had breached her defenses without even trying, he was in love with someone else.

And wrong for her, anyway. Too smooth. Too rich. Too...everything.

Dex pedaled harder. She flew past the entrance to the campus and down University Avenue to Sirius Street, where she turned left into the middle-class residential area in which she lived.

She tried to focus on how good it would feel when she finished her dissertation. She could devote herself to teaching, research and writing professional articles. At last, she would make her own place in the world.

The bike zipped past a cozy bungalow. In the porch swing, a young mother rocked her baby while watching a toddler splash in a wading pool.

Dex's heart swelled. Why did she keep torturing herself? It was inexplicable, yet since childhood, Dex had treasured forbidden dreams of domesticity.

She'd sneaked romance novels into her bedroom, and in the margins of school notes, invented elaborate baby names like Eldridge and Valeria. Isolated by the twin handicaps of insecurity and overweight, she'd found her greatest pleasure in reading and in babysitting.

But regardless of what her instincts told her, she wasn't cut out to be a mother. And while Jim Bonderoff might make a decent enough father if he had the right wife, he didn't, and he might never have.

What kind of girlfriend hadn't bothered to accept his proposal in three months?

What Dex wanted for her daughter was the one thing that had been denied to her: the chance to grow up loved and cherished and nurtured so she could pass those qualities on to her own children. And it was obvious that neither Jim nor his blundering staff members were equipped to give Annie this kind of upbringing.

She turned a corner and swooped down Forest Lane. Mrs. Zimpelman, who was leaning on her rake and listening on the phone, smiled when she spotted the bicycle. She began talking in animated fashion, no doubt boring a friend with the news of Dex's arrival home.

Across the street, Dean Pipp knelt in the garden snipping herbs into a wicker basket. She wore a floppy black hat, a gingham apron over a shapeless gray dress and a pair of skaters' pads on her knobby knees.

"Hello, there!" she called. "What did the lawyer want?"

Dex angled her bicycle around the side of the house and came to explain about Helene and Annie and Jim. By the time she finished, Marie had finished gathering her herbs and led the way into her book-filled house.

"I'll certainly miss you." The dean removed her apron and knee pads and hung them on a coatrack. "It's only for a week, though, you say?"

"Or less, if I can persuade him that adoption is the best course." Dex tried not to dwell on how difficult it was going to be to wrench her daughter away from one self-important father and a pair of no-holds-barred leathernecks.

The elderly woman frowned at a padded envelope lying on her hall table. "Oh, dear, I must have put the mail here and forgotten. What is this?"

Dex glanced at the envelope. It bore the return address of a rare books dealer. "Something you ordered?"

"Well, yes, of course," said Dean Pipp. "Now I remember. I asked for everything they had about the Richard Grafton controversy. I'm afraid there isn't much."

Knowing that her landlady wrote papers about obscure literary matters, Dex tried to dredge the name Richard Grafton from her memory, but failed. "Was he a poet?"

"Oh, surely you remember Richard Grafton." The dean rattled open a drawer, pulled out a sharp engraving knife and sliced open the envelope to reveal an aging volume. On the cover was imprinted Chronicles of England, by Richard Grafton. "He was a sixteenth-century writer."

"Refresh my memory," said Dex.

"It's all in here." Her landlady smiled and recited from memory, "'Thirty dayes hath November, Aprill, June and September, February hath twenty-eight alone, and all the rest have thirty-one.'"

"He wrote that?" Dex asked.

"Yes, but did he write it *first*?" The dean cocked an eyebrow as if inviting Dex into a fascinating mystery. "There's a similar poem by William Harrison, written at almost the same time, and rhymes of that nature pop up elsewhere in folklore."

"I see. So there's a controversy." Dex regarded her landlady fondly. Hardly anyone was likely to care who really wrote that bit of doggerel, but she had no doubt that it would make a fascinating article.

"Oh!" Marie dropped the book on the table with a thump. "I nearly forgot! There's a student in your apartment. She wanted to talk to you about something or other and insisted on waiting. Her name is, let's see, Coreen or Cara or..."

"Cora Angle." The student had asked to speak to Dex after receiving a D-plus on a paper. Dex had suggested she drop by so they could have some privacy, but they hadn't specified a time. "I'd better hurry. She's upset enough as it is."

"See you later." Clearly absorbed in her project, Dean Pipp wandered into the living room, reading the book out loud. She was still wearing her floppy hat.

Hoping that Cora hadn't been waiting long, Dex let herself out of the house and loped toward the freestanding garage. From the driveway, a straight, weathered staircase led to the apartment. She clattered up and opened the door, which she left unlocked during the day.

The single room looked smaller and darker than usual, by contrast to the expansive scale of Jim's house. Dex didn't see anyone, but she heard a tuneless mumble coming from the tiny kitchen. She had to close the door to take a look, because the kitchen was behind it.

Cora Angle, her large frame cramped in the small space, was wiping a dish and carrying on a conversation with herself. "I shouldn't hang around," she muttered. "She's obviously busy. She did promise to see you. I'll only be in the way."

One glance at the open cabinets showed Dex that her thrift-store dishes had been rearranged. They were stacked in an orderly manner, the plates and saucers on the lower shelf, cups and glasses on the upper one.

"Oh, hi!" The tall freshman stopped wiping and gave her a tentative smile. Pale blond hair straggled down Cora's pudgy cheeks, and there was a dust smear on the shoulder of her tan smock.

"You've been working hard." Dex decided not to point out that the new arrangement, while more efficient, put the cups too high for her to reach easily. She could always switch them back later.

"I like to organize things." The chubby girl watched her apprehensively, as if expecting a rebuke. She reminded Dex of herself not many years ago.

"Well, thank you." She indicated the half-full coffeemaker. "Care for something to drink?"

"Okay. Sure," said her guest. "I'm sorry for just showing up. I mean, I know you weren't expecting me."

"It's okay," Dex assured her. "I told you to drop by, right?"

"Right." Cora cleared her throat. "Listen, I just came to tell you I decided to drop out. I guess college is too hard for me."

"If you were smart enough to get in, you're smart enough to do the work." Dex frowned as she poured the coffee. She hated to see anyone leave, especially after less than a year. "A lot of people have trouble adjusting. How are your other classes?"

Cora put two spoonfuls of sugar in her coffee and slouched in a seat at the counter. "Cs and a few Ds. College is costing my parents a lot of money, and I'm not doing well enough to justify it."

"Do you want me to see if there's financial help available?" Dex refused to give up easily. True, the young woman's papers and tests had been mediocre and sometimes worse, but she might blossom.

"I've already got a partial scholarship." The young woman shrugged. "Originally, my parents said I should just get a job, but when I won the scholarship, they agreed to help. The thing is, I knew from the first few days that I made a mistake by coming here, but I didn't want to admit it."

"What makes you think so?" Dex asked.

The freshman's forehead wrinkled. "The other kids all seem so sure of themselves. I never know what the teachers expect. I keep trying to guess, and getting it wrong."

With relief, Dex realized that she might be able to help. "Maybe that's the problem. You're too busy trying to second-guess the professors instead of expressing your own point of view."

"But who would care what I think?" Cora nibbled at the split ends of her hair.

"I do," Dex said. "Listen, I'll make you a deal."

"What kind of deal?" The young woman fiddled with her coffee cup.

"You promise to stay in college for the rest of the semester," Dex said. "In exchange, I'll critique your papers in advance for your other classes. I can't in fairness help you prepare for Professor Bemling's class, since I'll be grading you, but what you learn should apply to everything."

"I—I can't afford to pay you much," the freshman said.

"No charge," said Dex.

"I can't accept such generosity." Cora pressed her lips together before continuing. "Besides, I'm sure there are more deserving students."

I'm going to rescue you whether you want me to or not. "First of all, you deserve my help as much as anybody. Second, I'm not being generous. Consider this a loan," Dex said. "Next year, you can tutor a freshman who's having problems, and she can pass the favor on to someone else the following year, and so forth. How's that?"

Reluctantly, the woman nodded. She must be eighteen or nineteen, and yet she seemed very young. At twenty-six, Dex had considered herself still a kid. Until today.

Now she was a mother. And a tutor. Next to Cora, she felt practically ancient.

Then she remembered that she was going to be staying at Jim's. "Let me give you another address. I'll be helping out a friend with some baby-sitting for a week. You can contact me there."

She hated to hedge, but people gossiped like crazy around campus. The discovery that James Bonderoff had a daughter by Helene Saldivar, and that the biological mother was a mere teaching assistant, would fan the flames to wildfire proportions.

Cora accepted the slip of paper gratefully. "I can't believe you'd do this for me."

"That's why I'm in the teaching field," Dex said.

After the freshman left, she mulled over the conversation. *Was* she in education because she enjoyed helping people? That hadn't been mentioned anywhere in her parents' expectations.

She did enjoy her time in the classroom on those occasions when Hugh was ill or at a conference. The problem was that college-level instruction required researching and writing professional papers, which she did *not* enjoy. Also, the lectures were often delivered to large groups of students with little or no personal contact and the grading left to an assistant.

Well, it didn't matter. She didn't belong in any other world, so she had better make the best of this one.

After tucking a few changes of clothes and her personal care items into a backpack, Dex opened her desk drawers and flipped through the notes she'd accumulated for her dissertation. She really ought to finish it this coming summer, which was only a few months away.

She'd chosen to write about how the structure of Shakespeare's plays prefigured movies and television. While watching Kenneth Branagh's movie version of *Henry V,* Dex had been struck by how visual it was and how well the scenes, with little adaptation, worked on the screen.

Her parents had agreed that it was an interesting subject. Her mother had sent a long letter with suggestions for how to approach the matter, and her father had urged her to publish the thesis as soon as possible to gain critical attention.

That had been a year ago. Since then, Dex hadn't been able to muster any interest in working on the dissertation. It seemed to belong more to her parents than to her.

Oh, grow up, she told herself. As soon as she returned from Jim's, she would buckle down and get to work.

A short time later, she locked the door and set off with her backpack. En route, she stopped at a baby store and bought a bicycle seat for Annie. It was quite an extravagance, since she'd only be able to use it for a week, but perhaps she could give it to the adoptive parents.

Maybe Annie would stay in Clair De Lune. Maybe Dex would see her from time to time, riding in this very bicycle seat, whizzing around town behind some bearded man or long-haired woman.

Unexpectedly, tears pricked her eyes. It must have been the wind.

5

AFTER HIS LUNCH with Dex on Friday, Jim Bonderoff returned to his office for two hours. In that time, he made one hundred million dollars.

That was how much his stock went up when news was announced of a faster, smaller computer chip developed by researchers at Bonderoff Visionary Technologies. The company's other investors became similarly enriched, and he declared a bonus for employees.

Word traveled fast. De Lune University President Wilson Martin was one of the first to call with congratulations and a hint about future donations.

Of course, he didn't ask Jim for money directly. What he said was, "I want to take this opportunity to thank you for your past generosity to our school."

"And I want to tell you how much I've enjoyed being an honorary Ph.D." Jim, who'd never completed college, had been thrilled to receive the degree at graduation ceremonies last June. It honored his achievements in the fields of business and technology.

"You earned it, buddy!" Wilson Martin spoke with a gung-ho attitude more reminiscent of a car salesman than of a university president. Right now, he would be sitting at his desk, brushing back the thick hair that he dyed silver to disguise the fact that he was only forty-two years old. "By the way, did you hear the tragic news about Dr. Saldivar?"

"Something about an elephant, I gather." Jim propped up his foot and retied one of his jogging shoes. He dressed comfortably whenever he didn't have an important meeting.

"Tragic loss," Wilson said. "It was her dream to someday see us establish a medical school on campus."

It hadn't taken the man long to work his way around to his longtime dream. Jim doubted it had also been Helene's, but obviously she provided a convenient way of bringing up the subject.

Well, Jim was a hundred million dollars richer, minus taxes. Why not make a sizable donation? He was on the verge of proposing it when something occurred to him.

He had a daughter. This money was hers, too.

Not that he intended to spoil her. He considered it foolish to give young people huge amounts of money. Still, he felt for the first time as if he were the custodian of his wealth instead of its outright owner.

"I'd be happy to look at some cost projections," he said.

"We'll get right on them," the president responded. "In any case, we're always glad to see BVT prospering. It's good for the community."

Jim was glad when the man rang off. Not that he disliked Wilson Martin, but Jim had other things on his mind. One in particular, and she was waiting in his outer office.

He strode across the variegated carpet and went into the adjacent room. Between the fax machines, copiers and computers sat a portable playpen.

Five women stood, leaned and knelt around the playpen, making cooing noises. Jim assumed they had wandered over to enjoy the unexpected visitor. He couldn't even spot the tiny figure inside until he got close enough to see over the women's shoulders.

Ignoring a pile of stuffed animals and toys, Annie sat regarding the women around her with mingled interest and uncertainty. Someone had fixed tiny yellow ribbons in her hair, one of which had fallen out.

As he approached, the little girl plopped onto her knees and crawled toward the fallen ribbon. Her audience responded with encouraging cries of, "Go for it!" and "You can do it, honey!"

Jim cleared his throat. The response was electric. The five women swiveled, straightened, or—depending on their starting position—leaped to their feet. They weren't afraid of him, but they did seem embarrassed to be caught making goo-goo eyes at a baby.

"Congratulations, Jim!"

"Way to go on the stock market!"

"I guess I'll be getting my new house soon!" This last remark was a reference to BVT's stock-option program, which extended to all employees.

Four of the women melted away and returned to their offices. Only his secretary, Lulu Lee, remained. "She's so cute! I can't believe how lucky you are!"

He hadn't told anyone who the mother was, only that he'd recently learned he had a daughter. People would talk, of course, but that couldn't be helped.

"I'm not sure those yellow ribbons are such a good idea," Jim said. "Couldn't she swallow one?"

"Oh!" Lulu leaned in and snatched the fallen ribbon from the playpen. Then she began removing the others from Annie's hair. "Willa from accounting put them on her."

Jim crouched next to the playpen. "How's it going?" he asked the baby.

"Ga ga da da." She hoisted herself to her feet, hanging onto the rim of the playpen.

He was lost. If there had been some other task Jim meant to accomplish today, he forgot it utterly.

"Look at her!" he said. "Nine months old and she's standing up! She must be some kind of genius."

"I wouldn't doubt it." Lulu gave him a teasing smile.

"You don't seem surprised. Do they all do that?"

His secretary, who had long expressed a desire to have children if her boyfriend ever got around to popping the question, nodded sagely. "According to the books, they often stand by this age. Some children are even walking by now."

"They must be freaks of nature," Jim said. "If Annie isn't doing it, it can't be normal."

"She's a bright child," Lulu said. "I wonder where she got that hair."

It was as far as his secretary would go toward prying. Jim made a mental note never to let her catch a glimpse of Dex. Lulu's hair was lustrously straight and black, bespeaking her Chinese heritage.

It was only natural for her to be curious about Annie's mother, he reminded himself. "Must be a throwback," he said, in response to her statement. "I think my great-grandmother stuck her finger in a light socket once."

Then he remembered that this little girl would someday inherit the company. It wasn't too soon to prepare her for taking the reins of command. "I'm going to give her a tour of the facilities."

"I'm sure she'll enjoy that," Lulu said.

Annie did. For the first five minutes, she took a keen interest in all the blinking computers and admiring employees.

Jim's tale of how he'd started the company in a garage, moved to a leased plant and finally built this facility quickly bored the baby. She yawned. Then she drooped against his shoulder.

"Nap time," said one of the women engineers.

Jim had forgotten that babies needed naps. No wonder this one was exhausted. She'd had a long day, and it wasn't even five o'clock yet.

He took her out to his covered parking spot. This afternoon, he'd brought the European sedan with an infant seat installed in the back. Strapping a sleepy baby into it turned out to be a challenge, but he was getting used to manipulating her tiny limbs.

When his nose brushed her cheek, he discovered that she smelled like Dex and was startled to realize he missed the woman. Missed her mentally *and* physically.

Thinking about her was dangerous. For safety, Jim tried to focus on Nancy.

As always, the image of his calm, self-possessed pal soothed him. After his mother died of cancer when he was fourteen, she'd been the friend he turned to for comfort and advice while his father worked long hours selling insurance.

In the month following his rendezvous with Dex, Jim had felt restless and off-center. That was why he'd flown to Washington and proposed to Nancy. It had been, he told himself, a wise step toward his chosen future, and the fulfillment of long-cherished plans.

He wished she had accepted immediately. Instead, she'd murmured that things were up in the air at her university and that her career was at a turning point. Jim hadn't wanted to press her, but for some reason, the knowledge that Dex would be living in his household made him more anxious than ever to set a wedding date.

Jim pulled the car out of the parking lot and glanced at Annie. She was dozing peacefully in the back seat as he halted for a red light. Impulsively, he dialed Nancy's number on the car phone. It was about eight o'clock in D.C., so she ought to be home.

"Hi, this is Nancy," purred her familiar voice. The sound was so smooth that he expected her to add that he should leave a message after the beep, but she didn't.

"Are you there?" Jim said into the hands-free speaker. "In person, I mean?"

"Jim?" Nancy said. "It's great to hear from you. What's up?"

He'd last called her about a month ago. She'd told him how well her parents were doing and had brought him current on the activities of her six younger siblings.

The topic of his proposal hadn't come up. Jim didn't want to broach it too abruptly this time, either, nor did he wish to brag about his stock coup. There was, however, other news he needed to tell her. "I wanted to let you know that I have a baby."

The silence lasted until the light turned green. Then she said, "A baby?"

As he accelerated north on Mercury Lane, he explained about Helene Saldivar. There seemed no point in mentioning Dex, so he didn't.

When he was done, Nancy said, "A baby. Well, that is a surprise."

"You don't mind, do you?" he asked. "I know you spent a lot of time taking care of your younger brothers and sisters, but you like kids, right?"

"Of course." Nancy sounded as if she were thinking things over. "You know, my current research involves babies."

"What sort of research?"

"I'm investigating how infants acquire language," she said.

"Annie says 'da da' quite clearly," he boasted as he drove through the gates of Villa Bonderoff.

"Specifically, I'm investigating how some babies acquire multiple languages. In any case, she's there and I'm here, so it's irrelevant," Nancy said briskly.

"How's it going with your grant? You mentioned something about problems."

"Nothing you need to worry about." She always changed the subject if there were any possibility he might make a donation to benefit her. Nancy never coveted his money, even though it was thanks to her encouragement that he'd taken the first steps toward success.

She was a great friend and a beautiful woman. Even in high school, she'd had an air of sophistication, and she was always coolly in control of herself.

He wished they were already married. He wished they'd been married for years. Then he wouldn't have to fight these confusing, maddening, tantalizing images of Dex, naked and eager, that kept sneaking into his mind.

He reached the main parking area in front of his garages. "I've got to go, Nancy. Just wondered if you'd given any more thought to our future."

"Lots of it," she said. "If things work out the way I plan, I should have everything settled within a week. We'll talk again."

The word *settled* could be taken in either of several ways. Would she settle matters in his favor or settle permanently somewhere else? "What do you mean by—"

"I have to run. Duty calls. Take care!"

"You, too." After he clicked off, it occurred to Jim that since he'd called Nancy at her apartment, she wasn't likely to have any test babies lying around needing attention. Had she deliberately cut off the conversation?

He lost his train of thought when he noticed the bicycle parked by the curving stone staircase. And here came Dex, trotting down from the rock garden above.

Leaves and blossoms—lavender, yellow, white— clung to her brown hair, and a frothy pink sweater hugged her curvaceous body above clinging jeans. With her eyes alight, she was the spirit of springtime.

Jim got out and stood in the driveway, feeling like a teenager again. Pure raw lust rampaged through him.

"Where's Annie?" Without waiting for a response, Dex flung open the car's back door and crawled in. Her rear end waggled invitingly as she fumbled with the snaps and straps and then, after a dazzling gymnastic maneuver, she emerged with the baby.

Jim dragged himself back to reality. He was supposed to be the suave, urbane host, not some overgrown adolescent tripping over his tongue.

"Did Rocky show you to a guest room?" he asked. "I hope it's big enough." There were four bedrooms on the second floor, in addition to the master suite.

"It's fine," Dex said as she carried the cooing baby toward the house. "By the way, Grace and Rocky are fighting again. You might want to stop them before they rupture something."

"Now you tell me." Jim broke into a lope.

Disputes were nothing new in his household, but they hadn't turned violent in a long time. Not since the first few days after Grace joined the household, when she'd insisted that Rocky cook hash and rock-hard biscuits the way she liked them. He'd not only refused but insulted her taste buds.

The two of them had known each other distantly in the service, but not until they were both working for Jim had they found themselves cheek by jowl. Each wanted to be top dog, and it had taken a while for them to learn to compromise.

Jim still winced at the memory of Rocky's black eye and Grace's limping from their early clashes. After a few painful days, they'd come to an agreement. Grace had relinquished mess food in exchange for the right to maintain such Marine traditions as sounding reveille at six in the morning. and hoisting the flag at eight.

Jim raced through the garden room and veered down the hallway into the kitchen. Cooking smells wafted from the stove, but he saw the burners had been turned off.

Wrestler-type grunts emanated from deep within

the house. Heading to his left, Jim passed the utility room and halted in the doorway of the den.

Light streaming through French doors silhouetted the hulking shapes of his two servants. Grace, the smaller of the two but by no means the weaker, had hoisted Rocky onto her shoulders and was twirling him around. Both of them groaned like hogs at feeding time.

"He gets seasick, you know," Jim said.

The only response was a couple more grunts. He interpreted them as meaning, "What kind of Marine gets seasick?"

"It only points out how dedicated he was," he continued. "By the way, what's this fight about, anyway?"

Grace stopped whirling and studied Jim blearily. It was the first time he'd seen the usually spotless maid in such a disheveled condition. Her determination to stick to Marine traditions had led her to insist on wearing a uniform in domestic service, too, although she'd bypassed camouflage for an outfit more consistent with her new duties. Usually she starched and ironed every stitch, right down, he sometimes suspected, to her underwear.

Now, however, her apron was ripped and flopping down at one side, she had a run in her stockings and the frilly white serving cap hung rakishly over her forehead.

"He told me to stick my can of disinfectant where the sun never shines," she growled.

Rocky, balanced horizontally on Grace's shoulders, made a low, wheezing sound. Jim interpreted it to mean, "But, chief, the whole house reeks!"

"Yes, I can smell it," he said, approaching them.

"Grace, it isn't necessary to sterilize the house. Babies aren't that delicate. Put Rocky down, would you?"

Grimacing, she lowered the butler to his feet. His face, Jim saw, had gone deathly pale.

With a low moan, the butler stumbled across the room and out through the French doors. Jim could hear him puking into the bushes.

"You wash that down with the hose!" Grace yelled. "No fair sticking Kip with your mess! He's weird enough already." Assuming a level tone, she addressed Jim. "Do you know, ever since Kip banged his head in that helicopter crash, he thinks letters and numbers have colors?"

"He's a good gardener," Jim said. "Now listen, you and Rocky have got to work things out."

"Just let me pound him a little more," said Grace. "He'll come around."

"That isn't the way it's done in civilian life." Before he could continue, Jim's spine tingled, and he realized that Dex was standing behind him.

Glancing back, he drank in the appearance of the two bristle-haired females, their lively faces so much alike. He hated to admit it, but the more time he spent around his daughter, the more resemblance he saw to her mother.

Maybe fifty percent, he was willing to concede. At maximum.

Annie beamed at Grace and clapped her hands. "More!" she said.

The room went utterly still. Even Rocky, staggering in through the double doors, paused in mid-stride.

"That was her first word!" Dex crowed. "Wasn't it? Did she say anything today while I was gone?"

"Just ga ga da da," said Jim.

"Ba ba," replied Annie, as if they were carrying on a conversation.

Rocky's face glowed like a Christmas candle. Grace blinked several times rapidly.

As far as Jim was concerned, the moment was worth more than a hundred million dollars.

6

A WARM GLOW enveloped Dex. Annie's first word!

True, she'd apparently been requesting more violence, which wasn't desirable, but she'd spoken. The person inside the cute little shape had communicated directly with them.

It was only a small step to more words, then short sentences. Soon a torrent of speech would spew forth insight into her daughter's mind and emerging personality.

It's a miracle.

Dex hugged the baby. How could she give her up?

Her throat clogged as she regarded the three faces watching her or, rather, watching Annie. Rocky's, pale but delighted. Grace's, sternly protective. And Jim's, the handsome features transformed by tenderness.

Was he right? Did their daughter belong here rather than with some adoptive family?

But if Annie were here, Dex wouldn't be able to stay away. She'd be underfoot, watching from close by as Jim married and as his new wife, no doubt a shining example of all that was nurturing, gave Annie the love and support that Dex couldn't.

It would break her heart. Dex yearned to be that perfect woman, but she didn't have it in her. Her fumbling attempts might fool other adults, but they would leave Annie's needs unmet. And Jim's, too.

Dex knew even less about relationships than about mothering. None of her boyfriends had lasted long, for reasons that eluded her.

In addition to not understanding men, she didn't understand herself. She didn't know, for instance, why Jim had scared her so much on their terrific night together that she'd lied to him about moving away.

She also didn't understand why he'd forgotten her so quickly and proposed to someone else. It was all too confusing, a swamp into which she would sink forever if she weren't careful.

Life for Dex was safest alone. And Annie would be safest with a new family. No matter how perfect Jim's bride-to-be was, surely she would resent being forced to raise another woman's child.

"I'll keep a journal about her first words," Dex said. "So her adoptive parents will have a record of them."

"Adoptive parents?" said Grace.

"Dex and I disagree on the subject," Jim told her. He gave no hint that it was out of place for a maid to question her employer's child-rearing plans.

"They could live here," Rocky suggested. "It's big enough."

"Live here?" Grace echoed in amazement. "What, a pair of adoptive parents move into the baby's father's mansion? You've been watching too many daytime talk shows!"

"I never watch daytime talk shows," Rocky replied stiffly. "And I refuse to be taunted into another fight."

"Because you'd lose," said Grace.

Jim held up his hands. "Rocky, how's dinner coming along? Grace, I believe you've got liberty call."

The maid stood her ground for a moment, then nodded. "Thank you, sir. See you at Colors on Monday, if not before."

"Good night, Grace."

Dex watched the maid depart through the French doors. After she was gone, Rocky headed for the kitchen.

"What's liberty call?" Dex shifted the baby onto her hip.

"Free time. It means she's off duty," Jim explained.

"And what's Colors?"

"That's when we raise the flag. Eight a.m. on weekdays," he said.

Dex wondered how the future Mrs. Bonderoff would enjoy living on a Marine base. On the other hand, maybe the future Mrs. Bonderoff *was* a Marine.

"Make yourself comfortable. Dinner should be ready soon." Jim gestured toward a couch.

"Thanks." Dex placed Annie on the floor and sat down. The baby crawled to a bookcase and examined the book spines.

"I think you mentioned that you're a doctoral candidate?" Jim relaxed into an armchair.

"Working on my dissertation," she said.

"Feel free to bring your materials here," he said. "I've got several computers in the house. You're welcome to use one."

"I'm working on my dissertation *slowly*," she clarified.

Annie crawled toward the open French doors. Outside, a man's slim figure materialized, closed the doors and vanished. Dex couldn't see his features clearly, but got the impression of a sensitive mouth and large, sad eyes. "Who's that?"

"Kip, the gardener," Jim said. "He used to be full of bravado, a real rock-'em-sock-'em type. Then he nearly died in a helicopter accident. The brain injuries changed his personality."

"How come your whole staff is Marines?" Dex asked.

"They're my buddies." Leaning back, Jim laced his fingers behind his head. "I was a real rabble-rouser when I got out of high school. Surfing wasn't enough of an adventure for me, so I enlisted."

"You postponed college?" Dex asked.

"Not exactly. I took some courses while I was in the service, in the computer field, but I never got a degree," Jim said. "Not unless you count my honorary Ph.D."

Dex supposed that wasn't unusual in his field. She'd heard that Bill Gates had dropped out of Harvard. "So when you left the service, your friends came with you?"

"Not right away," Jim said. "I mustered out ten years ago, when I was twenty-four. When I was twenty-eight, Rocky lost a leg in an amphibious assault. He wasn't adjusting well to civilian life, so a year later, when I was planning to build this house, I asked if he would manage it for me."

Come to think of it, Rocky did have a slight limp. No wonder Grace kept besting him.

"What about Grace?" she asked.

"She left the service four years ago, suffering from clinical depression," Jim said. "It's a chemical disorder. Under my employee health plan, she got the right treatment, and now she's fine."

"How long has Kip been here?"

"He came right after Grace," Jim said. "His doctors thought gardening would provide a stress-free environment, and it seems to be working. I think he's lonely, though."

It was an unusual household. Dex approved of Jim's loyalty to his friends, but she wasn't certain how this eccentric crew might affect Annie. She wanted her daughter to have the perfect home.

Rocky appeared in the doorway. "Dinner is served," he announced.

Dex and Jim went into the formal dining room. In one corner, a playpen filled with toys awaited Annie, and she slipped happily into place.

The long table was set with white linen, bone china and silver service. In the center, candles had been lit. Serving dishes lined a sideboard, offering T-bone steaks, glazed carrots, parsleyed potatoes and Caesar salad.

"Great!" Dex said. "Rocky, you're a gem."

The large man blushed. "I like cooking."

Dex was about to ask who the third place setting was for when Rocky helped himself to a plate and got into line first. Obviously, he was in the habit of dining with Jim.

"What about Kip and Grace?" she asked, falling into place behind him.

"Kip's too shy to eat in company." Jim stood close behind her. Dex could feel his warmth radiating against her bottom, and recalled that that had been one of the positions they'd experimented with during their night together. "Grace prefers canned beans and fruit to Rocky's cooking, or so she claims."

"Perverse woman," grumbled the butler as he piled potatoes alongside his steak. "When she wasn't barking orders at the troops, she used to be quiet and polite. I thought that was her real personality, and it suited me fine. I didn't know she was depressed."

"It's lucky Jim came along," Dex said. "She must have felt miserable."

"I wish she was still depressed," Rocky grumbled. "She didn't give me so much trouble."

Jim sat at the head of the table, with Rocky and Dex on either side. As the meal passed in general conversation, she was intrigued to hear that Jim's stock had shot through the roof, thanks to some new computer chip.

What was the man going to do with even more money? Buy a few new cars, build another mansion, plan the most fabulous wedding of the decade?

She didn't envy his bride. Dex hated pomp and ceremony. When she got married, she wanted a quiet service with friends and family.

What was she thinking? Of course she envied his bride. Not because Dex wanted to marry Jim, but because she wished she were the type of woman who could.

Being this close to him was agony. She kept wanting to touch his closely shaved cheeks and rumple his sun-streaked hair.

And she kept remembering how much she'd wanted to make love to him on a thick, soft carpet piled with cushions. She could think of so many creative positions, but her carpet was too short and scratchy.

He'd suggested they go to his house and mentioned that he had the ideal carpet in his bedroom. Under no circumstances, she told herself now, would she ever enter that bedroom.

"Looks like Annie's ready for bed," Jim said.

Dex gave a little jump. "Excuse me?"

"The baby's yawning," said Rocky. "I can take her upstairs."

"No, thank you." Dex wanted to enjoy every minute of the scant time she had with her daughter.

"We'll take care of her," Jim told the butler. "Go relax."

"I am relaxed." He eyed the child wistfully. "My youngest sister has a baby not much older than Annie. She should sleep on her back, you know, without a pillow."

"Thanks for the advice."

After he left, Dex said, "You mentioned that Kip is lonely. I think Rocky is, too."

"He'd like to have a family of his own," Jim said. "He got the idea, when he lost his leg, that women wouldn't be interested in him. I can't talk him into going to a singles mixer or a dating service. He's sure he'd be a complete failure."

"That's ridiculous," Dex said.

"I think so, too." Jim scooped up his daughter from the playpen and lifted her to his shoulder. The movement was surprisingly natural, considering that he'd had little experience with babies until this afternoon.

He was a born father, Dex thought with a twinge of guilt as she followed the pair out of the dining room and up a central curving staircase. But Annie needed a mother, too. A real mother who would love her, not merely tolerate her.

Dex needed to know more about Jim's almost-fiancée. She supposed she could ask him some discreet questions, but it hurt too much to think about the woman.

At the top of the stairs, they emerged into a central court around which opened a number of doors. Dex felt as if she were in a hotel.

Jim headed for the door next to Dex's. Rocky had pointed it out earlier as Annie's room, but she hadn't gone in.

Now she followed the millionaire into an airy chamber with pale yellow flowered wallpaper, canary-and-tan stripes around the upper moldings and a lacy canopy bed. A crib, which must have been delivered that afternoon, stood against the near wall, across from a rocking chair.

At the far end of the room, Dex could see the twilit sky through glass doors. Beyond them lay a rounded balcony edged by a wrought-iron railing.

"This looks as if it had been deliberately decorated for a little girl," she said.

"It was." Jim laid Annie on a changing table. "I've always wanted children. Now, how do you work this diaper thing?"

Dex showed him. Every time their hands touched, she had to fight down rebellious fantasies.

She imagined that the carpet in his room was tan, as in here. The pile felt thick beneath her feet. If only the two of them could sink into it, could feel it against their skin.

Nearby, Jim's breathing sped up. Was he thinking the same thing?

That night at the faculty party, they'd found themselves operating on the same wavelength. Noticing the brightness of the stars at the same time. Leaning toward each other as if they'd planned it. Dancing as if they were a team.

It was amazing, considering how different they were. And how incompatible.

I don't even know what I'm doing here, Dex thought, and inched away. She didn't belong with a sleekly sophisticated man who made millions in the wink of an eye, or in a mansion that might have been designed for a glittery home tour.

Her parents were bookish people, their house efficiently small and filled with well-organized paper clutter. They couldn't understand why anyone would waste time on appearances. They weren't impressed by designer labels or by the nouveau-riche club crowd in their Florida town, either.

Their ideal woman was Dex's sister, Brianna. The editor of a literary magazine, she was married to an investigative journalist and lived in a small apartment in New York's SoHo district. They lacked much money and didn't want kids, but they were the darlings of the intellectual set.

"How's this?" Jim hoisted their daughter aloft. A pink nightgown covered her neatly diapered body to her evident pleasure.

"Beautiful." Dex inhaled the scent of baby powder and innocence.

Jim placed Annie into the crib on her back, as Rocky had instructed. The only jarring note was the quilt, which had a geometric design worked in black, purple and white. "Dr. Saldivar's taste in baby decor was a bit different from mine," he said, noticing her reaction. "I'll have Grace pick up something more appropriate tomorrow."

"There's no sense investing a lot of money," Dex told him. "Annie isn't staying."

They faced each other from opposite ends of the crib. She could feel Jim seeking the right words, the right tone to change her mind.

"Why are you so determined to put her up for adoption?" Apparently he'd decided on the direct approach.

Because if I can't be her mother, I never want to see her again. It would break my heart.

She didn't say so, because she didn't expect Jim to kowtow to her feelings. He was the most powerful person in this town, and she was, if anything, the most powerless.

Dex struggled to find a more rational reason for her position. In what she hoped was a logical tone, she said, "You've got to see how hard it will be for her when people find out about her background. The gossip. The teasing."

"No one has to know her background," Jim said.

"The town gossips will want to know who the mother is. And plenty of people have seen Annie with Dr. Saldivar over the last nine months," Dex said. "Whether they learn the truth or imagine some affair between you and the good doctor, it'll still be a mess."

"People may talk," he conceded. "But..." Instead of completing his thought, he said, "Come here. I want to show you something." Jim walked to the glass doors, unlatched the slide lock from overhead and opened them. Cautiously, Dex followed him onto the small balcony and into a cooling breeze.

Below them spread the town of Clair De Lune. From this height, she could see the triangular Bonderoff Visionary Technologies plant on the left and beyond a sprawl of high ground to her right, the campus of De Lune University.

Directly ahead, sloping downward toward the distant freeway, lay the town itself. She scanned tree-shrouded neighborhoods, shops, city hall, even the twelve-storey structure where she and Jim had met Annie this afternoon.

"It's quite a view," she admitted.

"The view is as much symbolic as it is literal," Jim said. "I don't mean to brag, but in a lot of ways I control this town. The mayor consults me about ordinances that would affect businesses. The Chamber of Commerce uses my name to encourage new industries to come to town."

None of this was news to Dex. "So?"

"Exactly how hard do you think people are going to ride my daughter?" Jim asked.

He had a point, but she wasn't about to admit it. "Kids can be cruel," Dex said. "And I don't want her spoiled, either."

"You're making excuses. There's some other reason you want her to be adopted."

He was too perceptive, she thought with a flare of alarm. She dreaded having Jim see how vulnerable she was, how much she yearned for things she wasn't emotionally capable of handling.

"I don't think I'm cut out to be a mother," she said as casually as she could. "Lots of women aren't."

"But I'm cut out to be a father," he said.

"It isn't enough!"

"You want to keep me at arm's length because we spent a night together, don't you?" he pressed. "If I were a total stranger with no memories attached, you wouldn't be so opposed to my keeping her, would you?"

Although she supposed that did make a difference, it wasn't the real problem. "I don't hold anything against you," Dex said.

"There's no reason you should," Jim reminded her. "You're the one who said you were going away."

"We aren't suited to each other," she said. "I accept that."

"So do I."

"At least we agree on something."

He touched her shoulder. Prickles of fire ran across her skin. "Dex, whatever I did to annoy you, please forgive me. Our daughter's future is too important to throw away."

She lowered her face, blinking back an unexpected sheen of moisture. "There's more to happiness than a fancy house and a view from the balcony. There's love and understanding and emotional support."

"And I'm going to give them to her," Jim said.

But if she's like me, she'll know from the start that she doesn't belong here.

Dex had to trust her instincts. This house, and this man, filled her with such panic that she couldn't bear to leave her baby here. "Whether you agree or not, Annie's a miniature version of me. Anyone can see it," she said. "She won't fit in. And the other kids' digs and snubs will hurt more than you'll ever know."

"Annie's half me," Jim said quietly. "She will fit in. She'll love it here. Please listen…"

His grip on Dex's shoulder tightened just as she swung around to go inside. The contact threw her off balance, and she stumbled against him.

Instinctively, Dex threw up her hands and braced herself against his chest. She'd forgotten how clearly defined his muscles were, how solid he was and how secure she felt in his grasp, as if nothing could uproot her.

Jim's arms wrapped around her, and her chin lifted instinctively. His mouth closed over hers, tasting of wine and sultry longing.

Dex indulged herself by cupping his cheek in her palm and then ruffling his hair. Jim guided her inside the house, away from public view, then kissed her more deeply.

The sudden cessation of wind and the flick of his tongue sent heat flooding through her. Pulled tightly against him, Dex discovered that he was completely aroused and experienced the same rush of abandon as on the night of the party.

Feeling his hand move beneath her sweater and touch her bare waist, she ached for him to reach her breasts. His hard, fast breathing matched her own. Dex knew they ought to stop. But not yet.

A happy gurgling caught her attention. The baby! She glanced over and saw Annie standing in her crib, watching them.

"More," said the baby.

Dex didn't know whether to laugh or blush. Jim burst into a deep chuckle. "She's got that right," he said.

"No." With a sigh, she moved away. "We can't do that. You're practically a married man."

"I'm not even engaged," Jim said. "But even though Nancy hasn't made a decision yet, I do owe her my loyalty."

She was glad to hear that, despite being the town's best-known playboy, he had scruples. "In any case," Dex added for good measure, "we both agree that we're incompatible."

"Not in bed," he pointed out.

"We already have one child," she said. "Isn't that enough trouble for one relationship?"

Besides, now that she was regarding this tall, strong-featured man from a slight distance, she remembered all the reasons he intimidated her. And all the reasons she had no intention of showing it.

"I agree, the situation's complicated." Jim ran one hand through his hair. "You're right, I suppose. We need to keep things platonic."

Although he didn't look happy about it, he withdrew. Dex stood motionless until she heard the door to the master bedroom close.

"Da da," said Annie conversationally.

Dex scooped the baby from the crib and sat in the rocking chair, cradling her daughter. She couldn't believe she'd kissed Jim Bonderoff. If Annie hadn't interrupted, they might have...

She rocked slowly. Why did she nearly lose control around the man? No doubt he had that effect on a lot of women. She could understand why, but that was no excuse for her own weakness.

It wouldn't happen again. At least, she didn't think so.

The chair moved smoothly, lulling both the baby

and Dex. She discovered she was crooning a lullaby. She couldn't identify the song at first, until she came to the chorus. "Hi Lili, Hi Lo."

It was the theme from an old Leslie Caron movie, *Lili*. When she was a child, Dex had watched it on TV with her mother, who mentioned having seen it years earlier.

The theme song had sounded familiar then, and it had burst forth while Dex was rocking her baby. There was only one possible explanation. Her own mother must have sung it to her as a child.

How odd. Sarah Fenton wasn't the sort of woman one pictured singing to a baby. She wore her frizzy hair cut so short it was almost a buzz cut, and smiled only fleetingly. Her tastes in entertainment ran to Wagner operas and Russian ballet, and whatever tenderness she'd shown had vanished by her children's teen years.

Dex rocked the baby some more and sang some more and wished that, unlike her mother, she could nourish these gentle feelings forever. But history had a way of repeating itself.

When Annie fell asleep, she tucked her daughter into the crib and left the room.

7

ON SATURDAY MORNING, Jim nearly called Nancy again. He'd slept badly the night before, bedeviled by images of Dex and by the knowledge that she was sleeping down the hall.

His body was a traitor. Not only his body, but his thoughts and his feelings, as well. Dex was like a creamy lemon meringue pie with a dash of Tabasco sauce for spice. Unusual, and not something one would normally order, but she excited him as no other woman ever had.

After brewing coffee in his bedroom suite, Jim took his cup and his cell phone onto his balcony. It faced east, toward the university, with a view of the mountains to the north.

Settling onto a deck chair, he tried to decide what to say to Nancy. "Come rescue me!" didn't seem quite the right romantic note. Besides, he didn't need to be rescued. He could control his actions as he controlled the rest of his life.

Yet he naturally turned to Nancy when he needed a sounding board. She'd certainly helped him in the past. After his discharge from the Marines and his father's death from cancer only six months later, Jim hadn't known how to focus his energies. He'd been too impatient for college, eager to make money and full of ideas for new computer technologies but unsure whether he was ready for the risk of starting his own business.

His head had been ringing with his father's words, spoken from a hospital bed. The years and his fatal illness had showed in every line of Ben Bonderoff's gaunt face. "Don't end up like me," he'd told his son. "I never had the guts to follow my dream."

When Jim mentioned his father's remarks to Nancy, who was working on her Ph.D. at the time, she'd challenged him to take his father seriously. "Follow your own dream. You can borrow start-up money. You've got good ideas and the ability to make them happen."

"But I'd have to go into debt." His parents had always insisted that responsible people should pay as they go. "It feels like a trap, like getting myself into a rat race."

Nancy had regarded him steadily over her corned beef sandwich. They'd been eating at the Lunar Lunch Box near campus, he recalled. With her long legs and honey-blond hair, she'd attracted a lot of glances from other men, but paid them no attention.

"Debt is a trap, all right, but only if you spend the money." Her gray eyes had fixed him in their spotlight. "Investing is different from spending. Look at me, for instance. When I get my degree, I'll owe a ton in student loans, but I'll be able to earn enough money to pay them off instead of being stuck in some clerical job. I've invested in my future. How about you, Jim?"

So, bolstered by Nancy's confidence, he'd put together a business prospectus and found investors. Within a few years, they'd become millionaires many times over.

Jim had paid those debts, but he owed a different kind of debt to Nancy, a moral and emotional debt. If only she would allow him to fund some of her research, he'd feel better about it, but she'd steadfastly refused. "We're friends," she'd said more than once. "Let's not let money come between us."

Jim stared at the cell phone, but he couldn't figure out what he would say to her. She'd told him yesterday that things would be settled in a week, hadn't she?

While he was debating the matter, the phone rang. It was a colleague congratulating him on his new chip technology. By the time the conversation ended, Jim had wandered inside and was ready to take a shower. No doubt he'd be receiving a flood of calls before long.

He decided to wait a few more days before talking to Nancy.

DEX TOOK A PLATE of toast and her coffee into the rock garden. She was glad, for the sake of her waistline, that Rocky hadn't fixed a formal breakfast.

Grace, wearing jeans and a sweatshirt and explaining that she was off duty on weekends, had insisted on taking Annie for a stroll. On the verge of declining, Dex had remembered that she was supposed to be observing, not baby-sitting.

Now she savored the last of her French-roast brew and enjoyed the light breeze playing through a peppertree. There was something magical about this garden, with the flowers spilling over low retaining walls and a man-made brook vanishing and reappearing beneath greenery.

The fairy-tale setting meandered along the side of

the house, from the sunroom past a cellar door and around to the back patio. Dex had chosen a table and chair near the back corner from which she could glimpse the tennis courts behind the garage and, on the far side of the house, the swimming pool and whirlpool bath.

It was tempting to sunbathe. Her shorts and her blouse would leave odd tan marks, though. Besides, she had Professor Bemling's papers to grade.

Distantly, through the open window of a downstairs room, she could hear Jim on the phone. It sounded as if he were talking to a reporter. "Of course, I couldn't have done it without my brilliant technical staff...."

He didn't mention discovering that he had a daughter, and she was grateful he chose not to announce her in the press. Perhaps he was simply embarrassed about the circumstances. Dex hoped, though, that it meant he was considering her feelings about adoption.

With a sigh, she opened the backpack she'd dropped on a chair and took out the stack of papers. From the corner of her eye, she glimpsed a movement among some ferns, but when she turned, she saw only a bluebird pecking at the ground.

Dex blasted her way through the first couple of papers, correcting grammar and spelling and, more important, noting lapses in critical thinking. Few of the students knew how to think an original thought and develop it convincingly.

A rustling drew her attention to a clump of calla lilies. She could have sworn she saw an elfin face peering through the trumpet-shaped white flowers, yet before she could get it fixed in her mind, it was gone.

It was probably Kip, the gardener. Grace had said

he was weird. That might explain his lurking behind the bushes.

Dex returned to the papers and was almost finished when a small bouquet of white chrysanthemums, the ends wrapped in aluminum foil and tied with a wire twisty, dropped onto the table beside her. Dex looked up into a bright face with shy eyes, a pointed chin and a nose just crooked enough to be interesting.

"You must be Kip," she said.

"Yes." Too slim for his overalls and T-shirt, the man appeared small, although she guessed he was at least five feet nine inches. If he'd once been the macho type, as Jim had said, there was no sign of that now.

"I'm Dex." She raised the bouquet to her nose. "Thanks for the flowers."

He cocked his head, studying her. "Pink."

"The mums? They look white to me."

"They are. With a tomato-red haze around them," he said. "Your color is light pink. Quite charming."

"Oh?" She hoped he wasn't completely batty.

Kip sat down across from her. "Grace is mustard-yellow, which is not as unpleasant as it sounds, and Rocky's a kind of peaceful blue-green."

"What about Jim?" she asked, curious in spite of herself.

"An honest grass-green," he said. "The baby's lavender. Very sweet."

"Do you picture them as flowers?" Dex said. "Is that the idea?"

"Oh, no." Kip gave her a wary smile. "I didn't used to tell people, but I see everything in color, in my mind. I mean, in addition to the colors that are already there. Even numbers and letters and musical sounds have their own hues."

Here was a man in natural possession of a poetic soul, Dex thought, one that Hugh Bemling might envy. He also definitely walked on the cuckoo side. "Is this because of your accident?"

"No. It's just made me freer to tell people how I see the world. I didn't used to tell them because they'd think I'm crazy, but now they think that anyway." His light voice had a breathy quality. "I'm what the scientists call a synesthete. It's hereditary, I guess."

"What's a synesthete?"

"Someone who perceives the world differently than most people," Kip said. "In my family, we live in a rainbow. Other people, I've heard, actually taste shapes. It's completely individualized."

He froze, and then Dex noticed it, too—a kind of mumbling chant coming up the steps from the driveway. Gradually, the chant clarified into words. "She did tell you to come. Yes, but she didn't say it was a castle. You might be in the wrong place, that's what."

"Cora!" Dex called. "I'm over here."

A round face haloed by pale wispy hair came into view around the house, followed by a flowing muumuu. The colors were so bright that Dex wondered what effect they would have on Kip, but he wasn't fazed.

"Amazing," he breathed. "She's a stunning pale gold. Introduce me."

"Cora," Dex called. "This is Kip. Kip, Cora."

The chubby young woman stopped beside the brook that flowed next to them, clutching her notebook. As she stared at Kip, something like amazement lit up her expression.

"He's so cute!" she said.

Kip hopped to his feet and bowed. "Allow me to show you the grounds."

"I—I brought my history paper for Dex to critique." Cora didn't take her gaze off the gardener.

"I'll take that." Dex lifted the folder from the student's grasp and returned to the table. "Go on, have a look around."

Kip offered his arm. After a brief hesitation, Cora slipped hers through it. As they strolled away, they fell easily into conversation.

"Everything's so green." Cora said.

"Not only green. The leaves are many colors. So is the water." Kip's enthusiasm bubbled through the air.

"What a wonderful way to see things."

"It's the only way I know."

"Tell me what you're seeing, so I can enjoy it, too."

The words flowed so easily that it sounded almost as if Cora were still talking to herself. This time, however, there was no hesitation or self-doubt.

Dex opened the folder and read Cora's paper. The woman had some interesting points to make, but she didn't know how to organize them effectively. And she needed to stop apologizing every other sentence for daring to disagree with conventional thinking.

After making notes that she hoped would prove helpful, Dex set the folder aside for her friend to reclaim later. It was nearly ten o'clock, time for her to go deliver the campus mail.

Dex was heading for the driveway when she heard

a man call her name. Jim's voice quivered right into her bone marrow. "Where are you off to?" he said from the garden room.

"My job." Dex kept moving, although slowly. "I'm the only courier who works on Saturdays."

He came outside. "I'll join you."

"You can't," she said. "I have to ride my bike."

"Then I'll ride my bike, too." He loped down the curving stone staircase ahead of her and, from one of the garages, produced a racing bicycle and silver-blue helmet.

In his tight jeans, breathtakingly snug T-shirt and jogging shoes, Dex had to admit the man was better dressed for the role of bicycle courier than she was. On the other hand, she prided herself on being defiantly casual, and that included her lack of a helmet.

"I don't suppose there's any point in mentioning..." Jim began, eyeing her flyaway hair.

"Not if you want to come with me." She swung onto her beat-up three-speed.

"Right." He strapped on his own helmet.

She tried one more time to discourage him. "Are you sure you can spare the time?"

"I have to attend a formal dinner at seven. Cocktails at six. Can't skip, because I'm the guest of honor." Jim checked his watch. "That gives me nearly eight hours to get ready. Okay, I've got time."

She set out, coasting down the hilly landscape toward campus. He joined her with no apparent effort.

It was disconcerting, cycling along University Avenue on her clunky old bike while Mr. Tour de France skimmed alongside. Dex did her best to ignore him.

"By the way," Jim called, "what's with the child seat?"

"It's for Annie." That seemed obvious, Dex thought.

"I thought you wanted to give her up for adoption."

"It's just for this week." The truth was, she conceded silently, that she wanted it there as a reminder of her daughter, even if she never used it.

Jim didn't pursue the subject. Instead, he said, "I saw a woman in the garden with Kip. Is she a friend of yours?"

"That's Cora," Dex said. "I'm tutoring her. She wanted to drop out, but I'm not going to let her."

"They seemed to enjoy each other's company."

"I hope so."

The conversation lagged as they zipped down the long arcs of the boulevard. Not until they slowed at the entrance to the campus did Jim say, "I've been meaning to ask. Is the name Dex short for something?"

"My mother named me after her allergy medicine." It was a flip answer she'd developed to replace the boring truth, that Dex was a childhood nickname for Alexandria.

Skirting the parking lot, she shot into the quadrangle and whipped to the back of the administration building. "Fitz!" she yelled, and banged on his door.

"Do you always make this much noise?" Jim asked.

"He sleeps late on Saturdays." Dex kicked the door a couple of times.

"He lives here?" Disbelief colored Jim's face. "Isn't that against the rules?"

"Oh, Fitz has a home somewhere," she said. "But he says that, being director of maintenance, there's always something breaking late at night. So usually he sleeps over on the couch."

"How long has he worked here?" Jim asked.

Dex wasn't sure. She'd started working for Fitzgerald Langley as an undergraduate, and he'd been an institution even then. "Decades, I guess."

Noises issued from within the building, and the door began to shake. It rattled and groaned until the rusty lock finally yielded.

"If he's the maintenance director," Jim said under his breath, "why doesn't he oil that thing?"

"He says it's better than an alarm system for keeping thieves away." Fitz's leonine head appeared in the doorway. "Got any deliveries?" Dex asked.

"A couple." He grunted and reached inside. "You ever get hold of that lawyer fellow?"

"It's all taken care of."

Finger combing his shaggy mane out of his face, Fitz produced two interoffice envelopes. "One for the English department. One for administration."

"This is the administration building right here," Jim said.

Fitz stopped plucking lint out of his beard and regarded the newcomer coolly. "This here's the back of the administration building. That there's got to go around the front."

"I suppose on some level that makes sense," Jim said.

The maintenance department was, in fact, an add-on that connected to the main building through a squirrely series of corridors and staircases that were more trouble to navigate than simply circling the building. Fitz, however, didn't bother to explain.

Instead, he squinted at Jim. "You're that computer

guy. Seen your picture in the paper. Things must be tough if you're riding a bike these days."

"I guess I should work harder," said Jim, playing along.

"Let me give you a tip," said Fitz. "If your boss tells you to take the letter around to the front of the building, don't give him any lip."

"Thanks. I'll remember that."

Dex hid a smile. She was enjoying Jim's company more than she'd expected. In a mood to tease him, she decided she'd take the long route via the English department before making the administration delivery, just to make matters more confusing.

"See you Monday!" she called to Fitz, and set off. Jim caught up, and they rode side by side beneath arching jacaranda trees.

"What about the delivery?" he asked.

"I'll get to it later," Dex said. "Nobody's likely to open it today, anyway. Sometimes the big shots come in, but their secretaries don't."

The main quadrangle was almost deserted on this sunny Saturday. The library and student center might be busy, but they were located in a newer area, along with the university's theater.

As Dex whizzed past the faculty center, with Jim riding alongside and slightly behind her, she imagined she could feel his gaze searing across her bare waist. Was he noticing the tiny flower tattoo she'd foolishly inscribed at the urging of a former boyfriend?

Since freshman year, she'd had two real boyfriends, not counting casual dates who vanished from her memory like dreams upon waking. In retrospect, Dex supposed that she'd kept both her more serious beaux at arm's length and ended the relationships when they demanded too much of a commitment.

Well, she knew what she could handle and what she couldn't. The same was true with Jim.

Yet here he was anyway, four months after their affair, inviting himself to make the rounds as if he were part of her life. Which he wasn't, not in any permanent sense.

She wished he would get bored and go do something else. She was much too aware of the lean thrust of his legs as he cycled, and the breadth of his shoulders cutting through the air. And especially of the tight derriere planted on the seat of his bike.

Dex pumped harder, heading for the English department.

HOW HAD HE failed to notice the small tattoo on her lower back? Jim wondered. He'd believed he had memorized every detail of her body during their night together.

What he'd actually memorized, he admitted ruefully, were his impressions of her body. And they were indelible.

Every inch of her moved in unexpected ways, rubbing him, tantalizing him, squeezing him. She was a woman a man could get lost in and stay lost in.

The two of them dismounted at a bike rack. Despite Dex's discouraging expression, he followed her into the adjacent ivy-covered brick building.

The English department smelled of book dust and mimeograph ink that must have seeped into the floor before the age of photocopiers. Jim followed Dex down the corridor and into the cramped front office.

There was no one in sight. Dex called, "Hello, anybody home?" a couple of times, then dropped the envelope on the desk. "They must be out."

"Do they have classes on Saturday?" Jim asked.

"No, but a couple of the professors keep office hours," she said. "Mostly to meet with graduate students."

This, Jim recalled, was where she worked as a teaching assistant. He found himself intensely curious about every aspect of Dex's life.

They were emerging into the hallway when a bearded man scuffled down the stairs, his longish hair falling around a thin face. Through wire-rimmed glasses, he peered owlishly at them.

"Dex?" the man said. "Oh, dear. I thought it was Saturday. You've got the papers graded already?"

"It *is* Saturday, Hugh," she said indulgently. "I'm just delivering mail."

He sighed with relief. "Thank goodness. I was afraid I'd lost track and it might be Monday." His slow-moving gaze fixed on Jim. "Is this a friend of yours?"

"Hugh, this is Jim Bonderoff," she said. "Jim, Hugh Bemling."

The men shook hands. "Are you *that* Jim Bonderoff?" asked Hugh.

"I'm afraid so."

The professor took off his glasses and cleaned them on the edge of his untucked shirt. He seemed disconcerted, and Jim wondered if the man were reacting to his millionaire status until Hugh said, "So are you two, er, involved?"

It was a rather personal question, but any resentment dissipated when Jim saw the smitten way the man studied Dex. So the absentminded professor had a crush on her.

His affections didn't appear to be returned, because there was nothing flirtatious about her manner, nor did she reassure the man of her availability. "I'm helping Jim with a baby-sitting situation," she said. "If you need to reach me this week, I'll be at his house."

"I see." Hugh cleared his throat a couple of times, then bumbled back up the stairs as if he'd forgotten why he'd come down in the first place.

"He's sweet, but permanently befuddled," Dex explained as they went outside. "He keeps mailing his scholarly articles to the wrong magazines. He sent one called 'The Flower of Chivalry' to *Better Homes and Gardens.*"

Jim laughed. As he got on his bike, he realized he hadn't felt this lighthearted in years.

It was a joy to wander through Dex's world, meeting the Alice in Wonderland people who inhabited it and enjoying her comments. It made him realize how much he'd isolated himself in his wealthy, high-tech environment.

Annie, too, might feel isolated as she grew up. She needed an anchor, someone down-to-earth who could help her make connections with people. She needed Dex.

Jim shook his head. He *meant,* she needed Nancy.

At the front of the administration building, he waited while Dex dashed up the steps with the envelope. The brick building's imposing granite portico appeared more Southern Gothic than Southern California. It was the first time he'd noticed how pretentious it was.

Through the open front doors strode two men in business suits. Jim recognized the round, unlined face of President Wilson Martin, whose dyed-silver curls gave him the look of a prematurely aged Kewpie doll. The man with him was one of the university's vice presidents.

The pair didn't glance at Dex as she darted past them, nor at Jim, either. Apparently scruffy student types on bicycles were beneath their notice. They breezed by, discussing the chances of the campus basketball team in the league playoffs.

Jim sat motionless on his bike until Dex reappeared. "Close call," he said.

"President Martin?" she asked. "You mean he didn't hit you up for a donation?"

"He didn't even see me."

She stood on her bike pedals, using her full weight to get the contraption moving. "Maybe you can answer a question the campus gossips keep chewing over."

"What's that?" He glided alongside her.

"How old is President Martin?" Dex asked. "Rumor has it that he's either in his early forties and trying to hide it or that he's in his seventies and made a bargain with some evil wizard in the basement of the biology department to hide his age."

"The first part is true," Jim said, "but the second one is more interesting."

They'd reached the half-empty parking lot when Dex stopped abruptly. "Oh, my gosh!"

He halted and discovered his heart was pounding. "What's wrong?"

"Annie!" she said.

8

"WHAT ABOUT Annie?" Jim asked.

"I forgot her!" Dex cried. "I left the house without even thinking about her!"

Fear clenched inside him. "Where did you leave her? In the garden?" He wondered if the baby could crawl as far as the main retaining wall. A fall to the driveway would be devastating. "I'll call Rocky." He reached into his pocket for the cell phone.

"No, she was with Grace," Dex said. "They went for a walk."

His anxiety faded. "You didn't abandon her in the garden?"

"Of course not!" Dex replied indignantly. "But a real mother wouldn't simply ride off and forget all about her daughter. I don't know whether Grace is taking care of her, or Rocky, or maybe she's with Kip and Cora."

"In any of those cases, she's undoubtedly safe." He wondered why she was being so hard on herself.

"If I were a real mother—"

"But you aren't." Nor, he assumed, did she want to be.

"No," she said wistfully, "I'm not. It's pretty obvious, isn't it?"

They resumed riding their bikes. "I did the same

thing," Jim pointed out. "I left without asking where she was."

"Fathers are like that," Dex said. "Mothers aren't."

"I suppose not." His mom had been attentive although, if she'd worried about him, she hadn't shown it. But then, Jim only remembered her from his later childhood, not when he was a baby.

His thoughts returned to what Dex had said. She seemed to be chastizing herself for not being a better mother. Until now, he'd assumed she had no interest in taking on such a role.

Yet there'd been clues all along to another side of her. The tender way she held the baby, and how she took charge of the situation when Grace and Rocky quarreled.

Jim wished he understood this side of Dex. Heck, he still didn't know why she'd misled him about moving away after they spent the night making love. The woman was full of contradictions.

Dex flew along the avenue, going home. She must be eager to see that Annie was all right.

He wondered what it meant.

DESPITE the cool breeze, Dex's cheeks felt hot. She'd neglected Annie and then blurted it out in front of Jim.

Just because she could never be the type of smart, sophisticated woman he dated didn't mean she had to act like an idiot in front of him. If she made mistakes, she ought to keep them to herself.

As she pedaled, she reviewed their conversation. He was right, he *had* neglected Annie as much as she had. Dex could hardly blame him, though.

She'd known from his reputation that Jim was too absorbed in his playboy lifestyle to be a devoted father. Of course, he was showing some initial fascination with their baby, like a kid with a new toy, but that would pass.

She wanted Annie to have a deeply involved father. To have everything that Dex had yearned for as a child. After all, Annie *was* Dex, reborn with a second chance for a happy life.

Okay, she's only half me. But it's the better half.

As the more experienced cyclist, Dex should have arrived at the top of Jim's hill faster and with more reserve breath. However, he had the superior machine, and she was more anxious. They halted in front of the garages at the same time, with her panting harder.

"That was great exercise," Jim said. "It beats working out in my gym."

"You have a gym?" She hadn't seen one on the premises.

"Upstairs above the pool house," he said. "Do you work out?"

"Sure." Dex sometimes accompanied her landlady to a Jazzercise class.

"You can join me and try some of the equipment tomorrow." Without waiting for a reply, Jim wheeled his bike into one of the garages.

Did he have to be so domineering? Dex made a face at his retreating back and then felt embarrassed at her childishness.

Jim returned a moment later. "By the way, do you recognize that car?" He indicated a dented Volkswagen parked in a slot. Cora's bicycle, Dex realized, was gone, but someone else had obviously arrived.

"It looks like my landlady's, but it can't be." She hadn't memorized the license plate. On second glance, though, she recognized some of the dents. "Gosh, she must have come to see me."

"Let's go find out."

"Yes," Dex said pointedly, "and let's find Annie, too."

They located the dean and Rocky in the kitchen, making omelettes with fresh herbs. When the landlady spotted Dex and Jim, she poked ineffectively at her nest of gray hair. A purple, Oriental-style sleeved cape cascading over a baggy beige dress showed the effort she'd made to dress for her visit.

On being introduced, Jim and Marie Pipp shook hands. Then she returned her attention to Rocky. "That omelette smells fabulous."

"If not for you, I'd never have thought of using basil with eggs." The butler adjusted the ruffled pink apron tied around his camouflage fatigues.

"I brought your mail, along with a few things to eat," Marie told Dex. "I didn't intend to go out today, but I wanted to make sure you were all right."

The mail on the table, Dex saw, consisted of two advertisements and a credit-card solicitation. She guessed her landlady had been motivated more by curiosity than concern, but she was glad to see the elderly lady all the same.

"Now, what about these lentils?" Rocky began cutting open a package.

"Heat them in the microwave," the dean said. "They're from India. Very spicy. You'll like them."

"I've never eaten food from India," the butler admitted as he poured the prepared mixture into a bowl.

"Time to broaden your horizons." Dean Pipp patted him on the back.

A snort drew Dex's attention to the opposite doorway. Grace stood there holding Annie and glaring at Marie. "Who is this? Some friend of yours, Rocky?"

"She's my landlady." Dex took the baby into her arms and introduced the two women.

She was surprised at how standoffish the maid remained. Could she be jealous of the contact she'd witnessed between Marie and Rocky?

How ridiculous, when the dean was probably thirty-five years older. Besides, Grace and the butler hated each other.

Dex apologized for leaving the baby. Without taking her eyes off Rocky and the visitor, Grace dismissed her concerns. They'd enjoyed playing together, she said.

Soon lunch was ready. As the five of them proceeded into the dining room, Dex heard the misfiring sputter of an out-of-tune jalopy coming up the driveway.

"More company?" Grace asked sourly.

Rocky positioned the omelette platter on the sideboard. "You expecting anyone, chief?"

"Not me," Jim said.

The doorbell blared the opening notes of "From the Halls of Montezuma." Whipping off his pink apron, Rocky marched into the living room. "Keep your pants on, I'm coming!"

Dex heard the hum of voices, and then Rocky appeared with Hugh Bemling hemming and hawing alongside. "I happened to be passing by and... Oh, hello, Dean Pipp."

Amid greetings, the English professor babbled another apology for his unannounced visit. His motive had obviously been to check on her, Dex thought, amused.

Standing there with Annie in her arms, she remembered she hadn't told him that she had a daughter. She didn't see any reason to spread the information around campus, either, although it was sure to get there before long.

Besides, Hugh was paying her no attention. As soon as Jim introduced him to Grace, the maid's eyes lit up with fascination, although Dex thought she caught a trace of mischief, too.

Towering over the slight professor, Grace had linked arms with him and was drinking in his every word. Dex couldn't imagine what she saw in him, other than wanting to make someone else jealous. But if Rocky took notice of Grace's new interest, he didn't show it.

He grabbed a plate ahead of everyone else and filled it from the sideboard. The others queued up, with Grace pulling Hugh.

Dex lowered Annie into her playpen. It was amazing how much she'd missed the little girl in such a short time.

Despite her growling stomach, Dex lingered to coo at the baby until everyone else was served. Then, at last, she yielded to what was usually her most driving need: food.

During lunch, Marie discussed her paper on the question of who first wrote "Thirty days hath November." Rocky looked impressed. Hugh kept staring from Dex to Grace, stammered whenever he tried to speak and finally lapsed into eating.

Jim surveyed his uninvited guests with a smile,

clearly enjoying their interaction. Dex supposed the dinner table conversations around here were usually much more subdued.

For one outrageous moment, she wondered what it would be like if she lived here with Jim. If she belonged here and welcomed their friends.

It would be fun to turn this huge place into an intellectual salon, where quick-thinking people met and conversed and relaxed. The other graduate students would love lounging in the garden or the den. One or two might even work out in the gym or use the tennis courts.

Annie would relish the excitement. She would grow up stimulated and creative, but she'd also spend plenty of free time playing with her little brother or sister....

Brother or sister? Figurative cold water washed away Dex's daydream. She must be out of her mind.

She looked again at Jim. Angled forward in his chair, his handsome face merry, he listened to Marie and Rocky discuss their mutual favorite movie, *Shakespeare in Love*. In Rocky's case, his admiration had something to do with the nude scenes, she gathered.

What struck her was the way everyone focused, subtly or not, on Jim. Even when he was only listening, he was such a charismatic figure that everyone addressed him, or preened for him, or tried to entertain him.

He was as gracious with this motley assortment of luncheon guests as he would no doubt be tonight, as guest of honor at a formal dinner. The mayor might be there, she supposed, along with the town's leading citizens. They would lean toward Jim in the same way, exhilarated to have him in their midst.

He might fit as easily into either environment, but Dex knew she'd stick out like a sore thumb among his elegant friends. Oh, she could dress up—well, not with her current wardrobe, but she understood the basic principles—and she was well-enough educated not to make a complete fool of herself.

But she was too feisty, too outspoken. She couldn't beam decoratively or convey the correct amount of subdued elegance. If the newspaper took their picture, she wouldn't look tall and willowy, but short and busty.

Ruefully, she wondered about the woman Jim loved. She must look like a model, maybe a Grace Kelly type. She probably had a nice personality, too.

It was a good thing Dex had avoided any continuing entanglement with Jim. Otherwise she might have fallen in love, and it would have hurt terribly when, inevitably, she lost him.

"I'd like to take Annie to my sister's house for Sunday dinner tomorrow, if you don't mind, chief," Rocky said to Jim. "I think she'd enjoy playing with my two nieces. Miss Pipp, I'd be thrilled if you would come, and I'll bet my sister would love meeting you. She used to recite 'Thirty days hath November' when she was a girl."

"Well..." The dean's hands fluttered around her plate. "I hardly ever go out."

"It'll do you good." In Dex's opinion, her landlady needed to circulate.

"I'll collect you at noon," said Rocky.

"You can take the sedan. The child seat's already installed," Jim said. "We'll have to get a couple more for the other cars. I'm sure Annie will enjoy meeting other children."

"You can come with me tomorrow, too." Grace boomed at Hugh. "Remember what we were talking about? Don't worry, I'll drive. Pick you up at one."

"You said it was, er, what kind of show?" asked the professor.

"A gun show!" responded the former Marine sergeant. "You'll love it!"

Dex hated to leave this intriguing discussion, but she was scheduled to tutor underprivileged high-school students at a local community center this afternoon. This time, she made sure Rocky was free to watch Annie before she left.

Outside, there was a flurry of leaves in the garden, and then Kip appeared. "She's wonderful," he said.

"I'm glad you and Cora like each other," Dex answered.

"We're going to a concert at the university tomorrow afternoon." He frowned. "Would you mind telling me, what's chamber music? It isn't something you listen to in the bathroom, is it?"

She assured him that it was a small group of musicians playing classical music, and that the audience listened to them in a theater.

"Can you hold hands?" Kip asked. "Like in the movies?"

"Sure," Dex said.

"Then I'll enjoy it." He walked away whistling.

THE FORMAL DINNER Jim attended that evening was held at the palatial home of Clair De Lune's leading patrons of the arts, Bill and Vanessa Sachet. The social occasion was a fund-raiser for the town's proposed new theater. Jim knew he'd been chosen guest of honor in the hope that he would make a large donation, so he did.

He didn't mind the subtle coercion. What bothered him was seeing Bill Sachet, a real-estate developer who'd been one of Jim's initial investors, doting on his second wife.

Vanessa was beautiful, calculating and twenty-six years younger than the man whom Jim had long considered a friend. A year ago, Bill had married her right after his divorce became final, even though he denied having dated Vanessa before his separation.

Jim had been fond of Lynn Sachet, who had since moved away. He thought her husband had treated her very badly. A large financial settlement couldn't make up for an emotional betrayal after thirty years of marriage.

The entire evening had been smoothly orchestrated, perfectly catered, splendidly decorated—and heartless. Vanessa, a freelance publicist only a year older than the marriage she'd helped destroy, had paraded her husband and his friends like trophies in front of a photographer from the local newspaper.

A few years earlier, she'd made a play for Jim. He'd gone out with her a couple of times, until he realized she was only interested in his social status and fortune.

He wanted so much more, he reflected as he parked the sports car in the garage. He wanted a home alive with laughter, where people could be honest and unguarded.

As he let himself in through the den, Jim half hoped to find someone awake. It was only eleven o'clock. Perhaps Dex would be watching TV in the upstairs family room, or fixing herself a late-night snack.

No one was stirring, though. Only the safety lights along the baseboards saved the house from utter darkness.

On the stairs to the second floor, Jim became aware of a slight stiffness in his legs and buttocks. It reminded him that he'd ridden a bicycle this morning for the first time in years.

He'd enjoyed whizzing around like a kid. And having President Martin walk right by without gushing over him. Sometimes anonymity could be fun.

Mostly, he'd enjoyed hearing Dex's pointed commentary on everything and everyone. So Wilson Martin was reputed to have made a deal with an evil wizard to hide his age. So Hugh Bemling had sent an article on "The Flower of Chivalry" to *Better Homes and Gardens*. Jim wanted to hear more.

He wanted to meet her other friends, too, if they were anything like the eccentric Hugh and Marie and that Fitz character who lurked behind the administration building. What about this Cora, whom he'd barely glimpsed? What kind of woman could snare the elusive Kip LaRue?

Smiling, Jim popped into Annie's room and watched his daughter sleeping in her crib along one wall. Glossy curls tumbled on the pillow, and her cheeks had a cherubic roundness. Careful not to wake her, he tucked the blanket around her.

It seemed only natural to go to the next room and peek at Dex. He could see her clearly from the doorway.

She lay on one side in a tumble of crinkly hair.

Same cherubic cheeks as her daughter, but not quite as round. Same soft lips. Same blissful expression.

No wonder the absentminded professor had a crush on her. Jim was glad she didn't return it, though.

He didn't want anyone else touching her. It would be utterly wrong for some other man to kiss her and awaken the explosive reaction that had leveled him four months ago.

If only he could go back to that moment when they'd arrived at her apartment and found themselves mercifully alone. His body hardened at the memory.

He'd caught her face in both hands and stroked his thumbs along her jawline. She'd melted against him, mouth to mouth, firm breasts pillowing against his chest.

Jim swallowed hard and forced himself to step away from Dex's door. He had no business standing here fantasizing about Dex.

The longer she stayed in his house, the faster his self-control eroded. It was inexplicable. Jim prided himself on his discipline.

He looked forward to a long session in the gym tomorrow. Even with Dex around, he ought to be able to work up a sweat that would leave him too exhausted to think.

And that would be a relief.

DEX SLEPT LATE on Sunday morning. By the time she arose and ate breakfast, everyone had cleared out.

Except Jim. As she sat finishing a lemon Danish and coffee in the garden, she could hear the rhythmic thump of exercise equipment resounding through the open windows of the pool house.

Dex knew she'd promised to join him, but she

didn't feel like working out. The spring wind was full of honey and jasmine, and the tinkling of wind chimes murmured of some make-believe land. She wished she had a magic carpet so she could simply float away.

She shook her head to clear it. As she did, she noted that her hair felt springier than usual. Something about Villa Bonderoff was working a change on her, and she didn't like it.

The place stirred longings and fomented romantic pairings. Just look at Kip and Cora, and the way Grace was trying to make Rocky jealous. Or was she truly interested in Hugh Bemling? And what about Rocky's interest in Dean Pipp?

In any case, Dex had never before been susceptible to the usual spring Clair De Lunacy. Yet she felt lightheaded every time she got near Jim.

She'd come to his house to keep an eye on Annie. Or, rather, to fulfill a bargain so that Annie could be put up for adoption. Instead, Dex could barely tear herself away from either the child or the father.

This place was like some fairy-tale castle where visitors became spellbound. She ought to run while she could.

But she wouldn't abandon Annie. Some compromise had to be reached. Suddenly she had an idea.

Dex jumped to her feet and hurried toward the pool house, her tennis shoes slapping against the flagstone walkway.

9

THE LOWER FLOOR of the pool house comprised one large room furnished with a pool table, arcade-style video games, a bar and grill area, a large-screen TV and a curving sectional couch. But Dex's target was on the upper level, not here.

She mounted a set of stairs and emerged into a wood-floored gymnasium lined on one side by amber-tinted windows and, on the other, by tall mirrors. A treadmill, a rowing machine and a stationary cycle barely made a dent in the space.

On a mat in the center, Jim stood with his back to her, lifting weights. A skinny black undershirt strained across gleaming bronze muscles as he hefted a barbell overhead. Through his clinging black shorts, she could see his buns tighten. He held the weight to a slow count of five before lowering it to the mat.

Dex could smell his exertion, the musk scent mingling with his aftershave lotion. Beneath the stretch jersey of her halter top, her nipples grew erect.

This hadn't been such a good idea, joining him here. She took a retreating step toward the stairs.

The squeak of her sneaker made Jim turn. Sweat beaded his forehead, and his eyes had a heavy-lidded look as he took in her skimpy top and short shorts.

Dex wished she'd worn something more discreet.

A bra beneath her halter or, better yet, a sweatshirt and jeans. No, a burnoose.

"You planning to exercise in that?" His gaze lingered on her bare waist.

"Changed my mind," Dex said. "I just came to talk."

Charged particles vibrated between them. Jim waited, hands on hips. He could, she realized, grasp and lift her as easily as he'd hefted the barbell. She almost wished he would.

"What about?" he asked.

"Annie." Dex swallowed and discovered her throat was dry. "Her future."

"It's only been two days. Don't rush to judgment." A lock of sun-warmed brown hair fell onto his forehead, and he didn't bother to brush it back.

"A week or two weeks isn't going to make any difference." Dex forced herself to keep talking. "Your employees are nice, but they aren't parents. You need to—" she cleared her throat "—to find out how your fiancée feels. Whether she's willing to raise someone else's child."

The woman would probably agree to take Annie for Jim's sake, but a halfhearted response would bolster Dex's case for adoption. And maybe, just maybe, this career-oriented lady would say no dice.

"I've already told her I have a daughter." Stepping around the barbell, Jim grabbed a towel and wiped his face.

"You have?" Dex hadn't expected this reply. "What did she say?"

He slanted her a rueful smile. "That it was a surprise."

"That's all?"

Jim slung the towel over his shoulder. "She said her current research involves babies and how they acquire foreign languages."

Dex could feel her hackles rising. "Annie isn't a research project."

"No, she isn't." He walked toward her. Dex tensed as she waited for him to touch her, but he walked past, inches away, and went down the stairs. Annoyed, she followed.

Did he have to smell so tantalizing? And hadn't he even noticed her reaction to him?

But she didn't want him to. It was crazy, getting this mixed up over a guy she wanted nothing to do with. However, they needed to resolve the matter of their daughter's future.

When she reached the lower level, Jim was yanking a cold soda from the refrigerator. "So what about your fiancée?" Dex demanded. "Is she or is she not prepared to be Annie's mother?"

"Let's face it." He popped the top and took a drink. "This marriage isn't going to happen."

"It isn't?"

Jim shrugged. "She would have given me a response by now if she intended to marry me. Nancy's never wanted anything but her career. She's the closest friend I ever had and she's a terrific woman. She would have made a wonderful wife and mother, but I don't think she wants that."

So he loved Nancy, but she didn't love him. Or didn't love him enough. It amazed Dex that anyone could reject Jim Bonderoff.

Of course, she herself had, four months ago. But only because she knew that eventually she'd be the one who got dumped.

"Then you don't plan to keep Annie?" she asked.

He set the can on the counter. "I think you need to reexamine your own feelings on the subject."

Dex stood her ground. "I want what's best for my daughter."

"And you're certain you know what that is?" He moved closer.

"It isn't to be raised by a nanny," she said.

"We'll talk about that later." His hands circled her waist lightly. Quivers ran across her skin. "Turn around."

"Why?"

"I want to inspect your tattoo."

She turned, mostly because she couldn't bear the intensity of standing here facing him, especially while he was touching her. "It's nothing special."

"Why did you get it?" His forefinger traced the flower design on her right hip just above the waistband of her shorts.

"A guy I used to date thought it would be sexy," she said.

His cheek brushed her hair. "It is." His low voice tickled her ear.

Outside the glass doors, sunlight sparkled off the pool. A butterfly zigzagged by, heading for a clump of calla lilies.

Spring fever hit Dex like a wall of shimmering heat. She sagged against Jim, and her rear end discovered immediately that she was not alone in her arousal.

He groaned with the inevitability of their union. At the same time, his hands smoothed upward and untied the front of her halter. As her breasts fell free, he captured them and chafed the nipples.

"Didn't we skip something? Like a kiss?" Letting her top fall to the floor, Dex swiveled and draped her arms around Jim.

He shimmered with the glow of exercise and sexual desire, and his muscles bulged beneath her strokes as his mouth quested for hers. When their lips and tongues met, the connection jolted Dex all the way to her toes.

Jim wriggled off his undershirt and moved away just long enough to toss it. They were both naked from the waist up, which was only halfway naked enough, she reflected as she reached for him again.

Then she remembered that, if anyone returned, they might be seen. "Curtains!" She gulped.

"Right." Jim closed the floor-to-ceiling draperies, leaving the pool house bathed in a half-light. "How's that?"

"I'll tell you in a minute." Her hands grazed his hips and lowered his shorts. He fumbled with the snap on her shorts.

At the back of her mind, it occurred to Dex that they ought to stop. This was how people got into trouble.

But she knew how outrageously good Jim was going to feel inside her. And he didn't belong to anyone else, so for today at least he might as well belong to her.

He looked splendid with nothing on, taut and sculpted. And he wore the most wonderful smile.

"I've missed you," he said, and dropped to his knees to remove her shorts. On his way up, he got only as far as her breasts, which he mouthed with a sigh of pleasure.

"I've missed you, too," whispered Dex.

"Show me how much." Grinning, he stood, slipped his arms around her and carried her lightly to the couch.

Dex knew it could only be this once, that she didn't belong in Jim's world or he in hers. But none of that mattered.

She'd never felt so alive with anyone else, and she doubted she ever would. Some moments were simply meant to be cherished.

After lowering her to the couch, Jim rummaged in a drawer and found some protection. As he put it on, he studied her. It was a self-conscious moment, because she knew she wasn't his usual model type. But he seemed to relish the roundness of her body and to revel in her response as, ready for action again, he stroked between her thighs.

Self-consciousness vanished amid the waves of pleasure rolling through her. Bracing his powerful arms on either side of her like pillars, Jim bent and brushed his lips across her mouth.

She was on fire. Her knees massaged his thighs encouragingly, and his hardness probed at her. It found its sheath with a sudden thrust.

Dex clutched Jim's shoulders and wrapped her legs around him. They rolled together and, with a *whump!*, went right off the sofa onto the all-weather carpet.

It prickled Dex's side, but she didn't care. She was attacking Jim, wanting him inside her. He hung on to her, laughing as she climbed on top.

He entered her again, and from this angle she could feel him pushing right up to her chest. He was so big and so hungry that she could hardly hang on for the ride.

And then it was over. "Not yet," she said.

Jim shot her a rueful look as he removed the protection. "Sorry. It's been four months, you know."

"For me, too!"

"We'll do it again," he said. "You work on creative ideas while I recuperate, okay?"

The instant Dex's bare skin touched the prickly carpet, she knew what she wanted to do next. "Your room," she said.

"Excuse me?" Jim sprawled on the floor, boneless as a cat.

"Your carpet. It's rumored to be thick and deep with plenty of cushions on hand," she said.

"Where did you hear that rumor?"

"From you. How about it?"

Jim's eyelids drifted shut, and she wondered if he were falling asleep. Then they opened with a snap. "Yes!" He sat up and grabbed for his clothes.

Dex raced for hers. Without their exchanging a word, it became a contest to get dressed first.

She nearly tripped, trying to pull up her panties while reaching onto the pool table, where her shorts had somehow landed. "Hey!" She glanced at Jim. "No fair! You're not wearing underpants."

With a grin, he yanked on his exercise shorts. "It's not my fault if you dress inefficiently."

"Oh, yeah?" She kicked his black undershirt beneath the couch. "Go dig for that!"

Jim clicked his tongue. "I had no idea you were so spiteful."

"Just evening the odds a little." Dex struggled to tie on her halter. Her hands refused to make a proper knot, and the front kept falling open.

Jim knelt on the floor, his shapely black-clad buns in the air as he retrieved his garment. It came out dangling dust bunnies. "I'm going to have to speak to Grace about this mess."

"Really? Exactly how do you plan to tell her you discovered it?" Dex gave the fabric of her blouse another series of jerks. She heard the ripping noise even before she noticed the gaping hole at one seam.

"On second thought, maybe I'll mention it to Rocky and let him scold Grace." Jim pulled the undershirt over his head, dust clots included. "It looks like I win. I don't think we can count you as being fully dressed."

"You're heartless." The halter was ruined. Dex would have to hug the fabric into place around her chest to maintain public decency as she crossed the pool area.

"I've got an idea." Removing the skimpy black shirt, Jim plucked off the bits of dust and handed it to her. "Wear this."

Dex dropped her halter, and felt her nipples tighten as his gaze roved over them. Quickly, she pulled on the knit top.

Jim's scent clung to the fabric as it molded itself to her breasts. "Your room," she said, and ran for the door.

JIM HAD BEEN well-satisfied by their encounter moments ago and on the point of sinking into a snooze. Although thirty-four was hardly an advanced age, a man didn't have the perpetual readiness for action that had dogged him—or thrilled him—as a teenager.

Until now. At the sight of Dex's full breasts straining against the thin knit top, no adolescent had ever gotten hard faster than Jim did.

Her eyes flashed a challenge. When Dex turned and

ran, he raced barefoot after her across the concrete that abutted the pool. The spring breeze cooled his bare chest, but the sight of Dex sprinting ahead inspired new bursts of speed.

Jim remembered an image he'd seen once on a Greek urn, of a mythological satyr chasing a maiden. In that case, the maiden had trailed a scarf through the air. In this case, the maiden tossed her ruined top into a trash can by the patio and ran inside.

They pelted through the den, across the hall and up the circular main staircase. At the top of the steps, Dex headed to Jim's private chamber.

She halted so abruptly that he nearly toppled over her. With her hair defying gravity, she made a splash of color in the middle of the subdued decor.

"Wow," Dex said. "Your room is bigger than my whole apartment."

"It's a suite." Jim had grown accustomed to the conveniences, but now he saw the place through her eyes. It *was* large.

To their left lay the dressing area with its twin bureaus and triple-width closet. Beyond, partly visible, was a bathroom as large as many bedrooms.

On their right, the entertainment center dominated the middle of the room. It featured the latest in audiovisual equipment, a coffee bar and compact refrigerator and a large couch. Beyond, in an alcove, wall-to-wall built-in shelves surrounded the oversize bed.

But Dex took no notice of the furnishings. She was staring at the carpet.

The softness of it soothed Jim's feet. He'd chosen a self-indulgent deep pile without quite knowing why. Now he understood. He'd been waiting for Dex even before he met her.

"Now, *this* is a rug." She walked to the couch, then tossed a couple of accent pillows to the floor. His black undershirt bounced with her breasts. "As you promised."

"I never lie."

"Oh? You promised that sex on your carpet would be the best thing that ever happened to me."

"As I said, I never lie." When she faced Jim, he could clearly see each round orb, and the outlines of two erect nipples. "Leave the shirt on." He moved toward her.

Dex's breath came audibly faster. "What about the shorts?"

"I'll take care of those."

Despite his playboy reputation, Jim had no more than the usual single man's experience with women. He didn't imagine himself a spectacular performer, or a seducer of innocent women, either.

From the moment he'd met Dex, however, he'd discovered the rake inside himself. That first night, he'd realized how little they had in common, and yet he'd gone after her without a second thought.

And right now, he wanted her again. Every inch of her.

Two strides brought them face to face. Beneath the waistband of her shorts, Jim slipped his hands down the bare skin of her hips. At the same time, his mouth explored hers with a thrust of the tongue.

Dex groaned. He could feel the points of her breasts poke his chest through the thin fabric as she relaxed against him.

A fierce joy filled him, to hold her transfixed this way. She was such an elusive creature, but he had captured her, and he had no intention of letting go.

They sank onto the carpet. Her garments slid free easily, and she pulled his off, too. Jim's lips traced patterns around Dex's bosom until she caught his buttocks with sweet urgency.

This time, he had more control of himself. He put on protection, then teased and inflamed her before spreading her legs and making himself at home.

Her eager writhing sent flames roaring across his skin. Straining to keep control, Jim measured the pace of his thrusts until her movements grew faster and hotter.

Dex clutched his shoulders and moaned. Her rhythmic pressure against his shaft shot ecstasy through his body like a white-hot rod, and her eyes flashed cobalt-blue.

Then her lids lowered and she cried out wordlessly, sheathing him with one last lunge. Jim held himself stiffly on his forearms, relishing the waves of satisfaction that rolled through him and, quite visibly, over Dex.

At last he lay beside her. They were both quiet, their hunger satisfied.

It was a rare thing for Jim to lose control. It had felt wonderful, but he needed to gather his wits.

In the splendor of lovemaking, he'd forgotten everything else. They still hadn't resolved the matter of Annie's future.

Lots of divorced couples managed to raise their offspring with mutual cooperation. Now that the chill between them had evaporated, maybe Dex would accept a mature, civilized arrangement of that sort.

And if, on occasion, passion overwhelmed them, who was he to object?

DEX BURROWED into a cushion and tried to make sense of the wreckage of her universe.

Even as her body hummed with fulfillment, her emotions rampaged against her weakness. How could she have let down her guard for a second time with Clair De Lune's most notorious playboy? How could she have made herself so vulnerable to this man?

The last time, she'd fled and even lied to make sure she would never run into him again. Yet here she was, even more deeply involved and even more scared of her feelings.

She yearned to crawl back to the safety of her former life, except that nothing felt safe any more. She craved Jim, wanted to cuddle against him, yearned for his love and approval. And recognized, at the same time, that she must give no sign of how she felt.

She couldn't bear to see contempt on his face. And surely she would, if he discovered that she'd been foolish enough to let him inside her heart.

Beside her, Jim stretched languorously, oozing contentment. He showed no signs of suffering from any tempest like the one raging inside Dex.

"You know," he said, "I think we can work something out about Annie."

"Work something out?" A sudden dread gripped her, that Jim had engineered this encounter to manipulate her into yielding her daughter to him. But surely he would never sink that low.

He rolled onto his side, facing her. The man seemed even larger and more intimidating from this angle than when they were standing up. "You've been worried about Annie being raised by strangers. By people who don't love her," he said. "But that isn't necessary now."

"You said you were getting married, that she would have a mother," she countered. "Well, you aren't. So nothing's changed."

"We could raise her together," he said.

Dex caught her breath. She would love to stay close to her daughter. It would be wonderful to be able to guide her through the difficult adolescent years. And Jim appeared to have the makings of a loving father.

But not a husband. Not for Dex, anyway. He wasn't proposing it, and she didn't want him to. Not when he loved someone else.

"Even though things haven't worked out with Nancy, there's no reason Annie can't stay here," Jim continued in a persuasive tone. "I adore her. My servants dote on her. And you could stay involved. Visit as often as you like. I'll give you a key."

Was it possible they really could raise their daughter together? she wondered. She had no intention of serving as Jim's convenient part-time mistress, but if they agreed to resume a platonic relationship...

Except that I don't seem to be able to resist him.

Besides, she reminded herself, she might not always live in Clair De Lune. "I'll have to move away," she said. "After I get my Ph.D. and find a teaching position. Then Annie would be motherless."

Jim propped himself on one elbow. "I can help you find a job here."

"I couldn't accept it."

"Not even for your daughter's sake?" he asked. "No, forget I said that. I respect your pride. You could accept airfare, though, to come back and visit her whenever you want."

Dex sat up and hugged her knees. He was being so

reasonable, and she wanted desperately to be near her daughter. Why not agree to a compromise?

Yet her mind continued to throw up obstacles. "How would you explain me to your friends? I don't fit into your social circles."

Jim ran one hand lightly along her thigh. It was a possessive gesture, and in spite of herself, Dex relished it.

What she really wanted was a passionate declaration of love. She wanted Jim to be so swept away by his feelings that he no longer cared what anyone else thought. It was a ridiculous notion, of course.

"You underestimate yourself," he said. "A woman who's earned her Ph.D. can hold up her head at any level of society in Clair De Lune."

That was his response? He sounded more like her parents, or maybe a career counselor, than a devoted lover.

Dex didn't want a man who only accepted her because she met some external qualification. She had to deal with the reality that their relationship would never go beyond the level it had already reached.

And how could things be otherwise? For his social circles, she was too rough around the edges, too intense, too short and too inelegant. Her amount of cellulite alone would get her banned from the Clair De Lune Country Club.

Not that she was fat. But she wasn't rail-thin like a model or socialite, either.

Downstairs, a door scraped open. Someone was home.

"Oh, my gosh!" Dex grabbed for her clothes, then realized she no longer had a blouse. "I'd better get back to my room!"

Jim caught her wrist. "Promise you'll think about what I said."

"Maybe. No guarantees." She pulled free.

It was a totally graceless way to exit, she reflected as she scrambled down the hall. Jim was probably having second thoughts already.

10

ON MONDAY MORNING, Dex awoke from a restless slumber promptly at six. That was because someone was playing piercing notes on a trumpet outside her window.

"What the…" Grumbling, she ran to her balcony and peered down.

Below and to one side, on a small guest parking area in front of the house, Grace stood wearing camouflage-style pajamas and blowing "Reveille." The staccato sounds smashed the morning quiet.

It was worse than the rooster one of Dex's neighbors used to keep back in Florida. The noise was so earsplitting, some unidentified person had sneaked into the yard late one night and strangled the hapless fowl. Dex had felt sorry for the poor bird, which was only obeying its nature.

Grace had no such excuse. Or perhaps she did. Marine Corps traditions apparently meant a lot to her.

As the last note died, the maid waved at Dex. "Sleep well?"

"Not very," she admitted.

"You should get up earlier." Grace thumped her chest. "Early morning air is bracing. That and a few laps around the block will help you sleep better at night."

A wail from the next room drew Dex inside. The trumpet must have awakened Annie.

The little girl brightened as soon as she saw her mother. Standing against the crib rail, she threw up her arms, lost her balance and plopped down bottom-first onto the mattress.

The small face puckered. When Dex picked her up, however, she thought better of crying and began to play with her mother's hair instead.

It was absurdly early, Dex thought as she changed the baby, pulled on a pair of jeans and a blouse and took Annie downstairs for breakfast. Since she'd showered last night, she had nothing to do for two hours before delivering the graded papers to Hugh Bemling.

"Don't your neighbors throw a fit about the trumpeting?" she asked Rocky, who was making an omelette with some of Dean Pipp's herbs.

"We don't have neighbors," he said.

"I'll bet people can hear that thing all over town!"

"Nobody's complained." He produced a jar of baby food for Annie, who was banging on the tray of her high chair. "Mind if I ask you something?"

"Ask away." Dex sneaked a bite of the omelette. It was delicious.

"It's about Marie Pipp." Rocky fed the baby a spoonful of applesauce. "Somebody like her, you know, an intellectual-type person, do you think she'd mind if a guy like me dropped by for a visit?"

"She'd enjoy it." In the refrigerator, Dex found a quarter of a loaf of rye bread. "I'll bet she had a terrific time at your sister's yesterday."

"She seemed to." Rocky hesitated before asking, "Does, er, anybody else live with her?"

"No. Her husband died a long time ago and there were no children. She spends too much time alone, in my opinion." Marie belonged to a health club and attended a few university events as a faculty member emeritus. That was the extent of her activities.

"Marie's a nice lady," he said. "I'd like to know more about how she—"

"How she what?" Grace stalked into the kitchen wearing a starched white apron over a black dress. Since Rocky didn't wear a butler's uniform, Dex assumed Grace had chosen the costume herself. "You're making a durn fool of yourself, panting after that old woman."

"Who asked you?" He continued feeding the baby. "And she looks better for her age than you do."

"Did you have a good time at the gun show yesterday?" Dex asked, trying to forestall a wrestling match in the middle of the kitchen.

"Sure did! That Professor Hugh is great company." Grace sniffed at the omelette, wrinkled her nose and helped herself to some of Dex's toast. "He was as jumpy as a rabbit when we fired a few rounds on the practice range, but I think he enjoyed himself."

"Rabbit is right." Rocky sniffed. "That's what he reminds me of."

"Rabbits are cute." Grace snatched the jar of baby food from his hand. "Go eat your froufrou omelette. I'll take over from here."

Dex carried her coffee and toast into the dining room. She was sitting down when Jim breezed past, knotting his tie.

"How do I look?" he asked. "I've got a meeting with the city manager and some of the planning staff about building a second plant for my company."

"You look striking." All signs of their lovemaking had vanished from his formerly rumpled hair, now moussed and combed to perfection. A lightweight dove-gray suit skimmed his muscular body.

Dex scarcely knew this Jim Bonderoff. He belonged in the upper echelons, far away from her.

Her heart gave a twist. Somewhere between yesterday morning and today, she'd fallen in love with him. It was an alarming thought.

"Did you give any more consideration to what we discussed about Annie?" he asked.

"Other than not sleeping all night, no," she said.

"And your conclusion?"

"I haven't reached one." Every instinct screamed at her to get as far away from this house as possible. Yet she didn't know how she could bear to.

Jim grabbed a piece of her toast. "Sorry to eat and run, but it's a breakfast meeting."

"If it's a breakfast meeting, why don't you leave my food alone?" she demanded, too late. He was already loping through the sunroom toward the garages.

Scowling, Dex returned to the kitchen to make more toast. Rocky and Grace sat glaring at each other both of them holding spoons full of applesauce. Annie peered from one to the other, puzzled.

"You two are acting like children," Dex said. "Why can't you be pleased for each other, that you've both found members of the opposite sex you like?"

"She's too old," Grace grumbled.

"He's a wimp," snarled Rocky.

The door opened from the utility room and Kip edged into the room carrying a bouquet of delicate spring flowers. It was, Dex realized, the first time she'd seen him indoors.

"Do you think she'll like them?" he asked.

She sniffed the flowers. "She'll love them. How was the concert yesterday?"

"She held my hand." Kip gave the impression of floating inches above the floor.

"Who's 'she'?" asked Grace.

"Cora," he said. "She's spun gold."

"Has the whole world changed color?" Dex couldn't resist asking as the toaster popped up the last two slices of rye bread. "I hear love makes things look rosy."

"The colors haven't changed," Kip said. "But my heart has." With a shy smile, he snatched a slice of toast and vanished through the utility room.

"Wait!" yelled Grace. "It's nearly eight o'clock!"

Time to raise the flag, Dex remembered. She took the last piece of rye bread with her for safekeeping, and Rocky carted Annie on one hip as they went outside.

At the front corner of the house, Grace ran the flag up its pole and then played a fanfare on her trumpet. The adults saluted. After a moment's observation, so did Annie.

They were just finishing when Kip swooped by on Jim's racing bicycle. He waved the flowers at them as he went down the hill.

Love, Dex reflected, was certainly in the air.

After making sure Rocky and Grace could look after her daughter all day, she went to her room to collect the papers for Hugh. On the way out, she heard a ringing in the hall near Jim's room.

It was his cellular phone, lying forlorn in a corner.

It must have fallen from his pocket as he rushed to leave.

The call might be important. Dex could relay the message to his secretary at work, she supposed.

Feeling like a trespasser, she picked up the phone. "Bonderoff residence."

After a short pause, a woman said, "Is Jim there?"

"I'm sorry, he ran out and left his cell phone at home," Dex said. "Can I take a message?"

"Who's this?"

"Dex." Further explanation appeared necessary, so she added, "I'm here about the baby."

"Oh!" Relief colored the response. "You're the nanny! I'm so glad to meet you. We'll be getting a lot better acquainted from now on, so I should introduce myself. I'm Nancy Verano. Jim and I are getting married."

Her knees went weak, and Dex collapsed onto a small padded bench. "I didn't realize..."

A chuckle echoed over the phone. "He doesn't know yet. I'm sorry, I must sound like a real basket case, don't I? I can't tell you how super it feels, like this great weight's been lifted off me. I've had so many things on my mind. There, I'm being incoherent again!"

Through her numbness, Dex discovered a reluctant sympathy for this woman. She sounded as muddled as Dex felt. "So you've decided to marry him?"

"He asked me months ago and I couldn't say yes or no because my funding was being cut off and I had applications out everywhere. I nearly went to Alaska at one point, can you believe that? But it's so perfect! I'm coming to De Lune University! In fact,

I'm getting on a plane right now, and I realized I ought to call and let him know I'll be there tonight."

Dex's heart sank. Any small chance she'd had with Jim was gone. He'd loved Nancy for years. No one else could even hope to come between them.

Still, there was one matter she had to address. "What about his daughter?"

"Oh, yes, little—what's her darling name?— Ayoka!" Nancy said. In the background, Dex could hear a PA system announcing a flight. "I'm sure we can muddle through. I've got scads of younger brothers and sisters that I helped raise, you know. And I *am* a psychologist."

Jim had mentioned research experiments, Dex recalled. "A little girl isn't a...a test subject. She needs a mother." She tensed, expecting a heated response.

Instead, Nancy sighed. "You're such a devoted nanny. How lucky we are to find you! To be perfectly honest, I wasn't sure I wanted children, but now, well, it seems like part of a divine plan. I mean, what were the odds that I'd land a job in Clair De Lune? And that Jim would magically produce a daughter? It was meant to be. I'm sorry, I have to go, but I'm looking forward to meeting you!"

"Me, too," Dex said, although there was no one in the world she less wanted to meet.

Tonight, Nancy would be here. With Jim. In his arms and, no doubt, his bed.

Her throat clamped shut, and it was several moments before she remembered to click off the phone.

She wanted to blame Jim, but she couldn't. He'd made it clear that he loved Nancy, but had given up on winning her. Dex had known that before she fell into his arms yesterday.

She didn't regret what had happened between them. Once the pain faded, it would give her memories to treasure for the rest of her days.

Leaving the cell phone on the bench, Dex walked stiffly to her room and began tossing clothes into her backpack. She couldn't stay in this house another minute.

What about Annie? Should she take her daughter with her?

Her common sense uttered a resounding *no*. The little girl could hardly spend her days riding on the back of a bike and accompanying her mother to classes. A baby wasn't a toy to be carted around.

Nancy hadn't sounded enthusiastic about children, but she did have experience with her siblings. Once she saw Annie, how could she help falling in love?

Tears prickled Dex's eyes. Only a short time ago, she'd dared to hope she and Jim might be able to raise their daughter together. And now...

Her heart squeezed. She had to give up the man she loved and the child of her heart, as well.

But she would safeguard her daughter's best interests, Dex vowed. She'd keep an eye on Nancy. If Jim's wife-to-be wasn't a suitable mother, Dex would insist on adoption.

When she emerged into the upstairs hall, she found she couldn't even look toward Jim's room without her eyes brimming over. She was going to miss him so much more than he would ever know.

Taking a deep breath, Dex went downstairs. To Grace, who was spraying disinfectant around the vast living room, she said, "Jim's fiancée called. She's arriving tonight." Forcing back tears, Dex turned toward the front door. "It was nice knowing you." Then she fled.

THE CITY MANAGER and planners loved Jim's proposal to build a new plant on the site of an abandoned warehouse across from his headquarters on Constellation Street. Later, at his office, he found a long queue of congratulatory e-mails about his stock triumph. All in all, Monday was one of the best days he could remember.

As Jim drove home in his sports car, he could hardly wait to see Dex. Despite her initial reluctance, he felt certain he could persuade her that they should raise Annie together.

What a dizzying, delightful scamp the woman was, catching him off guard in the pool house and finding fresh ways to thrill him each time they made love. He'd never known anyone so sensuous.

Everything was falling into place. It confirmed his belief that, if a man seized the initiative, life was meant to run smoothly.

As his car whipped up the driveway, he spotted a wilted bunch of flowers plopped in an empty parking space. Someone had left Jim's bicycle outside, laid on one side where a less careful motorist might have run over it.

Perplexed, he pulled into the garage and put the bike away. There was no sign of Dex's bike, but it wouldn't be dark for another hour, so perhaps she was finishing up her work on campus.

He mounted the curving stairs to the garden. At the top, a dejected Kip sat on a low stone wall twisting his cap in his hands.

Here, Jim suspected, was the errant cyclist and flower tosser. "What's wrong?"

Slowly, the gardener's eyes came into focus. "Cora won't see me."

"Because of the age difference?" She had appeared rather young when he glimpsed her through the patio door, Jim recalled.

Kip shook his head. "No, no. She says it would be disloyal."

"To whom?"

"To...to—" With a grimace, the man fled into the bushes.

Grace had been right, Jim mused. Kip was getting weirder by the day.

Indoors, the smell of burned cinnamon greeted him. In the kitchen, he found Rocky stirring an unappetizing pot of sliced meat and vegetables.

Jim had never known his butler to ruin a meal before. "What's wrong?"

"Okay, so I'm no professor. That don't mean I can't figure out for myself how to use spices!" grumbled the former sergeant, who had tan splotches and grease spots on his usually pristine apron. "Them Greeks or somebody use cinnamon with their meat, so why not me?"

"You're not Greek," he pointed out.

"Neither is that Pipp woman," growled Rocky. "But she won't loan me her cookbook."

"Why not?"

"Because I'm the enemy." He smacked a large wooden spoon against the counter, sending grease flying through the air. Jim ducked. "One day we're best friends and the next day I'm the bad guy!"

He couldn't imagine how Rocky had alienated the dean. "Why..."

Grace marched into the room and thrust Annie into his arms. "Take her."

Warily, Jim gripped his daughter and regarded his maid. "Don't tell me you're having a problem with *your* new boyfriend?"

"Who?" she said, or perhaps she said, "Hugh?" Jim couldn't hear very well with Rocky thumping on the counter again. "Naw. But we leathernecks got to stick together against them intellectuals."

Something was missing from this conversation, Jim realized. Or rather, *someone* was missing. "Where's your mother?" he asked Annie. He didn't expect her to answer, but he was a bit surprised that neither Rocky nor Grace did, either.

Outside, a car purred up the driveway. Inside, everyone froze.

"What on earth is going on?" Going to the window, Jim glanced down and saw a neutral-colored sedan halt in a parking space. "Any idea who that is?"

"You asking me?" demanded Grace. "I'm always the last one to know anything."

"Her and me both," said Rocky. "We figure you must like surprises."

"Considering the way you surprised us," Grace added.

Jim had never seen his staff act this way before. He wondered if he'd fallen asleep at the office and was having a bizarre dream. "Surprised you with what?"

"For instance, nobody mentioned that you were getting married," Rocky said.

"Or that Dex was clearing out," snapped Grace.

"Dex left?" Below, Jim watched a stately blonde uncoil from the car and remove two suitcases from its trunk. Even at this angle, he recognized Nancy.

The computer in his brain clicked the fragments into place. His left-behind cell phone. Her promise that matters would be settled within a week.

He itched for a Delete button. Or, better yet, Escape.

This mix-up could be resolved, but the last thing Jim wanted to do was to embarrass Nancy in front of his staff. There'd be plenty of time later to straighten out matters privately.

He handed Annie to Rocky and hurried to the side door. Nancy had only visited this house twice, once while it was under construction and once during the housewarming party. He didn't want her to have to wander around looking for the front entrance.

She was at the top of the stone stairs when he emerged. "Jim! Hi!" Dumping her suitcases without ceremony, she flew into his arms. "Wow, you get better looking every time I see you!"

Instantly, he felt comfortable with his old friend. "So do you, by a factor of ten." He gave Nancy a hug and then stood back to take in the sight.

Her gray eyes glowed with enthusiasm and her blond hair flowed around her shoulders as smooth as honey. She wore a blue-gray pin-striped jacket and a matching skirt, with a soft pink blouse bringing out the color in her cheeks.

"I guess this is something of a surprise, huh?" she said. "I did call, you know. I talked to the nanny. She's wonderful! Is she around?"

It took only a split second for him to make sense of her comment. "You mean Dex."

"Right! I wasn't sure I heard the name correctly. It's so unusual." She reached for her suitcases, but Jim beat her to them.

"Dex isn't the nanny," he said, carrying the heavy bags toward the sunroom.

"She said she was here about the baby. By the way, where is Ayoka?"

"We call her Annie. She's in the kitchen." He'd forgotten how difficult it was to get a grip on the conversation when Nancy was around. "About Dex..."

"This way, right?" She breezed through the sunroom, down the hall and into the kitchen. "Oh, my gosh! What a little cutie! Is she drooling? Maybe I'd better not hold her right away. But she's such a doll!"

Rocky and Grace stared at Nancy with barely disguised hostility. "You've met Miss Verano before," Jim reminded them, over Nancy's shoulder. "At the housewarming."

"There were lots of people," the butler said stiffly.

"Skinny women all look alike to me," muttered Grace.

Nancy indicated the cooking pot. "Who's making dinner? It smells...interesting."

"Do you cook?" Rocky showed his first trace of interest.

"I can reheat with the best of them!" She wiggled her forefinger as if pressing a button on a microwave oven. "Isn't it awful, how little time we have for the finer things in life? I'm glad someone around here knows how to cook."

"If you think that smells good, we've got some

canned pasta we could feed you, too," grumbled Grace.

"Those little O-shaped things?" Nancy said. "They're my favorite. I do hope you have a juicer. That's mostly what I live on, carrot and orange juice with soy powder. But I'm easy to please."

She swooped out of the room. Jim slogged behind her up the stairs. What had she put in these suitcases—anvils?

"This is such a stunning house," his fiancée called. "I'm proud of you, Jim. I always said you could do it."

"Yes, you did," he agreed. "You encouraged me when no one else did." Guiltily, he conceded that he owed her a great deal, not that Nancy had been implying anything of the kind.

"Which room?" she asked at the top, gazing about the open expanse around the staircase.

Not his room, that was for sure. Jim had no intention of getting intimate with Nancy, and besides, there had always been a reservoir of space between them.

Not Dex's room, either. "Annie sleeps there," he said, indicating the door next to his. "How about one of the two bedrooms at the back? I'll have Grace make one up for you."

"I don't need to be waited on." Nancy sailed toward the two rooms he'd suggested and picked the larger one. "Oh, dear, I hope those suitcases aren't giving you a hernia. My laptop's inside that one and my books are in the other."

"Didn't you bring any clothes?" He grunted as he hefted them onto the bed.

"A few. I shipped the rest," she chirped. "Oh, Jim, it's wonderful to be here!"

Now, said an inner voice. *Tell her now.* He took a deep breath, which, after the struggle up the stairs, he needed. "Nancy, things have changed."

"Yes, they have." She dropped her clutch purse on the bed and turned to take his hands in hers. "Jim, can you ever forgive me for taking so long to answer you?" Vulnerability glinted in her gray eyes.

"There's nothing to forgive," he said.

"Yes, there is." Nancy studied him pleadingly. "I was confused. I had such mixed emotions regarding marriage and children. It wasn't until you called me about Ayoka that things started to come clear."

"They did?" His feelings certainly hadn't become any clearer to Jim in the past few days. In fact, they'd become a whole lot murkier.

"I've been giving this a lot of thought. I'm thirty-four, and what do I want from life? A bunch of scholarly papers with my name on them that nobody reads?"

"Your research has real value for people's lives," he said, although he had no idea whether it was true.

"Maybe so, but it isn't enough." Nancy swung their hands between them as if they were children. "I want what every woman wants, to have it all. Husband, family and career. But I didn't realize that until I heard about your daughter. It was as if fate were speaking to me!"

"Nancy..."

She pressed on. "I've always felt driven, that there was something I had to accomplish in this life and I needed to be perfect to do it. Can you understand that?"

"Yes." Jim smiled. "I'm like that, too."

"I know," she said. "And now a child's been

thrust upon us. It's as if God were trying to tell us that it's time to stop and smell the roses. We need this little girl, Jim, and we need each other. We always have. You were just smart enough to see it sooner than I did."

His chest tightened. Nancy didn't arouse the joyous, explosive, delicious feelings Dex did. But she was promising to stick around, to be there for Annie as the little girl grew up. And he could see that she meant every word.

Dex planned to move away from Clair De Lune as soon as she got her Ph.D. And she'd insisted she wanted Annie raised in a loving two-parent family.

Well, that's what Nancy was offering. Did Jim have the right to ignore his daughter's best interests and hurt this friend who trusted him simply because of his confused feelings?

He wished he knew how Dex felt about him. Until they had a chance to talk, it was best if he didn't discuss her with Nancy. Except, of course, to reveal the one truth that his future wife was certain to learn anyway.

"There's something I think you should know," he said.

Nancy released his hands and smiled brightly. "There's nothing you can't tell me. We're still best friends and we always will be. So, shoot!"

"Dex isn't the nanny," he said. "She's Annie's biological mother."

11

"OH." A SLIGHT FROWN wrinkled Nancy's symmetrical features. "She is?"

"Yes."

"So where does she fit in? In your household, I mean."

"She's been staying at the house to make sure I could take proper care of our daughter," Jim said. At least, the situation had started out that way, he amended silently. "I gather she left today."

Nancy regarded him assessingly, as if she were about to administer a psychological test. "What's the relationship between you two? I mean, you had a child together, even if Dr. Saldivar did facilitate the whole thing."

"At the time of Annie's conception, Dex and I had never met," Jim said. "Of course, we've become much closer since then."

It went against the grain not to be completely honest, yet it also went against the grain to hurt Nancy unnecessarily. He still thought it wise not to say more until he talked to Dex. However, if Nancy pursued the subject, he wasn't going to lie to her.

All she asked, however, was, "She doesn't want custody?"

He shook his head. "She's a graduate student."

"No money, and a lot of uncertainty about the future. I can relate to that!" Nancy said. "I hope she didn't move out on my account. I'll go invite her back, if you want."

"No, thanks," Jim said. "I'll drop by and have a chat with her."

"No wonder she was so protective." Releasing his hands, Nancy went to unlock her suitcases. "About Ayoka, I mean. Do you think she'd mind if I use the baby in my research project? Gee, I haven't even explained what I'm doing here, have I? Aside from marrying you, I mean."

"No, you haven't." Jim was amazed at her energy after the long flight from Washington. Nancy had always been a powerhouse, though.

He felt both relieved and a bit ashamed that he hadn't confessed the whole truth about Dex. Handling ticklish interpersonal situations was a new challenge for Jim. He was going to have to play this one by ear.

Oblivious to his internal debate, Nancy went on talking. "The university hired me as assistant professor of psychology." She set her laptop on the bureau and plugged it into an outlet. "Do you mind? I want to be sure I haven't lost any data. Where was I? Oh, right, so I'll be teaching and also I've got a new research grant."

"How babies acquire second languages," he recalled.

"Right!" The screen blazed and beeped as the operating system sprang to life. Icons winked, and Nancy clicked open a couple of files in rapid succession. "Doesn't look like I lost anything. But then, I'm sure you could recover it if I did, couldn't you?"

"We've got a new program that can recover almost

anything," Jim agreed. "We're debating whether to release it because it could be misused for snooping."

"Your ethics are one of the things I admire most." Nancy turned off the computer. "Anyway, I'm going to be showing babies foreign films during their nap time and testing to see whether they pay more attention to foreign words afterward than they did at the beginning of the experiment."

He was intrigued. "What kind of foreign films?"

"I had to choose a language that has a lot of films available, so I decided on Italian." She indicated a row of videotapes inside one suitcase. "Wouldn't it be great if Ayoka learned Italian? And having her with me in the lab will give her and me a chance to get to know each other."

Jim read a couple of the film titles. *Amarcord? La Strada?* "You're going to show our daughter Fellini movies?"

"They're my favorites. Besides, she won't understand the content," Nancy assured him. "Well, I hate to be a party pooper, but do you suppose dinner's ready? I'm starving."

"Let's go downstairs and see." Jim offered his arm and wondered how anyone could feel hungry with that burned-cinnamon smell polluting the air.

DEX TRIED HARD all day Monday to keep a cheerful expression on her face, but she obviously didn't fool anybody.

Fitz Langley slipped a chocolate bar in among the delivery packages. Hugh Bemling read her a poem he'd written on scraps of paper.

"Heart that flutters, porcelain-delicate among the

stoneware roughness of the world, I salute you," it began. Fortunately, he'd lost the rest of it.

Dean Pipp, outraged at what she considered Jim's duplicity, insisted on fixing a dinner "that ruffian cook of his couldn't even dream of." Cora brought a gallon of ice cream to soothe their sorrows.

"You guys shouldn't take this so personally," Dex advised over a plate of orange-sauced chicken, Bengal-style lentils and jasmine rice. "He asked Nancy to marry him before he even found out about Annie."

"He should tell her he changed his mind!" Cora helped herself to seconds. "I can't believe Kip defended him. I'll never speak to that poor excuse for a gardener again."

"You broke up with Kip?" Dex asked in dismay.

"A good thing, too, if you ask me." Marie passed around a pewter pitcher of ice water. "I don't believe in consorting with the enemy camp."

They were sitting in the dean's dining room, a dark chamber with cabbage roses on the wallpaper and dim light spilling from scalloped sconces. The antique-style sideboard groaned with piles of books, and on the opposite wall, three portraits of famous writers—Shakespeare, Edgar Allan Poe and Mark Twain—hung slightly askew.

Outside, it might be a clear Southern California spring evening. Inside, Dex wouldn't have been surprised to see flashes of lightning and hear a rainstorm beating on the roof.

"I don't want the two of you messing up your lives on my account," she insisted. "I'm perfectly okay with this. Jim's getting married may be the best thing for everyone." She barely squeezed out the words.

Marie added a dash of Tabasco sauce to her Bengal

lentils. Dex wondered if the Pentagon had anything as fiery in its arsenal as the dean had on her plate. "It's the kindness of your heart that makes you wish the best for your daughter. But if Mr. Bonderoff is going to wed, he should wed the woman he wronged."

"The woman he what?" Dex choked on a sip of water.

"You're the mother of his child."

"Helene Saldivar was the mother of his child, and she tricked him into it!"

"We're standing by you," Marie said, "whether you like it or not."

"What else are friends for?" Cora began clearing the table. "Ice cream, everybody?"

"I whipped up some caramelized mint sauce," the dean said. "I only wish I could wave it under Rocky's nose until he salivates. You know, he had the nerve to try to borrow one of my cookbooks, all the while swearing that his employer is the best boss in the world. That blackguard!"

As Dex helped carry dishes into the kitchen, every word made her feel worse. She'd introduced Cora and Marie to new friends, and now everyone was estranged because of her.

From the kitchen table, she picked up today's newspaper and opened it to a photograph she'd noticed earlier. It showed Jim at a recent fund-raiser for the town's new theater, posing between millionaire Bill Sachet and his stunning wife, Vanessa.

"Look," she said, carrying it to the dean. "This is the kind of society people he hangs out with. I'd never fit in."

Marie glanced at the picture. "Vanessa Sachet? I

remember when that woman was a publicist for the Cheez Pleez Dairy. She's no more aristocratic than I am, and a lot less moral."

"But she must have something I don't, or that millionaire wouldn't have married her," Dex insisted. "Of course, she's beautiful. Maybe she's kind and generous, too. Or just better at relationships than I am."

"You're kind and generous," Cora said.

"As for relationships," the dean added, "you have a completely inaccurate image of yourself, Dex. You're one of the most nurturing people I've ever met."

"Thanks, but—" The doorbell rang. "Shall I get that?"

"If you don't mind," said Marie.

Dex marched into the narrow hallway and opened the door without bothering to peer through the glass panes. She found herself staring into the melting brown eyes of Jim Bonderoff.

For a long moment, they stood there speechless. At such close range, Dex could smell his masculine fragrance and feel his body molding itself, without touching, to hers. She got hot and tingly all over, as if she were coming down with a fever.

Somebody needed to break the silence, so she did. "Congratulations on your engagement."

"I didn't think Nancy was going to accept." Jim regarded her warily. "It must have come as a shock when she called."

"She sounds like a nice person." Dex felt constrained, as if making conversation at a tea party. Yet only last night they'd twined together, doing fabulously intimate things.

Things they would never do again.

"If it weren't for her, I might not have had the guts to start my business," he went on. "I owe her a lot."

It was agony being so close to him and knowing he loved another woman. "You don't need to explain."

"But I do need to apologize," he said. "Some people might say I took advantage of you."

"I went into this with my eyes open," Dex retorted. "Nobody took advantage of me."

"Not intentionally, no." He stepped inside. They were only inches apart. "You made it clear you didn't intend to stay in Clair De Lune, but you weren't planning to leave right away, either. And I didn't want you to."

Dex blinked back a sheen of tears. Why did he have to act as if he cared about her when his heart belonged to someone else? Maybe that's exactly what it was—an act. "You're not getting off this easily, you know."

"About what?"

A twist of anger dispelled her weepiness. "About Annie. My daughter's not going to become some kind of guinea pig for Nancy's research. And I'm not handing her over to you on a silver plate, either. I still want her to be adopted."

She wasn't, Dex told herself, being petty or vengeful. Jim had no right to keep the child if he couldn't provide a proper home. Nancy seemed like a pleasant person, but she'd given no indication of motherly instincts.

He drew back. "I intend to keep my daughter, Dex. Believe me, she'll never find a family that loves her more than I do."

They faced off, neither willing to look away. Dex became peripherally aware of the objects crowding around them: stacks of books on the floor, raggedly opened mail scattered on the side table, a rack of Marie's old hats and gardening knee pads. Everything seemed to be holding its breath.

"Tell me one thing," she said. "Does Nancy cuddle Annie and fuss over her? Does she hug her and kiss her? Change her diaper and clothes?"

She could see the answer on his face. To his credit, Jim didn't waffle. "No," he said. "She isn't used to babies. But she can learn. You weren't keen on babies, either, when you first met Annie."

"Don't let her take the baby to her lab," Dex warned.

"I'll go with them and make sure it's safe," he said. "She's only going to show Italian movies—Fellini—during nap time. Besides, it'll give the two of them a chance to get better acquainted."

"What's next?" Dex challenged. "Running her through a maze? Dangling bananas from wires while Annie tries to learn some code to get her reward? She isn't a monkey!"

When Jim spoke, she could tell he was weighing his words. "I'm going to make sure our daughter has a happy, healthy upbringing. I know you care about her, and you can be a part of her life for as long as you want. Nancy says you're welcome to visit her on campus any time, so you can see for yourself what she's doing."

"Okay, I will." Dex would have preferred to dance the macarena on hot coals rather than to spend time with the woman Jim loved, but she would do it for Annie's sake.

His lips parted, as if he intended to say more, or perhaps to kiss her. Instead, he nodded briskly and walked out the door.

As Jim got into his sports car, he was so angry he wanted to shake the woman. At the same time, he yearned to grab her and never let go.

It hadn't helped that his stomach kept growling at the marvelous scents floating through the air. He'd hardly eaten a mouthful of Rocky's burned stir-fry, although Nancy had cleaned her plate.

Revving the engine, Jim resolved to stop for drive-through burgers. En route, his thoughts returned rebelliously to Dex.

He missed her tart honesty and stubborn refusal to yield to common sense. Villa Bonderoff no longer felt like home without her, while that cluttered old cottage redolent of curry powder and sugar had immediately become the place he belonged, simply because she was there.

Yet how dare Dex cling to the idea of putting Annie up for adoption? He would never let it happen.

Jim had to admit, though, that he had the same misgivings about Nancy and her research. Also, it was true that she hadn't even held the baby once.

Near campus, he pulled into a drive-through joint and ordered the Lunatic DeLuxe, which included a cheeseburger, chicken nuggets, onion rings and fried zucchini. "For the diner who can't make up his mind," read the pitch line on the lighted menu.

That described him perfectly, Jim thought. For once in his life, he couldn't make up his mind. Or, rather, his mind was having difficulty accepting the truth.

He wanted Dex, but he couldn't have her. She'd made that point clear. From the first time they met, she'd held him at arm's length. And maybe she was right. By any normal criteria, Nancy was a much more suitable wife.

But he'd been looking forward to tonight like a child at Christmas. He ached to hold Dex in his arms until morning, to feel the tickle of her hair against his nose and the deliriously soft contours of her body pressed against his.

He would have to settle for cherishing the part of her that lived in Annie. Although he wanted all of Dex, he could only have half.

THE NEXT MORNING, Jim fell back to sleep after the notes of "Reveille" died away. An hour later, a loud knock on the bedroom door woke him again.

Grabbing his bathrobe, he hurried to answer it. Nancy stood there, wide-eyed.

"There's something wrong," she gasped. As his mind flicked over the possibility that something had happened to Annie, she added, "Can't you hear that noise downstairs? It sounds like wild animals got loose."

Now he noticed the thuds spiraling up the stairs, accompanied by subhuman grunts. "It's Rocky and Grace," he said, relieved. "They're fighting again."

"You mean they do this a lot?" Nancy asked.

"Only when they can't agree on something." He padded down the hall to check on Annie. She wasn't in her crib, so she must be downstairs witnessing this display of immaturity. "I'll go break it up."

Nancy hurried alongside him. She'd dressed in a tailored suit and clipped back her blond hair with a barrette, he noticed. Ready for the first day at a new job.

"Jim, I know I just got here, but I hope you don't mind if I suggest a little therapy," she said as they descended. "These two people need a course in anger management, to say the least."

"They just need to duke it out." He followed the noises into the utility room.

From the confines of a portable crib, Annie watched with fascination as Rocky hefted Grace above his head and lofted her toward the far wall. She landed with a crash, but amazingly regained her balance and charged forward, head lowered.

With an *oof!* Rocky went down. Overshooting, Grace landed square on top of him. There followed a series of grunts and snarls that Jim interpreted as meaning, Get off me! and, It's your own stupid fault!

"Okay, you two." Lending a hand, he hoisted Grace to her feet. "What's going on?"

"He called Hugh a mental midget!" she cried. "Can you believe this, a guy who barely finished high school is sneering at a college professor?"

"The man can't hold a candle to Marie!" Rocky rasped the words out between harsh breaths. "Who is *not*, regardless of what anyone present may think, an old fogy."

"Is so!" said Grace.

"Is not!" said Rocky.

Nancy raised one hand. "Excuse me. I think we should all sit down and talk about this calmly, so—"

"Mama?" said Annie.

Her soft voice stopped them all. The little girl, Jim saw, was leaning on the rails of her crib with an air of dejection.

"I'm right here," Jim said, starting for the crib.

"She didn't say 'Dada,'" reproved Grace.

"She wants her mother," Rocky said.

Jim looked at Nancy. "Me?" she squeaked. "I'm not...I mean, of course I will be. Once I get the experience."

Clearly aware that some further action was called for, she walked to the crib and patted Annie's hand. "Good morning, cutie," she said. "Do you miss Dex?"

"Ba ba," was the unhelpful response.

"Ayoka and I need to get better acquainted," Nancy told Jim. "I'll tell you what. Grace, would you mind watching her this morning? This afternoon, she and I will go for a little tour of the campus and I'll show her where we'll be working."

Jim remembered his promise to make sure she was safe. "Call me at the office when you're ready to take her and I'll join you."

Relief showed on Nancy's face. "That would be fine."

After he got dressed and his staff ran up the flag, the two of them ate breakfast in the sunroom at Nancy's request. "I wanted us to have a chance to talk alone," she said over a slice of melba toast. "Something's bothering you, isn't it?"

As a psychologist, Jim reflected, she was trained to be observant. But then, she'd always been perceptive. It was one of the qualities he prized about her. "I suppose it is."

"About Ayoka?"

"Yes." That wasn't the only problem, but there was no point in telling her that he was half in love with Dex. Anyway, being mathematically fair, he was about a quarter in love with Nancy, which left twenty-five percent of him up for grabs. "You don't seem to take to the baby very strongly."

Nancy folded her hands on her lap. "It isn't because of anything about your daughter. She's adorable."

Enjoying a mouthful of waffle and syrup, Jim nodded and waited.

"As you know, I've got six younger brothers and sisters," she said.

"They used to drive you crazy," he recalled.

"Mom didn't let me near them when they were babies, but when they got older, she made me watch them every Saturday," Nancy said. "I love them, but there were so many of them and they were so loud."

"Watching your siblings is different from having a child of your own." Jim wondered how he could speak with such authority, since he had no brothers or sisters, but he knew instinctively it must be true. "I'm surprised by how much joy she gives me."

Nancy answered with a tremulous smile. "That's what I've been telling myself. Once Ayoka and I get better acquainted, we'll be best friends. I got burned out taking care of my siblings, but I knew the minute you told me about your daughter that she was here to bring me to my senses."

Much as Jim wanted to agree, he had to sound a note of caution. "I think it will work out that way, but an intellectual commitment isn't the same as one that comes from the heart. Don't talk yourself into something that'll make you unhappy."

Reaching across the table, Nancy cupped his hand. "I'm terrified of being one of those women who're married to their careers and discover when they're fifty that they missed out on having a family. I want to have it all, Jim. And I need your help."

Guiltily, he realized that he'd been hoping, at least a little bit, that she might decide to back out of the marriage. Instead, she needed his support to make her dreams come true. She'd done the same for him once, hadn't she?

"You can count on me," he said.

"I FOUND the rest of it," Hugh told Dex, following her up the aisle as she collected tests from his one o'clock class.

The few remaining students bent over their papers, comparing Jane Austen's and Charles Dickens's views of nineteenth century English society. "The rest of what, and are you sure you want to discuss it here?" she asked.

"The poem." He patted his pockets and produced a few scraps of paper. "Remember how it went?"

"Something about porcelain hearts," Dex muttered, and walked down an empty row picking up test booklets.

"Right." Hugh squinted at what he'd written, then took off his glasses and polished them on his shirt. "Okay, here goes." He took a deep breath and read, "O broken shards, who will collect you? Whose yearning will make you whole again?"

"Excuse me!" called a young male student. "I can't think with all this racket going on."

"You can't think, period," joked one of his friends.

"Would everybody please shut up? Some of us are trying to get a good grade here," snapped a young woman.

The bell sounded. Dex said a silent prayer of thanks and snatched their booklets right out of their hands. "I'm sure you've all done fine." The students sauntered out, grumbling.

"That man wasn't right for you, you know," Hugh said, oblivious to whoever might be listening.

Dex adjusted the papers into a neat stack and walked outside to her bicycle, hoping the professor would take the hint and go away. Instead, he accompanied her.

"Do you have deliveries to make?" he asked.

She'd done that earlier and didn't want to lie. "No, but there's something I've got to check out."

"I'll come with you."

"You don't have a bike."

"I can trot alongside," Hugh said.

Dex couldn't bring herself to be cruel to this bearded, forty-year-old puppy. "I'll walk my bike," she said with a sigh. Luckily, it wasn't far to the psychology building, where she intended to make sure no one was experimenting on her daughter.

The honey-scented breeze tossed Dex's mane as they walked. "Did anyone ever tell you your hair is like a hummingbird's nest?" Hugh asked.

"The term bird's nest has been used, yes," Dex said. "Tell me something, Hugh. What do you think of Grace?"

The thin man winced. "She's a bit bossy. And she made me shoot a gun! I could have hit someone."

"You're supposed to hit the target," Dex said.

"It nearly jumped out of my hand," the professor replied in bewilderment. "How can anyone fire those things? They're dangerous!" He gave her a rueful smile. "That was a foolish thing to say, wasn't it? Of course they're dangerous. Even *I* know that."

He had such an endearingly embarrassed look on his face that Dex warmed to him. Not that she could ever imagine herself kissing the man, much less introducing him to the wonders of carpets. "You know, Hugh, I like you a lot. It's just that, well, you need to find a woman with a more poetic soul."

"Not Grace!" he said with feeling.

"Agreed," she said.

At the psych building, Dex parked her bike and took the papers with her for safekeeping. Inside, she asked for Nancy Verano's office. "She's in the lab," said the secretary, and gave her a room number on the second floor.

On the way there, she explained to Hugh about Nancy's project. "I love Fellini movies," he said. "Maybe I'll watch one."

They slipped into the lab. It was dark except for a lamp glowing on a desk at one side and a flickering TV screen. Staticky voices spoke in the musical cadences of Italian.

Nancy hadn't wasted any time getting started, Dex thought, her gaze traveling across a couple of portable cribs. Apparently she hadn't had any trouble finding subjects, either. Professors and students had probably jumped at the chance for free day care.

Most of the babies were lying down, but one stood on wobbly legs and prowled around the railing. Suddenly a little voice said, "Mama!"

Dex's heart lurched. She couldn't help herself. She shoved the papers at Hugh and raced forward, into her daughter's arms.

12

PLUGGING IN his laptop and getting some work done in a corner of the lab had seemed like a good idea, and the dialogue didn't disturb Jim, since he couldn't understand Italian.

But he kept getting an uneasy feeling about this whole situation. For one thing, Annie didn't seem interested in taking a nap. And Nancy, although she did her best to soothe the child and the other infants she'd borrowed, was interested in creating the right test conditions, not in meeting the little girl's needs.

Still, he had to keep in mind that Nancy was newly arrived in town and understandably preoccupied with proving herself. She'd had to teach her first Psych 101 class this morning, replacing a professor who, seized by Clair De Lunacy, had run off with a student. From all accounts, Nancy had done an excellent job.

Now she was getting this experiment up and running. She would, Jim told himself, find her own way to motherhood, if Dex would be reasonable and not push too hard for adoption.

When the door opened, he noticed a woman in a flare of light. At first, he thought it must be Nancy, returning from the ladies' room, until he recognized the shapely figure as Dex.

She looked sweet and familiar and a little lonely, too. He wanted to hug her.

The man behind her held the door open, illuminating the mother-child reunion. Jim's throat clamped as Dex lifted the baby into the air, and Annie giggled in delight.

The two whirled around and then Dex gathered her daughter close. In the beam of light, their hair blended into a single riot of curls.

A disturbance at the door drew his attention. Nancy, entering, bumped into the man, whom Jim recognized as Hugh Bemling. An armful of papers shot into the air, and the two bent to pick them up.

Jim walked over to help. Then he steered the whole group into the hall, where he could make introductions without disturbing the napping infants.

The two women smiled warily at each other. "Your little girl misses you," Nancy said. "She asked for you this morning."

"She did?" Dex looked to Annie as if for confirmation.

"She said 'Mama,'" Jim confirmed.

Hugh blinked and nudged his glasses higher on his nose. It seemed to Jim that the man was staring at Nancy, but perhaps he was merely peering myopically into space.

"I'm afraid I don't know much about babies," Nancy went on. "I hope you'll give me a chance with her."

Dex glanced at Jim and then quickly away. "It's very important that she have two devoted parents. I think adoption is the best course, unless you're very, very sure you love her."

"I don't know yet," Nancy admitted. "Can I have a little more time, please?"

It wasn't solely up to Dex to decide Annie's future,

but Jim refrained from saying so. If she could accept Nancy freely as Annie's new mother, that would be the best thing.

Or would it? demanded an inner voice. *What about you and Dex raising Annie together?*

Jim shrugged off the question. Dex wasn't the sticking-around kind of woman. He needed someone more reliable, someone who could help keep his world on course.

He'd suffered through more than enough chaotic periods, including right after high school when he'd been angry, restless and confused. Then again, following his discharge from the Marines, he'd faced the hateful possibility of bouncing from one unsatisfying job to another. Ever since Nancy encouraged him to start his own business, everything had fallen into place. He intended to keep it that way.

"Nancy will make a wonderful mother," he said. "Believe me, Dex."

She swallowed before speaking. "I'll reserve judgment, then."

"Thank you," Nancy said. "May I?" She held out her hands to Annie. With only the briefest hesitation, Dex transferred the little girl to her grasp.

"You know, your skin is beautiful," Hugh told Nancy. "It reminds me of porcelain."

"How lovely. Thank you. I'd better get back to work now." With a vague smile, she went inside.

Dex took the stack of papers from the professor. "Don't you have office hours starting in fifteen minutes?"

"Oh!" He dragged his attention from Nancy's retreating form. "Thanks, Dex. See you tomorrow."

Jim stood in the hallway, inexplicably averse to

making his departure. "How about coffee?" Afraid Dex might decline, he added, "And pie."

"At Key Lune Pies?" she asked. It was a favorite spot near campus.

"Exactly what I had in mind."

They rode over in his sports car and found the restaurant nearly empty at this late-afternoon hour. After they ordered coffee and pie—lemon for him, pecan for her—he said, "Can I ask you something without making you angry?"

"That depends on the question." Dex toyed with a salt shaker.

"Why are you so dead set on adoption?"

"Because Annie deserves—"

"Two devoted parents. I know," he said. "But Sunday night, I asked you to raise her with me. You love her, and so do I. Yet you put me off."

"I'm not in a position to take on so much responsibility." She turned the shaker at various angles, studying it.

"There's more to it than that," Jim said. "Why don't you want to be a parent?"

"I can't explain," she said.

The waitress arrived with their food. After she departed, Dex stared at her pecan pie. She must really be upset if she wasn't eating.

"Please," Jim said. "I need to know."

She took a deep breath. "The idea of being responsible for a baby terrifies me."

"Why?"

Shadows deepened the blue of her eyes. "When I was eleven, I was watching my nine-year-old sister, Brianna. We argued and she said some mean things. Brianna always knew how to please my parents and

I never did, and she knew how to hurt me, too. So I was really angry."

Jim took a bite of pie and said nothing. He was learning that, around women, silence could be very productive.

"She went to play in the woods near our house. I was so mad, I didn't follow her," Dex said. "For a few minutes, I almost hoped she'd get lost. Then I started to worry."

"Did you call your parents?"

"I didn't dare. They were always scolding about how selfish and careless I was." She released a long breath. "I went looking for Brianna, calling and searching. It seemed like hours. I had this horrible sick feeling. Just in the few minutes I'd ignored her, something terrible might have happened."

"Did it?" he asked.

"I found her partly submerged in a creek, her clothes caught on a log," Dex said. "She was barely keeping her face above water. I got her out and took her home. For some reason, she never told our parents that it was my fault, even though she caught a chill and was sick for a week. We got along better after that."

"You're afraid something terrible would happen if you were in charge of the baby?" Jim asked. "That doesn't make sense."

"Maybe not rationally," Dex said, "but I get this awful feeling when I think about Annie depending on me. I might not be careful enough. I might get forgetful, just for a few minutes."

"That's why you don't want to be a parent?" Jim asked.

"That's part of it," Dex said. "At first, I was afraid

I wasn't capable of loving her, of showing that love in a constructive way. I thought I'd be too harsh and critical, the way my parents are."

"But you're not," he pointed out.

"I surprised myself." She gave him a rueful smile that made his heart squeeze. "Around Annie, I feel such love, it's overwhelming. But I'm still careless sometimes."

"Other than forgetting that she was with Grace that day when we went bicycling, what have you done?" he asked.

"Once when I was changing her diaper, I walked across the room to get something without thinking about it. She could have fallen off the changing table."

"No one's perfect," Jim said.

"It's just an example," Dex said. "I've never pictured myself as a parent. I don't think I have the right instincts."

"I think you have all the right instincts." He supposed he shouldn't be saying that, but it was true.

"Annie needs someone who's a natural mother," Dex said. "Someone who'll never be impatient or forgetful. That's what worries me about Nancy."

"I wouldn't let anything happen," he said. "Besides, she's a highly competent person."

Dex dug into her pie. "What if Nancy decides she wants a baby of her own? Or two or three? Then she'd be distracted, and probably bond a lot more strongly with her biological children. I know she'd try to do her best, but a mother who has to adopt won't be torn between her own birth child and Annie."

"Nancy and I will work it out." Jim finished his coffee. "She's a wonderful woman. If anyone can succeed, she can."

Dex stopped eating as if she'd suddenly lost her appetite. "Maybe so," she said. "Can we leave now?"

They drove back to campus through the fragrant spring landscape without saying another word.

THE NEXT DAY, two hummingbirds were chasing each other around a flowering bush as Dex came out of her apartment. Across the street, Mrs. Zimpelman was planting pansies and primroses along the sidewalk.

She smiled and waved at Dex, then pressed a rapid-dial number on her cell phone. The local member of the Clair De Lune grapevine was dutifully reporting the day's trivia, including the comings and goings at Dean Pipp's house.

Dex walked her bike across the street. "Excuse me."

With a startled expression, Mrs. Zimpelman rang off. "Is something wrong?"

"I was just wondering," Dex said. "Don't you get tired of spying on people? It must be so boring."

"Oh, no!" The elderly lady brushed a clump of dirt off her stretch pants. "My friend Sadie caught an assistant professor having an affair with a dean's wife! And you wouldn't believe what some of the teenagers do when their parents aren't home."

"I'd believe it," Dex said.

"It's better than a soap opera," confided her neighbor. "My one regret is that I've never had anything really juicy to contribute. Not like that psychology professor running off with the coed! That was on my friend Mariah's block."

"I'll try to cook up something exciting," Dex joked, and pedaled away. She was heartily glad that

Mrs. Zimpelman hadn't been at her self-appointed duties that night after the faculty Christmas party, when Jim came to Dex's apartment.

Jim. She couldn't stop replaying their discussion yesterday. It had hurt when he'd sprung so forcefully to Nancy's defense.

A wonderful person who could succeed at anything, that's how he'd described her. It hurt to realize that he was simply a man in love, talking about the woman he was going to marry.

When she reached campus, Dex met with her faculty adviser. She was glad to forget her personal troubles and talk about the dry, impersonal dissertation. She'd organized her notes last night and was ready to begin writing; the adviser agreed.

Once her thesis was finished, she could leave Clair De Lune. And Jim. She still wasn't sure what to do about Annie, though.

Dex was cycling toward the administration building when a fluttering piece of white paper caught her eye. The hand waving it belonged to Cora, she saw, and halted.

"Wait up!" The blond student trotted over. "Look at this! I got a B-plus on my Humanities 101 essay!"

"I didn't know you had a humanities essay," Dex said guiltily. She'd only edited one of Cora's papers, and that had been in history.

"Your comments taught me a lot," the young woman said. "I did it by myself this time!"

Dex reached over and hugged her. "I'm so proud of you."

"I wish I could tell Kip."

"You *can* tell him," she said. "Nothing's stopping you."

"It wouldn't be right." Cora held up her hand. "And don't argue."

"Just because Jim and I—"

"I have to be true to my team," said her friend.

"It's your life, but I think you're an idiot," Dex retorted good-humoredly. "Congratulations on the paper." Leaving Cora smiling in a confused way, she pedaled onward.

At the administration building, Fitz handed her a stack of deliveries. "Nothing for the psych department. I gave those to another courier."

"There's no reason I can't make deliveries to that building!" Dex admired loyalty, but her friends were carrying matters to extremes.

"I'm on your side," growled the leonine supervisor, and he retreated into his lair.

She completed her rounds in half an hour. The last delivery was to the fertility research center in the science quadrangle. Black crepe paper hung around the lobby, and a large stand of black artificial flowers reminded her that the staff was in mourning for Dr. Saldivar.

Had it really been less than a week since she died? It felt like a month.

LaShawna Gregory entered the lobby as Dex was about to leave. They exchanged greetings.

"I don't mean to pry." LaShawna glanced around to make sure no one else could hear them. "But I understand that Dr. Saldivar's daughter was born from one of your eggs. I always thought that hair looked familiar."

"You know Annie?" Dex asked.

"I used to baby-sit for Ayoka on the nanny's day off." LaShawna smiled dreamily. "What a cute little tyke! Her first nanny was sweet, but I couldn't stand that Smithers woman! She always looked as if she'd just drunk pickle juice."

"Annie's probably right next door at the psych building," Dex said. "Want to say hello?"

"You'd better believe it!"

On the way there, she told LaShawna an abbreviated version of what had happened during the past few days. "So Jim wants me to turn her over to Nancy. I'd appreciate getting your opinion of her."

"Glad to oblige," said her friend.

They found the lab darkened and *La Dolce Vita* unfolding on the TV monitor. This time, even Annie was snoozing.

Nancy, who was on the other side of the room, waved them over.

"It must be that melodious language," Nancy said. "It's better than a sleeping pill."

Dex introduced the two women and explained that LaShawna used to baby-sit for Dr. Saldivar.

"I've known Ayoka since the very beginning," LaShawna said.

"You saw her when she was a newborn?" Dex asked with a touch of envy.

"Even before that." LaShawna brushed back the rebellious bangs of her short, dark hair. "Since she was an egg. Dr. Saldivar let me watch the test-tube fertilization."

Dex was glad she hadn't been present. If she'd wanted to make a baby with Jim, there were a lot more enjoyable ways of doing it.

"You work in the fertility center?" Nancy clasped her hands together.

LaShawna nodded. "I'm a graduate student. Of

course, we're all grateful to Mr. Bonderoff for his contributions. I don't know where we'd be without his generosity."

"Jim gives money to the center?" Nancy said. "He must think I want—" She stopped in mid-sentence.

"He must think you want what?" Dex asked.

Nancy frowned. "A few years ago, I had to have surgery for a medical problem and the doctor said it would make me infertile. I don't know how Jim found out about it, though."

"There've been a lot of advances," LaShawna said. "Whatever's wrong, it might be reversible. And of course there are procedures for egg donations, if necessary."

Nancy shuddered. "That sounds, well, so intrusive! I don't think I could go through with it."

It hadn't occurred to Dex that Nancy might not be able to have a baby. "You mean Annie's the only child you and Jim can ever have?"

"It doesn't bother me," Nancy said. "I got sort of burned out helping raise my younger brothers and sisters, so I didn't plan on having children. Still, I wouldn't want to deprive Jim of the parenting experience. When he told me about Annie, though, it seemed like the perfect solution."

Nancy must be soft-pedaling her disappointment because she didn't want anyone to feel sorry for her. Dex's cheeks burned. She'd been selfish and quarrelsome, while Nancy was considerate and tactful. No wonder Jim was in love with this woman.

"I want my daughter to be cherished," she said. "And you will cherish her, won't you?"

"Of course," Nancy said. "I'm sure I will."

"I'll be happy to refer you to the best doctors if

you do decide to get pregnant," LaShawna said. "But right now, I've got to go to class. It was nice to meet you."

"Thanks so much," Nancy said.

Dex was sorry when her friend left. She didn't know what to say to Jim's fiancée, so she settled for saying, "I'll sign whatever papers you want. You'll tell Jim for me, won't you?"

"You can tell him yourself." The psychologist pointed to the door of the lab. Jim had just walked through, his achingly handsome face warming at the sight of his beloved.

"I couldn't." Dex's throat was so constricted, the words barely squeaked out.

"Dex, it's good to see you." He strode across to them. "I hope you two are getting to be friends."

"Why didn't you tell me?" she demanded.

"Tell you what?"

"That Nancy can't have children!" She could hear the quiver of hurt in her voice. "If I'd known, I wouldn't have been so stubborn."

His jaw worked, but no words came out.

"It isn't anyone's fault," Nancy said. "No one blames you, Dex. You don't have to make any quick decisions."

"Of course I want you to raise the only child you'll ever have!" she said. "I talked to my advisor this morning and I can finish my dissertation this summer and move on, so you'll have Annie all to yourselves. It's long past time I grew up, anyway."

The torrent of words choked to a halt. Before she could do something embarrassing like burst into tears, Dex hurried out.

JIM STOOD THERE, stunned. He hadn't known about Nancy's problem. And he desperately didn't want Dex to walk out of his life.

Still, he couldn't abandon his old friend, not when she obviously needed him so much. Even though it meant losing the woman he loved.

And he did love Dex, he realized with agonizing certainty. He'd been lying to himself. He wasn't half in love with her, he was one-hundred percent in love.

"I should have told you," Nancy said. "I'm sorry."

"It wouldn't have made any difference." Jim meant that. "If you've got a problem, we'll face it together."

"I was afraid you'd think less of me because I'm not willing to pursue infertility treatments."

Nancy looked so downcast that he put his arms around her and rested his cheek against her blond hair. It felt silky and cool.

This was the woman he was going to hold for the rest of his life, Jim thought. Things had happened so quickly during the past two days that the reality hadn't sunk in until now.

He and Nancy were going to walk down the aisle together. She was going to stay in his house and be Annie's mother.

And he was never going to see Dex again except flying by on her bicycle. And, before long, not even that.

He had lost her.

13

FROM A DISTANCE, Jim watched himself share a makeshift lunch with an uneasy Nancy and four restless babies in a darkened lab. He watched himself return to the office and review the plans for his new building without really seeing them. He watched himself forget his password on the computer and have to consult his cheat sheet. Twice.

Finally he gave up and left early. Jim didn't even register the drive home to Villa Bonderoff. It was only when he passed beneath the arching gates of his palatial home that the truth hit him.

He had everything he'd ever wanted. A beautiful home, business success, a delightful child and the perfect wife-to-be.

It didn't mean anything. Not without Dex.

After parking his car, he mounted the steps to the rock garden. He didn't even know how Dex felt about him, Jim admitted.

She'd pushed him away once and been reluctant to make a commitment as recently as last Sunday. How ironic that the richest, most envied man in Clair De Lune had lost his heart to a woman who might not even want it.

What should he say to Nancy? Everything depended on her, he decided. If she loved him and needed him, he would keep his promise to marry her.

But if she didn't...

A scream from deep in the house yanked him from his reverie. Jim broke into a run.

Through the garden room he went, and across the hall. Another scream resounded from the living room.

As he raced in, he registered the fact that Annie, safe in her playpen in the middle of the room, was staring upward. Jim followed her gaze to see Grace dangling from the balusters, kicking wildly at Rocky, who was hitting at her legs with a whisk broom.

"He is not!" shrieked Grace. "But she is!"

"You take it back or I'll run your stockings!"

At the top of the stairs, Nancy spread her hands in a gesture of pacification. "I'm sure we can talk this out if you'll stop—" She broke off at the sight of Jim. "Thank goodness you're here! They've gone completely around the bend."

Straightening, Jim bellowed, "Atten-shun!"

Rocky dropped the brush and saluted. Grace swung herself over the railing, scrambled onto the stairs and stood at attention.

"Dada!" said Annie proudly.

"Hi, honey." To the others, Jim demanded, "Am I safe in assuming that this shameful display of childishness has to do with Hugh Bemling and Marie Pipp?"

"She called the dean an old hen whose recipes taste like chicken feed!" said Rocky in a tone of aggrieved hurt.

"He said Hugh was a brainless peacock!" retorted Grace. "A peacock, of all things!"

Jim was weary of the whole debate. "I think the two of you are jealous," he snapped. "And I suggest you get over it."

They both stared at him.

Jim scooped up his daughter and climbed the stairs, maneuvering around the maid. "Take the rest of the day off, both of you."

"But I've got dinner to cook, sir," said Rocky.

"Fix whatever you like, or nothing at all. I don't want to hear any more of this quarreling."

"Yes, sir," said the crestfallen butler.

Jim was already starting to feel guilty. He hated being harsh with his old friends.

"Are you all right?" Nancy asked when he reached her. "You're not usually this testy."

He carried the baby into the second-floor den, a large, sunny room with its own entertainment center, kitchenette and balcony. A couple of oversize teddy bears had been arranged on the carpet, and he set Annie down next to them.

"I want to ask you something." He closed the door and turned to regard his fiancée.

Nancy had never looked more striking. Her tall, slender figure showed to its best in a tan skirt and matching jacket over a tailored blouse. Perfectly groomed blond hair belled over her shoulders.

"Is it about the infertility?" she asked. "I wouldn't blame you for being angry."

"No," he said. "I only want to know one thing. Do you love me?"

On the floor, Annie crawled to Nancy and grabbed her skirt, trying to pull herself to a standing position. Gently, Nancy disengaged the child.

"You're one of the people I love most in the world," she said.

Obviously, he hadn't made himself clear. "Let me rephrase that," Jim said. "Are you in love with me?"

Following Nancy as she dodged her, Annie tugged on the buckle of her patent-leather shoes. Taking a steadying breath, Nancy dislodged her again and took two long strides away from the baby.

"That's a complicated question," she said.

"It shouldn't be." He met her gray eyes squarely. And saw there a longing that touched his heart, except that he didn't believe it was a longing for him. "There's something you want, but I don't think you're going to find it here."

"You've changed your mind about getting married?" Nancy asked.

"Tell me the truth," he said. "Do you really want children?"

"In theory, yes," she said, and did a quick two-step around Annie, who was zeroing in on her ankles.

"Do you want a husband in theory, too?"

Nancy folded her arms across the front of her jacket. "Jim, I've always considered you the perfect man."

It struck him that the most perceptive woman he knew was clueless when it came to herself. "Nancy, what are you most afraid of? Is it turning fifty and discovering you never had a family? Or—"

"Failing," she blurted.

"Failing at what?"

"At everything." Her chin quivered. "Work, home, love. I want to get it all locked safe and tight. I want to be the complete woman so no one can find fault with me."

"Even if it makes you miserable?" Jim collected Annie and found a toy for her to play with. She turned it over and over, shook it and beamed when it rattled.

A strange expression crossed Nancy's lovely face.

At first, Jim couldn't identify it, and then he saw it was relief.

"You're right," she said wonderingly. "I don't really want children. I mean, they're wonderful and special, but I'm not interested in them."

"I appreciate your honesty," Jim said.

Now that she'd started confessing, Nancy couldn't seem to stop. "I had this image of myself—you know, a fantasy scenario—being named Mother of the Year in some glossy magazine. I could see the photograph of you and me and Annie, retouched to take out any blemishes. We looked so perfect."

"Blemishes?" Jim teased. "Me?"

"I'm embarrassed to admit that isn't all," Nancy said. "That same month, I would be on the cover of another magazine as Psychologist of the Year. Can you imagine? I must be the worst egotist of all time!"

"Quite the opposite," he said in a burst of insight. "You crave recognition from other people because you don't have enough respect for yourself. Nancy, you don't need to be mother of the year or psychologist of the year. You're a great friend and a terrific person, and you can be who you are without apologizing for it."

A fat tear rolled down her cheek. Then she threw her arms around Jim.

Before he could catch his breath, Nancy took a little hop backward. "Wait a minute." She started out of the room. "Or maybe a couple of minutes."

He was on the floor playing with Annie when Nancy returned nearly half an hour later. "I'm packed and I'm moving to my parents' house until I can find an apartment." Nancy handed him a folded piece of stationery with the name Dex written on it. "Please give this to her for me, will you?"

"Sure." He got to his feet. "Are you sure this is what you want to do?"

She grinned, looking happier than she had since she arrived. "I feel like an idiot for not being honest sooner, with you or with myself. I truly believed I wanted to make this work."

"Call me when you're settled. I don't want to lose touch," Jim said.

"You bet!"

She walked out of the room with a lilt to her step and grabbed her luggage in the hall. Jim followed with Annie.

In the kitchen, Grace and Rocky sat glaring at each other. Apparently they'd stopped fighting out of deference to Jim, but neither showed any inclination to leave the other alone.

"Why don't you two make this easy on yourselves and admit you're in love?" Nancy said as she passed them.

Grace shook her head in disgust. Rocky, however, looked thoughtful as he held out his arms to take Annie from Jim. "Are you leaving, then?"

"And a good thing all around," Nancy replied. "Sometimes it's hard to see the truth when it's right in front of you, isn't it?"

In the garden, Kip knelt with a spade, poking dejectedly at a weed. When Nancy went by, he said, "You're such a pretty shade of peach. But I'm glad you're leaving, if it makes you happy."

"Very happy." She kissed Jim's cheek lightly, loaded her suitcases into her trunk and departed.

Jim stood on the pavement, letting the April sunshine dance across his shoulders. There was enough daylight left for a bike ride, he decided, and went to change into jeans.

RESTLESSLY, Dex tried for the umpteenth time to think of an opening sentence for her dissertation. All the information she needed was in her notes, yet she couldn't focus.

Through the open window of her apartment drifted the scent of freshly mowed grass. In a late-afternoon breeze, lavender jacaranda blossoms whirled to the street below.

The tree next to the garage was dropping its purple blooms so abundantly that Dex knew it would soon be bare. Next would come the green leaves of summer, and another Clair De Lune springtime would end.

Never before had she regretted the transition from one season to another. She wanted to hold on to the brief enchantment of her twenty-sixth spring in case nothing like it ever entered her life again.

The swish of bicycle tires below told her someone was passing through the purple haze. Maybe Cora was coming to visit, she thought, and then she heard a baritone voice raised in song.

An old-fashioned song. "A Bicycle Built for Two."

Dex sat rooted to her chair, unable to believe what her heart told her. Surely Jim Bonderoff was not circling below her apartment, serenading her with lyrics about being half-crazy in love.

With an effort, she dragged herself to the window and peered out. The scene below was pure Norman Rockwell—the manicured cottages across the street, a cat sunning itself on the sidewalk and, directly below, a man on a bicycle gazing hopefully toward her.

When he saw Dex, he stopped in the driveway and waved a fat pink rose. "A flower for my lady!"

She wished she had a balcony like Juliet's. But then, what good was a balcony unless it had a trellis so he could climb up and join her?

This couldn't be happening, Dex thought. And she shouldn't let it happen. For one thing, the man was engaged to someone else. Furthermore, across the street, Mrs. Zimpelman had come onto her porch and was squinting at Jim, trying to figure out who he was.

"Hold on!" Dex called, and pelted outside. At the base of the stairs, Jim handed her the rose. "Kip grew it himself," he said, still straddling his bike. "I know it looks pink, but he says it's actually dark red."

She inhaled the rich scent of old gardens and new love. "What about Nancy?"

"She asked me to give you this." He held out a folded sheet of stationery with her name on it. "I took the liberty of reading it, and I agree with its sentiments."

Dex opened the paper. The bold straight handwriting said, "Will you please marry this man and come take this cute little baby off my hands? She's adorable, but I guess I'm just not mommy material. Love, Nancy."

Across the street, Mrs. Zimpelman's face lit up as she realized who had come calling on Dex. The woman was so excited that, for a long moment, she didn't move.

"I don't understand why she's being so kind," Dex said. "Especially when she can't have a baby of her own."

"She doesn't want one." Jim grinned at her. "She only loved me and Annie in theory. I'm free, Dex, and so is she. Which brings me to my purpose here today."

Dex's heart skipped a beat, but she tried not to let her feelings show. She didn't want to make a fool of herself. Just because a man sang a love song didn't mean he was declaring himself.

If only she didn't love him so wildly, this fellow with golden highlights rampaging through his brown hair and determination glinting in his dark eyes. Up close, he filled the horizon.

Her feelings alarmed her. The safe walls she'd spent years building, and which she'd been reinforcing like mad these past few days, were crumbling. Soon she wouldn't have any defenses left.

"You know," Jim continued, "I love the half of Annie that's you and the half that's me. And I think they go together perfectly."

"She's a great kid," Dex agreed. Was that why he'd come, to ask for full custody?

"You were right about one thing. She needs two parents," he said. "Two parents who love her and each other. And you know what? She already has them."

"She does?" Dex clutched the rose, afraid he was going to spring some other previously undisclosed fiancée on her, some woman even more perfect than Nancy.

Across the street, Mrs. Zimpelman opened her cell phone and pressed a rapid-dial button. Her gaze remained glued to Jim.

Keeping his back to the nosy neighbor, he tipped

Dex's chin up with one finger. "You're having a hard time accepting that I love you, aren't you?"

She couldn't nod and she certainly couldn't speak. Dex merely swallowed.

"For a woman who's fearless in practically every other situation, you're terrified of letting anyone close," Jim said gently. "But it's too late. You already love me and Annie, so what have you got to lose? Let's get married and call the whole thing even."

"I ... don't know," she managed to say.

He swung off the bike and loomed over Dex. "Are you going to walk upstairs with me, or shall I pick you up and really give that snoop something to gossip about?"

With rabbitlike speed, she turned and obeyed. He followed right behind. Inside, Jim had no sooner closed the door than Dex clung to him, frantic to touch his face and shoulders, to feel him against her.

A happy sigh issued from Jim as he kissed her. He moved her onto the couch, smoothing off her floppy sweater and frayed jeans and helping her remove his clothes.

She could hardly unbutton his shirt fast enough. Her erect nipples met his chest, and she could feel his hardness pressing against her.

"Will you marry me?" Jim asked softly.

Poised above him, Dex stroked the insides of his thighs, encouraging him. He was touching her most vulnerable point, ready for her, and she ached for him.

"Say yes," he whispered.

Dex's lips brushed the corner of his mouth. She wriggled atop him, her need nearly unbearable.

One arm encircled her, and Jim flipped them. Now he was in control, yet still he held back. "Say yes."

Safety was an illusion. She already loved him, and if she were ever to be a whole person, she had to open up and let him inside. In every sense of the word.

"Yes!" gasped Dex.

When fulfillment came, it was everything she'd anticipated. And much, much more.

WHEN THEY TROTTED downstairs, Dex was surprised to see that Mrs. Zimpelman had abandoned her station. Then she noticed Dean Pipp planting parsley in the yard.

"I sent that snoop packing," Marie informed them. "She had the nerve to walk over here and trespass on my property. Some people need to get a life." She smiled at the two of them. "I'm glad you worked things out."

"We're getting married," Jim said.

Hearing the words aloud sent a thrill of fear down Dex's spine. It vanished almost at once in an unfamiliar glow of happiness.

"Congratulations!" Reaching into the basket beside her, the dean extracted a cookbook. "Would you mind giving this to your butler? There are some recipes he might like."

"You're invited over to sample them as soon as they're ready," said Jim.

"No hurry." Marie smiled. "We wouldn't want to make your maid jealous."

She returned her attention to her parsley, and the pair glided away on their bikes into the last rays of afternoon sunshine.

Jim hadn't felt so deliriously out of control since he was a child. He had no idea what time it was, and he didn't care.

They pedaled past a bed of bobbing, brilliantly colored California poppies. Amid such fanciful long-necked flowers, they might have been following the yellow brick road to Oz.

Soon the whole town would buzz with news of his broken engagement and rapid courtship, Jim supposed. He and Dex would take their place in the annals of springtime Clair De Lunacy, but so what? Nothing mattered as long as she was flying beside him, right where she belonged.

At the top of his driveway, he heard Kip's rare laughter. Looking toward the garden, he glimpsed his friend walking hand in hand with a merry-faced Cora.

"Good news travels fast," Dex said.

"In this town, it does," he agreed.

Opening the door to the sunroom, Jim nearly choked on the scent of frying hash. It took him back, for one jarring moment, to boot camp.

Well, he'd instructed Rocky to cook whatever he liked for dinner. But his butler hated hash.

Grace, however, adored it.

With Dex beside him, Jim popped into the kitchen. There sat Grace, holding a dozing Annie, while Rocky flipped the contents of a large frying pan. Both butler and maid wore expressions of pure contentment.

Jim decided not to mention Dean Pipp's cookbook. There would be time enough for that later, after the couple's newfound bliss matured enough to preclude any misplaced jealousy.

Dex touched her daughter's cheek but didn't disturb her. "She'll never have to ask for her mama again, because I'll always be here."

"Not afraid any more?" he said.

"Of getting careless and critical?" She shook her head. "More likely, I'll be so overprotective that she'll have to push me away!"

They adjourned to the den. Through the French doors, they could see the frothy blossoms of a tulip tree. "This is wonderful," Dex said.

"Yes, it is," he said. "It's like coming home after a long journey."

"Remind me never to go away again."

Jim gathered her onto his lap. "Don't worry. I wouldn't dream of letting you."

Outside, a breeze shook the tulip tree, dappling the patio with white blooms like rose petals at a wedding. All was definitely right with the world.

Follow That Baby!

ISABEL SHARPE

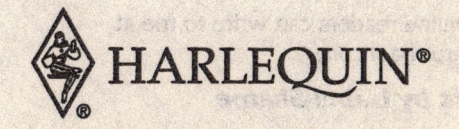

HARLEQUIN®

TORONTO • NEW YORK • LONDON
AMSTERDAM • PARIS • SYDNEY • HAMBURG
STOCKHOLM • ATHENS • TOKYO • MILAN • MADRID
PRAGUE • WARSAW • BUDAPEST • AUCKLAND

Dear Reader,

Before I met my husband, I used to think a lot like my determinedly single heroine, Melanie. I remember one day in particular when I lived in Boston, walking down Cambridge Street and hearing three different couples within fifty yards, all irritating the heck out of each other. I felt so free! So unencumbered by the endless compromises relationships entail.

Then I went home to my single-woman apartment and solemnly ate cold leftovers while watching TV. Okay, maybe there was something to be said for sharing life with someone.

Now, being the happily married mother of two young kids, that evening in front of the TV sounds like heaven. Sit down and relax, uninterrupted for an entire meal? Wow. There's a concept.

Of course, there is no perfect life. But as Melanie and Joe discover, better to hold your nose and dive in than stand on the side and risk having people see you in your bathing suit.

Cheers,

Isabel Sharpe

P.S. Online readers can write to me at IsaSharpe@aol.com.

Books by Isabel Sharpe

HARLEQUIN DUETS
17—THE WAY WE WEREN'T
26—BEAUTY AND THE BET
32—TRYST OF FATE

To my husband, Andrews,
who changed my thinking that alone was better.

1

"YOU WANT ME TO *WHAT?*" Melanie Brooks clutched the phone between her cheek and shoulder, teetering on the kitchen chair she'd set up to rescue her umpteenth spider this week. She could have sworn her friend Paige just asked her to toddler-sit for nearly an eternity. Paige lived in Philadelphia, Melanie in Birchfield, Wisconsin. Not the most practical child care arrangement.

"I need you to take Duncan." Paige sounded distinctly somber. "For a week...or two."

"You're joking." The spider crawled just out of reach. Melanie gritted her teeth. "You exasperating creature."

"Hey. You don't have to—"

"I wasn't talking to you. Listen, Paige, what I know about toddlers you could write on those holes you punch out of notebook paper." Melanie strained higher, swaying dangerously on tiptoe. "If you're burned out on motherhood, why don't you give Duncan to your parents?"

"I'm not burned out and I can't give him to my parents." Paige choked on a sob.

Melanie sighed. Choked-sob-inducing situations visited Paige several times a year. And getting information out of her was like shelling walnuts—you could never get the whole thing to emerge at once. "Okay, I'll bite. *Why* can't you give him to your parents?"

"His father would find him there."

"'His father.' Not 'my husband.' You and Lou are fighting again." Mosquitoes swarmed in the summer, thunderstorms followed heat waves.... Some things in life were entirely predictable. Served Paige right for breaking their Lifelong Bachelorettes pact and marrying Lou three years ago. Equally predictable, since the Great Betrayal Melanie only heard from Paige when something went wrong. Not one of Melanie's friends retained a shred of their celebrated independence once they enslaved themselves to men. Instead, they spent their lives catering to husbands who didn't lift a finger unless they had to change channels.

Well, not *this* woman.

The spider moved a centimeter closer. Melanie held up the small plastic container she set aside specifically for bug rescue. "Come on, sugar. Let's get this over with."

"Over with!" Paige gave a hurt whimper. "My problems may not be that important to you, but—"

"Of course they're important. I'm trying to rescue a spider. I was talking to him. Why are you trying to hide Duncan from Lou?"

"Oh, my gosh, you don't want to know." Her friend's dramatic whisper made Melanie roll her eyes and wish she had her hands free to play air violin. "It's so awful."

"Uh-huh." The spider took another few eight-legged steps toward the plastic container, then stopped. A drop of sweat formed and rolled down Melanie's forehead. Her shoulder ached from stretching out the cup. She could almost see the little spider tongue sticking out, the little spider lips forming the words, "Nyanny nyanny nyah nyah."

"I left him." Another sob, wrenching this time. "I left my husband."

"Again?" Melanie grimaced at the wretched arachnid. "*I'm* not little Miss Muffet," she whispered. "*I'm* not running away."

"I'm not running away, either—I left. He's having an affair. He deserves it."

"I meant..." Melanie sighed in exasperation. "Come on, Paige. Not a single one of Lou's 'affairs' has turned out to be anything more than mild flirting. Men have to feel ultra manly all day long. It's genetic." The spider crept to the rim of the container. Melanie nodded encouragingly.

"Ha! I could worship him on my knees twenty-four hours a day and he'd still say I was ignoring him." Paige sniffed despondently. "But that's not all this time."

"I'm listening." The spider delicately placed four legs inside the rim. Melanie grinned. "I'm not Miss Muffet," she crooned. "No tuffet...no curds..."

"Someone's hurting Duncan."

"No whey!" Melanie's attention snapped to the phone conversation. She knew enough to reserve full-blown protective outrage until she'd run the news through a Paige Melodrama Filter, but her adrenaline was ready and waiting. "You can't be serious."

"He has bruises everywhere."

"Don't all toddlers?"

"Not like this."

"You can't think Lou is responsible. You told me the man wouldn't hurt a—" Melanie scowled at her intended rescuee "—spider."

"Then how is my child getting bruised? Duncan's either with me or with his dad."

Melanie's mind spun a web of confusion that would have made her crawling friend envious. How could someone Paige described as an affectionate and devoted father suddenly turn on his only child? It didn't make sense. "All I know is what you tell me about Lou. He might not be the most sensitive man on earth, but he doesn't sound like a child abuser." The spider moved its final pair of legs into the container. Melanie snapped on the lid and heaved a sigh of relief. "Time to take a little trip, dearie."

"I'm going, but I can't take Duncan with me. I don't care if Lou finds me, but I can't let him have Duncan until I'm sure. Please, Melanie. You have to help."

Melanie walked toward her back door, off the side of her sunny yellow kitchen, shaking her head. Her friend's accusations seemed so theatrical, so sudden. Melanie had heard a lot of stories from Paige, but this was one of the strangest. "What makes you think Lou wouldn't come looking for Duncan here?"

"Uh. Well. He'd never expect me to leave Duncan with...with..."

"A single woman with no experience whatsoever taking care of children? Frankly, Paige, neither would I."

"Well, that—and, um, I...told him once you don't like kids."

"Don't like kids? I'm a teacher, for crying out loud. There's a vast difference between not liking them and not wanting any of your own." Melanie opened her back door and shook the spider into the geraniums growing on either side of her back stoop. She knew what her friend meant. Though she enjoyed the young minds in her classroom, the dynamic duo of female urges, maternal and marital, had completely passed her by. She wondered sometimes if she'd been given too many male hormones, except that then she'd probably be hairy and muscle-bound, which she decidedly wasn't.

"Besides, Lou hasn't ever met you. I don't think he even knows where you live. We haven't been in touch that much since I married him. Please, Melanie. I'm desperate. You're my only hope of keeping Duncan safe."

Melanie sighed. To her credit, Paige actually did sound desperate. But like the woodsmen ignoring the boy who cried wolf, Melanie had heard it all too many times. Child abuse was a new angle, but she even had trouble taking that very seriously, knowing Paige. Her friend probably wanted to get rid of Duncan for some other reason. Maybe she needed to break free of the mom and wife chains for a while and had simply overtaxed her parents' baby-sitting goodwill.

Melanie went inside. Her house still felt fairly cool

in spite of the early summer heat wave. Her beloved jungle of plants decorated every room. Her beloved knickknacks, collected during summer travels, graced her inherited or antique-sale furniture, and her beloved cats, Jezebel and Beelzebub, snoozed in a patch of sun on the worn living room rug. Birds chirped pleasantly outside in ivy-covered trees; the summery buzz of a lawn mower faded in and out from down the street.

She tried to imagine adding to her perfect, orderly, serene existence a screeching, careening, homesick toddler taking over her cherished free summer, upsetting her schedule and her possessions around the clock.

N-n-n-nope.

If the child were really in danger, she wouldn't hesitate. At least not as much. But Paige would have to do a lot better job of convincing before Melanie could be persuaded.

"Paige." She shook her head. "I'm sorry. I really am. But it's entirely out of the question."

"YOU WANT ME TO *WHAT?*" Joe Jantzen used the hand not holding the phone to pass an envelope of husband-compromising pictures across the desk to his sobbing client, then held up a finger to show he'd only be a minute. He could have sworn his friend Lou just asked him to find his wife and child.

"You have to find them, Joe. You're the only private investigator I can trust. Paige left me."

"Again?"

"Yeah, but this time she didn't go to her parents'

house. None of her friends has seen her. I can't find her anywhere. I think she might mean it this time." His voice cracked. "I can't lose Paige and Duncan, Joe. I can't."

"Uh-huh. Did you think of this before you got involved with Ms. Wonderbosom Two Thousand?" Joe tried to keep his voice down, but his client, Mrs. Glacker, burst into a fresh batch of he-done-me-wrong tears.

"That's right," she wailed. "Did he think of that? No, he didn't, the bastard. Just went for it with his…his testosterone hanging out." She blew her cosmetically altered nose and hiccuped. "But I'll get back at Hank. I will. I'm still young. I still have my figure. I'll…I'll have an affair, too. That'll teach him to—"

"Please, Mrs. Glacker. I'll just be a second." Joe sighed. Why did people persist in marrying each other when humans simply weren't cut out for monogamy? This business about true love had been cooked up by some ancient village elder to stop the spread of contagious disease and provide some measure of security for children. Other than that, marriage went entirely against human nature. The fact that Joe wasted the bulk of his detective skill tracking down unfaithful spouses proved his point: there was a sucker wed every minute.

"You mean Gina?" Guilt dripped off Lou's tone. "Nothing happened."

Joe rolled his eyes. "If you want me to help, you're going to have to—"

"Okay, okay. So we went out a few times for a

drink, that's it, I swear. You don't know what it's like being married to Paige."

Joe indulged in a private prayer of thanks that he didn't. He hated to admit it, but he couldn't exactly blame Lou for wanting a little innocent ego rebuilding. As long as nothing physical went on—that line he couldn't tolerate being crossed. Joe's ex-wife might not have been the answer to his dreams either, but he'd taken his vows deadly seriously—while they lasted.

"Let me guess. Paige doesn't like the way you live your life and thinks nothing you do is good enough."

"Yes. Yes. That's what Hank kept saying I did." Mrs. Glacker plucked a fresh tissue from Joe's desk with slender talon-tipped fingers and dissolved into it.

Joe nodded sympathetically at her, wondering how long she planned to stay and emit body fluids. He'd have to cut this call short.

"That's right," Lou said. "Nothing I do is enough."

Goes with the territory. "What about sitting down and thinking about what Paige might need? Maybe a night out to make her feel special. Women like that stuff."

"Oh! Oh, yes!" Mrs. Glacker looked up from her nose blow, eyes rimmed red and glowing, a small piece of tissue stuck to her upper lip. "That's it exactly. Such a small thing. If they only knew."

Joe smiled tightly. Sometimes he felt more like a marriage counselor than a detective. Though with a disastrous marriage in his own past, he knew talk was less than cheap. Men and women were simply and hopelessly unsuited. But for his friend's sake, he'd try.

"Lou, you need to romance her a little. Bring home some flowers. Hold her hand. Tell her she's beautiful. Do you ever do that?"

"No." Mrs. Glacker shook her head. "Oh, no. He doesn't."

"No." Lou's voice was low and husky. "No, I don't. Not enough, anyway. But while she's gone, I don't have the chance to make up for it. You have to find her."

"Unfortunately, I have something unusual and time-consuming coming up this summer. A vacation. Something I haven't done in over five—"

"Please. I'm begging you. If I don't get Paige back, I'll...I'll..."

Joe rested his forehead on his hand and shook his head. Time for *As Lou's World Turns*. "If you don't get her back you'll what?"

"Oh!" Mrs. Glacker's eyes widened. "He'll what?"

"I'll kill myself." Lou added an extra dose of his patented manly desperation to the statement.

"You are not going to kill yourself, Lou. You're not even—"

"Oh, my gosh." Mrs. Glacker gasped and clutched her designer blouse front. "Don't let him do that. He needs her. He loves her. You have to help him."

"Excuse me, Mrs. Glacker. Lou? I'll call you back in ten minutes." Joe hung up the phone and nodded at his client. "Don't worry, his wife leaves him a few times a year. Lasts about a week, then she comes back."

"Oh." Mrs. Glacker fanned herself distractedly with her hand. "Oh, thank goodness."

"So." He closed the file on his desk. "We're all set here. I'm sorry about your husband. I hope you two can work it out."

"Hmm." She appeared deep in thought.

"So, uh, I'll send you the bill."

"Yes." She nodded slowly, eyes wide, like a zombie on Valium. "The bill."

Joe stood and smiled. She stayed sitting. The silence lengthened.

"Mrs. Glack—"

"Are you married?"

He blinked. Where did that come from? "I was."

"You know a lot about being a good husband. What happened?" She dropped her eyes. "If you don't mind me asking."

Joe took a deep breath. There were few things he hated talking about more than the biggest mistake of his life. But Mrs. Glacker was hurting. Her misery would love a little company. "My wife left me."

"For another man?"

"No. She went off to find herself." He tried to keep the cynical twist from his voice and didn't remotely succeed. Marla had found herself the minute she was born. She'd just gotten bored. Of him. Let's face it, he wasn't exactly Mr. Excitement. And the minute men stopped making women feel like goddesses, they walked. Marla in one final exit, and Paige at regular intervals.

"What did she do?"

Oh, no, not this. He braced himself. "She became a tightrope walker with Barnum and Bailey." He grimaced, waiting. Lying about his personal life went against his nature, but he'd really have to think of some other answer. Mrs. Glacker would look surprised for a few seconds, take a breath and hold it, then say, "She ran away to join the circus?" and burst out laughing.

Mrs. Glacker looked surprised and held her breath right on schedule, but she only got as far as, "She ran away to j—" before she started laughing.

Joe ran his hands over his face and laced them behind his head. *Ha, ha, ha.*

"I'm sorry. I'm sorry." Mrs. Glacker wiped her eyes. "I'm a little hysterical. It's not at all funny."

"No, it's not." He smiled to let her know he understood, though he swore he'd kiss the first person who could hear about his painful past without cracking up.

Mrs. Glacker stopped laughing, then leaned forward, her not-very-discreetly-made-up features earnest. "Did you make her feel special?"

"I thought so. Maybe not enough. I don't know." No one could have made Marla feel special enough. No one could have thought she was as special as she did. With competition like that you were bound to lose.

Mrs. Glacker nodded again. "Do you...do you think...if I made Hank feel special he'd give up Lola?"

"It's entirely possible." Joe tried to sound sincere.

The truth was too sad to admit. As long as there were men and women, there'd be Lola and Hank. Hank hankering after hanky-panky and Lola getting whatever she wants.

"Oh, thank you!" She jumped up and grabbed his outstretched hand in both of hers. "Thank you, Mr. Jantzen. I'll never forget you."

She gathered her used tissues and purse and started to leave. At the door, she paused and turned. "If that doesn't work...can I have an affair with you?"

Joe almost swallowed his tongue. "I don't...think that would be such a good—"

"No." She sighed and gave him a wistful once-over. "No, I guess not. You're just so good-looking is all. And sweet. Goodbye."

Joe sank into his desk chair, which squeaked in outrage. Whatever. She wasn't the first woman who'd invited him to help recover her self-esteem. Of course under normal circumstances these same women wouldn't so much as cross the street to get to know him. He merely happened to be in the room when their lives fell apart and they needed someone handy.

But he wasn't in the business of repairing egos, though he was damn sick of being the medium through which so many were destroyed. He really did need this vacation. A road trip across the country. Man and his dog—only without the dog. He'd start getting ready this evening. Which meant laundry. Cleaning. He grimaced. Or he could just buy more underwear and—

The phone rang. He picked it up wearily.

"Joe, you said you'd call after ten minutes. It's been twelve. Tell me you've decided to find Paige and Duncan for me. I'm desperate."

Joe sighed. He had no idea why Lou was so worked up. Paige would be back in a day or two. She always was. And this was his first vacation in five years.

"I'm sorry, Lou. I really am. But it's entirely out of the question."

MOONLIGHT BATHED Melanie's room with a white-silver glow. The fan on her ceiling whispered mysteriously on its round-and-round journey. A breeze sighed through the leaves of the delicate red maple outside her bedroom window.

Melanie sat up, stretched, took in a long slow breath of the sweet night air and bellowed out a furious head-shaking roar of frustration. *"Insomnia-a-a-a!"*

She flung back the covers and stomped to the bathroom for her fourth cup of water. Not to mention the three cups of hot milk, six hundred and forty-two counted sheep and seventeen attempts at progressive muscle relaxation.

Too bad you couldn't do progressive relaxation of your brain waves. At least she couldn't.

Through all her attempts to sleep, she'd heard Paige's voice, the pleading, the desperation, the fear for her child. Paige had called again, barely an hour after the first time, and Melanie finally agreed to think about taking Duncan.

Well, she'd thought about it. And thought about it. And while she was thinking about it some more, she'd also thought about it again. With no resolution in sight.

Melanie sighed and crept to her kitchen to try another glass of milk. Moonlight spilled through the tall paned windows onto the kitchen floor, making shadows of the leaves in its way. The problem was greater than simply agreeing to care for a child. The problem involved Paige, her propensity for pumped-up drama and what constituted the boundaries of friendship.

But a child. A child who could be in danger, however remote the possibility. Melanie couldn't bring herself either to ignore or assume responsibility for that risk.

She opened the refrigerator door and scowled at the milk. Her stomach already sloshed like a water bed. Her eyes traveled next door to the freezer. What was ice cream, after all, but milk gone to heaven?

She scooped up a huge bowl and flipped on the radio on her way to the table. Her favorite nationally syndicated show came on in its wee-hours airing, an eclectic mix of show tunes, folk and only the best rock oldies, and with it the gravelly tone of Billy Joel singing a soft ballad. Melanie's spoon dropped into her bowl. One of her very, very favorite songs, "And So It Goes." The melody was so sweet, so moving, the poetry so wistful and tender. Tears welled in Melanie's eyes and dripped into her ice cream, making a sort of warm saltwater sundae.

By the time the song ended, Melanie was lost. Emotion swelled inside her until she felt there was no point going on in life since such beauty had already been attained. Who could be anything but ultimately satisfied and horribly empty listening to a song like that? She wanted to fight for world peace and hurl herself off a building at the same time; go out and find the love of her life and cloister herself in a convent for all eternity.

The announcer's voice came on. "That was a dedication of Marsha's favorite song from her widower husband, Mitch. Mitch writes, 'If I'd been there when you needed me, you'd still be by my side. Goodbye, darling. I'll miss you forever.'"

The end. The absolute end. Melanie's ice cream became cratered with tear marks, like some bizarre lunar surface. She tried to gain control of her sobbing and ended up sounding like a strobe vacuum cleaner. That was it. It.

Who cared if having a child around inconvenienced her? Who cared if the odds of his being in real danger were a zillion to one? Paige needed her. She had to help.

She put the half-melted bowl of ice cream in the sink and wiped her eyes. When the call came from Paige in the morning—she glanced at the clock—in a few hours, Melanie would say yes. Yes. Anything.

FOUR IN THE MORNING. Joe swung his legs out of bed, stalked to the tiny bathroom in his one-bedroom apartment and yanked open the medicine cabinet. He took three extra-strength antacids and groaned, wondering if his ancestors had somehow insulted pepperoni pizza so that it had pledged to exact revenge throughout time.

He ran the water until it was icy cold and sloshed

a few handfuls over his perspiring face. Okay, so pepperoni didn't always cause this kind of problem. In fact almost never. His mom called him "little goat" because his stomach could handle just about anything. If he were being honest, he'd admit the third call from Lou, about an hour after Mrs. Glacker left, had started his guilt machine humming along. The guy had been so insistent that this was not the usual Paige escape. So fearful of never seeing his wife and child again.

Joe gave a frustrated groan and buried his face in a towel. He needed that vacation. He deserved that vacation. He—

He wrinkled his nose and sniffed cautiously. He really, really needed to do laundry.

He turned to the hamper and groaned again. Clothes already spilled out of the top and onto the floor. *Okay, okay.* He gathered the pile, staggered into his bedroom and dumped the clothes on his bed. Why couldn't Paige have had the courtesy to leave Lou a month ago? Why now, when Joe had just wound down his last case and could turn his sights to freedom?

He added his boxers and undershirt to the pile and put on running shorts and a T-shirt. He pulled up the bottom sheet, wrapped the clothes into a huge bundle and swung it on his back, feeling a little like Santa Claus—or maybe Atlas, with all the world on his shoulders. All the way down in the elevator to the building's basement laundry room, he swore softly. Nothing worse in the middle of the night than a sackful of dirty laundry and a cloudy conscience.

The elevator landed. He strode into the laundry

room, surprised to see another nocturnal washer already down there—some guy in the building who worked weird hours, dressed in weird clothes and had a weird haircut, like a biker turned exotic dancer. Joe nodded curtly and scowled at the guy's radio, wafting gooey music through the room. He needed something stirring, like a Beethoven symphony or Twisted Sister.

He dumped a load of whites into one machine, colors in another. The whiny song ended. A Billy Joel song began—one he'd heard a couple of times, once in a terrific arrangement by the King's Singers. He sat down to listen and found himself strangely moved. He couldn't place it—maybe it was the exhaustion, the stress, but something made the tune call to him, touch him deeply. For some reason, he thought of his ex-wife and how their relationship had felt for the brief time things were good between them—maybe ten or twenty minutes' worth, right after the wedding. He was glad to feel that way again, even if he had to feel that way sitting in a basement doing laundry with some other pathetic chump.

He rubbed his chin back and forth in his hand, listening, listening. One thing you could say about love, it inspired some damn fine music.

The song ended. The feeling persisted in Joe's body, made him feel both maniacally high and depressively low, like he'd just fallen in love and been dumped at the same time.

The announcer came on, with some soppy dedication from one sop to another even soppier sop. *If I'd been there when you needed me, you'd still be by my side. Goodbye, darling. I'll miss you forever.*

Joe inhaled a breath that stuttered, as if he'd just finished crying. *If I'd been there when you needed me...*

Who was he to tell Lou not to trust his own instincts? Who was he to downplay his friend's anguish because it came at an inconvenient time?

Joe stood and clenched his fists at his sides. *I'm there for you, Lou. I'm there.*

2

"GENTLE. Ge-e-e-entle with the kitty." Melanie took Duncan's hand and pulled it in a soft caress down Jezebel's back. "Gentle."

Duncan grinned, swaying on unsteady legs, raised his arm and whacked Jezebel on the rear with all his sixteen-month-old might. Jezebel skittered away, gave him her best you're-not-worth-my-paw-nail stare and skulked out of the room.

"Ki-dee." Duncan chortled gleefully, launched himself in the cat's direction, tripped over an invisible dust mote and fell flat on his face.

"Oh-oh. Ka-boom." Melanie sighed and gave the wailing boy a hug. The child spent most of his day making violent contact between his head and whatever surface he could find. No wonder he had bruises. "Shall we play blocks?"

She dragged out the colored wooden blocks Paige had packed among Duncan's things, plunked herself down opposite him and made a three-square tower, which he immediately bashed to the ground. "Good," she crooned. "Make tower fall down, kaboom."

He laughed, tears already drying on his cheeks, and bounced up and down. "'Gain. 'Gain."

She reached for the blocks to build another impressive structure. Melanie had learned a lot since Duncan arrived the week before. Diapers went on best if he had hold of something utterly fascinating. Too much food on his tray meant most of it got flung onto the floor instead of eaten. Naps didn't go so well if she chose a time based on when *she* needed one. But the most important thing Melanie had learned was never to do anything to entertain him she wasn't willing to do again immediately at least six hundred times.

She got the tower to four blocks this time before Duncan sent the colored cubes sailing across the room. Melanie crawled wearily over to retrieve one that had shot under the couch. She'd always considered herself a hard worker, always made good use of her time. But now she saw clearly she'd spent most of her life lounging around on a chaise being fed peeled grapes, compared to this...this relentless need of her time and energy. Her respect for mothers had grown a thousandfold.

The third tower joined the others in a ruined mess on the rug. Sure, Duncan was cute. Those big baby eyes, dark lashes, pouty lips and astoundingly long, curling never-been-cut chestnut hair. After he'd stopped wailing for his mama for the first day or two, he'd even been pretty good company occasionally. But how could Melanie get anything done? The first day, she'd enthusiastically piled up some tremendously involving toys in the middle of the room, confident he'd sit and play happily for at least an hour, if not the rest of the afternoon, picked up the book she was reading and sat on the couch.

Twenty seconds later, she'd glanced up to find him standing next to her aloe plant, shoving dirt into his mouth with both hands.

And it had gone on from there.

She'd even made a desperate trip to the local toy store, but after long minutes staring at the toys, she gave up. Where to start? Which would be the magical product that would fascinate him for days on end? How could she tell when she was just lining the pockets of the television and movie industries instead of contributing toward Duncan's enrichment?

Melanie sighed. The one thing that hadn't changed was her conviction motherhood didn't suit her. She'd never been so busy and so bored at the same time. Baby games were stupefying, getting out of the house an endless procedure. She spent Duncan's naps in a desperate attempt at restoring her house to some kind of order, or apologizing to her cats for their new role as secondary characters.

Duncan picked up a block and held it over his head. She smiled encouragingly. He approached in his drunken sailor gait, grinning sweetly, and smashed the block down on her head. "Hi-*yah*."

"Ouch!" she yelled. Duncan burst out laughing and raised his arm for another strike.

"Oh, no, you monster." She took the block away and glared at him. Motherhood must be the absolute pit of existence.

He put his arms out and flapped up and down like a bird, so hard he bounced. "Ah, ah, ah, ah, *ah*." On the last "ah" he launched his little body at her and wrapped his arms around her neck.

Melanie froze for an instant, then folded his sweet soft form into her arms. He burrowed his head into her neck and held still. "Ba ba drrrrl bink."

Melanie closed her eyes. Oh, gosh. He felt good. He smelled good. He was such a sweet boy. So smart, and such a beautiful child. They'd had so much fun in the past few days. Being a mom must be so incredibly rewarding.

The phone rang. Melanie gave the warm body against her another squeeze and stood to take the call, bringing Duncan along with her.

"Melanie, it's Paige. We have a problem."

"We do?" Melanie suppressed a wave of irritation. She wasn't in the mood for more problems.

"Lou called me yesterday."

"And?"

Paige let out an exasperated moan. "Don't you get it? He's not supposed to know where I am. I'm thinking he hired that detective friend of his from Boston to find me. Two of my friends in Philly said some guy who looks like him came by, supposedly selling baby toys. He wanted to see their kids. They live on opposite sides of the city and he didn't visit anyone else in their buildings. I don't know if he can find you, but if he does, hide Duncan. Do anything you can, but don't let the jerk take him. Please, Melanie, I—"

A huge blast, like some enormous mechanical trumpeting elephant, drowned out the rest of her sentence.

"Paige, what the heck was that? Where are you?" Melanie wrinkled her forehead, rocking Duncan to keep him pacified. The sound was vaguely familiar.

"I have to go. I can't talk now. Please promise me you won't let him get Duncan."

Melanie grimaced at the ceiling. "I promise, I promise."

She hung up in disgust. Cheating abusive spouses, runaway wives and children, private investigators tracking them down. Paige's family was starting to sound like a rejected episode of *Law and Order*.

She lifted her shoulders in a frustrated shrug and let them drop. "Ridiculous."

"Dick-wess."

She blinked and stared at Duncan. Pride swelled in her as if she'd just found out her own son were Einstein the Second. "Yes, Duncan! Good! Ri-di-cu-lous."

He stared at her solemnly and scrunched his cute squishy lips. "Bun-ja mush."

"Okay, well." She kissed his soft hair. "You got it once. That's good enough for me."

The phone rang again. Melanie sighed and picked up the receiver, adjusting Duncan in her arms. She hadn't quite gotten the hang of the mom-hip thing, and twenty-six pounds got very heavy very fast.

"Melanie dear, it's Dot."

"Hello!" Melanie smiled just hearing her elderly neighbor's voice. Dot and Richard, sturdy and brilliant retired college professors, lived next door in an immaculate Victorian with gardens that put Versailles to shame. "How are—"

"I don't mean to alarm you, dear, but Richard very astutely noticed this morning that there is a *man* sitting in a car outside your house. He was asleep earlier, but now he's watching your door. I told Richard it was certainly nothing suspicious, but he *is* still there, and I thought you ought to know."

Melanie froze. "A man? Staring at my house?" Her mind scrambled to make sense of the information and jumped to an irrational conclusion. Lou's friend the detective? Could he have found her so easily? Could he have made it here this fast? Hardly possible.

Duncan reached for the phone and shook his arm so the instrument whapped her on the chin no matter how far away she twisted.

"Bungt blam di di *di*."

"What was that, dear?" Dot sounded a trifle alarmed.

Melanie got the phone away from Duncan. "I said 'bungt blam di di *di*.'"

"That's what I thought. Sanskrit, is it? No, not quite the proper verb forms. Have a baby recently, did you?"

"Dot, I'm going to need your help. Can you and Richard come over right now?"

"Of course, dear. Of course. We'd be delighted."

Melanie hung up the phone, adrenaline breaking all speed records through her body. For some reason, even though she still didn't believe Lou had hurt his child, the idea that he might have sent some...hound dog after Duncan made Melanie's protective blood boil. Paige and Lou should work their problems out for themselves. This stranger made the whole mess ten times more threatening.

Dot and Richard rang her front bell. She put Duncan in charge of demolishing another tower and ushered them in, peeking over their heads to see if the man was really there. She inhaled sharply. He was. Holding up a newspaper and peering nonchalantly at them around the side.

Melanie closed the door and rushed to the phone. This called for heavy artillery. She'd need help from her neighbors on both sides. "Peggy. Are you busy? Can you come over now? I need your help."

"Ha-appy to help." Peggy's high voice and strange intonation always reminded Melanie of the comedian Emo Phillips. The frail, tiny widow lived on the other side from Dot and Richard in an unkempt Colonial with a garden that looked like an unmown meadow. "So so happy to help. Be right there."

A short time later, Melanie's cast of characters had assembled in her living room, admiring Duncan, who immediately appointed himself host and began distributing blocks to each person.

Melanie gestured to him, not really sure what she planned to ask her neighbors to do but certain the job of protecting Duncan required more than she could manage on her own. "This is Duncan. His mother asked me to take care of him for a while. She...feels he needs to be protected from his father, because—"

"Oh, my." Dot put a pudgy hand to her heart; Richard patted her shoulder gently. They were practically indistinguishable—both short and stout, with masculine haircuts, khaki pants and polo shirts.

"Oh, dear, oh, dear, poor little tyke," Peggy sang. She shook her head, wig of gray curls on backward as usual so that the short straight hair at the base of the wig's neck stuck out over her forehead like strange horizontal bangs.

"I'm not convinced the father would hurt Duncan, but I think he might have hired a private investigator from Boston to find his son."

"And that horrible prying man outside is him?" Dot gestured contemptuously toward the front window.

"Is *he*, dear," Richard corrected gently.

Peggy frowned and cocked her head like a confused puppy. "Is he what?"

"Is *he*? Are you sure?" Dot drummed her fingers on her chin. "Yes, of course! The nominative case as a predicate complement, how silly of me. Is *he*."

Peggy looked from Dot to Richard and back. "Well, is he or isn't he?"

Melanie drew in a patient breath. Finishing sentences could be extremely challenging around her neighbors. "I promised his mother I wouldn't let the guy find him."

"So the question is, of course, how can we make sure he doesn't?" Dot pounded her fist on her palm.

"Right. To action." Richard leaped to his feet and began pacing back and forth, one hand at his chin, the other crossed behind his back. Duncan watched his pendulum progress in obvious delight. "We will not be able to pretend the child isn't here—"

"Due to the inherently noisy nature of children." Dot finished for him.

"So the thing to do—"

"—is make this man think the child is yours."

"Of course!" Richard looked approvingly at Dot. "Brilliant as usual, dear."

"Mine?" Melanie looked cautiously around the room. She'd been half-wondering how they could put Duncan in the attic and take turns feeding him. "But I'm a terrible mother. He'd be able to tell right away. And it's too much of a coincidence that I'd have a boy the same age as Paige's. He probably has a picture of Duncan anyway."

"Hmm." Dot jumped up and began pacing opposite her husband. Duncan crowed and clapped his hands at the cloned couple's energetic display. "Then we must either find another place for Duncan or disguise him somehow."

"Bwwwwwah," Duncan waved his arms to conduct Dot and Richard's pacing performance.

"Quite right, my dear." Richard tapped a finger to his rather enormous nose.

"I don't want anyone taking this child away from my house." Melanie scooped Duncan up, surprised at the vehemence of her feelings. "I promised to protect him and I will."

Duncan looked at her with serious, concerned eyes; his tiny lips parted, then blew a ferocious raspberry.

"How are we going to keep you safe, little guy?" she whispered.

"Oh, *dee?*" he answered in a soft squeak.

Melanie smiled tenderly at him while her insides contracted into a painful knot. She suddenly understood how a mother bear felt when someone threatened to come between her and her cub. Melanie hadn't even met the detective guy. He could be a perfectly lovely human being. But she still wanted to lumber out there and lacerate his face with her claws. No one would take Duncan away from her except Paige.

"You know there are men who love to dress as women." Peggy beamed and nodded. "Some of them are really quite lovely."

A short silence followed Peggy's statement, as short silences tended to do.

Melanie smiled at her dear friend. "Is that so?"

Peggy pointed at Duncan. "If he's your daughter, no one will suspect."

"Baa baa *bwah!*" Duncan flung out his arms to punctuate his proclamation and nearly smacked Melanie in the face.

"Splendid idea, Peggy." Richard snapped his fingers. "Dress little Duncan as a girl."

"Brava, Peggy. First rate." Dot nodded vigorously.

Melanie put Duncan on the floor and eyed him doubtfully. Could you do that without causing some kind of hormonal damage? Duncan beamed and stood to make a hands-out lunge at her nose, which she barely avoided. She studied him. His features were sweet and pretty enough, his hair long enough—but geez. He was too young to be a cross-dresser.

"What shall we call him—her?" Dot drew her thick brows down.

"I don't know...." Melanie still stared at Duncan, trying to adjust to the idea of having a little girl to look after. "I guess we could—"

"Baa bwah!" Duncan shouted and overbalanced onto his rear, grinning at the room.

"Barbara!" Peggy clapped her hands. "He wants to be called Barbara, the little dear."

"Settled." Dot rummaged through her pockets and came up with a small pad and the stub of a pencil. "Now. We'll need clothes. My son has an attic full of his daughter's outgrown stuff."

"Super." Richard whipped a pen and matching pad out of his shirt pocket and joined his wife in frantic list-making. "Pink toys..."

"Ribbons..."

"Party shoes..."

"Unisex diapers..."

"I'll bring the cello case." Peggy rubbed her hands together gleefully.

A pen and a pencil paused in their list-making. Four pairs of eyes swiveled to look at Peggy.

"Bung gwup." Duncan shook his head so hard his whole body wiggled.

"Cello case?" Melanie spoke gently. "Do you mean—"

"If you bring boxes into this house the detective will get suspicious. But if I make the rounds to give a little conce-ert..." She ended on a high singsong note and gave a knowing wink.

"Ha! Brilliant once again." Richard crossed the room and thumped Peggy on the back, nearly snapping her neck in the process. "Clothes in a cello case. Good thinking, old girl."

"So are we all set?" Dot closed her pad like Captain Kirk signing off from the *Enterprise*. "Richard and I will get over to Jon's and bring clothes back to our house. Peggy will bring the cello case to transport the clothes to Melanie. We'll meet back here in an hour. Then we can take Barbara out for a nice walk on the front lawn. Mr. Big City Detective will realize his mistake and leave."

Melanie nodded and let out her breath in relief. The plan *sounded* simple. It could even end up *being* simple. If luck went her way, the entire charade could be over by the time—

"Oh-oh." Dot peered out the front window.

"What?" Melanie's body tensed instinctively. Something told her the entire charade was about to become complicated. "What is it?"

"He's getting out of his car." Dot straightened and turned to face them, her features pale. "I think he's going to want to come in."

JOE RESTED HIS HEAD on his steering wheel and counted to ten. When the urge to run screaming out of the car, out of the town, out of the country didn't subside, he counted to twenty. At one hundred and forty-six, he gave up and got out of the car to stretch and inhale the warm, sticky air. He'd arrived here early after driving most of the night and had taken a nap in the car so his brain would have a better chance at functioning when he had his first shot at this Melanie Brooks person. Of course while he'd been mentally preparing himself to go in, the entire neighborhood had piled into her house. He wanted to speak to her alone.

He rolled his head around to get the kinks out of

his muscles. Some vacation. He'd started with a leisurely traffic jam from Boston all the way to Philadelphia to see Lou. After a day or two he'd traced Paige to Miami, though Lou had no idea why she'd be in Florida. The child, who Joe's sources reported was not with Paige, would be harder to find. When Lou ran out of Paige's friends to investigate, they pored over phone bills, and picked out a few numbers unfamiliar to Lou, including three here in Birchfield, Wisconsin, where Paige had lived as a child. Since Joe's planned vacation route went through Wisconsin anyway, he'd agreed to drive out and follow the leads personally.

So now he sat in annoyingly picturesque Birchfield, wanting to be just about anywhere else in the universe. Why couldn't Paige's friends live in New York or San Francisco? Maine or Washington State? Even Mars would be more interesting. Somewhere he could find relaxation, but which packed more excitement than counting Green Bay Packers flags sticking out of people's cars.

He stalked to the back of his car, opened the trunk and grabbed his traveling salesman kit, loaded with baby supplies and toys, and his summer jacket and tie—old but barely worn. He'd had it. In towns like this people could spend the whole day gabbing about peonies and lawn maintenance and the time Auntie Giselda's teeth landed in the punch bowl. If Ms. Brooks had the baby he'd find a way to see it whether she was alone or not. Then he had only to compare the little face with the blurry snapshot in his pocket.

After that, he could get the hell out of this cow town and back to civilization and his vacation.

If she had the baby.

He put on the jacket, barely managed the tie and walked up the front path—nicely mown, nicely planted, nicely edged, but not too recently. Could that be because a toddler came for a visit last week and interfered with her yard work schedule? He rang the doorbell, listening intently for signs of scurry or panic, though they'd have no reason to connect him with Lou.

After a minute of silence, measured, confident steps came toward the door. The painted wood swung open.

"Hello. What can I do for you?" A young woman, probably late twenties, stood with a polite, querying look on her face and a half-smile of cautious welcome.

Joe swallowed his surprise. What could she do for him? Right about now, anything. He hadn't realized Demi Moore had a twin sister. Light rosy skin, dark short hair, clear dark eyes under slender, shaped brows. She was slim, poised—with the promise of graceful movements. A long neck, bared by her shirt's wide neckline, medium bust, tiny waist flattered by high-waisted shorts, strong legs used to exercise. He swallowed again and pulled at his tie. Somehow he'd expected a friend of Paige's to open the door in spandex leggings and big hair, cracking gum and working on her manicure *du jour*.

"Hello, ma'am. I'm Joe Jantzen, traveling salesman for Baby Bliss Products." He gave his best aw-shucks grin. "May I speak to the baby of the house?"

"What makes you think I have a—" An earsplitting toddler shriek cut her off. She winced slightly.

Joe tried to temper his triumphant grin. Phase one complete. Baby on board. "I take it that wasn't your husband."

"No. I don't have a husband." Her eyes widened a fraction. "That is…not anymore. But of course I used to, with the baby…I mean he made the baby…that is, we did." The lovely Ms. Brooks made a few flappy, nervous gestures, looking as if she'd rather be the object of a shark feeding frenzy than continue this discussion.

Joe's instinct sharpened. Lou had been sure Ms. Brooks wasn't the marrying kind. In fact, Lou thought she was probably gay—but then Lou thought that about any woman not attracted to him. Lou was also sure she didn't like kids. Something certainly had this woman flustered. Either she hated talking about her ex as much as Joe did or she was lying about ever having had one. In light of his years of experience, and the fact that she stunk at it, Joe would pick lying. Which meant the entire project would be over very soon and he'd be off to the Pacific Northwest to—

"Anyway, the baby's napping. Or supposed to be." She gave a little shrug and a dimpled smile.

Joe nodded politely. Her scent reached him, floral, fresh, with a hint of baby powder. He took a deep breath and resisted the urge to let out a long, "Mmm." Baby powder on adult females just about did him in. He looked into the dark eyes facing him and felt his sexual interest stir out of its embarrassingly long hibernation.

"May I come back some time when your child is available, ma'am? I have some things I'd like to show the little one."

"Show the baby?" Her eyebrows shot up. "Actually, *I* make the buying decisions in this house."

He nodded, expecting her reaction. "We at Baby Bliss believe the bulk of our appeal comes from the customer viewing our products in direct interaction with the intended user. Ma'am."

She folded her arms firmly across her chest. Joe suppressed a grin. Hadn't Lou thought she was a schoolteacher? Joe would bet this pose made it regularly into unruly classrooms.

"You mean you want the baby to become attached to the toys so I'll feel obligated to buy them."

"Yes, ma'am." He nodded rapidly. "That's it exactly."

He grinned at her surprise and was rewarded with a smile that started out grudgingly and spread. He suddenly understood what people meant when they said a smile could light up a face. Hers was enough to make him remember he'd left his sunglasses in the car.

"Well, at least you're honest about it, Mr...."

"Joe. And yes, ma'am. I believe you get a lot further in life being truthful." He resisted the urge to smirk. Private investigators rarely let honesty interfere with their work.

"So I'd like very much to come back this afternoon and show your youngster some of what I've got. These toys are specially researched and proven to be more stimulating than the regular brand-name toys you find in the stores."

"Ha." She scowled. "That wouldn't be too hard. Most of them are more like advertisements than toys."

"Exactly, ma'am." He gave an internal cheer. Something that mattered to her; he'd found a way in. "Toys have become as enslaved to television and movie culture as the children who buy them. We at Baby Bliss believe the true value of toys is the associations the *child* develops from the toy, not ones preprogrammed by some Hollywood scriptwriter."

She looked at him critically. He kept his expression pleasant and neutral, afraid of communicating either his unexpectedly strong attraction or the fear she could tell he spouted prime USDA bull.

"If you'd just give our toys a chance with your child, ma'am, I think you'll open up a whole new world of creative and imaginative play."

"Hmm." She tilted her head to look at him harder, her jaw set. He got the feeling she was about to decide on a lasting impression. "How long have you been a traveling salesman, Joe?"

"Oh, gosh, uh…" He pretended to consider, rapidly calculating which angle to take. Directness had been the best entrée yet. Better play up the good old inexperienced boy. He consulted his watch. "I'd say…about ten minutes. New career for me, ma'am."

"Oh?" She slanted him a penetrating look that had him dry-mouthed for a few seconds. Whatever impression he made, the one he would keep of her was wholesomeness sexy enough to be unsuitable for family viewing. "What did you do before?"

"Before this job?" He made more calculations. A schoolteacher would like the intellectual type. "I had my own bookstore. Specializing in rare and out-of-print...nineteenth-century...American literature." His grin tightened. He pulled at the silk noose around his neck. Why the hell did he say that to a teacher? Ten to one she was some kind of specialist.

"Really?" Her eyes lit up to a dazzling dancing shade of brown. "I did my master's thesis on Mark Twain."

"Now that is amazing, ma'am." He barely kept from groaning in despair. Every second he'd planned for relax time would be spent cramming in the library—if Birchfield had one with more than three books in it. The humid summer air closed in another notch.

"Would you like to come in and talk shop?" She gestured behind her into the house. "I am absolutely starved for a long, deep conversation about Mark Twain. The baby might even wake up soon and want to look at your toys."

"Gosh, I would love to—" he swallowed "—but I really have to be getting on to see other customers. I would like to come back some time, though, ma'am. Maybe tomorrow afternoon?" He couldn't believe he'd said the words. He'd sworn *tomorrow* and *Birchfield, Wisconsin* would never have anything in common. But he'd need at least one night to reacquaint himself with the literature of Mark Twain or she'd peg him for the phony he was in five minutes.

"I'd like that." She gave him a grin that made him feel like he'd just come out of a coma and found that life was very, very good. "Do you have a card?"

He nodded and reached into his pocket. "Joe Jantzen, Baby Bliss toys. I'll stop by tomorrow afternoon, around three."

"I'll be ready for you." She smiled again and closed the door.

Joe went down the front walk, wishing her last words meant she'd open the door to him tomorrow wearing a smile and a lace teddy. Not that guys like him inspired women to such behavior. But the image was so engrossing, he nearly bumped into an old woman wheeling a cello case down the sidewalk. Wasn't she one of the neighbors who'd gone into Ms. Brooks's house? How the heck had she gotten out here?

"Hello, young man," she called. "I'm going next door now. To play the cello."

He nodded politely, wondering if she knew her wig was on backward.

"I like to play the cello for my friends. So that's what I'm going to do. Right now." She tapped the case. "Play the cello."

"Terrific. I'm sure they'll enjoy it."

She frowned. "Enjoy what?"

He pointed to the instrument.

"Oh, yes," she said happily. "My cello. I'm off to play this cello right now."

"Believe it or not, I'd heard that." He waved goodbye and walked to his car before he'd have to bear any more breathtaking installments of Woman Planning to Play the Cello.

He'd have to find a hotel now, and a library, and spend more time on stage in Nowheresville with its cast of intellectual giants, instead of wrapping up the two other leads in town and moving on as he'd hoped.

But he couldn't deny that the prospect of seeing Ms. Melanie Brooks again, even if she didn't come through with the lace teddy, promised to make his stay in Birchfield much more interesting.

3

MELANIE CLOSED the door, slumped against it and shut her eyes, trying to fight the impulse to open the door and run over a certain private investigator with a truckload of Beanie Babies. *We at Baby Bliss believe the true value of toys is the associations the child develops...* Blah, blah, blah. We at Baby Bliss are a mercenary, subhuman, wastebucket liar.

"Super job, Melanie." Dot and Richard crowded around and led her into the living room, Richard patting her back and Dot her hand.

"Absolutely stupendous. You had him going at the end there. Mark Twain!" Richard slapped his thigh. "Of course that bit about him running a bookstore was a load of hooey. Only had to take one look at him to know."

"He'll be in the library all afternoon studying." Dot leaned back, hands to her belly. "Ha! That's rich! What a lucky break you did your thesis on Twain!"

Melanie put tight hands to her temples. "I *didn't* do my thesis on Twain. I did it on James *Joyce*. I probably don't know any more about Twain than *he* does." She tried not to sound hysterical. She really did. But judging from the shocked look on Dot and Richard's faces, she hadn't quite succeeded. Or maybe it was the fact that she was blowing air in and out her nostrils like a furious bull.

Dot and Richard's laughter slowed to embarrassed chuckles, then faded into a couple of faint oh, dears and a shared sigh.

"I just wanted to make *him* squirm for a change." Melanie flopped down on an overstuffed floral print chair and folded her arms across her chest, jaw clenched. "I did so much squirming I felt like an earthworm on uppers."

The encounter had gone nothing like she'd planned—mostly because she hadn't had time to make a plan. She'd been composed enough when she answered the door, but when he asked about her husband, she'd lost it, thoroughly and without exception. Not until he started ladling on the toy philosophy extra thick had the realization come, along with mounting anger, that *she* had a weapon, too. She knew he wasn't a toy salesman. She knew he was a lying, manipulative "son-of-a" out to wrangle Duncan away from his protector without thought to the baby's best interests. Because he'd been paid to do it. From there, Melanie had no trouble going on the offensive, and happily attacked him with questions about his career.

She groaned and put her head in her hands. But then there was that other thing. The other little problem. The problem that began when this not-tall-enough, too-built-for-her-taste, professional slime puppy with dark curling hair and unremarkable features turned on her the bluest eyes she'd ever seen and brought her long-dormant sexuality absolutely screaming to life. She hadn't been instantly attracted to a member of the opposite sex like that since she first laid eyes on Billy Ehrgood in seventh grade—and he ate bugs for cash. Worse, under the guy's gee-whiz-ma'am salesman shtick, she'd glimpsed the hard edges of a man of experience. Experience in life, experience in passion...

Melanie swallowed. Maybe she'd lived in Birchfield too long. Maybe the nice, relatively wholesome small-town men had become familiar enough that a taste of anything different seemed overly exotic and compelling. But she'd spent the entire conversation wanting to touch Joe Jantzen, to be touched by him. Some way...any way...even Jell-O wrestling.

She raised her head to find Dot and Richard staring at her as if she'd become the star of some Kafkaesque insect novel.

"Uh. Where's Duncan?"

"I put him down for a nap. He objected strongly for a while, but he's settled now." Dot smiled as if she thought Melanie needed a long nap herself—after a sedative. "Peggy snuck out the back to get her cello. Are you all right, dear? You look as if you've seen some ghastly apparition."

She had. A wolf in creep's clothing. "I'm worried about our plan. There's no way—"

The doorbell rang. Someone opened the front door. The trio in the living room froze. Melanie's heart sank. He was back. Her heart leaped again. Oh, my Lord, he was back.

"'Tis I," Peggy called. "I can't give Dot and Richard a concert when they're not home."

"Oh, Peggy." Melanie rushed to open the screen

before her heart could sink again on the rebound. "It's okay. The man is gone."

"But where? He wanted to hear me play."

"You weren't going to play, Peggy," Dot said kindly. "The case was for clothes."

"The case was foreclosed?" Peggy blinked. "Does that mean we won?"

"No, no, Peggy." Richard cleared his throat and moved forward, prepared for a thorough clarifying lecture. "You see, we intended—"

"Yes, Peggy." Melanie put her arms around Peggy's thin shoulders, shaking her head surreptitiously at Richard. "We won. The first battle, anyway. But I'm afraid the war is—"

"Oh, good. Let's have a drink." Peggy sighed rapturously and rummaged underneath her skirt. She came up with a tarnished silver flask, opened it, flung her head back and tipped it over her mouth.

Melanie exchanged glances with Dot and Richard. No one knew what went into the concoction Peggy regularly indulged in. She claimed it was a long-held secret family recipe for a restorative tonic. Melanie just hoped it wasn't grain alcohol and food coloring.

She refused Peggy's offer of a swig and turned her mind to the problem of keeping Paige's child safe from Sleazelock Holmes. Dressing Duncan as a girl would only keep Joe off the trail for a short time. They had to find a better way.

"Listen, everyone, about this plan. Even if we can convince this guy Duncan is my daughter, he'll want the story corroborated. All he has to do is ask anyone in town if I have a child and the game's over."

"By Jove, then we'll tell everyone." Richard smacked his fist on his palm. "I'll start with the east side of town, Dot, you take the—"

"A bit impractical, dear." Dot patted his arm.

"Ah, yes, quite." He put his hand near his chin as if he were holding a pipe, which he no longer could since Dot insisted he quit. "If only there was some way to second-guess how a detective's mind would work and simply warn those people."

"Like Melanie's boss."

"Her co-workers."

"Her students."

"Stop! That's too many already." Melanie put her hands to her head in frustration, understanding for the first time why people were moved to tear out their own hair. "I can think of two people right off who Paige has kept in touch with—Wendy and Alison. He's probably got their addresses, too. But how can we make sure—"

"Ms. Brooks? You there?" A boy's voice came through the open front door.

"Hi, Kevin. Come on in." Melanie beckoned her student-slash-paperboy into the living room. "How are you doing?"

"Uh. Okay." He looked around uneasily, one hand shoved in the pocket of his enormously baggy pants, the other holding out a ratty newspaper. "Sorry your paper's late…again."

"It's okay, Kevin." Melanie took the dirty paper gingerly, her heart contracting with a strange combination of tenderness and exasperation. Kevin Ames was the classic case of a bright boy who didn't apply himself to anything but trouble. Nothing constructive seemed to grab that incredible mind of his for more than a few minutes at a time. Melanie had tried a dozen schemes to spark his interest in life, to no avail. "What happened this time?"

"My mom's boarder's moving out." His adolescent voice cracked. He pressed his lips together and shrugged as if he didn't care. "Had to help him start packing."

"Oh, Kevin—" Melanie bit off the rest of her sympathy—poison to a male teenager. But you had to be an idiot not to know how much Kevin wanted things to work out between his mom and Bill Stackman.

"We need a spy," Peggy announced calmly, and pointed a steady finger at Kevin. "To find out who that detective is going to talk to, so we can talk to them before he can talk to them."

"Peggy! Another super idea." Richard strode over and raised his arm. Peggy clutched her cello case between them to save her vertebrae from his exuberance.

Melanie frowned. A spy. Someone who could ingratiate himself with Mr. Jantzen on the pretext of friendship, and pass along his every intended move. It could work—if done carefully.

Certainly Kevin would be ideal for the job. If anyone had perfected the art of looking innocent while guilty, it was Kevin. Plus, he'd already had plenty of practice lying to detectives. He might even enjoy himself enough to stay out of trouble for a while. Melanie's excitement rose.

"Kevin, do you remember when Officer Williams

came to talk to us on Career Day?" She tried to keep her enthusiasm down. Anything that thrilled grown-ups had the potential to repulse teenagers merely on that basis. "Remember how cool you thought he was?"

"Yeah." Kevin's blue eyes brightened. "He pretty much rocked."

"I need your help." Melanie took hold of his shoulder and spoke earnestly into his not-quite-a-man face. "How would *you* like to be a detective? Right now?"

JOE WALKED UP the steps of the brick, ivy-covered Birchfield Library, wishing he was back at the White Birch Motel sleeping. He hadn't done too much of that last night, between studying his notes on Mark Twain, the two Quarter-Pounders he'd had for dinner, the people next door arguing over the best way to exterminate earwigs and a mattress that could have been used in the mogul competition at the winter Olympics.

Plus, he'd had a wildly erotic and strangely tender dream about Melanie Brooks, from which he'd awakened unable to get her either out of his mind or into perspective. He'd barely laid eyes on her yesterday, spent the entire time lying to her, and for all he knew she'd spent the entire time lying back. Not exactly the beginning of a beautiful friendship. But the dream had been so powerful, so real, he found it impossible to shake off its hold.

Then, when he'd finally fallen back to sleep close to dawn, he had a nightmare in which Mark Twain was hunting him with an ax, dressed in a black lace teddy.

Joe paused inside the building and followed signs to the fiction section of the library. He'd studied like mad until closing yesterday, biographies and analyses of Twain's work. Today he had to read at least one of his novels.

Someone fell into step beside him. "You new in town?"

Joe stopped and turned, instantly on guard. Only weirdos or fanatics spoke to strangers. Or was this some cute small-town-welcome thing? He nodded to the kid in front of him, thirteen, fourteen years old, ratty too-big Nike T-shirt, those god-awful baggy pants. His face, under its veneer of adolescent nonchalance, betrayed eagerness, an excited tension that revealed how young he really was.

"Yeah, I'm new."

"I'm Kevin. You need help finding something?"

"Hi, Kevin, I'm Joe." Joe offered his hand, impressed by the boy's intelligent eyes and firm shake. "I'm looking for books by Mark Twain. You know where those are?"

"Yeah. This way." He set off through the stacks, pants flapping like flippers on a seal. "So what are you in town for?"

"I'm a traveling salesman. I sell baby toys."

"Baby toys?" Kevin stopped and turned a look on Joe that clearly questioned his manhood. "I'm gonna be a detective some day. Those guys are tight."

"Really?" Joe grinned, assuming the meaning of

tight had changed since his youth. "One of my best friends is a detective, back in Boston."

"No way! That rocks." Kevin leaned on a nearby computer terminal. "So does he go after drug dealers and everything?"

"Nothing that exciting." Joe's mind spun into action. Small town, one school—the chances were good that Junior Detective here had had Ms. Brooks for a teacher. "You lived in Birchfield long, Kevin?"

"Only all my life." He turned his baseball cap back to front and front to back again in a smooth movement that probably had his female classmates agog.

"You might be able to help me."

"What, help you sell baby toys?" Kevin snorted. "I don't think so. Mr. Twain's books are over there." He jerked his thumb over his shoulder. "If your detective friend needs help, though, I'd do that."

"I'll pay you." Joe took out his wallet. "For information."

"Whoa." Kevin's eyes widened. "You mean like I'm your stool?"

"Kind of." Joe grinned. "The better I know my customers, the better I can sell to them."

"Baby toys." Kevin winced. "Can we pretend you're the detective and I'm your stool?"

"As a matter of fact, that would be completely...tight."

"Okay." Kevin's head bobbed. He grinned. "Okay. All right. You're on. Whadya want to know?"

"Ms. Melanie Brooks. You know her?"

"Yeah. She taught me last year."

"She have a baby?"

"Sure. A year ago. Maybe more."

Joe groaned in disappointment. One person's corroboration didn't prove the baby was hers, but things didn't look good for wrapping up this case quickly.

"What about the father?"

"Huh?"

"The father of her baby, Ms. Brooks's husband." Who Ms. Brooks had been extremely reluctant to discuss.

"Oh, her *husband*. Sure. Sure." He nodded repeatedly. "Great guy. Awesome guy."

"Tell me about him." Joe folded his arms across his chest to give the impression he wouldn't budge until he heard every detail of this man's life, aware on some level hearing about Melanie's true love was going to be irritating—if it turned out she'd had one.

"Well, he was a total brain—he wrote books on physics, a world-class rock climber, a triathlete, black belt in karate, headed some charity thing, too. And he did a couple of martial arts movies, but they never got to theaters."

"I see." Joe didn't know whether to laugh or be jealous. If Kevin was lying, he was good enough to realize his dream of becoming a detective some day. "What happened? Did they get divorced?"

"No way. He died while she was pregnant, rescuing Todd and Lee Jefferson when their house caught fire, down on Hawk Avenue. You can still see some of the charred-up trees on the lot."

The immediate rush of protective feeling at the

thought of Melanie pregnant and widowed was a complete waste of Joe's energy. Kevin had to be making this stuff up. Except Joe couldn't find any of the usual signs. Nothing in Kevin's voice or body language pointed to anything but a sincere recounting of fact.

"Were he and Ms. Brooks hap—" Joe snapped his mouth shut. What the hell did he care if they were happy?

"Happy? They were disgusting. He asked her to marry him at our high-school homecoming dance. Everyone went nuts. He sent her roses every week for her desk. He even had her name tattooed on his—"

"Okay, thanks, Kevin." Joe handed him a folded bill. The twinge of jealousy had become a gnaw. He wasn't sure when he'd started competing with the idea of Melanie's dead husband, let alone acknowledged such a person existed, but he felt distinctly like the loser at the moment. Damn those dreams last night. "That's all I need to know."

"Sure. Where are you going to sell next?"

"What?" Joe erased the mental image of himself skulking beside Mr. Superhero, blinded by the light of his halo. "I'm going to visit Ms. Brooks, then I'll probably try her neighbors, too, if there's time."

"Whatever. See y'around." He started to walk away.

"Kevin." The kid had pretty much convinced him, but Joe had to try one more test. "What was her husband's name?"

"Andrew." Kevin looked Joe straight in the eye,

his voice thick with emotion. "Andrew Brooks. Every kid in this town wanted to be like him."

That clinched it. No one could lie that well. Joe thanked him and walked down the stacks to look for Twain's novels, feeling absurdly deflated. Of course every kid wanted to be like him. Of course he'd been perfect. Of course he'd died nobly and left his perfect child and perfect wife, who would mourn his perfection to the day she—

The sight of Melanie coming around the end of the stack put Joe's body on instant sexual standby. Immediately he turned away. One look at him in the *Tw* section could blow his cover for the whole investigation.

A drinking fountain was set into the wall behind the stack. He moved forward, careful not to call attention to himself with abrupt movements, and started drinking. What was *she* doing here? Did she need to brush up on her Twain? Or was she looking for another author?

He peered under his arm to see. A pair of truly amazing legs, bared to mid thigh by navy shorts, distracted him from any thoughts of literature. He closed his eyes, desperately reminding himself his dreams had been nothing more than dreams, hating the irrational power they had over his feelings toward her, hating the false memories of the awe-inspiring gymnastics those legs were capable of.

He opened his eyes for another peek, unable to waste the chance.

He froze. Her legs had shrunk. They were covered in bruises and scabs. Instead of tapering into thin ankles, they descended into pink bobby socks and Rugrats sneakers.

"Mom, this man is going to drink all the water up. I'm thirsty."

He cringed. "Go away, kid," he whispered.

"No!" She glared and pouted. "I'm staying right here until you let me have some water."

Joe gritted his teeth, wondering if he could gag her with something and still appear to be a child-loving toy salesman.

"Are you all right, sir?"

The nasal voice of the little angel's mother sealed his fate. He straightened, wondering if he could convince Ms. Brooks he'd discovered the fountain in the fiction section had the best water. He smiled at the brat and her dowdy mom, turned to tackle Melanie—figuratively speaking, unfortunately—and stopped, mouth open, relief and regret rushing through him in equal measure.

She was gone.

MELANIE POISED the scissors over Duncan's curling bangs, hands trembling. The fear of snipping off some portion of the child's face, combined with the lingering shock of seeing Joe in the library after they'd spent the night tumbling lustfully in her dreams, had made her a little jittery.

Not to mention the fact that if he'd seen her in the stacks with the volume of Twain short stories in her hand, her plot to protect Duncan could have been irreparably damaged. Once he uncovered one lie, his big pointy detective nose would start sniffing around for others. Thank goodness little Donna Katz had been tenaciously and vociferously thirsty.

Melanie took a lock of baby hair between her fingers and snipped clumsily at the edges. Duncan immediately jerked his head to see what she was doing.

"Just cutting your bangs, love. Trying to make you look more...feminine." Melanie grimaced. She hated doing this to him. He wore a pair of purple overalls with a multicolored floral print shirt underneath—she couldn't quite stand the thought of putting him in a dress. Barbies, a pink dollhouse and Suzie Cute's Super Beauty Shop, all castoffs of Dot's granddaughter, surrounded him on the living room floor. Now if she could just trim his bangs a little so the rest of his hair would look longer in comparison...

"Hold still, Dunc—uh, Barbara." She took hold of another lock of hair and got the scissors ready. The minute the blades approached the soft curls, Duncan began shaking his head vigorously. "No, I need you to hold still, sweetie. The eensy-weensy spider went up the water spout. Down came the—Duncan!"

Melanie dropped the scissors at her side. Duncan grinned at her, his vanquished scissor-wielding enemy, and clapped his hands. "Bwee-bap!"

Melanie sighed. Chalk up another maternal failure to Melanie Brooks. His hair would have to stay as is. She gathered him for a hug and took him upstairs for his nap. Dot, Richard and Peggy would be by any minute to go over the next part of the plan. She'd already called Paige's other friends in town to warn them. Wendy had seemed more interesting in knowing if Joe was good-looking than in the details of the story, but agreed to help. Alison was safely out of town on vacation for the month. If anything else should be done to prepare for an afternoon of deception, Melanie didn't know what it was.

Duncan soon-to-be-Barbara gave her a rueful look as she set him in his crib, then fell over and wiggled his plump purple-clad body in preparation for sleep.

Melanie patted his back. "We'll keep you away from that evil though sexually desirable detective, Duncan. We'll figure out some way, I promise you."

"Bwum." Duncan rubbed his face against the sheet.

She covered him with a cotton blanket and quietly closed the door. The doorbell rang. Melanie's heart immediately jumped into a crazy ragtime beat. She lectured it sternly. No chance Joe Jantzen had gotten here already. She knew perfectly well it was her neighbors. Those dreams last night had blown her mild attraction—okay, major attraction—way out of proportion.

The worst part of the dreams hadn't been the sex, though she and Mr. Jantzen could have made the Olympic Dream Team, if such an event existed. The worst had been the tenderness afterward, the reverent, cherishing way he'd touched her, the possessive gleam in his eye, the whispered words of love....

Melanie bit her lip hard. *Grip thyself, Melanie.* It had been a dream. A dream. Whose power she had to be darn sure she'd shaken off by the time Joe got here.

She opened the door and ushered Dot, Richard and Peggy inside where they turned to her expectantly.

"Okay." Melanie did the mental equivalent of rolling up her sleeves. "I invited you over in case Mr. Jantzen plans to speak to you this afternoon after he comes here. We need to make sure our stories are straight. He'll be asking a lot of questions, and it could all get very complicated."

"Dear me, yes." Dot frowned and tapped a finger to her graying temple. "How can we cover all the information necessary? He could ask nearly anything."

"I know." Melanie glanced at the clock. In the next two hours she had to become conversant with a thesis topic on Twain and invent an entirely new past for herself. "It's going to be tough. But—"

"Tough? I'd say virtually impossible in the time we have." Richard gestured wildly with his phantom pipe. "The implications of what you are trying to accomplish are simply not in keeping with the reality of—"

"I heard of someone on te-levision," Peggy sang sweetly.

Melanie held up a hand to stop Richard's exasperated protest. Peggy might be about to offer another of her heavily disguised brilliant plans.

"Some gentleman had a stroke—" Peggy wandered to the far side of the room and sat down "—at a nice outdoor lunch. Hot dogs, I think it was."

Dot and Melanie exchanged shrugs. Once again a strange new adventure on the Starship Peggy.

"Yes?" Melanie prompted.

"Well." Peggy blinked her wrinkled lids. "From

that day on, the only words he could say were the names of condiments. For hot dogs."

Melanie's face twisted with the effort of trying to make sense out of that one. "Hot dog condiments?"

"I'm afraid I don't follow you, either, Peggy." Richard touched the side of his head as if to say he feared Peggy had finally become one with a black hole.

"If you asked this man how he was, he'd say *ketchup*. You asked him if he wanted water or milk, he'd say *relish*. You asked him his opinion of the situation in the Middle East and he'd say *sauerkraut*." Peggy gave a wink that would have been saucy in a younger woman. "That should fix your detective."

"You mean—" Dot shook her head. "I don't see what you mean."

"I think I see!" Melanie's brain had finally managed to bridge the Peggy Gap. "If we pretend something similar happened, we won't have to worry about what he asks!"

Peggy nodded smugly. "Mustard."

"But we can't all have had the exact same kind of stroke at the exact same moment." Richard threw his hands into the air as if he'd suffered the company of fools too long, and not at all gladly.

"No. But one of us can." Dot started pacing and pointed to her husband. "I nominate you, Richard. But not hot dog condiments, in case he saw the same program. Something else."

"What if he had a stroke watching a movie?" Melanie suggested.

"Yes! How about *Island Monsters of the Deep*? You saw that the other day, dear." Dot leaned confidentially toward Melanie. "Richard claims science-fiction B-movies cure insomnia, but I think he loves them."

Richard sputtered in outrage. "Are you suggesting that a man of my mental powers be reduced to quoting—"

"Perfect. Now what about you, Dot?" Melanie rubbed her hands gleefully. The odds against them were diminishing. Dot stood still for a change, frowning, apparently absorbed in her thoughts. Melanie touched her shoulder. "Dot?"

"What?" Dot shouted suddenly. "I can't hear you. I believe I'm going deaf."

"You're both wonderful." Melanie hugged them. "Thank you so much for this. Now what about Peggy?"

The three of them swung around to consider the elderly lady. Peggy's right eyebrow lifted. Her eyes, gleaming with mischief, turned suddenly dull and glazed, as if someone had unplugged her. She began to rock back and forth, staring at an apparently fascinating invisible speck in the air, mouth hanging open. The effect was startlingly moronic.

"People from big cities think we small town folks are not too bright." Her voice had become an uncharacteristic monotone. Her shoulder twitched a few times. "I think I will prove them right."

"You are *all* wonderful." Melanie's throat began to close on her. It was still a long shot, but at least they *had* a shot now, thanks to her friends. "So let's say the basic story is that my husband—let's say Michael—blew into town, swept me off my feet and left me for another woman when I got pregnant. Barbara and I have been living here happily ever since. The rest of the questions you can avoid. Now everyone go home and practice. I've got a thesis to write."

"Uh-huh." Peggy dulled her eyes and bumped into the door on her way out.

"What?" Dot winked and put a hand to her ear. "What did she say?"

"I hear strange sounds, Captain." Richard gave a sigh of resignation. "Dead ahead in the darkness of the swamp."

Melanie grinned and waved. The fact that Joe was from Boston would come in handy. If Lou had hired a local detective, they'd never pull this off. She looked at the clock again. Now she just had to get through some Twain.

Two hours and several discarded thesis ideas later, Duncan's I'm-awake squawk came through the baby monitor. Melanie brought him downstairs and fed him his afternoon snack, her apprehension rising. Any minute the man who had spent most of the night writhing naked with her subconscious would ring the doorbell and she'd have to spend the afternoon lying to him.

Nothing like a nice peaceful summer off.

She set Duncan, resplendent in his girlie outfit, on the floor amid the Barbies.

"These are dolls. You should be at least somewhat interested in them when our guest arrives."

Duncan looked at her scornfully. "Blump."

"I know, I know." She arranged his curls, wondering if she should have put a little pink barrette in his hair. "Gender stereotyping. It's ridiculous."

"Ah ah *ah!*" He grinned. "Dick-wess."

The doorbell rang, sending enough electricity through Melanie's body to light up the Birchfield baseball diamond. She tried to take a few relaxing breaths and succeeded only in alarming Duncan, who probably thought she had turned into some space alien unable to process oxygen. God forbid she got hysterical with laughter from the tension. She'd done that once, in college, and didn't care to repeat the experience.

She stood up, gave Duncan one last look and tried to get her mind to concentrate on the thesis she supposedly wrote on Twain, the lousy husband who loved and left her, the promise she'd made to Paige. Anything but the fantasy memory of skin to skin, mouth to mouth, groin to—

She yanked open the door and put on her best eager Baby Bliss customer smile.

"Hello, Joe. My daughter's waiting for you. Won't you come in?"

4

"YOUR *DAUGHTER?*" Joe stared at Melanie. His stomach plummeted. The kid was a girl? How had he and Ms. Brooks had such a long conversation yesterday without mentioning her? Hadn't he asked? Hadn't she said? Obviously not. He couldn't possibly have overlooked that vital tidbit.

"Come on in." Melanie gestured into the house, lips in a not-quite-relaxed smile, hand clutching the door. Something was making her nervous. He'd like to think it was his raw sexual power, but history usually proved otherwise.

He walked into the house, shamelessly relishing her baby powder scent as he brushed past. In the middle of her otherwise immaculate living room, a long-lashed, curly-haired toddler sat on a worn Oriental rug. Wearing flowery purple clothes. Clutching an obscenely stacked blond doll. He grimaced. A girl. Unless Melanie had stashed Duncan away in another part of the house or with neighbors, it looked as though Joe's stay in Birchfield would be lengthened to include checks on Paige's other friends.

Which, unless they were as fabulous as Ms. Melanie Brooks, was a decided pain in the cheesehead.

He glanced around the room, tastefully decorated

in turn-of-the-century single woman—the plant, book and knickknack look. No doubt she had at least one cat around somewhere, too. He noted a table of framed photos—most looked like family. If she did have a late husband, all evidence had been removed, from this room at least. Remembrances too painful? Or no remembrances?

"I'm so thrilled that you enjoy nineteenth-century American fiction. Twain's influence on the literature of this country was inestimable. I wonder if you ever came across my thesis." She smiled, easily this time. "It was called *Jumping Frogs and Connecticut Yankees—A Study of Twain's America*."

"No. No, I can't say I did." He pulled at his tie, the knot at his neck practically choking him. So much for hoping she'd been in the library for a brushup. Melanie was obviously completely at home in the subject. He'd need every ounce of his ability to shovel it with the best of them. "But I'm sure it was terrific. Uh, Twain led quite a wandering life. After being a printer's apprentice in the late 1840s, he became a river pilot in 1857, then a journalist."

She raised her eyebrows, as if she couldn't imagine a salesman, even one who used to be a bookstore owner, knowing anything of literary value. "Yes. A fascinating man. Such an engaging blend of humor and realism."

"Indeed." He drew his brows down into what he hoped was a tremendously intellectual expression as he tried to remember more from his notes. "Though after he lost his money on speculation and his wife and daughters died, his works became increasingly pessimistic and satirical.''

"You are so right. Of course since he'd already—Oh!" She jumped and gave a yelp of pain. "No, Barbara, dear. No bite Mommy."

Barbara emerged from between her legs, grinning like an evil sprite. Melanie rubbed her rear ruefully and sent Joe a calculating look. "'A baby is an inestimable blessing and bother.'"

He picked up his cue immediately, even in the midst of envying Barbara's teeth, and thanked the eternal soul of John Bartlett for his book of quotations. "From Twain's letter to Annie Webster, September first, 1876."

She grinned, probably delighted with his brilliance on the subject. "You know your Twain."

"Twai!" Barbara flung herself down and began pushing her doll along the floor, making choo-choo noises.

"Barbara." Melanie knelt next to the child and patted her back. "This is Joe. He has some toys to show you."

"Da da *da*." Barbara sweetly offered Joe the blond plastic centerfold, then repeatedly smashed it on the floor. "Bung!"

Joe chuckled at the baby's attempt to inflict dolly brain damage, immensely relieved they'd been interrupted before the discussion progressed to Twain's influence on adopted Midwestern vegetarian farmers. "How nurturing."

Melanie bristled. "All girls should be Mommy-in-training from the time they're born?"

"Of course not, ma'am." *Oh, brother.* Any points he'd scored avoiding a Twain wreck could be erased by one thoughtless comment. "We at Baby Bliss believe in gender neutral play. I was making a joke."

"Oh...sorry." Melanie smiled tightly and stood. "I admit to being a little touchy on the subject. Comes from being a single wom—parent for the last year or so."

"I understand." He smiled directly into her eyes and was pleased to see her color slightly and turn away. His sexual power might not be raw, but maybe it wasn't hopelessly overcooked, either. "How long since your husband...departed, ma'am?"

"He *departed* right after we found out I was pregnant."

"I'm sorry." Joe's instincts pricked up at the acid in her voice. "That must have been hard on you."

"It was."

Bitterness and barely controlled anger—she hadn't gotten past that stage of grief yet. Understandable, when her late husband essentially invented human perfection.

"I met a kid—Kevin—who knew your husband. Said he was quite a guy."

"He was quite a guy, all right." Sarcasm bunched her mouth into a tight package—then let go as she appeared to register something he'd said. "Kevin said that?"

Joe nodded, taken aback by her reaction. Something wasn't adding up in Happyville. "I got the impression he admired him tremendously."

"Oh, yes." She sank down next to the baby again. "Of course. Kevin did."

He was onto something. "I got the impression the whole town thought the sun set only at his command."

"Oh, yes." She smiled weakly. "Everyone loved Mike."

"Mike?" Kevin had called the guy Andrew. Joe shoved his jacket back, put his hands on his hips and planted himself firmly. An old cop pose, to send a clear message that he wouldn't tolerate bull. "That wasn't the name Kevin used."

Melanie busied herself pawing through the pile of pink toys in front of her daughter. "Mike was my name for him. Everyone else called him…the name Kevin used. Oh, Barbara, look! Accessories!" She handed Barbara a little pink plastic purse and hat that matched the tacky dress the doll wore.

The name Kevin used. Joe walked over and squatted on his heels next to her, ready to move in for the kill. If the husband turned out to be fake, Joe would bet he was on the right trail to Duncan, after all. And men the world over would celebrate their right to be average. "What was his other name again? I forget."

She turned her head, color high, eyes sparking total aphrodisiac anger. "Why do you want to know? I don't mean to be rude, but it's not really your business."

"You're right, ma'am. I was being nosy. It's just that your husband's story…touched me." And would touch him more deeply should it turn out to be a work of fiction.

Melanie handed Barbara a tiny pink car and let her hands drop. Joe moved slightly around her, ostensibly to engage the child but so he could see Melanie's expression better. She frowned, eyes distant and contemplative. Time to back off a little, before she started wondering further why a toy salesman seemed so interested in her past.

"I apologize, ma'am. I had no right to—"

"Andrew." She sat back on her heels and watched him, clearly apprehensive. "That's what Kevin called him. So did everyone else."

Disappointment delivered a solid kick to Joe's midsection. Not only was he getting further from finding Duncan, but the Flawless Wonder now looked to have really existed. He nodded, feeling like a kid who just found out Santa Claus was a fantasy. "Andrew. That was it."

She let out a long sigh as if she'd been holding her breath. "Andrew Michael Brooks. I called him Mike because...I have a brother named Andrew." She spoke in a quiet monotone, blinked repeatedly as if holding back tears and sniffed, lips trembling. "Mike was a physicist and an athlete. He made martial arts movies, though none of them made it into theaters. He died...saving two kids from a fire down on Hawk Avenue."

Joe took two clumsy steps closer on his knees, unable to look away from those clear, dark, mournful eyes, hating himself for pushing her past her pride, past her anger, to the breakdown point. But he had to be sure. It was his damn job to be sure.

"I'm...sorry." The words came out, hopelessly inadequate, and hung between them in the sunny room. She had no idea how much, or how hard he fought to keep from reaching out to her. If only he hadn't had those dreams the other night, his reaction might be tempered by something approaching normal behavior.

"Guh *dooj*." Barbara's triumphant shout broke the tension. She held up the doll, upside down with her dress over her head, pink cotton panties around her plastic ankles. The baby poked her bare bottom proudly. "Ba-ba! Ba-ba! Whoa."

Melanie gently took the doll and turned it back into G-rated material, smoothing the dress a few times. She cleared her throat and wiped one eye. "Why don't you show us what you brought, Joe?"

"Of course, ma'am." Joe took her cue and pushed himself into professionalism, still shaken by the fierce desire to comfort her. He tried out a friendly smile on Barbara, who scowled suspiciously. "I'll set up my display on the floor here."

He took off the blasted jacket, rolled up his sleeves, opened his case and took out the handmade wooden toys he bought from a shop near his apartment in Boston. A hopping frog with a pull string, a carved turtle with a ball shell that rotated against its wheel legs, a stacking puzzle with different hand-painted pictures on each level, a little truck loaded with wooden cows...

Melanie's face lit up. Joe grinned, irrationally pleased that he'd had a part in her transition to happiness.

"Barbara, look!"

"Ah-da!" The child crowed in delight, stood and headed determinedly toward the toys. Then past them. Then reached under a chair, pulled out a TV remote and hugged it passionately.

Melanie looked startled for a second, shook her head and laughed. "A house full of wonderful toys and she wants to play with the remote."

Joe nodded, wishing he could steer the conversation to the girl's mother, consumed by the force inside him, beyond professional interest, that wanted to know so much more about her.

He pushed the hopping frog toward Melanie, groping for the appropriate quote from *Bartlett's*. "'I'll risk forty dollars...he can outjump any—'"

"*The Celebrated Jumping Frog of Calaveras County*, 1865." She laughed.

Joe smiled until he felt their eye contact would damage his chances of further sanity and went back to rummaging in his case, willing himself to return to the safe cocoon of his real business here. He risked blowing his cover if he appeared too interested in Melanie's life. He had to get over his sudden uncharacteristic obsession with this woman, do his job and move on to somewhere he could really enjoy himself.

"Here's a special toy she might like." He held up a soft rag doll, almost as big as Barbara, with felt features and long yarn hair. "Her name is Hartley."

"Oh, how cute. Barbara, look at this!" Melanie took the doll from Joe, who tried his best to have their fingers brush, and regretted it the second the electricity jolted through his system. He was only making it worse.

Barbara paused in her exploration of the channel changer and came over to examine the doll.

"Dolly," Melanie said. "Isn't she sweet?"

"Bah." Barbara turned away, waved the remote at the TV and emitted a belch that would stun a frat party.

Melanie dropped her head into her hand. "I guess she's a bit of a tomboy."

Joe chuckled appreciatively, seeing an opportunity to take back some of the macho bumbling he'd done earlier. "She'll need that spunk in a man's world."

"You said it." Melanie watched the child protectively. "I could use more of it myself sometimes."

He braced himself, knowing he was about to boldly go where no sane detective would dare. "Bad experiences?"

"You might say that."

"You were lucky to find someone like Andrew—Mike." He winced. There. Was he happy now? He'd brought the damn water walker back into the conversation. Worse, he'd sounded wistful, like a jealous, love-starved geek.

Melanie's eyes flicked over him. His body contracted in self-disgust. She heard the wimpy tone in his voice. Any second now she'd embark on a long rhapsody of Saint Andrew's qualities to keep Lowly Joe in his place.

"Andrew...wasn't quite the saint everyone made him out to be."

Joe practically lost the ability to speak. "Uh, no?"

She leaned toward him slightly, making the nerve endings on his skin buzz with the desire for contact. "He was cheating on me."

He sucked in air between his teeth. "Oh, ma'am. I'm so sorry."

Ha! Sorry? He was ecstatic. Even better than if the jerk never existed at all.

"Two-timing." She drew Barbara into her lap. "With two women at once."

"Two!" He tried not to sound smug. "Doesn't that make it three-timing?"

"I guess so." She gave a small sad smile. "When he found out I was pregnant, he packed up and left for a business trip. Only...I don't think he planned to come back."

"The *swine*." He had to suppress the urge to do a victory dance around her living room. Even someone like Joe could compete against an unfaithful creep who abandoned his pregnant wife. Not that he was actually in the running.

"On his way out of town he saw the Jeffersons' house burning. He rescued the kids, then went back in to try and save their...Pokéman collection, and..." She spread her hands helplessly.

Joe's imaginary victory dance stopped cold. "Your husband *died* for Pokéman?"

"The kids had to have them." She shrugged as if she thought no further explanation necessary and gave a long, wavering sigh. "That's why I'm so interested in the Baby Bliss line of toys. I want to put off as long as possible the moment when my daughter is enslaved by popular culture."

She ruffled Barbara's hair and offered the rag doll again. Barbara stood, smashed the remote on Hartley's soft head, grabbed the long yarn hair in a plump fist and began walking around the room, dragging the body behind her.

Melanie groaned. "Did I say tomboy?"

"I think you meant cave boy."

She laughed a trifle nervously and gestured to the toys he'd brought. "Gender neutral time."

"Of course, ma'am." He pulled out the Baby Bliss paperwork he'd had printed in Boston. "You can place your order right now. We take cash or check."

He watched her try out the toys, methodically test their shape, their quality, their function. A precise, detail-oriented person who knew what she wanted. Someone like Andrew with his weekly roses and his public marriage proposal must have swept her off her feet—then let her down with a tailbone-shattering thud. Chalk another one up to the power of true love.

"I'll take these." Melanie held up the puzzle and the pull frog. Joe took down the order, lost in a surge of protective anger. Apparently he hadn't yet sunk to the absolute depths of cynicism if the old story of marital betrayal could still evoke a sympathetic response.

Or was it just Melanie? He glanced at her, keeping his head bent over his clipboard. That aura of strength in defiance of her inherent vulnerability, the slightly haunted look in her eyes, as if she were at constant war with invisible demons...

Or maybe it was the fact that she was the first

woman since his divorce to make him yearn for a long afternoon of premarital sin.

"Okay." He tore off a receipt copy, handed it to her and accepted her check. "You should receive the toys in two to three weeks. Thank you for your time, ma'am."

He packed his case, fighting the ridiculous feeling of oncoming emptiness. Melanie Brooks had produced a credible husband and child. He'd double-check with her neighbors tomorrow to verify the story, then proceed to Paige's other friends in Birchfield, one of whom doubtless had Duncan. Ms. Brooks would live on here with her daughter and forget he ever existed.

He put down the lid of his case with a thud. Why the hell was he doing all this whining? He'd known this woman for all of an hour. *Get over it, detective.*

He draped his jacket over his case, unwilling to subject himself to its unnecessary warmth, moved to the front door and held out his hand. "It was a pleasure to meet you."

"Same here." She gave him a firm shake, then didn't resist when he kept hold of her hand longer than a business relation warranted. "You off to visit the rest of the neighborhood?"

"I think I'll pack it in for the afternoon." Talking to anyone else today would spoil the glow of his experience here this afternoon. He drank in Melanie's dimpled smile, dark eyes, fair skin and sexy wholesomeness, and was nearly overpowered by the urge to kiss her. He dropped her hand, shaken, and stepped out the door. "Sensible Joe," Marla had called him, teasing him for what she called his lack of passion, or spontaneity. But here he was, very unsensibly tempted by intimacy with someone he didn't even know. Damn those dreams.

Melanie followed him out, smiled and parted her lips, looking as if she had something else she wanted to say. A ridiculous egotistical hope began building through him. Did she wish he'd stay longer? "I wish you...luck in your new career, Joe."

"Thanks." He took a step closer, watching her carefully for signs he was going too far. "It's a lonely business, traveling around so much, but I enjoy it."

"Lonely?" She swallowed abruptly and began examining her fingernails. "But don't you have a...someone to go home to?"

The blush that rose to her face had nothing on the heat that poured into his body at her question. "I'm divorced."

"Oh, I see." She nodded, still not meeting his eyes. Her scent rose between them. She bit her lower lip and held it between her teeth, further clouding his mind.

"My wife—Marla—left me."

She met his gaze so suddenly he jerked back to keep from leaning into her, astounded by the sexual pressure building in response to her nearness.

"I'm sorry. I know what that's like." Her brown eyes were full of sympathy...and questions.

He gritted his teeth. Why not? Melanie had had a tough life. She deserved some extended hilarity. "Marla ran away...to join a circus."

She gasped. "How awful!"

Joe took in a long, slow breath. She hadn't laughed. She hadn't even smiled. Her eyes were wide with genuine horror. And with her mouth open, Ms. Melanie Brooks's lips were full, round and inviting.

Holding back was a lost cause.

"Oh, Joe! You must have been—"

He practically crushed her against him, found her lips as if by instinct. She tasted fabulous. Her mouth was soft and warm and fit his to perfection. She was incredible. They were incredible. Fate had made—

"What the *hell* are you doing?"

He let go and stepped back, trying to clear his lust-colored brain. Hadn't she been responding? In the red haze of passion, he'd been sure. But for all he knew, the pressure he'd ascribed to an eager body could have been her struggles to get away—the twisting of her head an attempt to escape his kiss.

Joe let his head drop back to stare at the sky. A truckload of cold mortification pulverized his desire. Joe Jantzen, traveling sex offender. Nice one.

"I'm sorry." He brought his head down to look at her gorgeous, furious face. *I'm sorry.* How many times had he said those words today? He should have them tattooed on his chin. "I thought you...wanted me to."

"You thought...you thought incredibly *wrong.*" Her chest heaved with her breaths, slender body taut with outrage. "I don't even *know* you. Why on earth would I want you to kiss me?"

The truckload of mortification was covered by a fresh delivery of prime, grade-A humiliation. Joe's body grew heavy. His expression sagged. Why indeed? "I have no idea. Forget it happened. Just forget it happened."

He turned and walked heavily down her path, the stupid Baby Bliss case banging against his thigh. Who the hell did he think he was, Mel Gibson? He'd be in better company with Mel Tormé.

Marla was right about him. Sensible Joe couldn't excite a female mosquito.

5

FORGET IT HAPPENED? Melanie floated into her house, nearly tripping over Duncan, flat on the floor chewing hungrily on Suzie Cute's feet. Forget the most amazing, incredible, passionate moment of her entire life? Oh, man. She'd never forget. In fact she'd probably relive it every minute for the rest of her life.

She flopped onto her couch and gazed stupidly at the ceiling, her body thrumming and throbbing like some exotic instrument that had been taken out of a dusty attic and played for the first time in decades. *Why* did the most passionate moment of her life have to occur after she'd decided to move beyond passionate moments into a more meaningful existence? Why with the only man she didn't want to *consider* becoming involved with, even casually? He had to be kept as far away as possible so she could fulfill her promise to Paige and keep Duncan safe. Pressing herself close enough to leave concave imprints on his body did not count as keeping him away.

She closed her eyes and parted her lips, trying to recapture the memory of his mouth against hers. Her attraction had been building slowly but surely during their entire meeting. His clumsy efforts to interact with Duncan; his laughable but strangely endearing attempts to sound like a Twain expert; his righteous anger over her fake husband's treatment of her... She touched her cheek where he'd touched her, moved her head as if he were kissing her still, moaned softly as she had when he—

"Dick-wess."

She opened her eyes to Duncan pointing at her, shaking his head.

"Okay, okay. I'm ridiculous. I admit it." She sat up abruptly. But the kiss had been so damn good. Where she'd gotten the emotional strength to push Joe away she hadn't a clue, except it had suddenly occurred to her that a total stranger was kissing her and she was letting him. A total stranger she'd set half the town against, no less. Not tremendously smart. For all she knew, he had a dual career as a private investigator and serial rapist.

Though he didn't seem the type—not that she had a lot of serial rapist experience. But anyone who could tell her his ex had run off to join a circus and not make her want to laugh had to have a little humanity tucked away somewhere. Even as Melanie had been expecting to succumb to a gale of giggles, the sight of his face channeled her reaction into real, deep anger at the woman who'd left him, rejected and humiliated. Just like...Melanie had.

She dropped her head into her hands, still wanting to erase from her memory the way he looked after she pushed him away. As if she'd told him she was afraid of catching some disgusting disease. His circus ex-wife must have done a number on his confidence.

Tenderness she didn't want to feel welled up inside her. Poor Joe.

Melanie opened her eyes and glared through her fingers at the rug. *Poor* Joe? Poking around where he wasn't wanted? Taking her money for a fake toy company? The guy was slime mold. Okay...slime mold who happened to be a fabulous kisser.

She groaned and sprawled on the floor next to Duncan, who giggled and took an experimental bite of her nose.

"I'm beat, Duncan." She wiped the baby residue off her face. "*He* lies for a living, but it's new to me. If I had to reinvent my husband's personality one more time I think I would have passed out from the stress." Apparently Kevin hadn't thought it important to call and mention the story he told Joe about Andrew. She sighed. Typical Kevin. Other than that minor detail, he must have done quite well. Joe had been firmly convinced.

The phone rang. She went to answer, shooting a toy car along the floor to Duncan from the banished boy-toys box on her way.

"Ms. Brooks, this's Kevin." The words came out smoothly, but she could sense his uneasiness. "I, uh, saw Joe this morning."

"I figured as much."

"Oh...he came over there already?"

"Yes, Kevin, he did."

"Oops." His laughter cracked unconvincingly. "Guess I blew it, huh."

"Actually, you didn't." Melanie smiled, still amazed how it had all worked out. The last thing

Kevin needed was an easy excuse to label himself a failure. Not when she'd finally found something he could be good at. "Remember the composition you wrote for me? The story about your dad, how he was into all those sports and made movies and saved—"

"—the Jefferson kids from the fire, yeah!" He cleared his throat, apparently appalled he'd betrayed any excitement. "You remembered that, huh?"

"Of course I did. That essay hung over my desk all year. I must have read it a hundred times." She'd also cried nearly every one of those times. Andrew was Kevin's childhood creation, his version of the perfect dad he craved—part *Father Knows Best,* part superhero. Kevin's real father abandoned the family for a woman half his age, too early for Kevin to remember him. Now that his mom's boarder, Bill Stackman, was leaving, too, it was all the more important Kevin succeed as Melanie's spy.

"So, uh, he didn't figure it out?"

"So far so good."

"All right," he said coolly.

She smiled. Teenage translation—a huge whooping cheer. *Gotcha.* "Now I just have to warn Dot and Richard about the change in my marital history, since they were going to tell Joe I hooked up with a complete bum."

At least she'd added the infidelity bit in a desperate attempt to make her story jibe with that of her neighbors, in case Joe had been planning to talk to them immediately. Thank goodness he was going to wait one more day.

"Joe said he'd visit them tomorrow." She peeked

absently in on Duncan to make sure he hadn't engendered any new life-threatening situations. "So we have some time to make sure our stories still fit. He's a professional. We can't risk any inconsistencies. Even tiny ones can eventually add up to disaster."

"So I should go hang with my friends, or...you want me to look for him at his motel later?" Kevin's voice rose hopefully.

"Well..." Melanie grinned. She hated to disappoint him, but if he hung around too much, Joe might get suspicious. "It might be obvious if he bumps into you in too many places. Just try and hook up with him sometime tomorrow, after breakfast. See what he plans to do and when."

"Okay, Lieutenant. Whatever you say."

Melanie grinned at the careful lack of enthusiasm in his voice, and hung up. Eggshells were sturdy compared to what they were walking on, but so far they'd done okay—and Kevin might actually be enjoying himself.

She changed Duncan's diaper and tidied a little while he picked up cubes and circles for his shape sorter and with great concentration hurled them around the room. She hummed the Billy Joel song that had come on the radio the night she decided to take on this mess, "And So It Goes." She felt unusually light and radiantly alive, graceful and confident, except for knee-melting hormonal aftershocks when she thought about the kiss.

Joe probably wasn't such a bad guy. He had a job to do, after all. Besides the lies about the toy company, she felt instinctively that he'd been reacting sincerely. Maybe he was okay, under his strange mix of toughness and vulnerability. He certainly intrigued her more than any man she'd met in quite a while. Not that Birchfield boasted the most fascinating selection.

She plumped the sofa pillows and glanced dreamily out the window. In other circumstances, she'd probably like to—

Melanie squawked loudly, like a furious chicken. Heat rose through her body and burst over her face. Her fists clenched into angry circles at her side. So, the slime mold had oozed back into the primordial soup, where he obviously felt the most comfortable.

Gathered on the porch next door, all smiles and intimacy, were Dot, Richard, Peggy...and Joe Jantzen, private investigator.

JOE LEANED HIS HEAD against the steering wheel of his car, asking himself for the millionth time what the hell kind of demon had possessed his body ten minutes ago and forced him to kiss Ms. Melanie Brooks. Not that he'd been kicking and screaming to escape its evil hold.

He lifted his head a fraction of an inch and let it bump down again. Twice. He hated this feeling. This leaden, shameful, I-am-lower-than-dirt feeling. Though he should really be used to it. He'd felt this way for most of his married life. *I, Joe, take you, Marla, for fetter or curse, in slickness and in stealth, until stress do us part.* Stress and the echoing, amplified call of the Big Top.

A fly buzzed in through the open window, circled

the car and buzzed out the other side. Like Marla. Fly-through matrimony. He started the engine and pulled down the street in case Ms. Brooks saw his car outside and was tempted to call the cops. Halfway around the block, he pulled over. So what was he going to do now, go back and sit in his motel room? Beat himself up for the rest of the day?

Hell, no. He had to do something to break this strange spell Melanie had cast over him, put her and the kissing disaster behind him and remind himself he did have some worth on this planet. The last thing he should do was give another woman power over his self-esteem.

He put the car in neutral, yanked up the brake and popped the trunk. He'd pay that visit to Melanie's neighbors right now and confirm the facts she'd told him. Reimmerse himself in his mission, track Duncan down, then continue his vacation. The child was here in Birchfield, he could sense it. His instincts rarely lied, at least professionally. Romantically, they seemed to be on a permanently disabled list.

The toy case thudded against the side of the car as he hoisted it out of his trunk, the noise reverberating through the peaceful street. He walked the rest of the way around the block to avoid passing in front of Melanie's place. The warm summer air flowed around him; he inhaled the smell of cut grass and flowers. Nice to have green around, though Boston had some fine parks. Nice to be in a relaxed atmosphere for a while, though soporific might be a more accurate term. He couldn't picture himself in a town like this. How could you lose yourself here? Remain anonymous when you needed to? Not his style—but not so bad for right now.

He crossed the street toward Melanie's neighbor's house, hoping Melanie wouldn't choose this moment to bring Barbara outside. He had told her he wasn't making the rounds of her neighborhood today and would rather she didn't add *liar* to her long list of his faults. He walked up the wooden steps of the large, immaculately kept Victorian. Whoever lived here had plenty of money or time—or both.

"Hello? Can I help you?" A sturdy woman, late middle-age with cropped graying hair and mannish dress and bearing opened the door and stared inquiringly. Joe recognized her as half of the couple he glimpsed going into Melanie's house when he first arrived in Birchfield.

"Good afternoon, ma'am, Joe Jantzen, Baby Bliss toys. Is there a child in this house or one you love who you'd like to see with high-quality noncommercial playthings?"

Her thick brows drew down; she cupped a hand to her ear. "What?"

"I said—"

"*Richard.*" She called behind her in a voice that could stop a charging army.

From somewhere in the house, a male voice responded with something that sounded like, *Yes, Captain.* Joe narrowed his eyes. Captain? The guy would probably show up in a pink apron carrying a feather duster.

"This nice man wants something. Would you come

here?" She turned to Joe. "I'm so sorry. I lost my hearing aid. My husband will try to help."

"Try?" He said the word as loudly as he dared, in case Melanie decided to investigate what must sound like bedlam in this neighborhood.

"He had a little stroke a while ago. Has a hard time communicating."

Terrific. Joe pointed to his case and into the house behind her. He wanted to be out of Melanie's view. "Can we go inside?"

"Of course! Where are my manners! Come in, come in. I'm Dot. Rich—"

"Here, Captain."

No pink apron, but the degree to which he looked like his wife was astonishing, and a little unnerving. Same height and build, same graying hair, same plain clothes, both strangely androgenous. Tweedledum and Tweedledee—the Twilight Years.

"This nice man is here to show us toys."

"The ship is near to full, Captain," he bellowed. "We can take no more."

"There's always room for another toy." She turned confidentially to Joe. "We spoil our grandchildren terribly."

"Of course, ma'am," Joe shouted, eyeing Richard apprehensively. "That's what grandparents are for."

Dot escorted them into the living room. Joe glanced around at the Oriental rugs, the antique furniture, original paintings on the wall. Dot and Richard seemed bizarrely out of place among such tasteful elegance. Like they were curators in a domestic museum.

He unpacked three toys, anxious to get the demonstration under way so he could start questioning them about Melanie. "Now. What I have here is an assortment of—"

The doorbell rang. Richard leaped to his feet. "Alarm, Captain! In the forward deck."

"Well, go answer it, dear." Dot gestured him over to the front door and rolled her eyes laughingly at Joe. "He's a little dramatic these days. But it does keep life interesting."

"I'm sure it does, ma'am." Joe could only imagine—except that he preferred not to. He pulled at his tie and wiped the sweat from his forehead, despising every fiber of his salesman suit. How did people who had to wear this costume every day survive?

Richard returned, leading the backward-wig-wearing, cello-playing woman Joe had seen outside Melanie's house yesterday.

"An intruder requests permission to come on board. *Sir!*" He saluted smartly.

"Peggy! How nice to see you. This is Joe. He sells toys." She held up the pull frog.

Peggy turned eyes on him totally devoid of life or intelligence. "Nice toad."

Joe let out a short breath and smiled a greeting. This would undoubtedly take longer than he had the patience for. He laid out a few more toys and shouted a brief description of each one. Dot and Richard crowded around the Baby Bliss merchandise, while Peggy stared at him, unblinking, her mouth curved into a moronic smile. Funny, he remembered her more animated.

"So." He clapped his hands together, wanting to move on—and out. "I was just next door, at Ms. Brooks's house. She bought some—"

"The native girls are not here for your pleasure, my good man." Richard turned to him sternly. "They have hunting skirts to make for the menfolk."

Joe nodded politely. Clearly Richard was on some lovely island voyage and would not be back any time soon. "She bought some toys for her daughter, Barbara. Cute little girl."

"Yup." Peggy started chewing on one of her fingernails. "Cuter than mud."

Obviously there was a grandfather clock around somewhere, because its ticking became deafening in the sudden silence. Joe sighed. He'd hoped for loose tongues and gossipy inclinations.

"Has Ms. Brooks lived here long?"

Dot elbowed Richard. "What does he care about her lawn?"

"Long," Richard shouted. "Long rolls of thunder in the night. The waves tossed us around like seeds in a maraca."

"Longer than some." Peggy finished the nail and began on another. "Not as long as others."

Tick, tock, tick, tock. Joe blew out another exasperated breath. "I enjoyed talking with her," he yelled. "Did she have the baby here?"

"Baby hair? What would she want with—"

"Baby *here*," Joe bellowed.

"Oh, no." Dot looked around her, hand pressed to her chest. "She had it in a hospital."

Peggy rolled her eyes as if she thought Joe invented

stupidity. "Who'd come to Dot's living room to have a baby?"

"Blood and gore all over the scupper deck!" Richard sidled closer and waggled his eyebrows. "And me without my mop."

Tick...tock. Joe sighed. Forget subtlety.

"She told me about her husband. What a sad story." He shook his head to look supremely regretful, all the while taking in their reactions. Nothing from Dot, who obviously hadn't heard, since he forgot to bust a vocal cord when he made his announcement. Peggy began staring around the room, frowning in concentration, as if she were following the flight of a drunken insect.

Richard slowly raised his arm, finger pointed off into the distance. "It was *him*. The sea serpent of legends past. Caught in his coils, until hope itself fled in terror, lay the lovely maiden, Soom Tee."

"I'd love some tea." Dot smiled lovingly at him, then turned to Joe. "Won't you stay and have a cup?"

Peggy pulled a flask from somewhere under her skirt, belted back a swallow and offered it to him.

"No. No, thank you." Joe bowed his head for a second, trying to pull his frustration under control. "Did any of you know Melanie's husband?" he yelled.

"Yes."

"Oh, yes, we knew Michael."

"Aye, aye, *sir.*"

Joe blinked, astonished to have gotten a straight answer. By this point he'd abandoned any pretense at being a salesman. Somehow he doubted these people could put one and one together, let alone two and two. "So...what was he like?"

Peggy made a grab in the air as if the insect had come temptingly close, then threw it to the floor and stomped.

Dot's mannish face darkened into a sneer.

"Vermin *scum.*" Richard opened one eye wide and narrowed the other in an expression worthy of Vincent Price. "A *rat,* rife with disease, *gnawing* at the underbelly of the ship." He finished his sentence with a furious jerk of his head. The women nodded. The clock ticked.

Joe cleared his throat. "I take it...you weren't too fond of him."

Peggy drew her finger across her throat and spat on the carpet.

All three of them glared at him.

Joe opened his mouth and took in a long breath. Apparently they weren't as taken with Melanie's husband as Kevin was. Did being closer to Melanie mean they knew about his nickname, Michael, and his cheating heart? Or did the discrepancy indicate something amiss with Melanie's story, after all? He needed to confirm the facts. "His death was certainly tragic."

The three faces regarded him blankly.

Joe raised an eyebrow. Perhaps he *had* found a flaw in the armor.

"His death?" Peggy straightened slowly, raised her flask in a toast and had another drink. "You call that tragic? I'd say hallelujah, after what he did to her."

"Terrible way to die, though." He tsk-tsked, eyeing them speculatively.

"Ready...aim...*fire*." Richard waved his arms and fell to the floor. "Fire! Fire!"

Peggy watched him writhe, chewing her lip thoughtfully. "You're toast, Michael."

Toast? Joe shuddered. He'd hate to get on these people's bad side.

"Forgive us if we don't sound sympathetic." Dot spread her hands toward him. "Michael was a louse. He left Melanie when he found out she was pregnant. His death was poetic justice, if you ask me."

The three nodded emphatically.

Joe moved to pack up his toys. Enough. He was satisfied Melanie had told him the truth, and he was certainly anxious to get the hell out of this mental ward. "Thank you for your time, folks. Would you...be wanting any toys this afternoon?"

Dot shook her head. Richard saluted. Peggy nodded solemnly and pointed. At him. "I'll take the toad."

MELANIE SCOOPED UP Duncan and ran, out the door and across her front yard, the baby bouncing on her hip, yelling his delight. She had to get over there and see what kind of damage had been done, see how much she could undo. Maybe she hadn't convinced Joe, after all. Maybe he suspected she had to change her story and wanted to see her neighbors before she had the chance to warn them. With any luck, the inspirational manure about her husband's infidelity would bridge the gap if Dot, Richard and Peggy hadn't said too much. If Joe hadn't asked too much.

Duncan gave another happy screech, thrilled with his new mode of transportation. Melanie heaved him onto her other hip and decelerated slightly. Was she being paranoid? Would Joe's mind follow that train of thought? She couldn't tell. She had zero experience trying to fool private investigators.

She slowed her steps further as she approached the group so as not to appear frantic, though her flushed face and rapid breathing would probably give her away. Her neighbors smiled. Dot waved a greeting. Melanie dared to hope. At least if they'd blown it they weren't aware they had. She met Joe's eyes, afraid she'd see triumph or censure, afraid he'd come running over to strip off Duncan's diaper and take him away.

He stared back, intense blue gaze cutting across the porch, down the steps and through her body so that she felt stripped herself. She caught her breath, astounded by the man's magnetism. It didn't make sense. He really wasn't that good-looking. He wasn't more than four inches taller than she was, but he radiated enough masculinity to make a professional wrestler look like a kitty in need of rescue. More than that, the sensual energy seemed to be directed at her, not something he wore for his own testosterone rush. A heady feeling. Nearly overwhelming.

"Melanie! How nice to see you." Dot's cheerful shout brought Melanie's brain back into her skull where it belonged. "This nice man was just trying to sell us some toys." She gave Melanie a surreptitious thumbs-up sign.

Melanie nodded to Joe, wishing she could recapture

the nice healthy rage that had propelled her over here. But in his presence she'd been reduced to a quivering mess of hormones. The exact pathetic reaction she scorned in all her friends. This was ridiculous. She'd grown beyond such adolescent infatuations. "Yes, we've—" *kissed like starving animals at a feast* "—met."

"He asked us all kinds of questions about you." Peggy made a face at Joe's back, then returned instantly to village-idiot mode when he glanced behind him.

"Our ship steered clear of storm and reef to land in Happy Harbor, Admiral."

Joe raised his brows and walked down the steps until he stood next to her. "Admiral! You rate. His wife only made captain."

She shrugged, wondering why he'd come over to be with her. "I'm a damn fine sailor."

"Blap." Duncan took a swing and smacked Joe's shoulder with a plastic car.

"I wonder." Joe cleared his throat and pulled at his tie. "I wonder if I could talk to you for a minute. Maybe we could take a walk around the block."

Melanie's polite expression froze on her face. *Mayday, mayday. Prepare for enemy attack on Happy Harbor.* He found something out. The trio must not have done quite as good a job as they thought. "I guess—"

"Dow, dow, dow, dow, *dow.*" Duncan launched himself sideways.

"I'll watch...her." Peggy stepped off the porch and held out her arms for Duncan. "You two go on."

"Okay." Melanie handed the child over, feeling like a kid caught cheating on an exam. What gave her away to Joe? Something about her husband? Duncan? Herself? Which of them had blown it? How badly would Duncan have to pay? "Thanks, Peggy."

Joe sent Melanie a startled glance. "You leave Barbara with *them?*"

"They're harmless. Just a little odd."

"If that's a little odd I'd like to be in the next state when wacko shows up."

Melanie managed a wan smile, head spinning. Maybe when he confronted her, she should tell him the truth. Admit to the setup. Maybe she could get him to take her side so Duncan could stay until Paige was ready to get him.

They crossed the street and started around the block.

"I wanted to talk to you."

Melanie braced herself. *Here it comes. Here it comes. Please let me think fast enough to get out of this one with Duncan safe.*

"I wanted to apologize."

"Apologize?" Melanie stopped dead in the middle of the sidewalk.

Joe swung around to face her. "I figure you must think I'm some kind of weird stalker."

"A *weird* stalker?" Melanie stared at him. This was not what she expected. This was good. "Is there some other kind?"

"After what happened at your house and then Peggy telling you I asked so many questions, you probably think I fit right in with the little-odd trio."

The panic began to exit Melanie's system. She wasn't in trouble. She hadn't blown it. He thought *he'd* blown it. What kind of traveling salesman would go next door and ask all kinds of questions about his previous customer? No kind. She gave a hiccup of relief. She'd been so busy trying to figure out a way to dig herself out of whatever hole he'd found to bury her in that it never occurred to her he might have dug himself one.

"Yes." She nodded grimly. "I was terribly concerned. One has to be so careful."

"I can explain."

She folded her arms across her chest in a this-better-be-good stance, ready to enjoy watching him sweat, still barely able to believe *she* wasn't the one left shoveling her way out.

"Since telling people about how my wife left me is so tough, I had this...joke with myself that I'd kiss the first person who didn't laugh." He grinned sheepishly.

Melanie's eyelids shot wide. He kissed her for a *joke?* Her world had been turned upside down for a little private ha-ha?

Her lids rebounded into condemning slits. Not funny. "So why all the questions about me?"

He swallowed uncomfortably and examined the foliage overhead for a few seconds, then brought his eyes abruptly to hers, almost making her jump back. "I liked kissing you, Melanie."

"Oh." The word came out on a soft breath of air. Melanie clamped her lips shut, trying to recapture the make-my-day attitude she had down pat only a second ago. She was in trouble, after all.

"I wanted to know more about you. You're...different from the women I know."

"No tightrope potential?" She spoke gruffly to keep her insides from going any gooeyer than they already were.

He winced, then reached out and laid a gentle finger on her cheek. "I was trying to get to know you better."

Right. Checking up on her story, more like it. She moved back from his finger. "Find out everything you needed?"

"No." He took a step closer and planted his hands on his hips, pushing back his jacket so his shoulders and chest grew broader, more imposing. He was so close she could see the black flecks of stubble shading his chin gray, see the intricate patterns in the blue of his eyes, practically feel the heat of his body through his cotton shirt. "I want to know one more thing."

"Shoot," she mumbled. Only it sounded more as if she said a different word, one polite people didn't. It sounded like she said that word because she was completely flustered by this man standing so close to her. It sounded like she had no idea what to do with the silly hope he'd kiss her again and again, right here, until she fainted dead away on the hot sidewalk.

"I know you told me to get lost...and you had every right to. But it seemed to me, at first anyway, that you...liked kissing me as much as I liked kissing you." The vulnerability in his eyes and the hesitant flow of his voice kept the words from sounding as if he'd lifted them from a lounge-lizard instruction manual. "Is that true, Melanie? Or am I crazy?"

"You're...crazy," she said. But she said it breathlessly, with a slight hitch in the middle of the phrase, staring at him like a helpless puppy. So it didn't come out at all convincing. In fact, she might as well have said, *Kissing you was the most amazing thing that has happened to me since I was a multicelled zygote.*

She had to stop this. Any second she'd start tittering and batting her eyelashes. Next, she'd bake him cookies. Just one batch to start, maybe oatmeal or chocolate chip. Then it would be brownies—cream cheese brownies, butterscotch brownies, then entire brownie cakes and brownie pies à la mode with hot fudge. Next, she'd pick up a pair of his socks off the floor. Not much, just one pair. But then it would be two pairs. Three. Then shirts. Pants. Soon she'd be doing his entire laundry, cooking his meals, rubbing his feet, fetching him the newspaper from the end of the driveway in the dead of winter, with her teeth.

"You're crazy." She tried again, but this time was worse, because she could only whisper the words, and they practically sounded like *I love you, take me now.*

"I think you're right." He moved his head toward her and kissed her again. Only this time he kissed her more possessively, more passionately—probably because she'd just about launched herself at him, even while thinking she was trying to keep him at bay.

She threw herself into the kiss, pressing close to him for the second time that day, feeling the electricity zap through her body even more powerfully than before. In spite of the complicated mess she was in, in spite of the danger of slipping up with her brain turned to cooked wheat berries, in spite of any possible risk to Duncan, something entirely uncharacteristic was making her say, What the hell.

Sooner or later she'd wake up from this dream and return to who Melanie really was. And who Melanie really was never got the chance to do anything even remotely this fabulous. So she might as well indulge this stranger—the stranger she was right now to herself and the stranger she was kissing as if she hadn't been kissed in centuries and never would be again.

He raised his head and looked at her, his expression slightly awed, then wary. "Are you going to push me away again?"

"I should," she whispered.

"Why?"

"This is nuts."

"Why?"

"I barely know you. I don't even—"

"Shh." He stroked her hair. "Don't talk."

"Why?" She blinked at him, not quite yet willing to move away.

"Because, Melanie, I'm going to kiss you again." He cupped her head between his large, warm hands and caressed her cheeks with his thumbs, sending new thrills zinging through her. "I'm going to kiss you until you do know me well enough—and then I'm going to stand here, with you still in my arms, and kiss you some more."

6

I'M GOING TO KISS YOU until you do know me well enough....

Joe laughed out loud and pounded the steering wheel. He loosened his tie, rolled down the windows and cranked up the car stereo so the hammering, generic beat of whatever nauseating pop song was on would announce to Birchfield, Wisconsin, that he, Joe Jantzen, was *here*.

Damn, he'd been good. *I liked kissing you, Melanie*. He laughed again, the human equivalent of whatever makes roosters strut around the chicken yard racing through his body.

He'd been backed into a corner. Nearly revealed, when Peggy of the backward wig blabbed that he'd been asking questions, and Melanie's gorgeous eyes turned troubled and hunted. Immediately, he realized he'd scared her with his idiotic lack of control kissing her and his uncharacteristically careless assumption that the dimwits next door wouldn't question his interest in her.

So what to do? He snapped his fingers. Of course! What any brilliant private investigator would do. Play into the deception. Turn it to his advantage. Take the half-revealed truth and weave it into another part of the lie.

I wanted to know more about you. Sheer genius. She bought it, too. He could tell by the way her eyes had gone from hard and wary to soft and yielding. Her voice had turned breathless, and her body sagged toward him as if she could no more control her desire to be closer than stop the world spinning.

Wind tumbled into the car and ruffled his hair, rattled the papers strewn over the back seat. He pumped his fist in the air. What a rush! To use lines like that and have her melt, like he was some kind of Adonis. Like he reeled in whatever woman he wanted, whenever the urge hit. Jantzen. Joe Jantzen, double-o-seven. Vodka martini, shaken, not stirred.

She'd even given him just the line he'd wanted. "You're crazy." And he'd been able to say, "You're right," and kiss her again. And again. Ha! That time he'd really gotten to her. She'd been wild for him, her mouth hungry and sweet, her hips pressed to him without shame or restraint.

He shifted, his body remembering in the traditional male fashion. Wild? She'd been on fire. For Sensible Joe Jantzen.

He accelerated around a corner so his tires would screech and infuriate the good citizens of Birchfield. He even knew the actual second he had her, when her swallowing grew convulsive, her eyes both frightened and yearning, when she could barely get words out through her dismay, her helpless desire. *I don't even know you.*

Then he'd kissed her again, and whatever kissing

her had been like before paled in comparison to this meeting of their lips and bodies and, it almost seemed, their minds. The emotional power had elated and shaken him, left him triumphant and humble, pumped up and quaking.

Joe tried to laugh again, but the laugh came out strangled and unconvincing. He slowed to turn another corner, punched off the whiny crooning on the stereo. A leaf blew in the window and smacked his cheek. He rolled up the glass, punched the airconditioning button and drove in silence.

He'd done it, all right. Saved his skin and the investigation, convinced Melanie he was on the up-and-up and in the process, with lines worthy of Mr. Universe, recaptured more masculinity than Marla had ever guessed was there. Three for three. Unanimous victory.

There was only one little problem.

He pulled into the motel parking lot, slammed the car door, went into his room, sat on his bed and let that little problem hit him between the eyes.

He'd been telling her the truth the whole time.

Joe jumped up and began to pace the room. No. No. He wasn't doing this again. No way. He knew what these feelings led to. Infatuation. Love. Marriage. Then that peculiar but well-documented aspect of female evolution—the beautiful, passionate woman who made you feel on top of the world turned into a *wife,* whose only mission was to grind you under her heel until licking dust became a privilege.

She began the change right at the altar. Right after the priest pronounced you husband and wife. Her soft, loving eyes hardened into blame and criticism. Her tongue lengthened and strengthened for a lifetime of lashing. The mother part of her body prepared for conception and birth, while the wife part of her brain prepared to make sure you felt inadequate and humbled, grateful she was around, because who the hell else would put up with you?

I do became *you don't*. You don't do this, you don't do that, this is wrong, that is worse.

She entered your house and rearranged. First the furniture, then your life, your dreams, and if she'd really done her job well, your very soul. No matter how hard you tried, how much you changed, it was never enough. You could never be the man she was so sure you'd promised to be.

Joe clenched his fists. He knew. He'd lived it. No matter how far the earth moved when he kissed Melanie, he wasn't going there again. Not in a million years.

His cell phone rang. He punched it on, nearly pushing the button through the unit in the process.

"It's Lou. You find Duncan yet?"

"No." Joe forced himself to uncoil, rolling his shoulders and head in a therapeutic circle. "But he's somewhere in Birchfield, I'm sure. Melanie didn't pan out, but—"

"Melanie... Is she the one who hates men?"

"Yeah, Lou, that's her." Joe rolled his eyes. If Melanie hated men and kissed like that, he'd probably be charred to a cinder if she decided to like them.

"By the way, I found my lovely *wife*." Lou's voice broke bitterly. "One of her friends told me she's on a damn *cruise*. Leaves me, ditches our kid, all for some pleasure trip. She's probably cheating on me, too, Joe. Can you effing believe that? I'm her *husband*, for cryin' out loud. She can't just—"

"Uh, Lou?" Joe suppressed a weary groan. "Are we forgetting Gina D-cup?"

"Hey! I never touched her, I told you. It was all innocent. I'm a good husband...I'm an outstanding father."

"I know you are, Lou. I wouldn't be doing this for you if I thought you weren't." Joe sank into one of the room's peach velour chairs. "I'm sure Paige isn't cheating either, just off pouting. She'll come back when her cruise is over, I'll find Duncan soon and you'll all be together. I'm sure he's safe. This town is like a perky Packers theme park."

"Never get married, man, I'm telling you." Lou sniffed loudly. "It's not worth it. Nothing but a royal pain in the horse's rear."

Joe pulled off his tie and chucked it on the bed. If he ever needed extra confirmation he should forget pursuing Melanie, Lou and Paige had just provided it. The sacred union of man and woman, in all its many-splendored rot.

He clenched his jaw, covering memories of Melanie's kisses with the image of Marla's back going out the door. "Don't worry, Lou. I've been there. I remember."

"COME HERE, LOVE." Melanie teetered on the arm of her sofa, trying to persuade another spider that plastic container real estate was big in this year's webspinner market. "Into the cup, little one."

"Pi! Pi!" Duncan shrieked.

"Yes! Spider." She strained the cup closer, hand trembling. Body trembling. In fact even her brain was trembling. Fifteen minutes after Joe Jantzen finally stopped kissing her and left with the vague promise, "See you soon," she still lacked the ability to function normally.

This was nuts. This couldn't be happening. Not after she'd spent so many years convinced of her immunity to this type of schoolgirl infatuation. Convinced and proud of the fact. Parades of other women could simper and preen for the male of the species. *They* could all suffer the betrayal their hormones invariably let them in for when the attentive, courteous men in their lives became undershirt-wearing, beer-guzzling, chip-crunching television worshipers who eventually left them for their best friends' daughters.

She had something infinitely more steady and stable to depend on. Herself.

Melanie stretched her body to its limit, coaxed the spider into the container and snapped on the lid. She just needed a nice quiet evening to get over whatever these strange jitters were and remind herself what really counted in life. Friends, family, her career, her house, her travels...

She frowned. Since when did the list of what she treasured make her sound like president of the Drying Paint Watchers Club? She really, really needed some rest. The tension of the last two days had made her feel like the cork in a shaken champagne bottle. If she didn't get some relief soon, she'd lose it. Like that time Jon Barber, the love of her life in college, had *finally* asked her out—three days into exam week and the day before her thesis was due. At the end of the date when he tried to kiss her, out of nowhere she'd become hysterical with laughter and had to have water dumped over her head before she could stop.

She'd rather not go through that again.

Halfway to the back door to liberate her arachnid prisoner, the phone rang.

"Melanie, it's Paige." Her voice crackled faintly.

"I can barely hear you. Where are you calling from?"

"Uh...Miami."

"Can you give me a number so I—"

"How's Duncan? I miss him terribly."

"He's fine. Do you want to talk to—"

"Did that detective show up?"

"Yes. But he won't get Duncan, I promise."

"Oh, Melanie, thank—" A huge roaring blast drowned the rest of her sentence. "I gotta go. Thanks for taking care of Duncan. I'll be back in a few days."

"Paige, what the *hell* is... Paige? Paige?" Melanie punched off the phone in disgust. That furious elephant noise again, and then Paige disappearing. Like she was being summoned by some slave driver's horn. Melanie wrinkled her brow. Horn? It did sound like a horn. But what—

The doorbell rang. Duncan bounced up and down, waving his chubby arm. "Beow, beow."

"Yes, bell." Melanie sighed and opened the door

to Richard, Dot and Peggy, beaming at her as if they'd just saved the planet from destruction.

"Greetings, partner in crime." Richard strode in, pumped Melanie's hand and slapped her on the back, nearly sending the spider into orbit. "We didn't really chat when you got back from being with your detective. You seemed a little shaky. All went well, I trust?"

Melanie grinned weakly. "You might say that."

"Well, *we* were magnificent when he tried to sell us his toys. Dot couldn't hear a thing he said and Peggy made one of the most charming idiots I've ever had the pleasure to know."

"Why, thank you, Richard." Peggy beamed. "I thought your bad acting tour de force worthy of an Oscar."

"Hear, hear." Dot gave her husband's shoulder an affectionate punch. "Stupendously stupid, all of us. We fooled him completely, Melanie. He had no idea which end was up."

"That's wonderful, really." She smiled at her friends and took a suggestive step toward the door. Her gratitude wasn't quite as boundless as her need to be alone. "Thank you all again for your—"

"But I was so-o-o sorry to hear of your husband's death." Peggy's huge blue eyes blinked mournfully. "If we had known before…"

"I know, I know. It's a long story." Melanie groaned silently. This charade had become more of a strain than she'd ever have thought possible. Bad enough the detective Lou hired was the old millennium's sexiest man alive. But trying to get all of

Birchfield to lie for her had just about worn her out.

"But you got around it somehow?"

Richard chuckled his satisfaction and puffed on his imaginary pipe. "By gads, apparently so, apparently so."

"Anything for this little one." Peggy squatted beside Duncan, who solemnly offered her one of Suzie Cute's socks.

"I think we've earned a breather." Melanie glanced at her watch, hoping they'd take the hint and leave. Her body absolutely craved rest, and she still had some serious emotion sorting to do. "I've got to get Duncan ready for dinner and bed."

"Can we help?" Dot put a friendly hand on her shoulder.

"No, no, thanks." She moved them to the door. "I'll just—"

The phone rang again. She shooed the spider out, dragged herself over to the loathsome instrument and picked it up.

"Ms. Brooks, it's Kevin."

Melanie's body tightened at the alarm in his voice. "What is it? What's happened?"

"That detective guy, Joe."

"What, what?"

"I kind of...bumped into him at Anderson's restaurant. Talking to Mrs. Anderson."

"Oh, no." Melanie's heart rocketed downward. She slumped into a chair. Mrs. Anderson could sweep the world gossip championships. They'd been naive even to hope they could keep Duncan hidden from a professional detective. "She blew it, didn't she."

"Nope." Kevin gave a smug laugh.

"You're kidding!" Melanie jumped up, hope sending her fatigue packing. "How is that possible?"

"Joe started asking questions about your husband when he was paying at the register. So I stood behind him where she could see me and kept shaking my head and pointing at him. She looked kinda surprised, then she nods, not even looking at me. Then she tells Joe she won't ever talk about your husband 'cause he was supposed to marry *her* daughter, not you. Then she goes on and on about how Lalli is still single, like she does all the time. Then Mr. Harmon comes in and I start talking to Joe, and that's it. Joe never gets to ask about Duncan."

"I can't believe it. You saved the day." Melanie erupted in relieved laughter. Kevin felt proud of himself, and deserved to. She couldn't remember hearing that many consecutive sentences out of him in quite a while. Plus, he obviously hadn't been able to keep himself from following Joe even after she suggested he wait. The kid was hooked. "I owe you, Kevin. That's fabulous."

"Well, not quite. He's going over to see Ms. Decker next. Says he hears she has a little boy just the right age for his stupid toys. I tried calling to warn her, but the line's busy. I think her oldest kid is an Internet junkie."

Melanie whacked her fist to her forehead. Wendy Decker. Paige and Melanie's man-eating friend from grade school. Melanie had told her about Barbara when Joe first came to town, but hadn't thought to update her on the Michael-Andrew husband situation.

With three kids and a husband always traveling, Wendy would be more than willing to chat extensively with Joe. Melanie gritted her teeth. If not more. *Oh, man.* Trouble.

"You did great, Kevin. Really great. When is he going to see her?" Melanie made a desperate face at the ceiling, dreading the answer she knew was coming.

"Right now."

INTERESTING. Joe slid behind the wheel of his car and consulted the map of Birchfield the extremely talkative Mrs. Anderson had given him, with Wendy Decker's address circled. Very interesting. Downright fascinating, in fact.

He put the car in gear and started down Main Street toward Donald Avenue. Mrs. Anderson had lived here her entire fifty-six years. Mrs. Anderson seemed to know everything about everybody. But whether Kevin had been sending her signals or she was in on some plot, she fit the same mold as everyone else in Birchfield. Nobody seemed comfortable talking to him about Melanie. Something that went beyond small town suspicion or, in the case of Dot, Richard and Peggy, mental deterioration. He sensed tension, and both an eagerness to confide in him and a determination to hold back.

Something didn't smell right, and it wasn't the fast food wrappers in his passenger seat. Whatever it was, he'd bet it would lead him to Duncan. Soon.

He pulled into Ms. Decker's driveway, adjusted his tie and got out of the car. The soft summer evening air made him inhale and stretch his shoulders. Nice night. The smell and the silence reminded him of his grandparents' home in western Massachusetts. For one crazy minute he was homesick for the small-town upbringing he never had.

He walked up to the brick Colonial, stepping over toys scattered across the walk. At the front door, he reached into his pocket and checked out the blurry snapshot of Duncan smiling from the seat of a plastic airplane. What must it be like to have a little replica of yourself in the world? Someone you could teach about what it means to be human?

An unfamiliar longing prodded his heart. He tightened his lips. Thank God he and Marla never found out. They'd have to start a fund for therapy instead of college. He stuffed the picture into his pocket and rang the bell.

A petite attractive blonde peeped around the door. "Yes?"

"Evening, ma'am. Joe Jantzen, Baby Bliss toys. I saw the assortment of lawn ornaments you have out here and wondered if you'd be interested in some high-quality children's products."

"Oh, well..." She bit her lip and studied him. "I'm not sure."

"Our products are guaranteed for the life of the toy. You break it, we replace it." He sent her his best double-o-seven smile, afraid she'd growl and slam the door in his face.

"Okay." She smiled shyly and opened the door, revealing a stunning figure clad in a low-cut skintight outfit that apparently contained hydraulic lifts for her breasts. "My husband's out of town. You can understand me being cautious."

"Of course, ma'am." He followed her through the portrait-laden hall and into a luxurious living room, a little bewildered by her reaction. Since when did dressing in homage to your cleavage, announcing your husband's absence and inviting a strange man into your home count as being cautious?

"So, Mr.—"

"Call me Joe."

"Call *me* Wendy." She sat on the sofa, arranged shapely legging-clad legs and swept her hand caressingly over the cushion beside her. "Sit here…and show me what you've got, Joe."

Joe pulled at his tie. Was she— Nah. A hot number like her? Impossible. He sat next to her and put his case on the coffee table. "What are the ages of your kids, ma'am?"

"Eight, four and two." She pushed herself closer to the table, and closer to him in the process. Her perfume clouded around him. Her breasts seemed ready to jump out and play. She tipped her head and peeked at him coyly. "All boys. My husband's away practically all the time."

"Yes, ma'am." Joe pulled his tie again. Holy moly. He had to be imagining this. "Is your two-year-old around? We at Baby Bliss like to see our products in direct interaction with the—"

"I think he's watching TV. *Landon! Come see Mommy!*"

Joe jumped, resisting the urge to cover his ears. She

probably won the annual Birchfield cow-calling competition every year.

Footsteps sounded running along the hallway. A curious two-year-old poked his head around the doorjamb. Joe's heart sank. Blond. Like his mom. Duncan was dark.

Which meant Paige's other friend, Alison, must have Duncan. Which meant Joe would have to extract his body from this uncomfortable proximity to Ms. Decker's and get the hell out of here.

"Hello, Landon." He smiled at the child's sullen expression and removed his thigh from contact with Wendy's. "Would you like to come see—"

A battery of knocks at the front door was followed by the sound of it being shoved open. Joe braced himself, expecting the man of the house to burst in with a shotgun and spill detective guts all over the carpet.

Instead, in a rush of night-scented air, Ms. Melanie Brooks swept into the room.

"I tried calling, but Hayden must be online, so I—" She stopped short and made a not-very-good attempt at pretending to be surprised to see him. "Oh, Mr. Jantzen."

Joe's every nerve ending prickled with instinct, complicated by a healthy dose of sexual energy. *She knew he'd be here.* How? Mrs. Anderson? Kevin? That other guy in Anderson's restaurant? Why would they tell her—

The truth smacked him in the head like it had been hurled by a professional discus thrower. *Melanie knew his real reason for being in Birchfield.* How long had she known? From the very beginning, when she grilled him about his former career and his love for Mark Twain?

Of course.

Man, she'd played him well. Beaten him at his own game time and time again. If he wasn't so full of admiration, he'd be completely humiliated.

Melanie glanced at Wendy's mammarial display, then at Ms. Decker's thigh, which had followed his toward his end of the sofa. Her eyes turned frosty. "Well. Looks like you've come to the right house for what you're selling."

Joe ignored the stab of pleasure at her jealousy. His decision had been made where matters concerned Melanie Brooks. He stood and took a step toward her, trying to intimidate the hell out of her with his best talk-or-I-pump-you-full-of-lead stare. "What an amazing coincidence to bump into you here."

"Indeed." She narrowed her eyes but didn't quite hide a flash of alarm. "I didn't mean to interrupt. I'm sure you were making excellent progress."

"Would you like some coffee?" Wendy glanced between them, clearly unable to decipher the tension. "I have decaf already made in the kitchen."

"Sure." Melanie whirled toward her. "I'll help you."

So she could feed Wendy some party line? *I don't think so.* Joe picked up his case. "Why don't I bring my things and we can *all* go to the kitchen."

Wendy shrugged, scooped up Landon and smiled. "Whatever you say, Joe."

She led the way, depositing Landon in the TV room to watch with two vacant-eyed, slack-jawed siblings.

"Pokémon. They're addicted. Always telling me something about Charzard or Jigglypuff."

Jigglypuff? "How difficult that must be, ma'am." Joe grinned sweetly at Melanie, who sent him a low-browed thundercloud glare in response. He followed the two women into the kitchen, trying to keep his eyes off Melanie's indignantly swaying backside.

Paige must have found out he was coming to Birchfield and warned Melanie. All her fancy footwork must be an attempt to keep Duncan away from him. Which would explain why people seemed ill at ease talking about her and her strangely hard-to-pin down past. Most people were uncomfortable lying, even if they thought the lies justified.

But if Melanie's current state of near panic was anything to go by, Joe had found in Wendy a citizen of Birchfield unsullied by prior coaching.

"So!" He settled himself onto a stool and folded his hands on the counter. Now to figure out what was at the bottom of all this and where Melanie had hidden Duncan. It had something to do with her husband—the block everyone kept stumbling over. He had no idea what, but he had to lead the conversation there before Wendy tuned in to Melanie's danger signals. "Have you known each other long?"

"All our lives." Wendy beamed at Melanie. "Kindergarten up to college—she went on, I didn't."

"You knew Melanie's husband, I take it?"

Wendy's eyes opened wide, but not as wide as the pleading ones belonging to Melanie. "Y-yes. Her...husband. Of course I did. Yes."

"Joe, I'd...rather we didn't talk about him right now." Melanie shook her head meaningfully at him.

Of course not. He grinned at Melanie, who turned an angry pink that made her brilliant, sexy eyes blaze out of her face and forced him to beat back some seriously primal urges. Judging from the fact that Wendy had been broadsided by the mention of a husband for her lifelong friend, Joe could finally conclude that Michael-Andrew was a fake.

"Why not talk about him?" He raised his eyebrows, prepared to enjoy himself. "The guy's dead. What do you think of what he did to Melanie, Wendy?"

"Uh." Wendy darted several glances at her friend. "I...can't believe she told you about that."

Joe took a slow swallow of coffee, smug satisfaction oozing out of every pore. "I was surprised, too, Wendy, because—"

"Joe." Melanie's quiet voice stopped him. "This is awkward for us."

No kidding. He turned toward her, ready to claim his prize. At long last—confession. "I can certainly—"

"Because Wendy was one of the women Michael had an affair with."

Joe's stomach stopped processing his coffee. *Oh, no. Oh, man. He'd done it now.* How could he read people in this town so consistently wrong? Had he lost his touch completely? This case had him going in circles like an amateur.

He looked to Wendy for confirmation, eyes narrowing when he saw the shock on her face. Shock that

Melanie had mentioned it? Or shock because it never happened?

"Right. Right! An affair. Of course we did." Wendy got a faraway look in her eye and clutched her cup to her considerable assets. "I miss him. We both do, don't we, honey? He was so thoughtful, so...giving."

"Wendy." Melanie's voice implied she had a clear vision of Wendy's imminent demise.

Joe stared at Wendy speculatively. Lucky for him the woman went to the Professional Football Players School of Acting.

"I miss his laugh, his smile, his...expertise." Wendy sighed languorously and flicked a seductive glance at Joe. "We were so—"

"*Wendy.*" Melanie made a cutting motion across her throat.

Joe hid his smirk, no longer buying it. He glanced admiringly at Melanie. She was certainly a shrewd one, hanging tough in some pretty tricky situations. This time, however, he had her. The husband was definitely out. But why fake him in the first place—he could see no connection to Duncan. Was she worried what Joe would think of her having an illegitimate daughter? He couldn't imagine why she'd care. But maybe she preferred a tale of a marriage gone wrong to a story of the love 'em and leave 'em type? A husband over an accidental pregnancy?

Possible. More likely something else was going on here. If the husband never existed, then...

Joe stiffened. Maybe Barbara wasn't her daughter. But how would that tie in to Duncan's disappearance?

His brain sped up as possibilities tumbled through it. Maybe it didn't. Maybe Melanie was protecting Barbara for some other reason and didn't know anything about Duncan, after all. Maybe Joe had stumbled onto something else that needed investigating. Illegal adoption? Could easily be the case. Maybe he should steer the conversation that way and see if Wendy's overstimulated hormones could help him out again.

"Who's baby-sitting your daughter tonight, Melanie?" He raised his eyebrows, watching carefully for any reaction out of the ordinary.

Wendy's eyes shot open. She gasped. Clapped her hand to her mouth.

"Peggy's watching her." Melanie kept her gaze firmly fixed on Wendy.

Wendy doesn't know about Barbara. A slow smile spread across Joe's face. The familiar joy of victory close at hand burned through him. He'd been a complete fool. Wendy knew nothing of Barbara because Barbara wasn't Melanie's daughter. Barbara wasn't a *daughter* at all. Any second, Wendy would say it and clinch the whole thing. *Who's Barbara?*

"I can't believe I forgot." Wendy took her hand off her mouth and reached to the cabinet over her head. "Hayden and I baked some cookies today and I set some aside for Barbara. They're her favorite—oatmeal chocolate chip."

Joe's jaw dropped. Damn. Damn. Damn. *Damn.* She even knew the child's name. No way could Melanie have communicated that information over the counter without him being aware of it. So Barbara wasn't Duncan? Then why Melanie's apprehension?

Why the fake husband? Joe was back where he started. Except that Melanie obviously knew Lou had sent him. So he could lose this damn suit and get some real answers to direct questions. He loosened his tie and stood. As soon as he could get Ms. Melanie Brooks outside.

"Thanks, Wendy." Melanie accepted the plate of cookies with a strained smile. "That was awfully nice of you. Barbara loves your cookies."

Joe gulped his coffee and plunked the mug on the counter. "So, Wendy. Would you be interested in any of these toys? I don't want to intrude for too long—and I have other visits to make tonight."

"Oh, you're not intruding." Wendy smiled—a long, slow, sweet smile. "It's nice to have a man in the house."

"Wendy, you have three boys." Melanie rolled her eyes. "You need more Y chromosomes than that?"

"Boys don't count." She leaned across the counter toward Joe. "It's tough to be alone so much. I crave *adult* company."

"Gee, Wendy, *I'm* here."

Joe looked at Melanie warily. If she were a train she'd be giving off enough steam to curl Wendy's dyed hair.

"You're sweet." Wendy sent Melanie a smile that could cause serious frostbite. "But I don't want to keep you from your *daughter*."

"She's in good hands, *thanks*."

Joe sighed and started to unpack his case. What the hell must the men of Birchfield be like if *he*, Joe Jantzen, inspired a catfight? Maybe they were all too busy in their cheesehead hats, eating bratwurst and watching Packer games taped last season to pay attention to women. Whatever the reason, he wasn't as delighted as he should be. Ms. Brooks had spoiled the Wendys of the world for him. In fact, if he were being honest, she'd probably spoiled most of the women on the planet. And since he had excellent reasons for staying away from her, now would probably be a good time to consider the priesthood.

Wendy came around the counter and pressed herself close. Melanie came around the other side and hovered furiously. Joe held up the pull frog and pasted on his most earnest salesman smile.

It was going to be a very long evening.

7

MELANIE shot her car into the garage, stopped just before she went through the back wall and yanked up the parking brake. This had been the longest day of her life. She pushed out of the car and slammed the door behind her. But instead of being ready to crawl into bed, she had a hankering to go down to J.C.'s Bar and pick a fight with Chuck Benton, Birchfield's ex-professional boxer.

Joe Jantzen, private investigator and lying, sneaking, no-good, rotten...potted meat product. How dare he kiss her, then cozy up to Wendy Decker a few hours later? How dare he mix up her hormonal structure, alter her view of the world order, then show all too clearly he'd only been after information? As soon as she convinced him Duncan wasn't with her, he'd turned his manly charm on the next suspect.

Her shoes pounded an angry rhythm on the pavement. If he'd been sitting any closer to Wendy when Melanie walked in, he would have achieved human fusion. Of course Wendy hadn't exactly helped matters by practically wearing a sign that said, Married Only in the Legal Sense. Nor had she helped matters by employing the Melodramatic Society method of lying. The Birchfield elementary school kids could act rings around her.

A car pulled up to the end of her driveway. Melanie stopped in her tracks, then whirled and bolted for her front door. Joe. He'd followed her home after she wouldn't talk to him when they left Wendy WonderBra's house.

Body trembling, she reached the door and yanked at the handle. *Damn.* Peggy had locked it. She jammed her key into the dead bolt, every nerve ending registering his approach. *Turn, key...turn...*

Too late.

She peered over her shoulder to find herself face to face with Detective Jantzen, his breath coming hard, eyes blazing.

"What the hell are you running away from?"

"You." She whirled and struggled furiously with the key. *Work, damn you.*

Strong hands closed over her shoulders and turned her. "Mind telling me why?"

"Let go." She put her arms between his, elbows together, and chopped outward to free herself, the way they did in the movies. Only his arms barely budged. His hands clamped down harder. Time for a new tack. "One scream and half the town comes to my rescue."

"Who, Peggy? Richard?" He laughed scornfully. "What'll they do, *idiot* me to death?"

"Let go!" She folded her arms across her chest, leaned as far away as his grip would let her and fixed him with a killer glare, trying not to notice how incredibly sexy he looked with his tie loose, collar unbuttoned, hair disheveled and blue eyes snapping anger. "I said—"

"Okay."

He released her so abruptly she reeled back, appalled to find herself a little disappointed at the loss of contact. Great. Now she could add submissive masochism to her list of Joe-inspired neuroses.

"I'd like some answers to a few questions, Ms. Brooks." He put his hands on his hips in that intimidating cop pose. "And may I suggest a little honesty for a change?"

"Oh! I forgot! You're the great and powerful Keeper of Truth." She turned to her door. "Blow it out your...pull frog, Joe. I don't have a thing to say to you."

He pressed himself close behind her, trapping her against the door with his hard, male body. Melanie inhaled enough oxygen to inflate her like a parade float. Man, he turned her on. After years of lukewarm romantic encounters, she responded to Joe Jantzen as if she were born to be his love slave.

He turned his head so his mouth hovered near her neck, exposed by her scooped T-shirt. "Where's Duncan?" he whispered.

Melanie crossed her eyes and prayed hard to the gods of sexual forbearance to quiet this crazy ant farm of hormonal activity. "Dunc—" She cleared her throat. "Duncan who?"

"Enough. Paige warned you about me. Where's Duncan?"

His whisper barely sounded. His breath caressed

her neck, sent shivers down her back that set her body on fire. "I have no idea what you mean."

"Come on, Melanie." His lips touched her skin. His words sounded like a sexual invitation. "It's over."

Melanie opened her mouth and released a word her mother probably heard halfway across the country and was calling right now to make her wash her mouth out with soap. *Damn.* Damn him. Damn her. Damn Wendy and her...Jigglypuffs.

She took a deep breath and wiggled around to face him, jamming her arm up so she could point in his face. "You will never get him. In fact you will never get anything from me again. Especially using that sleazy seduction thing."

His face froze, then registered a flash of mortification before he froze it again—the same look he'd worn when she pushed him away after kissing her the first time.

He stepped back, the light gone from his eyes, the masculine confidence gone from his posture. Melanie gaped at him. How could she possibly have hurt him that badly? A professional? He looked as if he'd taken a personal blow to his manhood, not a slam on his detecting technique.

"Joe." She couldn't help reaching out. She hadn't meant to emasculate him. "Duncan's safe. He's... He's with Paige's friend Alison. On vacation in...Istanbul." *Istanbul? For crying out loud, Melanie.*

He gave a weary smile. "In a word, Istan-*bull*."

She stared at him in the twilight, unable to give

him what he wanted. She'd promised Paige that Joe wouldn't get Duncan—it wasn't up to her to decide if Lou could have him or not. In a few days the little guy would be with his mom, and Melanie had no doubt his mom would be with his father a few days after that. No reason to get Joe involved in this.

He pushed his hands into his pockets. "I'm not leaving until you tell me where he is."

"Then you'll be out here a long time." She turned and tried the key again, without success.

He came up behind her, keeping his distance this time. "Car key, Melanie."

Melanie gave her mom another reason to wash out her mouth and selected the correct key, hands shaking. "Sorry I can't invite you in. The neighbors would talk."

She opened the door. His hands shot out on either side of her and shut it again. "Turn around."

She turned, slowly, unable to fight the feeling that something was about to happen that would affect the rest of her life. She dared a glance at him, then raised her head to meet his eyes fully. The look on his face was like nothing she'd ever seen. Hope, despair, fear, desire—and vulnerable tension excruciating enough to make her shudder.

Instinctively she knew this was Joe. The real man. Not the womanizing salesman, not the detective. Joe Jantzen who, unless every female receptor in her entire body had gone haywire, was dying to—

"I want to kiss you."

She sucked in a quick breath that was released just as quickly, along with most of her ability to stand.

"I swore I wouldn't, but..." He ran his hand across his jaw. "I want to kiss you for real. No lies. No acting. I want to know if you really want me, the way I want you, or if it was just...Istan-bull."

Melanie tried to say many things. She tried to explain that she hadn't meant to call him sleazy. She tried to say she'd never been acting when she kissed him. She tried to say she was sorry for all the lies. But all that came out was, "'S'not bull."

He laughed. The best laugh she'd ever heard come out of a man. Rich, free, happy. "Snot bull will do, Melanie."

Then he kissed her, and Melanie was completely lost.

All the kissing that had gone on before between them, which had been amazing enough to expand the entire concept of kissing, had nothing on this sensual, passionate—

The front door flew open and Peggy emerged from the house, waving her flask. "I *thought* I heard voices! Care for a drink? I was just giving some to the baby to help her sleep."

Melanie stared at the flask in horror, then pushed Joe away and hurtled past Peggy into the house as if she had a horde of demons in pursuit.

"I'm sure she's okay." Joe raced up the stairs with her, his voice a good deal less than sure.

Melanie flung herself into the spare bedroom and gasped. The crib was empty. "She's gone!"

"Melanie." Peggy's singsong voice floated up the stairs. "She's down here, in the—"

"Kitchen!" Melanie barreled downstairs, barely

registering that Joe wasn't quite as close behind her as before. She stopped short in the kitchen to see Duncan, in only a diaper, smiling broadly amid a sea of pots and pans. A bright orange stain ran from his lower lip onto his chin.

"Peggy." Melanie whirled on her friend. "What's in that stuff?"

Peggy raised her chin, the flask nowhere in evidence. "Nothing harmful. But it's a family secret."

Melanie forced herself to take a long, calming breath, except that it stuttered up and down her trachea as if she'd inhaled several Ping-Pong balls. "How much did you give him?"

Peggy opened her eyes wide and tilted her head toward the stairs where Joe's tread could be heard coming down. "I gave *her* enough to help her sleep."

"That's it." Melanie grabbed the phone. "I'm calling poison control."

Joe reached the landing and closed his hand over her wrist. "And tell them what? That your daughter drank something which is probably just fruit juice?"

"No." Peggy frowned. "Not *just* fruit juice. But it won't hurt her. I wouldn't hurt her."

"Look at Barbara." Joe put the phone in the cradle and gestured at Duncan, who stared at them, clear-eyed and smiling. "No sign of an altered state."

He walked over and crouched next to Duncan, then leaned forward and sniffed the baby's chin. "Sweet. And something orange. No booze, no arsenic. We'll watch her, but my guess is the worst thing we'll have to deal with is a toddler sugar high."

Melanie bit her lip and tried not to think how wonderful it sounded when he said *we*. Duncan grinned at her, waved both arms and burped. He did look fine. Not even remotely poisoned. Joe was probably right—she'd overreacted. "I'm sorry, Peggy. It's been a long day. I'm sure she's fine. But I would feel a lot better if you'd tell me what's in that stuff."

Peggy shook her head emphatically. "Can't say a word. Except that it's all natural ingredients from God's good earth, nothing bad for anybody—even a baby. Why, I grew up drinking—"

"Okay, Peggy, thanks." Joe took the old woman's arm and escorted her firmly to the front door.

Melanie watched in relief as he said good-night to the old woman and closed the door behind her. The thought of losing Duncan had made her feel more vulnerable than she'd ever felt in her life.

Just this once, it was nice to have someone to share the burden. That much didn't make her a disempowered oppressed female, did it?

She scooped Duncan up, held him tightly and buried her nose in his soft neck, wondering how his skin could smell so delicious all day long. The floor in the hall outside the kitchen creaked. She looked up to see Joe watching them with a hungry, yearning expression that took her so far aback she was pretty sure she'd never return. Worse, her own needy feeling jumped into the fray at the sight of him. Needy for what? She was unwilling to put it into words after she'd known him such an unbelievably short time, but it smacked of long-term sharing and intimacy, and it scared the bejeezus out of her.

Joe came into the kitchen and took Duncan from her.

"I should put her to bed...." She trailed dumbly into the living room after the cozy pair, adrenaline supply exhausted, wondering who had just replaced her brain with bologna. Joe set Duncan down in a pile of toys and pulled Melanie onto the couch.

"Melanie." He spoke quietly, reached out and stroked her hair off her forehead, expression serious. "Could you tell me why Barbara's room looks like a guest room with a crib thrown in it instead of a nursery?"

She looked into his eyes, so hopelessly sick of lying she wanted to throw up. "Well, Joe...after his father died, I...couldn't bring myself to—"

"The husband's out." Joe gestured over his shoulder like a baseball umpire.

"Out?" Melanie raised her eyebrows. *Uh-oh.*

"I've eliminated him. He never existed. Your friend Wendy convinced me."

I'll bet she did. Melanie set her jaw, trying to summon the energy to cope with whatever came at her next.

He pressed a finger to her mouth. "Remember what Twain said? 'When in doubt, tell the truth.' I won't lie to you again, Melanie. Please do the same for me."

She scrunched up her face in an agony of indecision. How much more would he swallow? Not much, from the look of him. But she couldn't let her promise to—

"Di-buh! Di-buh!" The baby's triumphant shriek

pulled Melanie's head around. She gasped. Stared in horror. *Oh, no. Oh, no.*

Duncan walked toward them, diaper held aloft in a victory salute, his gender bared for all the world to see.

Joe threw back his head and gave another wonderful shout of laughter, then pulled Melanie close for a brief, hard kiss she could barely take in.

"You are a master." He kissed her again. "I'd guessed, anyway, but you probably could have convinced me he was your daughter—in fact you probably still can, even with his...evidence hanging out."

She struggled to make her mind-turned-bologna comprehend what he was saying. "When did you figure it out?"

"I suspected at Wendy's house. But the nursery—or lack thereof—upstairs did it. Show me a mother who hasn't decorated her baby's room, and I'll show you a temporary parent."

"Bum." Duncan glared and pointed at Joe, his point falling in the vicinity of Joe's lap. "Dickwess."

Joe laughed again. "I can't say the same for you. You did the right thing, buddy. Obviously Peggy's hootch hasn't harmed you any."

He picked Duncan up and put his diaper on with only minor fumbling, then handed him to Melanie, who still sat there as if the bomb Duncan dropped had her shell-shocked. "I think this little guy should be in bed."

"Yes." She took Duncan upstairs to put him to bed, her movements slow and deliberate, as if she were afraid speed would shatter her. So the game was over. All her efforts of the past forty-eight hours finished, with only weak success. Maybe Joe would take Duncan back tomorrow; maybe he'd let her keep him. But after this week, nothing would ever be the same.

She'd put Duncan to bed. Go downstairs. Maybe Joe would kiss her again. Maybe they'd even make love. Then what? He'd leave, return to Boston. She'd stay, and start classes at the end of the summer. Everything else would be as it always was. Except her. Because even though he might be a womanizing professional liar, Joe had opened up an entire new world of feeling—scary some of it, worrisome a lot of it, but so deep, and so exciting, and so *alive*.

She kissed the baby extra long and laid him in his crib. He snuggled down with his stuffed bear and wiggled his body back and forth to settle himself. She turned out the light, half closed the door and stopped at the top of the stairs, picturing Joe in the living room.

Was he waiting for her? Or *waiting* for her?

A thrill rose through her like springtime sap in a sugar maple. She could make his wait worthwhile. The amount of romantic excitement she could expect to encounter in Birchfield after Joe left was negligible. Bob Radmer would buy her a cream puff at the Wisconsin State Fair. Colin Cairns would invite her to the Packers' season opener. Ian Rosner would take her on a brewery tour so he wouldn't have to pay for the beer....

In many ways she preferred her life that way. Peaceful. Nonthreatening. Noninvasive.

Melanie dropped her head back and closed her eyes. But a chance like this, to indulge this new sense of living life to its fullest, might not come again. And a man like Joe wouldn't feel he had to propose marriage in the morning. He wanted her. She wanted him.

Go for it.

She tiptoed into her bedroom and dug out a Victoria's Secret nightgown she bought for her birthday. She slipped into the clingy, apricot-colored sexual invitation and peeked at herself in the mirror. Her eyes peeked back from her flushed face, shining with feverish anticipation. *Hello. My name is Melanie, may I pleasure you?*

She crept halfway down the stairs to the hallway, trembling from nerves—and suppressed a giggle of excitement. *Oh, no. Not that. Not now.* She brought herself under control and sighed with relief. She could do this.

"Joe?"

"Yeah." His voice floated in from the living room.

She batted down another giggle, waited a few seconds, then tried again.

"Joe."

"Yeah?"

She frowned. The seduction stuff was not easy.

"Joe."

His footsteps sounded. He was coming. She tried to strike a sexy pose. The giggles rose more forcefully. *No. No laughing.*

When he appeared, she would arch her body suggestively, pitch her voice to a husky murmur and invite him upstairs for playtime. She would *not* crack up.

His steps sounded louder. She pressed a shaking hand to her mouth. *Here we go.*

Joe came around the corner; he stopped; his eyes shot open; his breath shot in.

Melanie arched her body suggestively, opened her mouth to emit the husky murmur...and burst out laughing.

"WHAT THE..." Joe stared at her, collapsed helplessly on the stairs in the sexiest nightgown he'd ever seen, gulping and choking on her laughter. Tears streamed out of her eyes. Above them, from the baby's room, came Duncan's wail of protest.

He stepped forward, hoisted Melanie in his arms and took her upstairs.

"Oh... Oh... Make it stop. It *hurts.*" She went off into another spasm, her body tight with hysteria.

He strode into her bedroom, chuckling from the contagious sound, dumped her on her bed and walked toward the baby's room, shaking his head at the helpless gasps still coming from behind him. He'd give her something to get serious about very soon. First he had to comfort Duncan, who probably thought Melanie was preparing to journey to the Great Beyond.

Duncan sat in his bed, holding out his teddy for inspection, his eyes bleary from fatigue. Joe touched his shoulder gently; the baby fell over onto his face and wiggled for a few seconds, then lay quiet. Joe lingered, watching him sleep. The yearning hit him again, stronger this time. Was he nuts? Babies required mothers. Mothers required marriage. Marriage required sacrifice—your time, your sanity, your manhood.

He backed away from domestic temptation, the urge to investigate the enticing change in Ms. Brooks's attitude and outfit luring him to her room. He'd keep this simple. Melanie obviously wanted sex—at least before she began her laugh track audition. Sex could be simple. No strings. No heartache. No Marla. Joe Jantzen had the chance to prove he could handle a one-night roll in the hay with the best of them.

The gales of laughter continued full force. He stood at the foot of her bed and pulled off his shirt, grinning at Melanie's helpless struggle with hysteria.

She shook her head wildly. "Oh... Oh... This isn't the...way I wanted... I was supposed to—" She convulsed into a fresh spasm.

Joe pulled out his wallet and extracted a condom, which had probably been there since the Civil War. He had no idea why a female body writhing in hilarity at the sight of him undressing turned him on so much, but with Melanie it did. He also had no idea how he'd dug up the courage to kiss her again outside her front door after she called him sleazy.

But somewhere, from the depth of his humiliation, had come determination so forceful he'd been unable to quell it. He *would* have this woman. He *would* get to the bottom of why her kisses did things to him no kisses had ever done to him before. He wouldn't let the lies and the stories interfere with what could be the best thing ever to happen to him. Even if it only lasted tonight.

He took off his pants, then his undershirt, bunched it into a ball and tossed it aside. Maybe *because* it would only last tonight.

If you were with someone only one night, they could remain forever a perfect memory, like a precious keepsake cemented in Lucite. No contempt born of familiarity. No creeping boredom, no feelings of inadequacy. For Melanie, tonight and ever after in her fantasy, he could be everything she ever wanted. The thrill of discovery without having to get to the disappointment of knowing too much.

If she ever stopped laughing.

"Joe... I'm so sorry... I... *Help me.*"

He took off his boxers and lunged, caught himself on his hands above her and lowered himself gently onto her body. She was perfect, held him perfectly. The shiny slippery-smooth fabric of her nightgown caressed his skin as he moved against her.

Her laughter died, faded away to soft hiccuping gasps. He kissed her throat, the swell of her breasts above the lacy edge of fabric.

She stretched against him, caught a long, shuddering breath and let it out. "This is much better than having water dumped on me."

He lifted his head and raised his eyebrows. High praise, indeed. "Not to brag, Melanie, but lots of women tell me that."

She smiled dreamily and pulled his head down. "That's how they got me to stop laughing last time

I did this," she whispered. "I think all the tension of the last week got to me."

"I guess." His voice came out low and husky. She was magnificent, all baby powder warmth and softness and silk underneath him. He pulled the nightgown away and down from her incredible breasts, drew his tongue slowly across them, trying to control the fierce need to possess her completely right that second. "Are you tense now?"

"Y-yes." She arched against his mouth, pushed her hands through his hair and down his back. "But only because I'm crazy to have you inside me."

Okay. That pretty much did it. He rolled off her, pulled the skimpy straps from her shoulders and worked the nightgown down the length of her body, pausing with a hiss of indrawn breath when he saw what she wasn't wearing underneath.

He pulled the gown off and drank in the sight of her. His brain turned to caveman mode. Skin. Curves. Woman. Want. Now.

No. He owed her at least another half hour of foreplay. Marla constantly complained that he hadn't spent enough time—

"Joe." His name came out pleading, nearly frantic. Melanie reached for him, opened her legs, then closed them as if her boldness embarrassed her. "What are you waiting for?"

The glimpse of ecstasy drove him over the edge. He kicked Marla out of the bedroom, put on the condom and stretched over Melanie, reaching down with his fingers to make sure she reached the same peak of pleasure he'd be heading for the minute he entered her. About twenty seconds later she sank her nails into his shoulder. "Now. *Now*."

Well, okay. He sank into her glorious heat with something like relief. She was so perfect—tight, willing, fiery, meeting and matching his strokes. He kept them slow at first, savoring the motion, savoring the woman, savoring the taste of her mouth and the sensations in his body. Then tension crept in; urgency flared. His thrusts quickened; the need to stay rational fled. His mind became selfishly full of her effect on him; his body took over the rhythm and the need to spill into her.

He clenched his teeth and waited, waiting for her, fighting instinct and his own release, until she cried out and her muscles tensed under and around him. He let go then, allowed his climax to burn through his body until it swept him away. He said her name, whispered it, buried his arms under her to gather her close, to pull their shared intimacy in so tightly it wouldn't stop; wouldn't ever stop...until he chose to let it go.

8

MELANIE STRETCHED and yawned, feeling every bit as sappy and sated as the morning-after cliché described. She turned dreamily toward her bed's other occupant and smiled. Joe still slept, dark hair even darker against the white pillowcase, his magnificent shoulders and chest bared by the rumpled sheet. Last night had been fabulous—a passionate, erotic adventure she'd treasure for the rest of her life.

Joe stirred; her smile grew tender. In sleep he lost that I've-got-to-prove-myself intensity and his features relaxed into boyish peace. Melanie's mom always said no matter how much children aged, they always looked the same sleeping. No doubt Joe's mom would recognize her darling little boy in his—

Joe emitted a loud snort, then wrinkled up his face as if he smelled something foul. His eyes half opened; he wiped his mouth and squinted at her as if he had no idea where he was.

Melanie giggled. So much for Prince Charming. Fine by her—she preferred her slippers flat and fuzzy, not high-heeled and glass. And fancy dress balls made her cranky. Better still, she didn't have a life she needed rescuing from. Last night gave her just what she wanted. Now she only had to make sure Joe left Duncan behind on his way out the door.

"G'morning." Joe pulled her to him so her head rested against his shoulder. "Sleep well?"

She shook her head. "Someone kept waking me demanding carnal pleasure."

"What a jerk." He squeezed her closer and kissed her temple. "Did you give him any?"

"Not on your life." She rolled onto her elbows. "I told him you had first dibs, but to come back tonight."

"Tonight?" His eyebrows shot up. "You get bored quickly."

"Yeah." She yawned and feigned intense *ennui*. "I go through men so fast they call me Pell Mel."

He chuckled and drew her to him, ran his hands over her body, sending new shivers across skin that had shivered for him all night long. "Well, Pell Mel, I better make the most of the moments left...a'fore the sun come up and I gots to move on across the open prairie."

She ran her hands through the hair on his chest, traced it across the wide expanse, fighting the annoying ache at the reality of him leaving so soon. She'd *counted* on him being anxious to return to the city where he belonged—to close the Lost Duncan Case with a night of ecstasy and get back to work. Kind of a James Bond thing.

One night had given her everything her life in Birchfield lacked. If he stayed more than one night, when he left she'd probably try to follow him on her knees.

She stroked her hand up his arm, across hard biceps to a powerful shoulder, remembering the warmth and excitement of being in those arms, the rapturous female thrill of learning how to drive him wild, teasing, then giving everything she promised.

"You know, Melanie," he whispered, "I'm surprised Birchfield doesn't do a booming tourist trade. I mean, the locals are so friendly, so warm and giving."

He grinned at her rolling-eyes expression and slid his hand down, making her breath hitch and making her wonder if he wouldn't mind cloning his hands and leaving them behind when he left.

"I'm thinking I might have to visit again sometime," he murmured.

"Oh," she breathed. What the heck else could she say with his fingers working magic on places she'd have thought too sore for any more magic this entire week? If this is how he'd make her feel, he could visit every day for the rest of eternity.

His fingers worked faster, made her writhe and push rhythmically with her hips. She reached for him under the sheet—smooth, hard, ready—curled her palms around him, stroked, pulled, caressed. The rhythm of their hands and fingers meshed. Their desire climbed together, straining, rising, then headed inexorably to the peak of—

"Ma-ma! Ma-ma! Dow, dow, *dow!*"

Melanie groaned and lay still. "I don't believe it."

"Just what we didn't need." Joe drew his hand up her body and sighed. "The toddler cold shower."

"Dow! Dow! Dow!"

"I'm coming!" Melanie dragged herself from the bed and sent Joe a wistful look. "Well, I almost was."

She took three steps; her feet tangled in something soft. She stooped to pick it up and tossed it on the bed. Joe's undershirt. He must have thrown it on the floor last night.

Body still throbbing from his touch, she headed for the baby's room. Then stopped. What had she just done? One night together and already she was picking up his clothes. A bad sign.

She went in and greeted Duncan, lifted him out of his crib for a morning hug, laid him on his changing table and took off his pajamas.

"Bum." Duncan pointed over her left shoulder.

Joe came up behind her, already dressed, and encircled her with his arms, making her have to work a little harder to want him to leave, undershirt notwithstanding. "The name's Joe, Duncan. Joe."

"Doh." Duncan clapped his hands, immensely pleased with himself. "Doh!"

"Anything's better than 'dick-wess.'" Melanie taped the diaper, trying not to lean back against that incredible chest, and pulled a navy cotton outfit covered with white elephants over Duncan's soft, chubby body.

"Whadya know, he owns boy clothes." Joe bent closer and kissed Melanie's neck hungrily. "I'm starving. Since I can't have you, what's for breakfast?"

Melanie's upper lip curled on its own initiative. What did he want, a menu? "Well, I hadn't really—"

"I'm thinking bacon. Eggs, over easy. Buttered toast. Hot coffee..."

Which you can order from Anderson's or make yourself. "I don't have any bacon."

"I'll go get some." He squeezed her and let go. "I confess I'm not much of a cook...."

Melanie tugged Duncan's shoelace tight. What a surprise. Next he'd ask her to wash his clothes. *I'm not much of a launderer....*

"But I can make bacon and eggs that'll knock your socks off."

She picked Duncan up and turned to him in astonishment. "Really?"

"Oh, ye of little faith." He grinned and started downstairs. "You like toast or English muffins?"

"English."

"Plain or wheat?" His voice rose from the stairwell. "Jam or honey?"

"Wheat. Honey," she yelled.

"Hey, sorry I left my clothes all over. I was a little...impatient last night. Back soon." The front door slammed.

Melanie frowned at Duncan, checking her internal functions for any urges to start baking cookies. This was bad. Very bad. A man who apologized for leaving his clothes strewn around the room and offered to cook. She could get entirely used to this. Which made the fact he'd be movin' on across the prairie a very very good thing.

Women had fallen into this trap since Org brought home the first mastodon haunch for Orga. Oh, how she'd blushed and beamed with happiness. Such thoughtfulness! Such consideration! How envious her friends would be!

Then, two years later, he's stretched out on the bearskin rug staring at cave paintings while she's hauling in the haunches herself, with three screaming cave kids in tow.

Melanie wasn't falling for it. Like peacocks, men only brought out the beautiful feathers at courting time. Once they got what they wanted—free lifetime maid, mother and prostitute service—down went the splendid feathers to reveal an ordinary, screechy bird.

She glared at Duncan. "You'll do it, too, someday, you little rat."

"Wat, wat!" he crowed, and smacked her on the shoulder.

The phone rang. Melanie hoisted Duncan to her hip and raced downstairs, making him bounce and giggle. She put the phone to her ear and ruffled his hair. She'd miss this guy when he left, in spite of his impending rathood. Not that she entirely minded getting a life back. But having Duncan around definitely softened her position on never wanting children.

"Ms. Brooks, it's Kevin. I'm at the pay phone at Bosworth's. Uh...how did things go with Ms. Decker last night?"

"It's over, Kevin." Melanie held the phone away from Duncan's groping hand. "He found out."

"You're kidding." Kevin sounded completely astonished. Poor kid. He'd miss his detecting assignment—it had obviously meant a lot to him, and done a lot *for* him. If only there were some way to channel his enthusiasm into something similar.

"You did great." Melanie gently pinned Duncan's wandering arm to his body. "I was really proud of the way you—"

"That makes no sense."

Some ancient instinct rose up and commanded Melanie to give Kevin her full attention. She put Duncan down in spite of his screech of protest. "What makes no sense?"

"If he knows, then why..."

"Why what?" Melanie clutched the phone to her ear. Something weird was going on. Something she wasn't going to like. The doorbell rang; she clenched her fists. "Why what, Kevin?"

"Why did he just tell Mr. Bosworth he's staying in Birchfield indefinitely?"

JOE TOSSED the bag of groceries into his passenger seat and waved at the car waiting politely for his spot. The driver waved back and smiled as if he thought Joe was some long-lost relative. In Boston the guy would lean on his horn, shout at Joe to hurry up already and ask what-was-he-an-idiot? Joe smiled, enjoying the civility of the moment. Obviously, more than one aspect of Birchfield had seduced him.

He eased into the driver's seat, his body protesting slightly. Last night's activities had made him feel every one of his thirty-five years. At his age he didn't think he was supposed to be able to perform at that level. But he'd put Viagra to shame. Even now, thinking about Melanie, he was ready to go again.

He pulled the car out of the space and shot it forward toward the street, impatient to get back to see her. Hold her. Watch her smile. What a fool he'd been, thinking all he wanted was a one-night stand. Who could ever get enough of Melanie Brooks, in the sack and out?

He'd never experienced passion like that. During sex, Marla always acted as if he had ten times more fun than she did, making the entire event an extended, athletic apology. Melanie had been incredible, insatiable; orgasms became secondary to the intensity of their physical sharing. Not that he minded having them, of course, even secondary ones.

But he'd finally figured out that Melanie wasn't anything like Marla. And he couldn't walk away from something this special this soon. After one night, the only thing he wanted was another. And another. And another. Until eternity stared him in the face. Joe shifted into fourth gear and roared up her street. Facing eternity with Melanie Brooks? All he could do was smile and say, bring it on!

He pulled into her driveway, grabbed the grocery bag and hightailed it up her front path. Should he ring the doorbell? Knock? Or just walk in? He tried the front door and pushed it open. Why not? He could play master of the house and see how it felt.

"Hi, honey!" he boomed in his best 1950s husband voice. "I'm bringing home the bacon. Drop your pants and I'll—"

Dot, Richard and Peggy swiveled and stared at him, blinking in surprise.

"Doh! Doh!" Duncan pointed and clapped.

"Oh, my." Peggy put a hand to her heart.

Melanie sighed. "I was just getting to the part where you were coming back."

"But this is fabulous!" Richard jumped out of his seat and nearly attacked Joe with a handshake. "How thrilling you found each other!"

Joe narrowed his eyes. Had Richard's ship finally come back from Happy Harbor?

"Hear, hear." Dot swaggered over and clapped him on the back.

Joe narrowed his eyes further. *Hear?* He raised his eyebrows at Melanie, who shrugged and gave a sickly smile.

"Would you believe miraculous recoveries?"

He shook his head and grinned, sending the depth of his admiration out to her in his eyes. "You had me going on all fronts."

Peggy gave his wrinkled clothes the once-over. "Apparently."

"Now." Dot took the groceries out of his hands and passed them to Richard, who relayed them to Melanie. "Come over here, sit down and tell us all about it."

"Uh…" Joe swallowed and sat on the couch, images of Melanie writhing naked underneath him playing through his mind. "All about what?"

"Last night. Your proposal. Her acceptance. The wedding date. Everything."

Joe twisted to look at Melanie, who appeared to have gone into shock. What the hell had she told them? Not that he minded she'd been dreaming. Hell, he'd been dreaming, too, but he'd rather actually fall in love and propose before the news made the *Birch-*

field Gazette. "There's...not exactly a wedding date yet."

"Yet?" Melanie's eyes became perfect panicked circles. Maybe she hadn't been doing that much dreaming.

"Well, there's still plenty of time, then." Dot pulled a pad and pencil out of her shirt pocket. "Now. Were you planning to live here or did you want a larger house?"

"The Placeks are selling." Richard pulled out a matching pad and a pen. "And I think the Watts house is still on the market, also Charlie Hu's place."

"Good thinking, Richard." Dot scribbled furiously. "In the meantime, Bill Stackman is leaving the Ames's apartment. Joe can stay there for appearance's sake."

Peggy came up with her flask and held it aloft. "A toast to the bride and groom."

Joe smiled weakly and glanced at Melanie to see how she was taking the news of their engagement.

She stood stock-still, clutching the bag of groceries as if it were a life preserver. Not exactly the blushing bride.

"So that's Placek, Watt and Hu." Dot brandished her pencil. "Who shall we talk to first?"

"'Whom,' dear." Richard puffed thoughtfully on his imaginary pipe.

"Of course, of course. *Whom* shall we talk to first?"

Peggy finished a swig and wiped her mouth. "Talk to Hu."

"No, dear, the objective case of the pronoun. Talk to *whom.*"

"On my list—" Richard checked his pad "—Hu's on first."

"I've got Placek." Dot tapped the pencil on her pad. "Watt's on second. Third?"

"I don't know," Joe said automatically, and cringed. Even when they were no longer trying purposefully to confuse him, the trio managed pretty effectively. "Look, I think it might be better if—"

"This soup has too many cooks," Peggy announced. "Come along, Dot and Richard. I'll take the little darling home with me for a bit." She beamed at Duncan, who sat serenely attempting to insert a block up his nose. "And no tonic this time, I promise."

Joe extracted himself from the wedding planners' couch and went to Melanie, wishing the nuptial chatter hadn't made her look quite so horrified. "Think Duncan will be okay with Peggy?"

"Oh. Yes. I'm sure he'll be fine." She turned strange, empty eyes to his. "Peggy's trustworthy. I just freaked last night."

And this morning, too, apparently. "Look, everyone seems to think—"

"I didn't tell them anything about a wedding."

"I know." He leaned forward and kissed her, then wished he hadn't when his entire body started hungering for something that wasn't bacon. A long collective sigh sounded from the living room, followed by the noises of Peggy urgently shepherding the group from the house.

Melanie called out a feeble goodbye, then looked at Joe as if she thought he was about to turn into a werewolf and trash her house. He forced a grin and caressed her cheek, trying to tamp down his panic. "Is it so terrible, thinking about being together?"

"No. Well, no. that is—"

"It's not what you want?" He asked the question lightly so she wouldn't be afraid to answer with the truth. But several functions vital to his continued health and sanity stopped while he waited for her answer. After last night he'd been so sure she wanted as much more of him as he did of her. How sickeningly ironic to have finally shaken off his fear if the woman who banished it suffered from the same misgivings.

"I want—I want..." Her eyes widened. "Oh, no."

"What is it?" He took her arms, the panic swelling, instinct preparing his heart for a serious crushing. "Sweetheart, tell me."

She looked at him with eyes full of anguish. "I want to make you breakfast."

He felt his face go incredulous. "And...that's bad?"

"I thought it was, but...now I don't know." She glanced side to side, frowning in concentration, as if she were testing for internal injuries. "It doesn't *feel* bad."

"Well...good. That's good." He nodded stupidly, fishing around for some explanation that made sense. "Making breakfast shouldn't feel bad."

"No," she said doubtfully.

He took her shoulders and turned her in the direction of the kitchen. "Let's try it out. Bacon, then eggs. If either of them becomes painful or life-threatening at any time, you let me know and I'll take over."

She grinned over her shoulder and let him propel her to the counter, where she dumped her combination bag of groceries and life preserver, and pulled out the carton of orange juice.

"Are you...really planning to stay in Birchfield?"

He gritted his teeth. Her enthusiasm wasn't exactly sweeping him away. "Would you like me to?"

"It's just that I thought when you were talking about moving on across the prairie..."

Oh, that. "I was kidding. Last night wasn't something I want to walk away from, Melanie."

"No." She shook her head. "Do you want juice? I guess I'm a little...scared."

"Of having juice?"

She didn't crack a smile. Joe started to sweat. He stood behind her as she poured from the carton, feeling as if he had less of a right to touch her now than he did the first day they met. Who or what replaced their easy intimacy with this blind-date relationship? "I'm scared, too, Melanie. It's normal to be scared. This has all happened so quickly."

He started counting the days since they'd met. One. Two. Oh, man. Microwave dating. Not his usual style at all. Did that mean this was right? Melanie was the one? Or had he just gotten horny and careless?

He put his hands to her waist as she unpacked the groceries, reassured a little when she leaned back against him. She pulled out the boxed package of English muffins he'd chosen and set them on the counter.

"I should have told you to get the muffins at the bakery department."

He took his hands away from her body. "What's wrong with these?"

"Nothing." She turned and handed him his juice, smiling brightly. "I love these. They're perfect."

He drained his juice and ran over the warning bell in his mind with a steamroller. They were talking about English muffins. He could handle being told he'd screwed up with baked goods. It didn't mean she was mutating into his ex-wife. "You want me to make the coffee?"

"No, no, I'll do it." She reached up and started rooting through her cabinets. "You know, I have a muffin mix in here somewhere—hey, and I have dried cranberries, too. I can whip up a batch of cranberry muffins in a jiffy. Or maybe I should make some—" She froze. "What am I doing?"

"Melanie." He came up close behind her and squeezed her shoulders. "Unless a meadow of green mold is growing on these English muffins I'm betting they're fine. Next time I go to the store I'll buy the bakery ones. Now, *I'll* make the coffee. Relax."

"Yes. Okay. You're right. Coffeemaker's in the top cabinet." She reached for the bacon and flipped on her radio as she walked to the stove.

Joe winced at the deejay's hearty stream of inane chatter. Why did she want to invite *him* into their morning after? Something was seriously bugging Ms. Melanie Brooks. He'd bet it was his impulsive decision to stay in Birchfield. He should have let well enough alone. Should have gotten up this morning, smiled, kissed her and walked out, like the love 'em and leave 'em cowboy she thought he was. But who the hell could leave what they had last night alone? And why hadn't last night spilled over into this morning?

"So what about your career?" She glanced at him with eyes that only told him she was not currently being consumed by adoring passion. "I mean if you stay. Will you start up another detective agency?"

"I don't think so." He measured ground coffee into the paper cone filter, wondering if he should run out the door or attack her with kisses until he rediscovered the woman he'd had in bed upstairs. "I'd burned out by the time I left Boston. Tracking deadbeat dads and taking pictures of people having affairs isn't exactly uplifting."

"I can imagine." She put strips of bacon onto a large iron griddle where they started to spit and shrink. "So what do you want to do?"

"I think I'd like to go back to being a cop." He methodically measured water and poured it into the coffee machine. Given his precarious mental state, the mundanity of the conversation was so surreal that continuing it was his only option. "That experience taught me—"

"You know—" she turned toward him, eyes finally alight "—I think Bob Toffey is retiring from the force this summer. He had a great job working with kids, educating them on safety, drugs, etc. I think you'd be great at that."

The warning bell resurrected itself. "I hadn't really—"

"In fact, he did a lot of the programs last year in conjunction with a student volunteer." She clapped her hands together, face aglow. "Kevin Ames! He'd be a natural. It would give him something important and worthwhile to do. Something he likes and could be good at. You could move into his mom's place after her boarder leaves and start planning with him. That would help him over the hump of Bill Stackman moving out. It's perfect."

Joe stared at her in horror. It was happening. It was happening already. They hadn't even made a commitment, let alone journeyed to the altar, and she was organizing his entire life. Where he'd live. Where he'd work. Who he'd work with.

He tried to shake off the panic. He was overreacting. Her idea was perfectly plausible—an understandably helpful suggestion. "I'll give it some thought. Thanks for the idea."

"How do you like your eggs?"

"Over easy."

"Bacon?"

"Crisp. I thought *I* was going to make breakfast."

"I know, but I just got going. Sit down and get comfortable. I'll serve you when it's ready—" She cringed as if she regretted something she'd said.

Joe turned on the coffee machine and sat, wondering if Marla in all her duplicity had ever bewildered him quite this much. If Melanie resented cooking for him, why insist? He tried to get in touch with his earlier romantic optimism, but all he could dial into was a little voice whispering that he might want to get the heck out of here before he got seriously hurt. Now that he'd found Duncan, he was—

"Oh, man." How could he have forgotten? "I have to call Lou and tell him I found his son so he can come and get him."

Melanie frowned. "Can you wait until I hear from Paige again?"

He stared at her. "Why? The guy's wife essentially kidnapped their kid. He's been frantic."

Melanie broke two eggs onto the griddle, concentrating on the simple task as if she were performing brain surgery. Joe's instincts kicked in. She was holding something back. "What is it, Melanie?"

"I don't want Duncan back with Lou until I hear from Paige." She turned down the heat and faced Joe, eyes serious and pleading. "She took Duncan because she suspected Lou was hurting him."

"*Hurting* him? Hurting Duncan? Lou? What kind of—" Joe got to his feet, blood and adrenaline rushing to his right fist. Only Paige wasn't around to be the recipient of what she deserved. He took a deep, enraging breath. "Listen. As far as Lou's concerned, that child wouldn't get wet crossing a river. I'd be less surprised if Lou hauled off and socked Paige for mental anguish."

"Mental anguish?" She slapped her tongs on the stove and put her hands on her hips, eyes shooting off more burning heat than the bacon. "Exactly what kind of mental anguish did she inflict by not being able to trust her husband with their child?"

"She's a manipulator. She wanted you to take

Duncan so she could go on a cruise, probably with some lover."

"A *cruise?*" Melanie's face twisted in horror. "A lover? How can you say such a thing? She was afraid for her child and she couldn't stand Lou's cheating anymore."

"He did *not* cheat on her. Lou's got a lot of integrity. All he did was have a few drinks with a friend."

"Oh, right. And can I interest you in some nice coastal property on Jupiter?"

He gestured impatiently. "The guy tried to get a little of his ego back from under Paige's boot. If it takes an innocent drink to do that, then I think he's entitled."

"Innocent, my rear."

"If I thought Lou was anything but innocent, I wouldn't be here. I've seen what cheating can do and I don't want any part of it. Paige treated him like—"

"If he'd stopped treating her like a *slave* for two seconds he would have gotten a little more of...more of what..." She turned her head toward the radio.

Billy Joel's deep voice filled the room with the song Joe had heard only a week ago. "And So It Goes."

He turned, too, and listened. The song flowed on, filling and emptying him the same way it had the last time, making him feel horrendously conflicted, as if life and love, risk and commitment were something to be grasped close, indulged, cherished forever—and avoided at all costs.

Melanie stared at the floor for a full minute, then

met his eyes a little sheepishly. "I guess maybe we're letting other people's problems tear us apart."

His mind cleared; he walked over to her, cupped her chin and tilted it. "I guess maybe I don't want us to be torn apart."

"No," she whispered. "I guess I really don't, either."

Her lips parted; her eyes closed. He brought his head down, aching for physical contact to erase the lingering fear and doubt. The song played. The kiss began.

Two phones abruptly filled the air with obnoxious electronic summonses.

Joe pulled back wistfully, touched her mouth with his fingers and dug his phone out of his pocket. Melanie smiled, gave a resigned shrug and went to answer hers in the hall.

"Joe, it's Lou."

"Paige," Melanie cried.

"Lou! I was about to call you. I found Duncan. He's fine."

"I knew you'd find him. Joe, I'm doomed."

"What's wrong, Paige?" Melanie covered her ear and bent into the phone. "Where are you?"

"Doomed?" Joe rolled his eyes. He wasn't in the mood for Lou's theatrics. "What happened?"

"A *cruise!*" Melanie shrieked.

Joe couldn't help smirking. About time she discovered the truth about the way Paige had used her. You couldn't be too careful about the friends you kept. Especially female friends. Good thing he'd trust Lou with his life.

"Gina just called me, Joe."

He frowned. "And?"

"You gotta help me." Lou's voice shook with emotion. "She's pregnant. And I'm the father."

9

MELANIE HUNG UP the phone, feeling like her last meal was fighting to see daylight again. Joe had been right. Paige ditched Duncan with Melanie so she could go on a cruise with her boss. A friendly trip at first, a bonus for the good work she'd been doing, a fatherly gesture—the gift of escape from tough and confusing times with Lou. Then one thing had led to the proverbial other....

She gripped her fingers into fists, still torn between anger at her friend's betrayal and sympathy for the confused desperation and shame in Paige's voice. Marriage—bah, humbug. Lou cheating on Paige. Paige's boss seducing Paige at her most vulnerable, cheating on his own wife. Joe's wife walking out. Kevin's father and a bimbo half his age. Wendy...well, Wendy deserved what she got.

Melanie looked at Joe, the man who'd spent the night in her bed. Such sweetness; such passion; such reverent tenderness. What a naive idiot she was, even wondering if they might have something special when the odds were so against it. Like she and Joe would be picked to win a super jackpot out of some couples lottery with billions of participants. Because *their* blossoming romance transcended all the pettiness *other* people stooped to.

Right. And the tooth fairy was coming to dinner.

Paige had thought her love with Lou was perfect, too. So had Kevin's mom, Joe's wife and, yes, probably even Wendy, and every other woman starting out a relationship. Melanie was no different. Once the shine wore off, once being with her inevitably stopped making Joe feel like Mighty Manly Man, he'd get restless, dissatisfied, no matter how hard she tried to please him. *Sorry, honey, but your hardware is outdated, your software is sagging, and your ports no longer appeal. Next!* Leaving Melanie bitter, broken and worst of all, dependent on someone else for how she felt about herself. She hadn't spent twenty-eight years fostering independence to throw it away on the basis of a good feeling bound to be temporary.

Joe shoved his phone into his pocket and sank down on the couch. Concern crept into Melanie's indignation. He looked like someone had taken a bat to his kneecaps. "What happened?"

"That was Lou." He ran his hand over his face. "You were right. He was cheating. Worse, he was careless. His *friend* is pregnant."

Melanie opened her mouth for triumphant venting and found she was too disgusted and upset to feel any. "I'm sorry, Joe. I...wish I'd been wrong." God, how she wished she had been. Then she might have one little shining example of loyalty to cling to.

She went over to him, wanting to touch him but knowing whatever they had last night had been poisoned beyond hope of antidote. "You were right, too, about Paige—the cruise, the lover..."

"Lou sounded miserable."

"So did Paige." She sank down next to him on the couch. "I knew her best before she met Lou—she was one of the most indomitable people I'd ever known. Now she sounds as if the entire planet were sitting on her shoulders."

Joe leaned back and stared blankly at the ceiling. "Lou used to be able to stay out all night, outparty, outdance, outcelebrate all of us. Now he sounds like an old man."

He turned his head toward her. They stared at each other hopelessly. Not even Billy Joel could save them now.

"It's not what I want," Joe whispered.

Melanie swore she heard the cracking sound of her heart breaking in her chest. "Me, neither."

He pushed himself off the couch and looked at her with pain in his eyes. Tears filled hers. She stood; he leaned forward and kissed her once—soft, lingering, then straightened, closed his eyes and tipped his head back, as if summoning the strength to walk out.

Melanie pressed her lips together to try to keep the feel of his kiss there as long as possible. The solid warmth of his body only inches away and memories of last night's passion threatened to come between her and her sanity, erase her rational and sound reasons for Joe to leave Birchfield and her life. She knew she was doing the right thing. Staking her fulfillment on another person could lead only to disaster. Her happiness had to stay her own responsibility.

She drew her hands down the hard muscle of his arms. A traitorous part of her wanted more of Joe Jantzen. Wanted the way he made her feel, wanted the way they felt together to go on longer. A day, a night, even just an hour—to lie in his arms, to know his body again, make him laugh, make him lust and maybe...maybe even bake him one tiny quarter-batch of cookies, just for the road.

Joe exhaled, opened his eyes and peered dully over her left shoulder. "Uh...spider on your wall."

"Wha—" Melanie glanced behind her. "Oh. I'll get it." She started toward the kitchen for her rescue container, feeling as if weights had been hung off her limbs and internal organs.

"Don't bother. I got it."

Thwap.

Melanie froze. Turned on the balls of her feet and stared in horror at the dark smear on the white plaster. Just like that. Not even a thought for the spider's life or the value of its mission on earth. Not a thought of anything but Joe. Joe's desire to rid himself of its presence. Joe's decision that the creature was useless. Served no purpose. In the way. A pest. *Thwap.*

A perfect metaphor for the male attitude, and a timely reality check. *Sweetheart, you've been putting on weight. Thwap. Sorry, dear, have you been talking for the last half hour? Thwap. Didn't you know I wouldn't feel like meat loaf tonight? Thwap. You've tried soaking, scrubbing, but I still have ring around the collar. Thwap. Thwap. Thwap.*

"Joe." She spoke quietly, looked him square in the eye, all weakness gone from her resolve. "I've loved knowing you. It's been great between us and I'll remember you forever. I wish you nothing but a long, happy life—out on the prairie.''

JOE SET HIS BAG on the bed in his motel room to pack, neatly, carefully, as if keeping his movements controlled and precise could hold his feelings in check—keep his eggshell mental state from cracking and spilling out a gooey, emotional mess.

He'd set up a mantra, which he chanted over and over, balling his socks, rolling his T-shirts, folding his jeans. *I'm doing the right thing; I'm doing the right thing.* The only problem was that at the same time every atomic particle in his body screamed that he was making a stupid, ridiculous, colossal mistake.

He pulled the battered lid down on his clothes and zipped the case shut. Of course he was having second thoughts. Transitions were always hard. Transitions that involved leaving a woman who could turn him on until the end of time were particularly difficult. Especially given that he'd only had a tiny and tantalizing taste of what it could be like to be with Melanie.

All the better. The deeper they got in, the harder to dig themselves out and the more painful when eventual disillusionment hit. This way the misery would be minimal. He could continue his vacation and lose himself in the sights of the country. Return to Boston refreshed and ready to decide where he wanted to go with his life. The possibilities could be endless. He could open another agency. Or rejoin the force. Or take up some...hobby or...something.

He lifted his suitcase off the bed and let it thud down in the middle of the room. Okay, so the possibilities might not seem exactly endless now, but he could expand them given a little time. He'd be fine. Lonely, maybe, but sane, in control of his own destiny and thoroughly unemasculated. He could live with that.

A tentative knock sounded at the door. He jerked his head toward the sound, bracing himself against the heart-racing rush of adrenaline hope. It wasn't going to be Melanie. It wasn't. He walked to the door and turned the handle. It wasn't going to be Melanie.

It wasn't.

Peggy stood outside, blinking at him in confusion. Had she expected someone else?

"Joe." She stared at the number on his room as if it had changed when she wasn't looking. "Oh, my. I've come to the wrong room."

"Oh?" He couldn't help being curious. Who the hell was Peggy meeting at a motel? "You here to see someone?"

"Yes." Her wrinkled face took on a becoming shade of rose. "Mr. Parsons and I meet once a week for…for a game. A game of…"

"Chess?"

"Yes!" She smiled at him. "Chess. That's it."

Well, who would have guessed? "What room is he—"

"But you know I'm early. Very early. So I'd love to come in and chat, thank you." She walked into the room, past his rolling-eyes expression, and stopped short at the sight of the suitcase. "Oh! You're leaving town already."

Joe narrowed his eyes. Why hadn't she assumed he was packing to move in with Melanie? "I'm actually—"

"And I thought things were going so well between you two." She sat primly on the edge of the bed.

"How do you know they're not?"

She raised her eyebrows calmly. "Because a man who is packing to move into his lover's house does not look as if he'd eaten several bowls of Mrs. Anderson's eight-bean chili and subsequently entered a Charleston marathon."

"Oh." She had him there.

"So." Peggy reached under her skirt and handed him her flask. "You need a drink."

He laughed humorlessly and accepted the tarnished silver bottle. What the hell. How bad could the stuff be if Duncan swilled it with no ill effects? He raised the flask in an ironic salute and tipped it back.

A flaming torrent seared its way down his throat. He coughed and clutched his neck, half expecting to turn plaid and shoot flames out his mouth like a cartoon character.

"What...what..." He sputtered and coughed again. He'd guess grain alcohol, gasoline and about a cup of cayenne pepper. "You drink this stuff? You...you gave this to the baby?"

"Lands, no!" Peggy clapped her hands to her cheeks. "That's Uncle Jim's special. He called it heartbreak tonic."

Joe gasped in a few raspy breaths. Heart *attack*

tonic, more likely. "Then what did you give Duncan?"

"Look." She reached down with both hands and lifted her skirt to reveal five identical silver flasks strapped to her legs, room for three on each side. "Something for everyone. My family has always been very particular about what we dish out, when and to who—" she frowned, then closed her lips "—m."

"Well, thanks, Peggy." He handed the lethal potion back to her, hoping his throat wasn't permanently lacerated.

"You won't have more?"

"Not in this life, thanks. Maybe the next one." He gestured to the door, itching to be loading the car so he could leave the pain and ecstasy he'd encountered in Birchfield far behind him. "I'm sure you don't want to keep Mr. Parsons waiting."

"Oh, yes, I do. The anticipation is good for him. Keeps our...game...nice and fresh. After all these years, too." She nodded significantly. "It's possible to keep chess exciting, even after a long time. I would have thought you two would know that."

Joe smiled uncomfortably, wondering how to tell her—gently—that he wasn't interested in discussing his love life with a pleasant but mentally dubious old woman. "I'll keep that in mind."

"Life is full of surprises. You're young and healthy now, but you never know when you'll be crossing the street and the bus from the Birchfield Sweet Life Senior Center will come tootling around the corner a bit too fast."

Isabel Sharpe 357

He sighed. "I've heard it all before, Peggy. I should seize the day, not risk living a life of regret. I understand. But it doesn't change what I need to do right now."

She frowned, pressed her thin lips together and regarded him thoughtfully. "When I was eighteen, Mr. Parsons and I were engaged. I loved him, but he hated traveling, and I wanted to see the world. He was very understanding, so I went—intending a short visit."

"You went alone?" He couldn't imagine a young woman traveling the world by herself in that era.

"Oh, er, no. I had a...friend with me. But once I got there, Mr. Parsons and Birchfield seemed so dull that I stayed. I saw Florence, Paris, London, Athens, Beirut." She sighed dreamily. "I was gone for almost a year. Then one day I woke up and realized I'd been living in a lovely soap bubble. Can you beat that?"

"Uh, no, Peggy." He rubbed his forehead impatiently. "I don't think I can."

"I was observing life, not really living it. Life without someone to share isn't really life at all. So I came home. And you know what?"

"Mr. Parsons had married someone else."

Her mouth dropped open. "How did you know about that part?"

"Detective Joe Jantzen misses nothing." He tapped the side of his head. Not too hard to figure if she had to meet him in a motel room.

"His marriage was miserable. Then his wife got ill and slipped into a coma fifty years ago."

"Fifty!" He gaped at her.

"Oh, dear, is that too long? Well, anyway, for

years and years we've been meeting for...chess. Once a week. Then I go back to my house. He goes back to his." She dabbed at several tears Joe couldn't quite see. "I've never lost my feelings for him, nor he for me. But we wasted our chance for happiness." She shook her head and gave a peculiar-sounding sob.

Joe's stomach tightened in spite of his suspicions about her story. For some reason when he'd thought all this through, the slow, inevitable passage of the rest of his life alone hadn't really sunk in.

"I'll never know what it is to wake up beside him. We'll never be able to build any kind of life together." Peggy's voice grew louder, her expression absurdly mournful. She tipped her head and clutched her hands together over her heart. "Alone! Always alone! While the love of my life waited for his wife to die, the best years of my life slipped by...alone." She peeked at him, then resumed her yearning gaze at the wall.

"Peggy?" Joe grinned. Sweet old lady. B-movie actress.

"Yes?" Her eyes swiveled apprehensively.

"There is no Mr. Parsons, is there?"

Peggy sighed. "Not exactly that way, no. I like being alone. But I'm a weird old nut and you're not. I'm only trying to tell you that you won't be young and tremendously virile forever. You and Melanie should at least give it a chance. Maybe it will work out, maybe it won't. But—"

"At least we'll have tried, I know." His confusion increased a billionfold, along with a healthy dose of irritation. Why did she have to show up and unsettle him like this? He'd be on the road by now, his decision firmly behind him, instead of here in this Wisconsin cheesy motel, wallowing in renewed uncertainty.

Peggy leaned closer, eyes earnest. "You have nothing to lose...but your freedom and happiness." She giggled. "I'm joking, dear. I'm really the wrong person for this job. I wouldn't enslave myself to a man if you paid me."

"For heaven's sake, Peggy." He didn't know whether to laugh or slug her. "Then why are you wasting my time?"

"Dot and Richard made me promise to talk to you, and I *do* think—"

Joe's cell phone shrilled from his pocket.

Peggy started and clutched her heart. "Oh, my...oh, I see, the phone." She pointed to the bathroom. "I need to go anyway, so you'll have some privacy."

Joe nodded, still sick from the sour taste of indecision, and put the phone to his ear.

"Joe! God, Joe, it's Lou. Turn on CNN. It's Paige. I know it is. Oh, God. This can't be happening."

Joe lunged for the TV set and turned it on. A helicopter view of a smoke-blurred cruise ship filled the screen. "Passengers are being evacuated as quickly as possible. Again, if you're just joining us, a fire has been burning out of control on a Happy Times Cruise Line ship since early this morning. We have unconfirmed reports of possible casualties. We'll be bringing you more information as soon as it's available."

Joe switched the set off, his only thought to get to

Melanie as fast as possible. She'd need him with her. "Lou, it's going to be okay. There are thousands of people on that ship."

"I know. God, I know. It'll take forever to evacuate them. The fire..."

Joe winced. He'd meant to point out that the odds of Paige being one of the casualties were small. "The evacuation will be done in a flash. Paige will be fine, Lou. I feel it. I know it."

"I can't lose her, Joe. I love her. She's my whole life, she and Duncan. If she dies, there's nothing for me. A lifetime of nothing."

Joe winced as if he'd taken a right hook to the jaw. *A lifetime of nothing.* He hadn't known Melanie long enough for her to be his whole life, but he was pretty sure he was well on his way to being in love with her.

"I'll call you back in ten minutes." He punched off the phone. Peggy emerged from the bathroom. He grabbed her arm, dragging her after him.

"Where are we going?"

"You're going home. I'm going to see Melanie."

"Oh, good. Did I change your mind?"

"No." He pushed her through the door and closed it behind him. "But Lou and Happy Times might have."

Not that it would make the slightest difference if Melanie didn't change hers.

"I'M AFRAID I still don't understand what is so terribly threatening about all of this." Richard fiddled absently with his equally absent pipe and stretched his legs on Melanie's couch. "If you are fond of the man, then why not explore the possibility that you belong together?"

"Because." Melanie took in a deep breath and sighed. For some reason this was very hard to explain. In spite of the fact that it all made perfect sense to her, every time she tried to talk about it with someone else, she ended up sounding like an extra large chicken. "Because...well, like this morning he killed this spider...and—"

"Ah. That *is* something. A spider killer."

Melanie rolled her eyes and blew a ferocious raspberry of frustration. "I don't want to lose my freedom. I don't want to become like all my friends and spend every waking minute adapting my life to my husband's, then ten years from now have the marriage end in betrayal and bitterness."

"Hmm." Richard stroked his chin. "I guess you do have a—"

"But you're not your friends." Dot elbowed Richard in the stomach, then made an abortive grab at her pocket as if she couldn't stand not documenting the conversation on paper. "If you don't *want* to be like them, you won't be."

"What about all these weird urges to cook for him?" Melanie jumped up and started pacing the room, gesturing like a wild woman. "To take care of him? Put his happiness and needs ahead of mine? It's like after one night with him I became Donna Reed."

"Hmm." Dot whipped out her pad, obviously not able to stand the strain any longer. "Wants to take care of him."

Richard was one step behind her, scribbling with his pen. "Puts his needs first."

"Aha!" Dot showed her pad to Richard.

"Brilliant, dear." Richard nodded excitedly. "Exactly my conclusion."

"What?" Melanie stopped pacing and squinted at them suspiciously. She was going to hate this. She could just tell.

"You're in love." Dot walked over and patted Melanie's shoulder. "Congratulations."

"In *love?* After three days?" Her legs chose that moment to do their impression of rubber bands. She sank into a chair. She was right; she did hate this.

"It happens." Richard got off the couch and put an arm around his wife. "It happened that fast for us, didn't it, my lovely?"

"Indeed." She patted his cheek.

Melanie covered her face with her hands. "This is a disaster."

Dot leaned down to her. "Would you like us to call nine-one-one?"

"I'm serious." Melanie put her hands down and glared. "I might as well kiss my identity goodbye."

Dot and Richard exchanged glances.

"Phineas?"

"Absolutely."

Dot put a kindly hand on Melanie's shoulder. "You know what your trouble is?"

Yes. After she'd finally figured out love didn't exist, she'd most likely fallen head over heels—for a man who didn't believe in it, either. "What?"

"You've never had a railroad spike through your head."

Melanie gave her forehead a furious whack, as if she had no idea why she hadn't figured that out sooner. "Oh! You are absolutely right. I've never had a railroad spike through my head. That's my entire trouble."

"Phineas Gage!" Richard made a grand gesture, as if he were taking center stage for a performance-art extravaganza. "A railroad worker in 1848. Prepared a charge to blast rock and pounded down the powder with a metal railroad spike."

"Boom!" Dot smacked her fist into her hand. "The spark touched off an explosion that blew the spike clear through his head."

Melanie cringed and put a hand to her stomach. "What a charming story."

"But the most amazing aspect—" Richard lifted a dramatic finger "—is that he survived the accident."

"Instead of being a nobody railroad worker, he became one of the most famous neurological cases of all times, inspiring countless medical works, such as *Recovery from the Passage of an Iron Rod through the Head*."

Melanie gave a sickly groan. "I'll recommend it to the school board."

"The point is, you can't make assumptions about the future," Dot said. "You can't even assume a railroad spike through your head will kill you."

"So you're telling me that being with Joe is like having a spike through my skull."

"Exactly." Richard put his air pipe in his mouth and nodded smugly.

"Not quite." Dot gave Richard a glassy stare, then smiled at Melanie as if Melanie needed immediate medical treatment. "We mean that you don't always get out of life what you expect, even if it seems inevitable. Nothing is entirely predictable."

"Phineas was a triumph of the human will to survive and flourish in the face of certain doom."

"Richard..." Dot shook her head warningly.

"Flourish?" Melanie gaped at him. "He flourished with a hole through his head?"

"Actually—" Richard rubbed his hands together, oblivious to his wife's warning tugs on his jacket "—he went a tad berserk and died thirteen years later, penniless and epileptic."

"Oh, Richard." Dot smacked her hand on his thigh as if she'd prefer Richard's head was the target. "That wasn't the part we wanted her to—"

A heavy pounding shook the front door. Melanie jumped up, heart pounding almost as loudly. A vision flashed through her mind of Joe back, mad with desire, ready to break the door down if need be, to make her his for all eternity.

She moved to the front door, fighting the traitorous hope, telling herself she was being a complete—

"Melanie!" Joe's voice came through the door, muffled, emotional.

Melanie's heart exchanged pounding for pogo-stick jabs. *Oh, man.* There wasn't enough strength in the universe to help her withstand that kind of passionate assault. To be brutally honest, she wasn't entirely sure she wanted to withstand it.

Doomed. She was doomed.

She reached for the knob, glancing at Richard and Dot for support to find they'd sneaked out of the house through the kitchen. *Damn the torpedoes. Full speed ahead.*

She summoned every ounce of her for-the-most-part impressive self-control, braced her body for the impact when he burst through intent on crushing her to him and opened the door.

"Melanie." He rushed past her into her living room and turned on the TV.

Melanie froze, waited until her brain caught up to her emotions and whipped around, folding her arms across her chest in her most furious teacher pose.

Joe came back and practically broke down her door because he had a frantic need to watch television? Was some Boston team playing this evening? Had he a desperate need to see the pre-pre-pregame show? Would he soon be sending her out for chips and beer?

She slammed the front door behind her and advanced on him. What had Twain said? *If you're angry count to four; if you're very angry, swear.* Joe deserved more than a mere piece of her mind. He deserved at least two-thirds. The part without the spike through it.

The TV showed a ship in open ocean, smoke billowing from its stern. Melanie's arms abandoned their indignant pose. "What..."

He rushed to her, took her shoulders, breaths accelerated, blue eyes filled with anxiety and concern. "Paige's ship, Melanie."

She gasped. "Oh, Joe!"

He tightened his hold on her. "Lou called me. I came back here because I thought you might—" he looked panicked for a second, then set his jaw "—need me."

She stared at him, completely unsure how to respond. Did she need him? No. But she was starting to think she really, really wanted him. Maybe even loved him, though time would tell whether that was meant to be. Right now she had some serious worrying to do.

"What happened? Where's Paige?"

"There's a fire on board. They don't know how it started. I was in the motel packing when Lou called to—"

Melanie's phone rang. She flew across the room and lunged for it.

"Melanie, it's Paige." She was sobbing.

"Paige!" Melanie's eyes filled. "Paige, are you okay? What happened? Where are you?"

"I'm fine. I was one of the first evacuated. They brought us to the Miami airport. My plane is about to leave—for Milwaukee. I have to see my family, Melanie. My baby. My husband. Is Duncan there? Can I talk to him? Please?"

"Yes, yes. Oh, Paige, I'm so glad you're safe!" She sniffed and wiped her eyes. Joe came in from the kitchen holding a tissue, which he handed her with a grin followed by a hands-clasped victory salute. Melanie blew her nose and smiled. Maybe she *was* in love. She certainly felt goopy enough.

Joe's cell phone rang, interrupting his cheering pantomime. Melanie watched him answer, wondering if she could ever survive him leaving again.

"Lou!" He listened for a moment, then his grin grew wider; he gave her a thumbs-up and a wink that made her start mentally sifting through her recipes.

She pulled herself together. "Paige! Lou's on the other phone."

"I just called him. Did he tell you that woman lied about being pregnant to see if he'd leave me?" She laughed, still crying, so that she sounded vaguely demented. "As if! He really loves me, Melanie. He's flying out to Milwaukee as soon as he can get a flight. I'm so happy! Put Duncan on, please. I want to talk to my baby."

"Melanie." Joe held his phone out. "Lou wants to talk to Duncan."

"Peggy has him," Melanie whispered, then spoke to Paige. "My neighbor is watching him."

"Oh, gosh." Paige sounded heartbroken. "Can you get him? I'll call back in five minutes."

"Sure, Paige, I'll—"

"Uh, Melanie?" Joe tapped her shoulder.

She held up a finger to tell Joe to wait. "I'll run get him, Paige. Talk to you in five."

"Melanie."

She hung up. "What?"

He covered the mouthpiece of his phone. "Peggy came to see me at the motel. She followed me back here and went home. Duncan wasn't with her."

Melanie's mouth dropped. "She wouldn't leave him alone in her house...would she?"

"Maybe she gave him to Dot and Rich—"

"No! They were just here. Oh, my God, Joe." She sprinted for the front door, Joe close behind her, cell phone in hand.

"Lou, Duncan's next door, I'll call you back." He punched off the phone and followed Melanie across her front yard. They hurtled up Peggy's stairs and pounded on her door.

After several centuries, she opened it slowly, backward wig tilted slightly over one ear. "Yes?"

"Peggy, where's Duncan?" Melanie resisted the urge to grab her by her skinny shoulders and shake until her wig came the rest of the way off.

"I don't get visitors often." She gestured into the house. "Would you like to come in?"

"No, Peggy." Joe took the old woman's arm and stopped her retreat inside. "Did you leave Duncan here when you came to see me at the motel?"

"Oh, no. I wouldn't leave him." She shook her head and grinned. "I took care of him."

For some reason, her words brought to mind tiny cement shoes and a wading pool. Melanie shrugged off the thought. Peggy was odd but not twisted. "What did you do with him?"

"Let's see. First, I gave him some happy pills."

"Oh, no—" Melanie clutched her heart "—she drugged him."

"Sugar pills, dear! Just sugar." Peggy adjusted her wig, mumbling something about paranoia.

"I'm sure Duncan's fine." Joe put his arm around

Melanie and squeezed. She leaned into him, relishing his protective— No. No, it wasn't going to be that way. She wrapped her arm around his waist and hung on tight. If only he'd allow it, they could be a damn good team.

"*What* did you do with Duncan?" She only just managed to swallow the urge to scream in Peggy's face.

"Oh, I gave him to my friend."

"What friend, Peggy?" Joe's body felt stiff under her touch; his voice sounded as badly controlled as hers. "What friend is that?"

Peggy smiled and put her hands on their shoulders. "It's so nice to see you two back to—"

"Peggy!" Melanie gave in and screeched her name like a rabid monkey. "Where's Duncan?"

"I told you. He's perfectly safe." Her smile faded into an injured pout. "But Joe was in such a hurry to come back from the motel, I got flustered and I forgot."

"Forgot where you left him?"

"Oh, no, dear. I just forgot that he's still with Mr. Parsons."

Beside her, Joe's body convulsed; he made a sound in his throat that suggested he required emergency intervention.

"Joe!" Melanie gasped. "What is it?"

"Stay calm." He turned toward her, looking anything but.

"Who's Mr. Parsons?"

Peggy gave a musical laugh. "My paramour, of course."

"Melanie." Joe gripped her shoulders, his eyes willing her not to panic. She panicked anyway. "Melanie, Mr. Parsons doesn't exist."

10

MELANIE SAT on her couch next to Joe and watched, numb and exhausted, while Paige, Lou and Duncan demonstrated the most nauseating family lovefest since *Little House on the Prairie* went off the air.

If she had to watch much longer she'd probably need medication to keep her lunch down.

She grimaced, annoyed at herself. Okay, she was a teensy-weensy bit jealous. Or maybe a majorly-wajorly lot jealous. Because since she and Joe found Duncan playing happily with a very real Mr. Parsons at the Birchfield Motel, spent forever stuck listening to his stories, came back to explain everything to Dot and Richard, coordinated phone calls and rides to the airport and back to pick up Paige and Lou, Joe hadn't touched her again or given the slightest indication that he'd changed his mind about leaving. Obviously, *he'd* had no epiphany finding out he was falling in love with her. No discovery of a deep, burning determination to make their future work. As far as he was concerned, the L word contained as much poison as it always had.

Joe stirred beside her; she glanced at him.

"Are you thinking what I'm thinking?" He jerked

his head toward the slobbery reunited parents and rolled his eyes.

She doubted it very much. "You're thinking, 'How long is it going to last this time?' Aren't you?"

He nodded, watching her carefully. Too carefully for someone who didn't care enough about her to stay. She sat up and took notice.

"You know—" he rubbed his hand along his chin "—Peggy and Mr. Parsons had the right idea—having that weekly chess game at the motel. Neutral territory. None of this love and commitment stuff to complicate matters. Ideal. Don't you think so?" Again, that careful stare.

"Oh, yes. I do." Her agreement sounded as vehement as she could make it, which wasn't very. Peggy's arrangement sounded almost as lonely as Melanie's life would be without Joe. But what was the use groveling and begging him to stay when he was set on leaving? "Thank goodness Duncan was safe. I almost had a heart attack when you said Mr. Parsons didn't exist."

"Peggy never actually said that. I misunderstood. Mr. Parsons didn't exist the way she described him originally—all this baloney about their being engaged, her trip to Europe, his marriage to an invalid. She was just trying to convince me to...give you and me a chance." His voice became low and husky.

Melanie sat straighter and took more notice, still not quite sure what to think. Was he testing her?

They watched in silence while Lou and Paige swapped enough spit to fill Lake Michigan, Melanie furiously devising a plan to find out if Joe had feelings for her that went deeper than lust.

"Crazy, isn't it, the idea of giving our relationship a chance." She laughed as if it were the stupidest idea she'd ever heard, hoping he'd turn and say, "Well, actually, I—"

"Nuts." Joe shook his head, eyes still glued to Lou and Paige. "Totally nuts."

Well, *that* made things clear as mud. Melanie sighed. Joe sighed louder.

Lou finished inhaling his wife's face, grabbed Duncan and twirled him around, then tossed him up and down until the boy screamed with laughter and waved his chubby arms as if he intended to take off. Paige hugged them both, cheeks flushed, eyes bright with happiness.

Melanie caught her face dissolving into envious misery and forced it to scowl in cynical disgust. Joe turned abruptly toward her, blue eyes dark and intense. Her scowl fled. She stared back, flooded by a shockingly strong urge to hurl herself in his arms and beg him to handcuff her to his side and make her his forever.

Whoa, there, girl. She didn't care to risk rejection from Mr. Thought-I'd-Stay-Then-Changed-My-Mind. Not until he gave some indication he thought men and women could inhabit the same square mile without jousting to the death.

"You know, Joe, I got the same lecture from Dot and Richard. About how we were making the biggest, stupidest, most irresponsible mistake of our entire lives, sacrificing the possibility of years of incredible, passionate happiness together for the certainty of an eternity of dismal heartbroken loneliness." She tried to laugh again, this time disparagingly, while peeking at him for his reaction. "Can you believe that?"

"That's nuts." He gave the same laugh. "Isn't it."

"Yeah. Nuts." She sighed again. He did look slightly miserable, but—call her greedy—she needed a little more progress than that before she could begin the groveling and pleading.

The doorbell rang. Richard and Dot came into the living room, not waiting for her to answer, wrapped in each other's arms and beaming identical beams.

"Guess what?" Dot gazed lovingly at her husband. "Richard and I have decided to renew our vows! After thirty years of marriage we want to celebrate our love all over again!"

"How fabulous!" Paige threw herself at them as if they had all been born and raised next door to each other. "Us, too! And we decided to have another baby!"

"Congratulations!" Dot and Richard exchanged handshakes and backslaps with the soon-to-be-expecting couple.

Melanie sent Joe a sideways glance. Another baby? This sounded serious. This sounded like a real reconciliation. For all their recent pettiness, Lou and Paige weren't stupid enough to bring another child into the world unless they were sure their marriage was strong.

"Wow. Romance all around." Joe shrugged and cleared his throat. "Must be something in the water."

Isabel Sharpe

"Yeah." She peered at him again. Was it her imagination or did he look a trifle wistful?

"Knock, knock!" Peggy came waltzing in, stars shooting from her eyes. "Guess what? Mr. Parsons asked me to marry him...and I said, yes!"

Dot and Richard, Paige and Lou exploded into hearty cheers and crowded around her, accepting various flasks for the celebratory toasts.

Huh? Melanie checked in with Joe again, this time through narrowed eyes. "Is there a full moon tonight?"

He shook his head slowly. His thigh crept closer until it made contact with hers. Melanie swallowed and stared at it, long and strong and male. *Oh, yes. Oh, yes. Please let this be what I think it is.*

She shifted closer to him, hope making its first recent appearance in her emotional repertoire. Whatever was going on, and whoever had staged today's episode of the Love Files, she prayed there'd be more of it—enough to push Joe over the edge, to join her at the bottom of the right-now-lonely Chasm of Commitment.

"Anyone home?" Kevin came through the front door, a huge grin plastered to his face. "Guess what? Mr. Stackman decided to stay! He and my mom are getting married!"

Another cheer sounded throughout the house. The throng surrounded Kevin for an extended hugging marathon.

Joe draped his arm casually around Melanie. Melanie put her hand casually on his long, strong, male thigh. *Oh. Oh, yes.* "Geez, Joe, what the heck is going on?"

"I don't know—" he looked at her mouth, sending hot electric shivers through her body "—but I'm starting to think it might be contagious."

"Ding dong, anybody home?" Wendy wiggled into the house and stopped short in surprise at the crowd. "Wow, everyone's here already...well, guess what?"

"What?" the crowd roared.

"My husband quit his job—and he's taking me on a second honeymoon!"

Joe shook his head and laughed amid the general Hallelujah Chorus of excitement. "Okay. That's it. I can't take this any more. I give in."

He pulled Melanie to him and kissed her hard and possessively, letting loose so much passion and feeling in her body that she practically climbed on top of him trying to kiss him back.

What the hell had she been fighting this for? This incredible merging of their mouths and bodies and souls? How could she have wanted to spend the rest of her life trying not to think about him? Trying not to want him? Trying not to wonder if Joe Jantzen could have taken her life in directions she never thought possible?

Forget it. She was through fighting.

Joe raised his head and looked at her with so much tenderness that tears spilled from her eyes and surfed down her cheeks.

"Oh, Melanie," he whispered.

"Oh, Joe," she whispered back.

A huge, long, eight-person sigh made them both freeze, then turn their heads. They had an enthralled audience. Eight enraptured faces, glowing as if they were watching the end of *It's a Wonderful Life*.

"Oh, Menny. Oh, Doh." Duncan threw his arms around his father and deposited a wide-mouthed gooey mess of a kiss on his face. The room erupted into laughter; Duncan clapped his hands and smiled as if he'd just won a lifetime supply of animal crackers.

"I think that was our exit line." Richard saluted Joe and Melanie, then ushered Dot and Peggy through the front door. Kevin, Wendy and Paige's family exchanged hugs all around and see-you-soons, and we're-so-psyched-for-you-guys, and followed them out.

Melanie closed the door and threw herself into Joe's arms, hardly able to take in that she belonged there now. She kissed him, happiness making her giddy and giggly, like those disgusting spineless friends of hers she was endlessly thrilled to be joining. "So who do you think planned that outrageous parade of devotion?"

'I'm betting Dot and Richard had the whole thing sketched out on their mighty notepads." He puffed on a non-pipe and consulted his palm. "Let's see here. Kevin enters at three-sixteen and announces maternal reconciliation. Wendy jiggles in at three twenty-two.... I wonder how much of it was real?"

"I can't quite see Peggy as a bride, or Wendy's husband giving up the corporate life. But I know Lou and Paige were real, and I think Kevin's mom probably did make up with Bill Stackman." She laughed, unable to control her joy overload. "They've been good friends to us, Joe. All of them."

"So what about us?" Joe pulled her to the couch and brought her down to sit in his lap, stroking her back with strong, warm hands. "Still think I should become a Birchfield cop and hire Kevin?"

She smiled, knowing he had to be the one to decide and knowing, too, deep in her heart, that if he didn't want to stay she'd find some way to kidnap him and chain him to her bed. "It's your life, Joe. I'd like you to stay in Birchfield, but only if it's what you want."

"It *is* what I want. I need Birchfield at this point in my life—and I need you." He kissed her gently, slowly, until her breathing all but stopped. "Just don't expect me to become a Packer fan."

She laughed again. "I promise."

He tilted her chin and looked into her eyes, his expression serious, tender and full of the love they'd both been so afraid of. "What do *you* want, Melanie?"

She tried to smile again, but the emotion ran too deep, too strong. He was going to stay. They'd have time to work on forging their own version of commitment that could beat the odds, that could last.

"What do *I* want? Hmm. Well, I certainly want to know you...I definitely want to kiss you...and I absolutely want to make love all night long." She arched her back and sent him what she desperately hoped was a smoldering gaze. "But most of all..."

He toppled her onto the couch, settled his body

over her, burned kisses up the column of her throat. "Mmm?"

"Most of all—" she traced a finger along his jaw, trapped beneath his weight, feeling freer than she'd ever felt in her life "—I want to make you a giant, colossal, stupendous batch of oatmeal peanut-butter marshmallow chocolate-chip cookies."

Author in the Spotlight

In February 2001

HARLEQUIN
Duets

brings you

The Swinging R Ranch
&
Whose Line Is It Anyway?

Both by

Debbi Rawlins

Both available in one book for one low price!

Available at your favorite retail outlets.

Visit us at www.eHarlequin.com

HDAS-DR

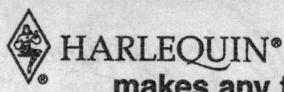

HARLEQUIN®
makes any time special—online...

eHARLEQUIN.com

your romantic books

- Shop online! Visit Shop eHarlequin and discover a wide selection of new releases and classic favorites at great discounted prices.

- Read our daily and weekly Internet exclusive serials, and participate in our interactive novel in the reading room.

- Ever dreamed of being a writer? Enter your chapter for a chance to become a featured author in our Writing Round Robin novel.

your romantic life

- Check out our feature articles on dating, flirting and other important romance topics and get your daily love dose with tips on how to keep the romance alive every day.

your community

- Have a Heart-to-Heart with other members about the latest books and meet your favorite authors.

- Discuss your romantic dilemma in the Tales from the Heart message board.

your romantic escapes

- Learn what the stars have in store for you with our daily Passionscopes and weekly Erotiscopes.

- Get the latest scoop on your favorite royals in Royal Romance.

HINTA1

Harlequin proudly brings you

STELLA CAMERON
Bobby Hutchinson
Sandra Marton

in

MARRIED IN SPRING

a brand-new anthology in which three couples find that when spring arrives, romance soon follows...along with an unexpected walk down the aisle!

February 2001

Available wherever Harlequin books are sold.

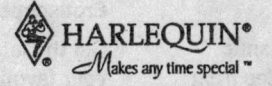

HARLEQUIN®
Makes any time special ™

Visit us at www.eHarlequin.com

PHMARRIED

#1 *New York Times* bestselling author

NORA ROBERTS

brings you more of the loyal and loving, tempestuous and tantalizing Stanislaski family.

Coming in February 2001

The Stanislaski Sisters
Natasha and Rachel

Though raised in the Old World traditions of their family, fiery Natasha Stanislaski and cool, classy Rachel Stanislaski are ready for a *new* world of love....

And also available in February 2001 from Silhouette Special Edition, the newest book in the heartwarming Stanislaski saga

CONSIDERING KATE

Natasha and Spencer Kimball's daughter Kate turns her back on old dreams and returns to her hometown, where she finds the *man* of her dreams.

Available at your favorite retail outlet.

Silhouette
Where love comes alive™

Visit Silhouette at www.eHarlequin.com

PSSTANSIS

CELEBRATE VALENTINE'S DAY WITH HARLEQUIN®'S LATEST TITLE—

Stolen Memories

Available in trade-size format, this collector's edition contains three full-length novels by *New York Times* bestselling authors Jayne Ann Krentz and Tess Gerritsen, along with national bestselling author Stella Cameron.

TEST OF TIME by Jayne Ann Krentz—
He married for the best reason.... She married for the only reason.... Did they stand a chance at making the only reason the real reason to share a lifetime?

THIEF OF HEARTS by Tess Gerritsen—
Their distrust of each other was only as strong as their desire. And Jordan began to fear that Diana was more than just a thief of hearts.

MOONTIDE by Stella Cameron—
For Andrew, Greer's return is a miracle. It had broken his heart to let her go. Now fate has brought them back together. And he won't lose her again...

Make this Valentine's Day one to remember!

Look for this exciting collector's edition on sale January 2001 at your favorite retail outlet.

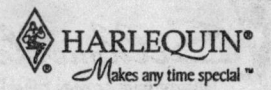

HARLEQUIN®
Makes any time special ™

Visit us at www.eHarlequin.com

PHSM